DELANEY'S SHADOW

INGRID WEAVER

BERKLEY SENSATION, NEW YORK

THE BERKLEY PUBLISHING GROUP
Published by the Penguin Group
Penguin Group (USA) Inc.
375 Hudson Street, New York, New York 10014, USA
Penguin Group (Canada), 90 Eglinton Avenue East, Suite 700, Toronto, Ontario M4P 2Y3, Canada
(a division of Pearson Penguin Canada Inc.)
Penguin Books Ltd., 80 Strand, London WC2R 0RL, England
Penguin Group Ireland, 25 St. Stephen's Green, Dublin 2, Ireland (a division of Penguin Books Ltd.)
Penguin Group (Australia), 250 Camberwell Road, Camberwell, Victoria 3124, Australia
(a division of Pearson Australia Group Pty. Ltd.)
Penguin Books India Pvt. Ltd., 11 Community Centre, Panchsheel Park, New Delhi—110 017, India
Penguin Group (NZ), 67 Apollo Drive, Rosedale, Auckland 0632, New Zealand
(a division of Pearson New Zealand Ltd.)
Penguin Books (South Africa) (Pty.) Ltd., 24 Sturdee Avenue, Rosebank, Johannesburg 2196,
South Africa

Penguin Books Ltd., Registered Offices: 80 Strand, London WC2R 0RL, England

This is a work of fiction. Names, characters, places, and incidents either are the product of the author's imagination or are used fictitiously, and any resemblance to actual persons, living or dead, business establishments, events, or locales is entirely coincidental. The publisher does not have any control over and does not assume any responsibility for author or third-party websites or their content.

DELANEY'S SHADOW

A Berkley Sensation Book / published by arrangement with the author

PRINTING HISTORY
Berkley Sensation mass-market edition / August 2011

Copyright © 2011 by Ingrid Caris.
Excerpt from *Dream Shadows* by Ingrid Weaver copyright © by Ingrid Caris.
Cover art by Trevillion.
Cover design by George Long.
Interior text design by Tiffany Estreicher.

ISBN: 978-0-425-24268-1

BERKLEY® SENSATION
Berkley Sensation Books are published by The Berkley Publishing Group,
a division of Penguin Group (USA) Inc.,
375 Hudson Street, New York, New York 10014.
BERKLEY® SENSATION and the "B" design are trademarks of Penguin Group (USA) Inc.

PRINTED IN THE UNITED STATES OF AMERICA

10 9 8 7 6 5 4 3 2 1

DREAM LOVER

Max took her chin in his hand.

She pressed harder against the tree. A piece of bark crackled beneath her back. Delaney caught another whiff of the pond, but the smell of the mud didn't turn her stomach anymore. It was countered by the clean tang of Max's soap. Her flesh tingled where he touched her, even though she knew it wasn't really a touch. That made no difference to her pulse.

Max brought his face to hers. His eyes gleamed. "We don't have to talk."

She moistened her lips. "Uh, Max . . ."

"There are plenty of more interesting things we could try."

"Let's stick with talking."

"If I were a real man, I would kiss you."

"If you were real, you wouldn't want to."

He smiled and stroked his thumb across her lower lip. "Don't bet on it."

Pleasure shot through her body. Her legs shook. She locked her knees to keep herself upright . . .

This book is dedicated to Mark, my husband,
my partner in dreams and in life.

PROLOGUE

❧

ON THE DAY JOHN MAXWELL HARRISON TURNED SEVEN, he knew he would kill Virgil Budge. He knew it with the same conviction that led other children to believe they would be astronauts or cowboys. Killing Virgil was more than a dream for Max; it was his purpose, his duty. His destiny.

Moving slowly, biting his lip to keep the whimper inside, Max grasped the willow trunk for balance and eased himself down. The moss was thick and spongy here in the shadows. It took only a few minutes for the cool to seep through his jeans and numb the place where Virgil's belt had left a trail of blood.

This morning, when the old man was snoring too loudly to hear the floor creak, Max had gone into the bedroom and picked up that belt. He'd liked the way the leather had felt in his hands. It had made his hair tingle and goose bumps rise on his arms, like the crackle of power in the air before a thunderstorm. And while he'd stood there, feeling the power, he'd watched the splotches of beer on Virgil's undershirt quiver, and he'd watched the spit trickle out of the corner of Virgil's mouth, and he'd wondered what it would be like to hit him.

Would he scream, the way Mommy always did? Would he cry until his nose ran in messy streaks into his mouth? Would he turn purple and then blue and have to hide in the trailer until the marks on his face went away?

Max had wanted to kill him then. He'd wanted it so badly his tongue had tasted like rust and his hands had shaken until the belt buckle chattered like teeth. The picture in his head had been so clear. He saw himself wrap one end of the leather around his fist the way Virgil did, and he saw himself lift his arm and whip the other end down again and again and again and then climb on the sour-smelling sheets and kick the middle of that sagging belly and jump up and down on that sneering mouth. He wouldn't have cared about the blood and tears and snot that would get on his clothes, because he'd be glad; he'd be glad.

Max sniffed and wiped his eyes with his T-shirt. Virgil was right. He was just a dumb chickenshit. He hadn't been able to do it. He'd put the belt back on the floor. He'd run out of the trailer. Then he'd climbed over the fence and crossed the old tracks and taken the path to the edge of the pond to the place where no one would find him.

A jay squawked from a branch overhead. Max willed his tears away and tilted his head back against the bark to look up. One of these days, he was going to be like that bird. He was going to fly away. And he'd take Mommy with him. After he killed Virgil, they would live in a house with white curtains and a brand-new fridge that didn't smell like beer. They would get a puppy and call him Skippy.

Max closed his eyes and let the picture build in his head. It was a trick he had learned to make the pain go away. He'd discovered it the first time Virgil had broken his arm. If he concentrated really hard, he could pretend he was someplace else.

Before the picture was halfway done, there was a rustling from the shore of the pond. Max blinked, squinting against the glare from the water.

A girl tiptoed along the edge of the mud. She was so small the bulrushes almost hid her, but he could see flashes of her blonde hair and sky-colored dress.

He knew who she was. She lived in the big Wainright house on the other side of the woods. He had seen her down here with some old lady lots of times when he was hiding in his secret place. She wasn't supposed to be at the pond by herself. She was even too little for school. She was just a baby.

She bent a cattail downward, her face scrunched up as she twisted it off the stem. The brown velvet puffed its cottony seeds into her hand, and she laughed, startling the jay out of the tree.

Max eased back into the shadows. This was the Wainrights'

property. Max didn't want to be caught here. Old man Wainright was even bigger than Virgil, and he looked awful mean the way he walked bent over that cane. Max was glad that Virgil didn't have a cane. It would hurt worse than the belt.

The girl lowered her face to study the fluff in her palm, then pursed her lips and blew it into the air. Taken by the breeze, the tiny seeds drifted over the pond in a speckled cloud, and she laughed again.

Would old man Wainright hit her when he found out she was here by herself? Max hoped not. From what he could see, her skin didn't have any bruises. She laughed a lot, too. He liked her laugh. It sparkled on the air the same as those cattail seeds.

A train whistle whined in the distance, its notes trailing off like a deflating balloon. A cicada did its buzz-saw noise from the grass, startling the girl into dropping the rest of the cattail. It bounced into the water at her feet. Heedless of her white shoes and lacy socks, she stepped into the mud after it.

Max frowned as he watched the dark water creep up her legs. She would get in trouble for sure now. Despite the ache in his ribs that made it hurt to move, he braced his palm against the tree and stood.

Someone would come to get her soon. Max wanted to warn her, but he wouldn't want to be caught trespassing, or they would take him home. And Virgil hated getting woken up when he was sleeping off a bender. Max should have hidden that belt. Or used it. Someday, he would. Yes, after he killed Virgil, he wouldn't have to sneak around in the bushes like this; he'd be far away with Mommy and Skippy in the house with the white curtains—

It happened so fast, Max would have missed it if he hadn't been looking right at her. One second the girl was reaching for the cattail; the next second there was a splash, and she sank under the water.

The bulrushes whispered together in the breeze. The cicada hummed. And Max was alone.

He ran to the edge of the pond. "Hey!" he yelled. "Hey, kid!"

The surface of the water bubbled upward in an oily bulge at the spot where she'd gone under. Ripples spread outward to lap at his running shoes. But the girl didn't reappear.

Max toed off his shoes and waded out, sinking to his ankles in the muddy bottom. The fresh welts on his back stung as the water reached his armpits, but he blinked away the tears and waved his arms through the murky water in front of him. "Kid!" he called. *"Hey!"*

He was getting scared. He didn't know what to do. He could run up to the big house and ask for help, but that would take too long.

And Max knew better than to trust anyone to help.

They never did.

Taking a deep breath, he dove under the water. Weeds brushed his face and wrapped their slimy fingers around his legs, holding him down. He struggled in panic, bursting to the surface to gulp in more air, then dove under again, fighting the mud and the weeds until his chest ached and tiny lights flickered behind his eyes. He couldn't give up yet. She was so little. She must be more scared than him.

His hand struck something smooth and cold. Kicking his way closer, he reached out and grasped a tiny arm.

He ran out of air and swallowed water by the time he got the girl to the surface. Panting, fighting against the pull of the mud, he dragged her to the shore and laid her on the grass.

Last year, just after Halloween, the police had pulled a dead body from this pond. Max had seen it all from his hiding place behind the willow. At first he'd thought the police were after him for trespassing, but then he'd seen the boat and the bar with the chains they'd dragged through the water. It was just getting dark when they'd hooked Donna MacGregor. She'd been a skinny woman, but her corpse had looked like a sausage that had puffed up too big for its casing.

Max wiped the water from his face and looked at the little blonde girl. Her hair straggled like seaweed against her shoulders. Her lips were blue. And her chest wasn't moving.

She was dead. As dead as Donna MacGregor had been. As dead as Max wanted Virgil to be.

"No." His voice cracked. Why did this kid have to die? She wasn't the one he wanted dead. Was this his fault?

Max put his mouth over hers and blew his own breath into her lungs, like he'd seen people do on TV shows. Nothing happened. He tried again. And again.

But the skin beneath his lips remained soft and cool and lifeless.

No! He wouldn't give up. He couldn't let her die. It wasn't fair. She didn't deserve it. She had been laughing. Please breathe. *Please.*

He didn't know how long it took. He was getting almost as cold as she was when, finally, her chest heaved by itself. He lifted his head just before streams of muddy water spurted out of her mouth and nose. She started to cough.

Max wiped her face with the bottom of his T-shirt and sat back on his heels, uncertain what to do next, when she opened her eyes and looked straight at him.

Her eyes were the color of new ferns. It was a weird thing to notice, but he'd never seen eyes that color before. They were beautiful . . .

And she was alive. He'd done it! He'd saved her. Maybe he wasn't a dumb chickenshit all the time. He grinned. "Hi."

Her mouth trembled. Tears rolled from the corners of her eyes to fall into her hair. Any second now she would start wailing.

His grin faded. "No, don't cry. You're okay." He touched a fingertip to her temple, stopping one of her tears.

She parted her lips, and he braced himself for a scream, but the only sound that came out was a hiccup.

"Thatta girl," he said. He helped her to sit up and patted her back. "Uh, do you hurt someplace?"

"I s-scared."

"I was scared, too. You're okay now, though. What's your name?"

She hiccupped again. "Deedee."

"My name's Max, Deedee. Don't worry. You won't get in trouble. No one's gonna hit you. I won't tell anyone what you did; I promise."

She turned her face to his chest. Even through his damp shirt he could feel the warmth of her tears.

Max didn't know what to do now, either. He didn't know how to offer comfort. He'd had far more experience being on the receiving end of cruelty than kindness. Once more he let his instincts guide him. He lifted his hand to cradle the back of her head.

Just like a kitten, she curled trustingly into his arms. He felt her shivering, and he forgot about the aches in his body so he could pull her closer. He decided to help her the only way he knew how.

He painted the picture in his mind, the place he went when things got real bad. And he took her with him. "Don't cry, Deedee." He bent his head to whisper in her ear. "We aren't really here. We're far, far away. Nothing hurts. Nothing bad happens. See the dog? His name is Skippy."

She turned her head. "D-doggy?"

"No, close your eyes, and then you'll see him. He's big and black with floppy ears and a long tail. Now he's licking your hand. That's how you know he likes you."

"I like doggies."

"Can you smell the cake? It's chocolate. My mommy made it. That's her at the table. Do you hear her? She's singing. She does that when she's happy. She's always happy here."

"She's pretty."

Max squeezed his eyes shut and concentrated harder. He saw Deedee pet his dog. He heard her laugh. Her blue dress and her white socks were clean again as she ate a piece of cake. She clapped her hands and smiled, her lips dotted with chocolate crumbs, as his mother sang "Happy Birthday."

This was nice. He'd never brought anyone with him before.

"Delaney? Baby, where are you?" The cry came from the woods on the other side of the pond. More voices called, getting closer. "Deedee?"

Max blinked and came back. But the picture he'd built was so strong this time, traces of it still remained, swirling like mist around him. Deedee squirmed out of his arms, stretching to reach for the dog.

"Over here!" someone yelled. "It looks like her hair ribbon."

"Oh, sweet mother of God! She's gone to the pond! Delaney? Answer me!"

Deedee twisted around, confused. "Gramma?"

The familiar, sick-sour taste of fear gathered at the back of Max's throat. If anyone caught him here, he was going to get in trouble. It never occurred to him that the adults might want to thank him. They'd call the police and take him home to Virgil. He stuffed his feet back into his shoes and stood.

Deedee scrambled up and grabbed for his hand. "Can I have more cake?"

He leaned over to put his finger against her lips. "Don't tell on me."

"Wanna play," she said.

"Promise you won't tell."

"Want doggy!"

"Promise, Deedee! Or I won't play."

She nodded quickly. "'Kay, Max."

He tugged his hand out of her grasp and backed away. "I gotta go."

"Play!" Her chin trembled. "Ple-ee-ase."

Something flashed between them. A surge of energy, like lightning, like holding Virgil's belt. In Max's mind, the picture built again, the same but different. Everything looked bigger, as if he were smaller.

He staggered, staring at the girl. This wasn't his picture. She was the one doing it. How was it possible? How could she be in his head?

She closed her eyes and smiled, holding out her arms.

Shouts echoed from the woods, along with the noise of heavy footsteps crashing through the underbrush.

Max turned and ran.

He never saw Deedee again. She didn't return to the pond, but until she grew up and no longer wanted to play, he visited her often in his mind. Like a blue jay in the willows or cattail seeds drifting on a summer breeze, she became part of the place he flew away to when he painted pictures in his imagination.

It wasn't until years later, after his parole hearing, that Max recognized the irony of how he had spent his seventh birthday.

On the very day he had decided to take a life, his destiny had been to save one.

ONE

❧

HE CAME BACK TO HER IN A DREAM. YET EVEN AS DELANEY sensed his presence in her head, the watchful, grown-up part of her knew he couldn't be real. This couldn't be happening. He was the boy of make-believe.

"Max?" Her lips mouthed the name. She hadn't spoken it aloud since her childhood. It belonged to the past, to the girl who used to sleep in this ribbons-and-bows room, to the days of laughter in the kitchen and bees in the roses and sheets snapping in the sunshine.

She couldn't remember when he'd first appeared. It seemed as if Max had always been with her, in some corner of her mind. Whenever she'd needed him, he would show up, the skinny little boy with dark hair and a crooked front tooth.

Oh, the times they'd had, the games they'd played. Racing along the lane, their arms extended like airplane wings, they would fix their gazes on the horizon and pretend to soar. Or quietly, so quietly, they would creep past Grandpa's room to the attic for rainy afternoon treasure hunts. There had been safaris in her grandmother's garden, elaborate banquets on the playroom floor, and gleeful, giggling slides down the curving oak banister.

But the best times, the very best ones, had been when he'd taken her to their own special world, the place they made up together, where nothing bad happened and nothing ever hurt.

She breathed his name again. Max. He'd been her partner in mischief, her secret confidante, the imaginary friend she had created to become her playmate. The first time she'd insisted on setting a place for Max at dinner, Grandpa had banged his cane on the floor and had told her to quit making up stories or by God she would turn out as flighty as her mother. Grandma had just winked at her and slid an extra plate beside the butter dish.

But then Delaney's mother had died, and her father had returned for her. They'd moved to the city. She'd tried to bring Max, too, but there hadn't been a banister or extra plates in the apartment, and Mrs. Joiner said that imaginary friends weren't allowed at school.

And eventually Delaney had stopped believing. She'd grown up and left Max behind.

Yet if she'd left him behind, how could he be here?

It was a dream, she reminded herself. And unlike the other ones, this dream wasn't filled with images of twisted metal and death.

Why hadn't she realized it before? Max would be able to keep the nightmares away. He could do anything.

"Max," she whispered.

His presence strengthened until the air around him seemed to reach out in a welcoming smile. He stood in the shadow beside the bedroom doorway. A stubborn, wayward lock of hair hid one eye, but the other sparkled in a conspirator's grin.

What would they do today? Where would they go? What games would they play?

It didn't matter. As long as he kept her safe from the nightmares.

She had always felt safe with Max.

He shuffled forward, his sneakers making stealthy squeaks against the floor. As usual, he wore jeans that looked a size too large, the denim hanging loosely from his hips. His T-shirt bore a smear from the mud pies she'd made him the morning she'd left Willowbank. He had the same hopeful smile, the same live-wire sizzle of energy, that clean, fresh-air feeling of sunshine and summer breezes . . .

The watchful, grown-up part of her stirred once more, but she kept her mind focused on Max. He was a part of the past that it didn't hurt to remember, part of the days of innocence, when life stretched out before her in endless possibilities, and pain was no worse than a skinned knee. Sleep hadn't been something she dreaded then.

She splayed her fingers, reaching toward him. "Let's play, Max."

His image wavered.

"No, Max. Stay!"

Like a shadow glimpsed on the edge of vision, like the dream he was, the little boy faded.

She fought the return of consciousness. "Not yet," she urged. "Not yet."

Through the open window came the cheerful lilt of a robin, as persistent as an alarm clock. Against her closed eyelids, Delaney could feel the tentative warmth of sunrise.

The presence that was Max trembled, then silently flickered out.

Sighing, Delaney rolled to her back and opened her eyes.

Something was wrong. Where was the shelf with her dolls? What had happened to the lacy canopy that sheltered her bed?

It took a few moments for her brain to catch up with her senses. Books lined the shelf, not toys, and a dieffenbachia filled the corner where there had once been a rocking horse. The dolls and the lace were gone. They had been packed up decades ago, along with her fairy-tale books and her frilly socks. The canopy bed had been replaced by a cherrywood four-poster. A matching, grown-up-sized dresser stood beside the plant. Her grandmother had redecorated the house when she'd converted the front half into a bed-and-breakfast.

Delaney sat up and raked her hair off her face. Instead of the typical sleep-tangled lengths, she felt stubby chunks slide between her fingers. There was another one of those moments of puzzlement. What had happened to her hair? She slipped her hand beneath the neckline of her nightgown. Scar tissue ridges as fine as stretched crepe paper slid beneath her palm. The burns no longer hurt. She could barely feel her own touch.

Full wakefulness hit her, bringing a spurt of panic. It had been more than six months since the accident. The changes to her life were so enormous, she still had trouble absorbing the full scope of them. She understood what had happened to her body, just as she was aware of what had happened to her husband. The doctors at the clinic had explained it. So had the police. But it wasn't the same as *knowing*.

Maybe today would be the day that she actually remembered.

After all, she had remembered Max, hadn't she?

Ah, Max. She'd had such a vivid imagination when she'd been a child; her make-believe friend would have been able to help her.

Too bad she'd grown up and was beyond all that.

"THOSE MUFFINS SMELL DELICIOUS, DELANEY, BUT YOU know I don't expect you to cook."

"I like to cook, Grandma, and besides, I have to do something to earn my keep." Delaney picked up a quilted pot holder and started transferring the muffins from the cooling rack to the napkin-lined basket she'd prepared. "These are apple oatmeal. I left out the walnuts in case any of your guests have sensitivities to nuts."

"No one alerted me about any allergies, but I'm glad you left out the nuts anyway. There always seems to be one piece that gets under my dentures. It's so annoying. It isn't very good for business, either, since for some reason the customers don't like seeing me take out my teeth at the table and give the underside a good swipe with my thumb. Seems to spoil their appetite."

Delaney rolled her eyes at her grandmother's humor. "I can't imagine why."

At seventy-two, Helen Wainright had the same twinkle in her gaze that she'd had at fifty, although her long, once-blonde hair was totally white now. Today she had styled it in what she called her Katharine Hepburn pouf. It suited her. She had the kind of presence that would have dominated a stage if she'd chosen to pursue acting. But Helen's passion was people—she would have balked at the separation between performer and audience. Besides, Delaney couldn't picture her assuming a role. She was far too honest to be anyone other than herself.

Helen pointed to the basket. "I hope you're going to have some yourself. You made more than enough."

"Maybe later."

"You should eat more, honey. You're too thin."

"Haven't you heard?" She transferred the last muffin to the

basket and covered them with another napkin. "There's no such thing as being too rich or too thin."

"If that were the case, you'd be turning cartwheels out in the yard instead of baking muffins and looking as if you haven't slept in a week."

"Grandma, I always look like this before my coffee kicks in."

"The weariness I see has nothing to do with caffeine addiction." She motioned toward the stools that were tucked beside the work island in the center of the kitchen. "Sit."

"The muffins will get cold."

"I can heat them up."

Delaney glanced at the swinging door that led to the dining room. The low murmur of voices came through the wood panels. "But your guests—"

"They've got yogurt and a fruit platter. That should hold them for a while. Please, Delaney. I'm worried about you."

"I'm fine. Really." She crossed the floor and perched on the nearest stool. "Please, don't worry."

Helen took the stool beside her and reached for her hand. There was a breath of hesitation as her fingers closed over the patches of new skin. She recovered quickly, turning the motion into an affectionate pat instead of a squeeze. "Leave the cleanup for when Phoebe comes in."

"I made the mess. I can manage."

"It's what I pay her for. The girl's already lazy enough. No point spoiling her."

Delaney did another eye-roll. From what she'd seen, her grandmother treated the college student she'd hired for the summer more like another granddaughter than an employee. "You're not fooling anyone with that tough talk, you know."

"Rats. How did you sleep?"

"Fine. That new bed is really comfortable."

"I heard you down here at dawn."

"I've become an early riser," she said, trying for a casual shrug. "Sorry if I disturbed you."

"Was it a nightmare?"

"No, just a dream this time."

"That's good."

"Mm-hmm. I'm making progress. Not ready for the loony bin yet."

Helen withdrew her hand. "There's nothing crazy about needing a rest. Give yourself time to heal, Deedee, both inside and out. Grief doesn't work on a timetable."

The sound of her childhood name brought tears to her eyes. She'd had more than six months to mourn, but there was something about coming home that lowered the defenses. A kind word, a loving gesture, and years of adulthood collapsed. "Stanford had always been afraid of growing old. He used to joke about how he would prefer to go out in a blaze of glory. God, it still seems unreal."

"Of course it does. It takes years to accept the fact that someone we love is gone. The sorrow does fade eventually, and you'll remember the joy instead."

Helen spoke from experience. She had outlived not only her husband but her daughter as well. Delaney wished she had a fraction of her strength. "I'm sorry, Grandma. You've gone through so much more than I have. I shouldn't be leaning on you."

"That's the wrong way to look at it. What I've gone through has made me a good listener, so don't give it a second thought."

"If only I could remember."

"Oh, honey, what difference would it make? Accidents simply happen sometimes."

Yes, the official ruling was that the car had left the road and struck the utility pole by accident. For lack of solid evidence to the contrary, that was what the police had concluded when they had closed the investigation last week.

Unfortunately, the ruling hadn't satisfied everyone. Only ordinary people died in accidents. Stanford Graye, the billionaire director of Grayecorp, hadn't been ordinary. Neither was the Jaguar XK that he'd died in, so there had to be more to the story. The rumors had been impossible to ignore. They'd run the gamut from a murder conspiracy to a foiled contract killing to a failed suicide pact. "I don't think that Elizabeth's going to let it rest."

"She's grieving, too, Delaney. He was her father."

"Of course, and I understand how she feels. Losing him would have been devastating under any circumstances, but the unanswered questions only make things worse. It must seem suspicious for the only eyewitness to claim amnesia, especially in light of Stanford's will."

"She wants someone to blame," Helen said. "She might be

behaving like a spoiled brat at the moment, but that's how she's handling her grief."

"I guess so."

"You both need time to heal. Be patient."

Delaney rubbed her eyes. Be patient. Right. That had been the motto of her life. It seemed as if she'd always been the one to let things go. If something hurt to look at, she looked at something else.

Helen took Delaney's hand and eased it away from her face. "This is about more than the memory loss, isn't it?"

"That's just it, Grandma. I'm not sure. I feel as if there's something more I'm missing that I should know."

"You and Stanford were happy, weren't you?"

She didn't pause to think about the answer. It was the one she always gave. "Yes. Of course we were."

"But?"

"But there must be some reason why I've blocked his . . . his last moments."

"Some reason besides the crack on the head you took when his car hit that pole? That might be all the explanation you need."

Then why do I keep having those nightmares? Delaney thought. But she didn't ask the question aloud. She hadn't yet described the details of her nightly horrors to her grandmother, and she didn't intend to. She'd already placed enough of a burden on her by coming here.

"I'm not going to push," Helen said. "As long as you know that whenever you're ready to talk, I'll be here to listen."

"Thanks, Grandma." She leaned over to kiss Helen's cheek, then rose from her stool and retrieved the basket of muffins she'd prepared. "Here," she said, holding it out. "I've kept you from your guests long enough."

"Why don't you join us? The Schicks come every year. The other couple, the Reids, are looking for a cottage near Willowbank. They're interesting people."

"Thanks, but I thought I'd take a walk in the yard before the sun gets too hot. It's a beautiful morning."

"If that's what you want."

"Yes."

"All right." Helen took the basket from her hands. "The fresh air will do you good."

"Probably."

"Make sure you put on some gardening gloves if you decide to weed the roses again. I keep them in the shed."

"I will."

"And take your sun hat in case you're out longer."

"Gramma, I'll be fine. Really." Delaney tipped her head toward the dining room. "Now go feed the customers before they start chewing the furniture."

Helen chuckled and crossed the kitchen, picking up a jug of orange juice with her free hand as she passed the counter. She turned around, mimed a kiss to Delaney, then used her backside to push open the dining room door. A welcoming chorus of voices greeted her arrival.

Only two of the four guest rooms had been occupied the night before, but none would be empty by the weekend. This was the busiest season in Willowbank. The annual waterfront festival was due to begin in two weeks. The influx of tourists provided a needed boost to the local economy.

Raymond Wainright, Delaney's grandfather, had made a fortune dividing his lakefront property into parcels for cottages back when the city people had first discovered the beauty of the area. He'd left Helen comfortably well-off, so she hadn't turned her house into a bed-and-breakfast solely for the income it provided. She'd needed something to fill her time, and she thrived on the contact she had with her guests. Like the Schicks, most were repeat visitors.

Delaney never had learned to appreciate the lake that drove the town's tourist economy. She didn't know how to swim. For as long as she could remember, she'd had a deep-seated aversion to water.

A burst of laughter drifted into the kitchen. Delaney took her sun hat from the coat tree beside the back door, settled it on her head, and went outside. She walked past the beds of roses at the edge of the terrace—even if she'd wanted to weed them today, she wouldn't have found anything to pull out. The lawn was over an acre in size and was just as well tended as the garden. It stretched in a freshly mowed carpet between high cedar hedges on either side of the yard to the wrought iron fence at the back. Sticking to the shade as much as she could, she wandered among the shrubs and beds of annuals until she found herself at the oak tree in the center of the lawn that used to hold her swing.

Like the other remnants from her childhood, the swing was gone, its ropes rotted long ago. Yet as Delaney paused beneath the oak, drawing in the smell of the leaves and the damp earth that mounded around the base, the past rose effortlessly to her mind. She could remember what it had felt like to sit on the swing, kick her feet free from the ground, and give herself up to the sway of the ropes. She remembered the half-scary, half-giddy sensation of leaning backward so far that her hair swept the ground. Sometimes, if her mother was having a good day, she would come outside and push her, but most of the time, she had played alone.

The Wainright house was on the outskirts of town. That fact, combined with sheer size of the property, had meant they had no close neighbors. There had once been a trailer park and a set of old train tracks beyond the wooded area, but the kids who had lived there had tended to stay on their own side of the tracks. Delaney's mother hadn't had energy to spare for socializing during her final years, and her grandparents hadn't had friends with children her age, so it wasn't surprising that she had invented a playmate of her own to fill her solitude.

Max. After lying dormant for so long, that was the second time today thoughts of him had surfaced. It wasn't exactly what she'd hoped for, but it was progress. If she could uncover memories that were buried as deeply as her imaginary friend was, could the others be that far behind?

Delaney rested her palm against the tree. As she'd done at least a thousand times since she'd first awakened in the hospital, she sent her thoughts back to that night last winter. She felt the bite of cold air as she stepped out of the restaurant, the warmth of Stanford's grip on her elbow as he helped her into the car, caught the scent of his lime aftershave and the faint aroma of wine . . . and then . . . and then . . .

Nothing. She shut her eyes and shoved against the closed door in her mind. Why hadn't they gone straight home? What had they done for the next four hours? And why on earth had she ended up behind the wheel? The details had to be buried in her brain—the fragments that had been surfacing in her nightmares proved that. She needed to push herself harder.

A breeze stirred the branches overhead, and the trace of Stanford's lime aftershave was replaced by the acrid scent of oak leaves. She couldn't hear screeching brakes, only a warbling robin. No thud of metal, just the sound of her heart.

Delaney curled her fingers into a fist until the backs of her knuckles prickled. Trying to remember the accident had become a daily routine. She should be accustomed to the frustration that followed, but she had hoped things would be different now that she was in Willowbank. If only she could find the key . . .

She strained, *willing* her mind to open.

Still nothing. Damn.

She sighed and opened her eyes. Maybe she was trying too hard. She'd never had to try hard to conjure up Max. He would simply appear.

A blackbird squawked from the woods beyond the fence. Delaney moved her gaze to the line of trees there, picturing Max's shuffling walk as he emerged from the shadows that hid the path. His hair had always been uncombed and a little too long, but she'd loved the way it had gleamed in the sun. She'd loved his smile, too, and the way it had never failed to wrap around her like a hug . . .

Her vision blurred, melding the manicured green lawn she saw with the one she remembered. And in the center of both there was Max. He had already passed the gate and was walking toward her, his hand lifted in greeting . . .

The lawn was empty. Of course, it was empty. No little boy, imaginary or otherwise, was coming to visit. It must be some trick of the sunlight, or a streamer of mist that had drifted in from the pond, that made the spot in the center appear blurry. It gleamed like something solid, yet she could see right through it, as if she were looking into another dimension . . . or a make-believe world.

Delaney's palm slid down the tree as she sank to the ground. She dug her fingernails into the arch of a root, anchoring herself in the here and now.

Yet the budding vision persisted. A feeling of warmth, of unconditional welcome, was enveloping her. Although her mind was alert, her body was relaxing as if she were once again on the wooden seat of the swing and had kicked free from the ground. Her limbs tingled. This was how it used to feel when she had summoned her imaginary friend.

This was pathetic. A grown woman reverting to the crutch of her childhood.

Yet what did she have to lose? Summoning Max wasn't that different from the hypnosis Dr. Bernhardt, the clinic's chief of psychiatry, had attempted. Maybe her subconscious was trying to tell her something. If she could free her imagination the way she had as a child, perhaps she could push past her mental block.

Delaney glanced around to ensure she was still alone, then drew her knees to her chest, wrapped her arms around her legs, and focused her thoughts on Max.

The picture of him wavered, then re-formed, stronger than before. Blotches of crimson and yellow sparkled against the sky. The mist around him thinned, as if stirred by the same wind that rustled the leaves over her head.

Instead of coming closer, the figure in the center turned away from her.

"Hey, Max," Delaney whispered. "Don't go yet."

The shape that was Max appeared to stiffen. He paused where he was and tilted his head to one side, as if he were trying to hear her.

"That's okay, Max." Incredibly, she heard a chuckle bubble past her lips. How long had it been since she had laughed? "Talking to myself is bad enough. I don't expect to get answers."

The light around him brightened, and details began to appear. He was still turned away, so she couldn't see his face, but his hair was the same dark brown it had always been, gleaming with streaks of auburn where the sun touched it.

He was taller than she remembered. Much taller. As a matter of fact, he was far too tall to be a boy. And he was no longer skinny. His shoulders had the breadth of a man's and his biceps stretched out the sleeves of his white T-shirt. He stood with his feet braced solidly apart in a stance filled with self-confidence.

Delaney blinked. Her imaginary friend had grown up.

This time, her laugh came more easily. It was bad enough to regress to her childhood by imagining Max. It was downright pitiful to fantasize about him being a fully grown man.

But what had she expected? She wasn't a child any longer, either.

"Deedee?"

The voice startled her. She hadn't heard it; she had felt it. It was inside her head. It was deep and rough, stroking through her senses like summer heat.

Years ago, she had imagined Max's voice in her head, too. They had giggled together as they'd played their pretend games, and sometimes he would join in when she sang her nonsense skipping rhymes. Back then he had sounded like a child. Now his voice was as unmistakably mature as his appearance.

This was some fantasy, Delaney thought wryly. The doctors would have a field day if they knew. So would Elizabeth. She'd haul her into a competency hearing so fast . . .

But no one had to know. That was the beauty of having a secret friend. "Long time no see, Max," she murmured.

There was a pause; then the spots of color that surrounded him began to move, elongating and twining around themselves. Sunshine gleamed not only from his hair but from his broad shoulders. The image was strengthening. His arms became more defined. She could see a smear of crimson on his sleeve, and a streak of blue on his jeans.

Max pressed the heels of his hands to his temples. "Deedee?"

The distress in his voice took her aback. "I know it's been a while," she began.

"What the hell is going on?"

"I just wanted . . ." She caught herself. He was a figment of her imagination. Why was she trying to explain anything to him?

He dropped his hands and half turned toward her. There was a hint of a sharp cheekbone and strong jaw, but she still couldn't see his face. "Go away, Deedee. I don't have time to play."

"Play? I don't want to play, Max. I only want to remember."

"I don't."

"But you can help me."

"No." He strode away. The colors whirled around him, melding with the shades of green at the edge of the lawn.

"Max, wait!"

"No."

"Max—"

"Dammit, Deedee. Get the fuck out of my head!"

TWO

❧

THE CONNECTION SNAPPED. MAX DUG HIS FINGERS INTO his scalp and stumbled backward, his mind recoiling. Wood splintered as he fell against the easel. He didn't hear it. His foot came down on the wet canvas. He barely felt it. His senses were still clinging to the feeling of *her*.

She'd come back. She was here. The bond hadn't broken.

How was that possible? More than two decades had passed since she'd left him. He'd stopped looking for her a long time ago. He'd stopped needing her. The bond should have been as dead as the boy he used to be.

He pressed the heels of his hands to his eyes, as if he could rub away the mist that had stolen into his mind, but it was as useless as trying to rub away sunshine. Or shut out the echo of laughter. *Her* laughter.

Deedee. He would have known her anywhere. She'd been his special playmate, the baby sister he'd never had. He'd felt the touch of her warmth even before he'd heard her voice calling his name. It was the name he used to go by, not the one on his paintings or his prison record but the one he kept for himself. As it had all those years ago, her presence had tingled across his nerves like the brush of a butterfly just out of reach. He'd needed only to turn around and he could have seen her . . .

"No." It had been a fluke, a trick of his mind, like the phantom twinge of an amputated limb. Max dropped his hands and forced his eyes open, grounding himself in reality. A cerulean sky spread beyond the windows. Stark, whitewashed plaster covered the walls. There were his shelves of paint, the jars of brushes, and the rolls of canvas waiting to be stretched. Nothing remained that didn't belong. He kept this room stripped down to the bare necessities, because that was how he lived his life.

This was what he needed. Peace. Sanctuary. He sure as hell didn't need that voice in his head, stirring up the past.

I only want to remember, she'd said.

Well, he didn't. What was there to remember? What a fool he used to be? How naive and trusting he'd been? How much he'd loved? How much it had *hurt*?

He looked down. A smear of crimson slithered over the maple planks. More paint of the same shade clung to his heel. The canvas he'd been working on lay in a crumpled heap, a deflated, dead skin over the broken skeleton of his easel.

It was gone. Ruined. But it had already been ruined before his foot had gone through the canvas. The shimmering image, the vision he had painstakingly built in his head, had slipped from his grasp the moment *she* had barged into it.

Max aimed a kick at the pile of debris. The remains of the painting skidded across the room, bleeding more smears of crimson until it came to a stop against the far wall.

Instead of relieving his frustration, the kick only fed it. He followed the trail the painting had left, his bare feet leaving bloody red footprints. He snatched up what was left of his work, twisting it between his hands, snuffing out the last possible spark of life until the paint oozed between his fingers . . .

The hair rose on Max's arms. He went motionless, fighting to contain the rage that waited to be released. He could feel it pulsing through him, tempting him, tightening his fists until the muscles in his arms started to tremble.

It would be easy to let go. It would feel good to let the ugliness out. It had felt so good before . . .

Max looked at the crimson that spattered his shirt and stained his hands.

And he remembered the second time he'd picked up Virgil's belt.

Bile gathered in his throat. He dropped the canvas and backed away, coming up against the wall with a thud. He crossed his arms, tucking his hands high into his armpits as he pressed into the unyielding plaster.

"Damn you, Deedee," he said through his teeth. "I'm not that boy anymore."

He had thought the past was under control. And it had been, until she had slipped into his mind and right through the walls that preserved his sanity.

Max didn't want to remember. Forgetting was how he survived.

THREE

❧

THE SCREAM RENT THE MORNING. DELANEY JERKED HER head up, sending her sun hat tumbling to the ground behind her. The blackbird at the edge of the woods took to the sky in a sudden blur of wings, and Delaney struggled to breathe, unable to draw enough air into her lungs. What was that? What on earth had just happened?

There was another scream, this one followed by high-pitched squeals of laughter. Delaney leaned to her side to look past the trunk of the oak tree. A pair of children raced around the house, their giggles trailing like banners behind them. A plump woman in shorts followed, calling their names as they dodged behind the roses, admonishing them to behave. Her words sounded as if they were coming through a tunnel. Delaney watched her usher the girls back to the veranda, distantly aware they must be some of Helen's guests, yet the scene seemed as unreal as the vision of Max.

Was this how insanity started?

She dropped her head into her hands. *Think logically*, she ordered herself. There had to be a reasonable explanation for the . . . the incident she had just experienced.

Yet her mind was still reverberating in shock from the loss of contact with Max.

No, she hadn't lost him. He had severed the link himself. This hadn't been any gentle fading, the way it used to be. His image hadn't gradually dissolved into the mist when they were finished with their game. He had rejected her.

What did this say about her ego, her self-esteem? Her own

fantasy had told her to get lost. Worse than that, he had told her to get the *fuck* out of his head.

Her Max never would have said anything like that. Sure, he used to be mischievous at times. That was all part of his charm. But he was never bad or mean or . . .

She pressed her fingers to her eyes. Stop. Max wasn't real. He was imaginary. He was a creation of her own subconscious. He had no free will, no control, no existence. Therefore she was the one who had rejected herself.

Did this mean she had created a tall, well-muscled, dark-haired man as a fantasy and then had made him reject her? Why? Because there was some suppressed prude inside her who felt guilty over the fantasy? Because she didn't feel she deserved it? Because she felt disloyal to Stanford?

No, that was all wrong. She was doing this because of Stanford. She *had* to remember. She owed him that much.

Then why had her subconscious severed the link with Max? Was there something buried there that she would be better off *not* remembering?

Delaney choked back a sob. If the incident didn't indicate insanity, then trying to explain it could drive her there. She concentrated on her breathing, trying to bring it back to normal.

There had to be a simple explanation for the . . . the hallucination. It might have been a vivid, fever-dream kind of phenomenon. It could be hotter out here than she'd thought. It was only mid-June, but the humidity could be a factor, especially to someone who hadn't spent much time outdoors lately. Or it could be even simpler than that. Her blood sugar might be too low, and she'd slipped into a semi-doze when she'd started to relax. Yes, that seemed plausible. She should have taken her grandmother's advice and eaten a muffin.

A hand settled on her shoulder, squeezing lightly.

Still strung tight, Delaney cried out and jerked away from the touch.

"Sorry. I didn't mean to startle you."

A man in navy blue coveralls stood in front of her. His eyebrows were bushy and steel-colored, as was the hair that poked out from beneath his John Deere baseball cap. His face bore the kind of deep creases due more to weather than to age.

He peered at her with wary concern, his brown eyes looking familiar . . .

Once again, the present merged with a vision from the past, only this man was real. "Edgar?" Delaney asked.

He nodded, a curt, energy-conserving motion of his chin.

Edgar Pattimore had been a frequent sight around the place in the old days. Each fall when the rain gutters had needed cleaning or the porch had needed painting, Edgar's blue pickup truck with the toolbox and ladders would clatter up the driveway. He'd seemed ancient to her when she'd been a child, probably because he'd been friends with her grandfather, yet he didn't appear to be much past Helen's age.

Or Stanford's.

The realization shocked her. She didn't know why it should. Age had been irrelevant when it came to her feelings for her husband.

Delaney got to her feet and combed her hair from her face with her fingers. It took a second to remember there wasn't enough hair to comb. It took several more to register the fact that her hands were shaking. She retrieved her sun hat from the ground and set it back on her head. "You might not remember me, Edgar. I'm—"

"Deedee," he said. "Your grandmother said you were coming."

He was the second person in the space of an hour to call her by the childhood name. The third, if she counted Max.

But Max wasn't real. So he didn't count. Or maybe he did, because he was a product of her subconscious mind . . .

Enough already, she told herself. Contacting Max had been an experiment. It hadn't worked. Time to move on. "Yes, I arrived here yesterday." The wind picked up, moving the boughs overhead. A shaft of sunlight struck her cheek, and she adjusted the brim of her hat to protect it. "The place looks wonderful," she said, gesturing around the yard. "I should have realized that you'd still be helping out."

"My nephew takes care of the heavy work now, but I do what I can." He slapped the work gloves he was holding against his leg, knocking off a shower of dirt. An electric hedge trimmer dangled from his other hand. "You didn't see anyone else out here, did you?"

She started. "What do you mean?" Her voice sounded shriller than she'd intended. She took a calming breath. "Uh, no, other than those girls and their mother. Why?"

Edgar used his chin to point toward the small wooden structure that was nestled beside the hedge on the far side of the roses. "Some of the stuff inside the garden shed was moved around. Looks like someone was inside before I got here."

"Was anything taken?"

"Nope. Besides the tools and a few bags of fertilizer, the only thing worth stealing's the lawn tractor, but it's still there."

"It could have been kids."

"I suppose. I don't like to think someone's been snooping around. That shed should be locked."

"Has Willowbank changed that much?"

"Used to be we knew everybody. Not now. Lots of new people building around the lake. Kids cut through here on their way into town. They figure everything is public property." He slapped his gloves against his leg again, then shifted his gaze from the shed to her. "You need some help?"

"Help?"

"You didn't look so good a minute ago. You need help getting back to the house?"

"Thanks, but I'm all right. I was just . . . reminiscing. This garden used to be one of my favorite places."

Another chin nod. "Sorry about your husband, Deedee. Or I guess I should call you Mrs. Graye now."

"No, Delaney's fine. And I appreciate your sympathy, Edgar."

The creases in his cheek tightened in Edgar's version of a smile. "It's good you came home, Delaney. We missed you."

Oh, God. Were those tears starting again?

Before she could embarrass herself, he pulled on his gloves and turned toward the driveway. "Watch out you don't step on any broken glass when you're wandering around. I picked up more'n half a case of empties last week. Kids," he muttered, moving away. "Some of 'em need a good swift kick."

She waited until he had left, then returned her gaze to the back fence. Not that she expected to see anyone. Not again. Not unless she summoned him, and she wasn't about to do that. She'd gotten carried away with the reminiscences, that was all.

As if to prove it to herself, she left the shelter of the oak tree and crossed the lawn, walking directly through the spot where she'd seen Max.

Nothing was there. No mist or shimmers in the air, no warmth other than the sunshine. Good. She continued until she reached the gate.

Like the fence, it was only as high as her waist and would present more of a nuisance than an obstacle to an adult, but it had been an effective barrier for a toddler. Her grandparents had always been adamant about keeping this gate closed. With the woods so close and the pond only a short walk down the path, their concern had been understandable. Helen would want it closed now, too, with those children of her guests running around.

Yet this morning the gate was unlatched, as if someone had passed through in a hurry and hadn't bothered to close it completely. Someone flesh and blood, like whoever had been in the garden shed.

Or someone with no substance at all, like a figment of an overactive imagination . . .

Delaney grasped the top of the iron gate and yanked it toward her. The latch clicked with satisfying finality. She returned to the house without looking back.

The kitchen was empty when she stepped inside. Judging by the silence in the dining room, breakfast was over. A tray full of dirty dishes rested on the counter, so evidently Phoebe hadn't yet arrived. She wondered briefly where her grandmother was, but then she heard a thump from the direction of the front of the house, followed by a pair of shrieking giggles like those she'd heard in the garden.

Those girls must be continuing their game of tag inside, which explained what Helen was doing. She would be running after them, trying to minimize the damage, but the children would be able to see through her scolding. Delaney certainly had. She wouldn't be surprised if the girls had already discovered the banister. She left her hat on the coat tree, found a pair of rubber gloves under the sink, and started on the dishes.

Though it had been years since she'd needed to do any housework, she welcomed the chore. Regardless of what Helen said, Delaney intended to help as much as she could, for as long as she was here. Besides wanting to ease her grandmother's workload, she did need to keep busy, or she would likely go nuts for real.

That was one of the few things she and Stanford had disagreed about. She'd been a successful real estate agent when she'd met him. He hadn't been able to understand why she didn't want to lead a life of leisure and simply enjoy the wealth he'd spent his lifetime acquiring. His first wife had filled most of her days with bridge games and shopping, and had apparently been perfectly content. Mundane necessities like cleaning, laundry, menu planning, or caring for her child had been handled by the household staff. The only occupation Constance Graye had undertaken seriously had been playing Stanford's hostess. She'd excelled at that, working her social connections with the zeal of a politician. The parties she'd given had been legendary.

Or at least they had seemed legendary to Delaney the first time she'd attempted to host one of her own. She'd wanted to make Stanford happy. That was why she'd eventually given in about her career, too. She'd directed her energy toward being a good wife. She hadn't quite believed him when he'd sworn he didn't expect anything from her except her love.

"You're beautiful, Delaney." That had been Stanford's reply to everything, and he'd considered the answer sufficient. "You make me feel young. That's plenty. How could I want more? You've already given me more than I'd ever dreamed."

She took a brush from the edge of the sink to scrub the baking tin she'd used for the muffins, and her gaze strayed to the gloves that protected her hands. They were yellow and clumsily ugly, but they were necessary. The current round of skin grafts was healing well. The doctors had assured her the lines would be practically invisible when they were done, and the Frankenstein patchiness over her knuckles would fade with time, but that didn't concern her. All she'd cared about was regaining the full use of her fingers. The burns to her body had been superficial compared to the damage done to her hands.

There was no way Stanford would have found her beautiful now. No one would. How could she ever have resented the way he'd admired her appearance?

Her stomach tightened at the thought, so she automatically pushed it away. Stanford had been a good man. He'd loved her, and he'd been kind to her. And it could very well be her fault that he was dead.

The dining room door squeaked open.

Delaney bent over to fit the muffin tin into the dishwasher. "I'm almost done here, Grandma. Do you want some help making up the rooms?"

Someone cleared their throat. The sound was distinctly male.

Delaney closed the dishwasher door and straightened.

A short, middle-aged man stood in the doorway. He had a symmetrical, unremarkable face that would be difficult to describe and would fade into a crowd. His round-shouldered posture and toed-in feet seemed to reinforce his apology. He kept his attention on the brochure he was holding. Helen displayed an assortment of them on the table by the front entrance. Some advertised local businesses and tourist attractions. This was one she'd had printed to promote her business.

"May I help you?" Delaney asked.

"Yes, I'm sorry, miss. I'm looking for Mrs. Wainright."

"I believe Mrs. Wainright is busy upstairs. Were you interested in booking a room?"

He nodded and stepped forward hesitantly. "Yes, I was driving by and saw the sign for the Wainright House on the gatepost. This is lovely. When was it built?"

Odd that she hadn't heard the front doorbell. Perhaps she'd been running the water. "Sometime in the early nineteenth century. The history is in the brochure you're holding, if you'd like more details."

"Of course, of course." He fumbled to open it. "Yes, I see. And it was built by a Wainright. How fascinating. Then Mrs. Wainright must have been married to a descendant of the builder. Mother would be thrilled to meet her. She's a history buff, but she gets out so seldom. Arthritis, you know."

Delaney pulled off her gloves and set them on the counter. "If you'd like to wait in the dining room, my grandmother should be down directly."

"Your grandmother? Oh, this is fabulous. Then you're a Wainright, too. Another generation still living in the same house. It says here this was triple brick construction. They built them to last back then, didn't they?"

"Please, help yourself to some coffee while you're waiting. We keep a fresh pot on the sideboard in the dining room. It's through that door behind you."

Instead of taking the hint, the man clutched his brochure and moved farther into the kitchen. "Will you look at these ceilings. They must be fourteen-footers. Or is it fifteen?"

"Fifteen, I believe."

"Marvelous." Tipping back his head, he turned in a circle to admire the ceiling. When he stopped, he was only a few steps away and was looking directly at her. "Oh, I know who you must be. You're Delaney Wainright Graye, aren't you?"

She was too surprised to deny it. "Yes. How would you . . ."

"Here," he said, placing the brochure in her hand. "This is for you."

"Excuse me?"

He smiled and continued across the kitchen to the back door, his gait no longer hesitant or apologetic in the least. "You've been served, Mrs. Graye." He gave her a jaunty wave and stepped outside.

Delaney regarded what she held. Wedged between the glossy pages of the brochure there was a stiffly folded piece of heavy, legal-sized paper.

"Delaney?" Helen swept into the kitchen. "I thought I heard voices. Did someone come back here?"

"Yes. He left."

"That's strange." She went to the window that overlooked the yard. "My guests know they shouldn't come into the old section, but sometimes they make themselves too much at home."

"It wasn't a guest, Grandma." She opened the paper. "It was a process server."

"A process . . . Here in my house? The nerve!"

Delaney wondered if the man had been watching the place from the garden shed, waiting for the best time to slip inside. It was a disconcerting thought. She was thankful he had missed seeing her in the yard. She'd had enough people materializing out of thin air for one morning.

"I'll bet it was that man who came here yesterday," Helen continued. "He seemed wrong somehow so I lied and said we didn't have a vacancy. What did he look like? Pale? Big and jowly?"

"No, he was short and very ordinary."

"He must have been looking for the Schicks. I'd heard they were having trouble with their former business partner."

"He was here for me."

"*You?*" Helen turned. Her gaze went to the paper Delaney held. "Why ever in the world would someone sue you?"

She steadied her hands so that she could read the print on the summons. Having it served this way had taken her by surprise, but she realized she felt no shock at what it said. In fact, she should have expected it. Now that the police had closed their investigation, there would be no criminal charges laid. A civil suit was the next logical step for a woman who was bent on revenge. "It seems as if I was right," she said. "Elizabeth's not letting this rest."

"Oh, no. She's not contesting the will again, is she?"

She's not allowing me bury my husband. She's forcing me to keep ripping open the wound that won't heal . . .

Delaney swallowed hard as she refolded the paper and placed it next to the rubber gloves on the counter. They seemed to belong together. Both were ugly reminders of the new reality of her life.

Messes that she'd made and needed to clean up herself.

"Delaney? Honey, what is it?"

"My stepdaughter is suing me for the wrongful death of her father."

ALL OF THIS SHOULD HAVE BEEN HERS. FROM HER FATHER'S collection of first editions and the burled walnut bookcase that enclosed it, to the trio of Picasso sketches that hung over the leather couch, it rightfully should have gone to her. Even the desk she was lying on ought to have been hers.

"Elizabeth?"

Elizabeth Graye summoned a reassuring smile. It wouldn't do to let Alan Rashotte know her mind had wandered. He used to be arrogantly proud of his lovemaking skills.

In that regard, Alan hadn't changed. He knew how to ensure a woman's physical pleasure. He was as tireless as a machine and just as reliable. His only flaw was his naked ambition. No, that wasn't his only flaw. He also considered himself to be smarter than her. He probably believed this interlude had been his idea. He might even have assumed that she'd been overcome by passion.

She'd been taught better than that. Emotions were good tools as long as you knew how to use them. Relationships should be maintained only as long as they were advantageous.

Alan pushed aside her pearls to nuzzle her neck. "That was great."

She murmured what he took for agreement as she flattened her palms on the desktop. Even without seeing it, she could appreciate the patina that gave the wood its depth. Her mother had been particularly proud of this acquisition. She'd outbid several dealers in order to bring it home. Elizabeth had slipped away from her governess to watch from the second-floor gallery as the chauffeur had maneuvered it up the stairs to her sitting room. One of the gardeners had been pressed into service to help. That had been a sight. Constance had made him remove his boots before he set foot on the marble floor of the foyer with no more than a lift of her eyebrow.

But the desk hadn't remained at the house. The moment her father had seen it, he'd decided to have it for himself and had it moved to his office.

Stanford Graye had had a weakness for pretty things. Like the desk and the Picassos. And his new wife.

Elizabeth curled her nails against the wood and moved her gaze to the window. The Manhattan skyline twinkled like jewels in a giant crown. It was a clichéd comparison, but she'd always thought it fitting since her father had ruled his kingdom from this place. The power he'd wielded had intoxicated her. He'd seemed invincible. His greatest strengths had been his exceptional memory and his knack for recognizing an individual's weakness. He was a master at manipulation. People lined up for the privilege of letting him have his way and believed it was their idea. He'd been a modern-day Tom Sawyer, reaping profits while others painted his fence. All her life, she'd watched and learned and dreamed of being just like him.

How many times had he sat behind this desk at the end of the day, his sleeves rolled up, the ice cubes tinkling as he sipped his drink? He used to ask her opinion. He'd pretended to listen to her, because he'd known that's what she wanted. Then had come the day when he actually *did* listen to her. She'd never been prouder. She'd never felt more loved. What shall we do, Bethie? What do you think?

Alan rubbed his cheek against hers. "Come home with me. Let's finish this on a bed."

Elizabeth tipped her head away. Alan's skin was like sandpaper. He should be shaving twice a day, but he rarely did. She should have remembered that. She put her hands on his shoulders, using the movement to ease back the cuff of her jacket so she could check her watch. "I can't. I have some things I need to take care of here."

"They can wait."

The self-satisfied tone drove away any lingering pleasure. Suddenly, she couldn't bear his touch on her flesh. She gave Alan a firm push and twisted her hips to dislodge him. She stood, turning her back while she straightened her clothes. "No, I'm afraid I need to deal with them now. You might as well go home."

"Are you sure that's what you want?"

The sound of his zipper set her teeth on edge. "Yes, Alan. It is."

He brushed aside a lock of hair that had come loose from her twist. "I thought what we did here meant you'd changed your mind about us, Elizabeth."

She didn't like his tone now, either. It implied an obligation she'd never agreed to. She and Alan had indulged in a casual affair a year ago. For a while, perhaps, she had deluded herself into thinking it could be more, but he hadn't really cared for her. He'd believed he could advance his career by romancing the boss's daughter. She'd realized that even before her father had pointed it out.

"Come on. We used to be good together."

"This isn't the right time for me. I can't afford any more complications."

"Then what was this about?"

She smoothed the wrinkles from her skirt, pressing her palms hard against her thighs so he wouldn't see that her hands were shaking. "Does it matter?"

Alan stroked her cheek. He laughed. "Not a damn. I love you anyway. I'll see you tomorrow."

She nodded and locked the door behind him.

There was a difference between making love and getting love. One didn't necessarily lead to the other. Alan was too arrogant to love anyone. It would be stupid to believe him, so it was good that she hadn't. The cologne he wore was too cloying. His laugh grated. His fingers were too bony and his lips were too stiff when he kissed. She didn't even like him that much.

Elizabeth returned to the desk and sat in Stanford's old chair. She curled her hands over the ends of the arms, exactly the way her father used to. Technically, this furniture belonged to Delaney, like all the other personal items in his office, although she hadn't yet bothered to claim any of it. Elizabeth had done it instead. Alan wouldn't have understood the subtlety of using the desk as they had. He'd thought he was simply screwing *her*.

She'd moved into the office gradually, bringing some files one day, holding a few meetings another. Her actions had produced rumblings of discontent among some members of the board, but no one had dared oppose her openly yet. That had been her primary reason for getting Alan on her side. She needed an ally. Sex had only been the opening gambit, though. The best way to ensure his cooperation was to promise him what he really valued, which certainly wasn't *her*.

The tears came without warning. She blotted them on her jacket sleeve, then used her cuff to rub off the palm prints Alan had left on the desktop.

What the hell *had* this been about?

Revenge. Power.

And proving to herself that she was indeed just like her father.

FOUR

❦

EVEN BEFORE SHE UNDRESSED THAT NIGHT, BEFORE SHE
dutifully rubbed the cream the doctor had prescribed into each
line of the healing sutures, before she slid between the sheets
and reached out to turn off the lamp on the beside table, Delaney knew the nightmare would find her.

The reprieve she'd had when she'd first come home was
over. It wasn't only the added stress of Elizabeth's lawsuit. Deep
down Delaney had known there was no escaping what haunted
her, no matter how far she went. She couldn't get away from it
because she'd brought it with her.

The dream started as it always did. She saw a road through
a tunnel of headlights. Or it seemed like a road, winding ahead
of her in a shiny ribbon of bluish gray, but it was narrow like a
path. She shouldn't be going this fast. The branches and leaves
were slapping her face and shins. She shifted her legs, pressing
back into the seat, into the mattress, trying to stop her forward
momentum. She didn't want to see what was around the next
bend. She didn't want to reach the end. This was the wrong way.
She had to turn back.

But she only went faster. Her hair was blowing across her
eyes, and she lifted her hand to push it away, but now it felt as
though she were moving through water. She couldn't breathe.
She fought to turn her head, to ask Stanford to help because it
was dark and she was cold and why couldn't she slow down?
This wasn't the way home and oh God what was that sound?

Delaney curled into a ball in the center of the bed. The top
sheet was wrapped around her calves but the rest of the covers

had slid to the floor. No breeze came through the window, no noise, no light. The moon had not yet risen, and the maples beside the house hid the stars. There was nothing to wake her up or to guide her back.

So she hurtled forward, through the cold and liquid scene, until the pale gray path turned shiny, then white, then fireball red, and suddenly she wasn't moving anymore because she was outside, freezing and burning and helpless to block out those sounds.

Metal screeched as it buckled. It moaned and cried like a living thing. Glass sang when it burst, a high-pitched pulse that stung the scalp behind her ears. Fire laughed and cackled as it ate flesh. Bones crunched like stalks of fresh celery.

Delaney pressed her face to her knees. The sheet beneath her was damp from sweat. So was her skin. Slick and hot like the blood that ran from her hands.

No. Please, no. Not again. No more.

The worst noise was yet to come, the heart-rending sound of a man screaming.

Stanford.

He was dying.

Again.

She tried to move, but her legs wouldn't work. Something held them down. Strands of seaweed curled around her ankles like slimy fingers. She tried to free herself but she couldn't get any air even though she could feel the bubbles brushing past her lips as they rose through the water.

Delaney was dying, too. Through the hell of her nightmare, that certainty reached her consciousness. Her mind cried out in desperation.

No! Not again. Please!

Someone settled on the bed beside her. She could feel the mattress dip with his weight and sensed that she was no longer alone.

Yes, oh *yes*! He'd come back. He couldn't be dead if he was here with her. Delaney moved toward the presence that she felt and spread her fingers to capture the warmth that flowed from his body.

Odd, though, that the place where Stanford was lying didn't smell of lime aftershave. It smelled of sunshine and fresh air and . . . turpentine.

*   *   *

MAX SURFACED SLOWLY. HIS MIND WAS AS LAX AS HIS BODY, and both were urging him to sink back into sleep. His dreams, on the rare occasions when he did dream, were merely random firings of his synapses, kaleidoscope patterns behind his closed eyelids with no purpose and little form. His subconscious got sufficient exercise while he was awake and painting, so he usually slept like the dead.

But this dream was prodding him forward, refusing to let him rest. It encompassed his senses as well as his mind. He was positive he was no longer alone. He was just as sure there was no one else in his bedroom, because he'd never yet allowed a woman to spend the night. But there was a presence in his bed, an unmistakably female one.

Max felt no alarm at first. Having the woman here seemed right somehow. He could sense her weight on the mattress beside him and felt the warmth of her breath on his neck. He turned his head, and her hair tickled his chin. She smelled sweet, like roses.

Like Deedee.

Max's eyes drifted open.

The dream didn't fade. Neither did the sensation of the woman's presence. He swept his arm across the bed beside him. There was nothing in the space, and yet he could feel a resistance, as if the air was thickening . . .

His pulse picked up. He looked around. The bed was cloaked in shadows. So was the entire room. The only illumination came from an orange glow that seemed to float in the corner. It was centered between a bookshelf and a potted plant.

He had no bookshelf in his bedroom. He kept no houseplants. His bed didn't have wooden bedposts, either. What the hell . . .

The glow shimmered in midair, appearing to come from a dimension that wasn't bounded by distance. He began to hear noises now. Crunching metal. It sounded like something was crashing over and over inside that light.

The woman beside him pressed closer, as if he could protect her, just as Deedee used to . . .

Finally, the pattern of what was happening registered in his brain. The last traces of sleep fled.

Hell, this was no illusion. Deedee had returned, but instead of crashing his painting, she'd stolen into his sleep.

Max sat up fast, pulling away from the presence on the bed.

He didn't move quickly enough. Something tingled across his back. Not a touch, yet deeper than a touch. It held him where he was as her voice slipped into his mind. "Don't go. Please."

He felt himself start to soften, to lean into her, the way he used to. It was a reflex response. He gritted his teeth and held himself rigid. "What the hell do you want this time?"

"Max?"

"Who else did you expect?"

"Max?"

She sounded surprised. He didn't know why she would, because this sure hadn't been his idea. She'd been the one to bring him here.

But where was *here*? She'd drawn him into her grandparents' yard this morning. He'd recognized the scene as it had formed around him, because she'd often played with him there. He glanced at the corner again. The plant and bookshelf seemed real, but the rest had the wavering haze of an unfinished dream. He swung his legs over the side of the bed.

"Max, wait!"

"This has to stop, Deedee. Quit barging into my head."

"Don't leave me."

"Hey, you were the one who left me."

"What?"

"Forget it. Go back to wherever it is you've been all these years. We're done."

"Help me, Max. I . . . need you."

"What? To remember? I told you—"

"No! I don't want to remember this part."

The sounds of crunching metal grew closer. The glow in the distance—in the corner—brightened until flames covered the plant and licked up the walls. At their core was a dark mass, part car wreckage, part seaweed, writhing in rhythm with the screeching metal. As he watched, it stretched tendrils across the floor toward his feet.

This wasn't a dream; it was a nightmare.

Deedee's nightmare.

Max twisted to look at the bed. In the flickering light of the flames she had created, he could see the outline of her shape beside him. She had curled into a ball, her face pressed to her knees as she shivered and gasped for air. Someone was screaming, but it wasn't Deedee; it was a man.

The dark tendrils from the mass in the corner reached Max's toes and flowed upward. Cold slime, like the muddy bottom of a pond, enveloped his ankles. He was being drawn toward the core of the nightmare.

"Make it stop, Max. Please!"

He could free himself with a snap of his thoughts. She was the one who was generating this image, not him. He could break the connection between them as he had before and be back in his own bed in the next second.

That was what he should do. She didn't belong in his life. This was the second time she'd ambushed him when his mental defenses were down, and she had no right. The boy she was looking for didn't exist any longer. He owed her nothing.

"I'm begging you, Max." She was shaking so badly her teeth chattered. "I can't do this alone. Help me. Keep me safe."

For all its urgency, the plea was silent. It was here and yet not here, like all the other words she'd spoken and the bed he sat on and the room he was in.

Yet it held him in place as firmly as her touch that hadn't been a touch . . .

Damn. *Damn!* Max kicked loose from the slime that gripped his feet and swung his legs back onto her bed. "You're okay, Deedee. It's only a dream."

She moaned. "It's real."

"It's a dream," he repeated. "It won't hurt you."

"It will. It always does."

Always? Had she experienced this horror before?

Light flared from the corner, sending the flames racing along the ceiling while the dark seaweed tendrils crept over the edges of the mattress and up the bedposts. Deedee wrapped her arms around her legs and curled more tightly into her ball.

Max inched closer and leaned over her until he sensed the curve of her ear beneath his lips. "Deedee, you have to stop this."

"How?"

The slime touched his feet again. He braced his hands

beside her and shifted to his knees. "You know how. Go somewhere else."

"I can't."

"We'll go together. Think of sunlight. Birds. You like birds, don't you?"

Fire billowed through the air, curling above the bed like a living canopy. The man was still screaming, only the sound was turning guttural, liquid, melding with the whoosh of the flames.

"Think of roses, Deedee. I can smell them on your hair." Max pulled out a memory to build the picture in his head. "Look, we're in your grandma's garden. Here's a bud that's almost open. Aren't the petals soft?"

Cold was spreading across the sheet as the glistening, wet darkness advanced. Overhead, the flames screamed in harmony with the man.

Max lifted one hand to her shoulder, holding his fingers close enough for her to feel his warmth. "Deedee, you have to let go of this dream before it swallows you."

"I can't."

"You can. What color is the rosebud?"

"I don't know!"

"I think it's yellow. Sure, it's the color of soft butter."

"I don't see it."

He concentrated harder. "There's dew on the petals."

"It's around my ankles. It's wet and cold and—"

"No, that's only dew. Let go of the bad part and see the good."

"Max, I *can't*. I forgot how."

He moved his hand down the shadow of her arm. Energy sparked along his palm. "Feel the moisture on your skin."

"Max!"

"Use it. Make it do what you want."

Her breath hitched. "My skin's burning. Don't you smell it?"

He did. He could feel his own skin puckering. He had nothing to shield himself. She'd brought him into this dream as naked as he'd been in his own bed. "Think of the dew. There's rain, too. It's going to put out the fire."

"But—"

"You're safe, Deedee. Nothing hurts here. Nothing bad happens."

"Nothing bad."

"It's our own special place, remember?"

She unlocked one of her arms from around her legs.

"That's it. Snuff the flames, Deedee."

She extended her hand past his shoulder. "I still feel them. They're hot."

"That's the sunrise."

"Is it morning?"

"Sure. The night's over. The sun's coming up. It's shining through the rain."

"On the roses?"

"Right. Whatever you want."

Inch by inch, the wet blackness receded from the bed and drew back to the corner where the plant stood. The screams took longer to fade, but they did in time, taking the flames with them.

In place of the nightmare, a rainbow-tinged mist spread through the air. From it came the lilting call of a robin, the whisper of raindrops on leaves, and finally, the image of a rosebush in a slanting beam of sunlight.

Max sat back on his heels and rubbed his palms on his thighs. His skin was damp. He was breathing as hard as Deedee now, but it seemed as if the worst was over. Details continued to appear in the scene that was forming. Sunshine spread past the raindrops to warm his skin. The scent of earth wafted past his face. She was assuming control of the dream herself, as he'd known she could. Her mind had been almost as powerful as his when it had come to building their play world.

She used to love playing hide-and-seek with him among her grandmother's rosebushes. It had worried him, because she would often snag her clothes on the thorns and sometimes she'd get scratches, but she hadn't cared because she never got punished. She'd giggle when he found her and raise her arms to him for a hug.

She'd felt small and solid, or the next best thing to solid, since he hadn't actually been able to touch her. The sense memory of holding her that first time by the pond had been enough to make her real in his mind. That, and the power of

Deedee's own imagination, had given substance to what had happened whenever their thoughts had been together, just as it had tonight. At times, she'd been as pesky as a real little sister, but he'd never been able to refuse her.

Apparently, that hadn't changed. He could be anywhere, and he'd sense her touch. He would know he was alone, and yet he would feel and hear and smell her so vividly that often he got confused.

His fantasies didn't confuse him these days. They were what powered his art.

Max returned his gaze to the bed. The sunlight Deedee had imagined was spreading across the mattress, giving him his first clear view of her. Apart from a sheet that was wrapped around her ankles, her legs were bare. So were her arms. A satin nightgown was twisted in tight folds around her waist and hips. It revealed a woman's body, not a girl's.

The sight jarred him, but it shouldn't have. Time hadn't stood still for her any more than it had for him. She would be close to thirty by now. There was no trace of the baby fat that had rounded her limbs when she'd been a child. Her calves and thighs were slender. So were her arms. He could see the ridge of a hip bone beneath her nightgown and the sloping, feminine curve of her buttocks.

The differences in her weren't only physical. The child he had known would never have produced a nightmare like the one he'd just witnessed. She'd been pampered and doted on. She'd embodied everything peaceful and good to him because she'd had no concept of evil or of pain. When had that changed?

Deedee rolled to her back on the mattress beside him and flung out her arms, as if abandoning herself to the pleasure of the scene she had imagined. The neckline of her nightgown was twisted to one side, revealing the graceful length of her throat. Ivory satin pulled taut across her breasts and outlined the contours of her nipples.

Max sucked his breath through his teeth. No, she wasn't a little girl anymore. She wasn't his sister, either.

"Can you taste it?" she asked.

"What?"

"The rain. Tip your head back."

"Deedee—"

"Don't you remember how we used to catch the rain on our tongues?"

He slid his gaze from her breasts to her mouth. "Game's over, Deedee."

"C'mon, Max." She opened her mouth and touched her tongue to her lower lip. The motion didn't appear childish in the least.

Max felt an unaccustomed stir of conscience. He ignored it and leaned closer.

That was when he saw the strip of raised skin that curled around her right arm from her elbow to her shoulder. It had the shiny pink tightness of a healing burn. A similar, wider scar crossed her collarbone and split into ragged white fingers that disappeared beneath the edge of her nightgown. The satin was pulled taut across that, too. The puckered edges of the scar extended to the upper slope of her breast.

What the hell happened to you, Deedee?

Her eyes opened fast, as if his thought had been a shout. She stared at him.

He soaked in the contact as he soaked in the sunshine. Her eyes were the same warm green he remembered, the color of new ferns, but there was an unfamiliar murkiness in their depths. The nightmare was still there. Waiting. He touched his fingertips to her scarred shoulder. "What the hell happened to you?" he repeated.

The garden vanished, along with the mist and Deedee. And just like that, Max was back where he'd started. In his own bed. Utterly alone.

He reached for her instinctively, extending his mind into the darkness to follow her warmth, but she had shut herself off, curling her mind into a defensive ball the same way he'd seen her curl her body.

He pushed harder, trying to get her back. He needed more. He needed her. He couldn't lose her this time . . .

Max drove his fist into the mattress, then rolled to his back and dropped his forearm across his eyes.

No.

He didn't need anyone.

FIVE

❧

DELANEY SCOOPED A FISTFUL OF CLOTHESPINS AND LIFTED a sheet from the wicker basket by her feet. Like so many things here, the smell of fresh air and her grandmother's lemon detergent took her back to her childhood, effortlessly calling up the days when she'd run along the row of laundry, her hands slapping against damp cotton. She had read somewhere that scent memories were the strongest. They bypassed the reasoning part of the brain and went straight to the vestigial animal brain that governed emotions.

That was probably why she imagined lime aftershave when she thought of Stanford.

Then why did she smell paint when she thought of Max? Why had she smelled it on her sheets when she'd awakened this morning?

She brought the damp fabric to her nose.

It smelled like fresh air and lemon detergent; nothing more. Of course, it would. It had gone through the cotton cycle of Grandma's heavy-duty washer. There was nothing like hot water and twenty minutes of agitation to get rid of a few leftover molecules of imaginary turpentine. It used to do the trick with imaginary mud pies, too.

Delaney pressed her lips together as she hung up the sheet. She wished she could smile, but she wasn't quite there yet. A five-year-old believing in a pretend playmate was considered cute. A thirty-year-old doing the same could be considered troubling, to put it mildly.

Her latest encounter with Max had been a dream, she

reminded herself. Overall, it had been a positive one, and she should be grateful for that. In fact, she'd awakened feeling refreshed instead of worn-out. For the first time in six months, she'd managed to take control of her recurring nightmare. She'd turned its familiar elements of fire and water into something she could deal with. Sunshine and rain. It was actually very clever, the kind of thing Dr. Bernhardt might have suggested. He would have approved of her progress.

But what would a professional have said about the man she'd glimpsed in her bed when she'd awakened? The *naked* man? Delaney wasn't sure that she wanted to know.

While she'd been asleep and battling her terrors, Max had been a hazy presence, more of a feeling than a form. Yet the moment she'd opened her eyes, the image of him had solidified. For a flash, Max had been *there*. The image had lasted only a split second, yet she'd had enough time to see his familiar blue gaze and the lock of hair that always flopped over his forehead. She'd gotten the impression there had been a lot of bare skin, too.

Apparently, her subconscious had decided that the adult Max slept in the nude.

Max the boy had worn grubby T-shirts and jeans. He would have been too shy to show up with nothing on. The new version of Max seemed to have acquired an attitude along with his height and his muscles. A man like that would have no problem with his nudity.

What the hell happened to you, Deedee?

He'd sounded as surprised by her appearance as she'd been by his. The reaction had made him seem even more real. She'd heard his voice as vividly as she'd felt his touch. Skin that had been as good as dead for months had tingled beneath the warmth of his fingers.

That alone proved it had been only a dream. For one thing, a real man would have been repulsed by the scars on her body. For another, she hadn't enjoyed a man's touch in ages.

The thought gave her pause. It was true, she and Stanford hadn't made love as often in the last few years as they had in their early days, but that was only natural. No one could honeymoon forever. She reached for a pillowcase and gave it a brisk flap to knock out the wrinkles. The back of her hand smacked hard against the clothesline.

The pain knocked her breathless. She dropped the pillowcase and cradled her hand to her chest, blinking away tears as she waited for the stinging to fade. An image of roses and rainbows flashed through her mind. It was the place Max had taken her the night before, where there hadn't been any scars or skin grafts. There hadn't been any vengeful stepdaughters or lawsuits, either.

Could that be why her mind was returning to him? Was it a sign she couldn't cope with her real life?

Possibly. He'd certainly helped her cope with her nightmare, even though she'd had to plead with him to do it. That was an improvement over the way he'd rejected her outright yesterday.

But she had made him up; therefore *she* was the one who had rejected herself, and now *she* was the one who was coping.

This was getting far too complicated. Of all the things she had to worry about, the return of Max shouldn't be one of them. It simply meant her imagination was functioning again. Hopefully, her memory would follow suit.

She flexed her fingers and leaned over to retrieve the pillowcase.

"Hey, Delaney."

She turned toward the voice.

Phoebe Spencer, the student who was helping Helen for the summer, was hurrying toward her from the direction of the back door. Along with her usual outfit of cut-off shorts and a tube top, she wore one of Helen's ruffled gingham aprons. She waved one hand at the laundry basket. "Mrs. W.'s going to kill me."

"Why?"

"I was supposed to hang that stuff up."

"I'm almost done. You can pretend you didn't see me."

Phoebe shook her head, knocking loose a clump of hair. She'd pulled it into a spiky, magenta-streaked version of Helen's pouf this morning. "No, that's not why I came to find you. You've got a visitor."

Delaney immediately envisioned a tall, dark-haired man with broad shoulders and a go-to-hell attitude. Her pulse skipped. "A visitor?"

"He said his name's Leo Throop."

A flesh-and-blood visitor. "He's my lawyer."

"A lawyer? You're kidding. He looks just like the algebra

prof I had last year." She gestured at her elbows. "His jacket has those things on the sleeves."

"He cultivates the rumpled look. It makes some people underestimate him."

"I guess that's why Mrs. W. made him show her his ID. She wanted to be sure he's who he said he is."

"Leo must have loved that."

"I couldn't tell. I know Mrs. W. enjoyed it." Phoebe took the pillowcase from Delaney's hand. "I'll finish this up for you."

"Thanks." She turned toward the back door.

"He's on the front veranda."

Delaney nodded and changed direction, walking across the terrace and around to the front yard. The veranda was considered a second sitting room during the summer. Leo was in one of the wicker chairs that were grouped to the left of the front entrance. He was a plump man, so it was a tight squeeze. A tweed sport coat with suede elbow patches was draped over the back of the chair and a bulging leather briefcase rested on the floor beside him. He used the chair arms to push himself to his feet as she climbed to the veranda. "Good morning, Delaney. I hope I haven't caught you at an inconvenient time."

"Hardly. I was hanging up the laundry."

He regarded her over the tops of his glasses and widened his eyes in mock horror. "You?"

"I need to exercise them," she said, waggling her fingers. "Consider it therapy. Clothespins work just as well as the rubber ball they gave me in rehab."

"How are you feeling?"

"I'm fine, thanks. How was the flight?"

"Aside from the uncivilized earliness of the departure time, it was pleasant. I learned a great deal about outboard motors from my seat mate, who was a sales rep for your local factory. I didn't have the heart to tell him I loathe boats."

"They're not my favorite mode of transport, either. Thanks for coming so quickly, Leo."

"It was my pleasure. I was planning to drop in during the weekend to check up on you anyway. This way I can bill you for the trip and the hotel."

It was an old joke. Leo had been a frequent visitor during her initial stay at the hospital and later during the months at the clinic, both as her friend and as her lawyer. They'd first met when he'd gone to work at the same firm as her father. She could have afforded to hire a more high-power attorney, yet there was none she trusted as much as Leo, especially when it came to dealing with her stepdaughter. Stanford's lawyer was an old friend of the Graye family and had known Elizabeth all her life, so she couldn't gamble on his loyalty. She took the chair beside Leo's and waited until he'd seated himself again. "I heard about the welcome my grandmother gave you. I hope you didn't take it personally."

"I thought for a minute she might frisk me."

"She's not usually suspicious of people, but the way that process server got into the house yesterday upset her."

"I take it there was some drama?"

"I can't blame the messenger. He was only doing his job."

Leo took off his glasses, polished them with the end of his tie, then set them back in place, his way of signaling the conversation was turning to business. "I want to assure you, Delaney, Elizabeth has no case."

"As far as we know."

"There is no evidence of any wrongdoing or negligence. I've studied the police reports as well as the transcripts of the official inquiry and found nothing that could support her claim of wrongful death."

"There's nothing that contradicts it, either."

"That reasoning will get her nowhere."

"The 'innocent until proven guilty' principle doesn't apply to civil cases, does it?"

"Correct, it's decided by a preponderance of evidence, but the result should be the same. You weren't responsible for Stanford's death. It had been snowing, the road was slick, the bend was sharp, and there were no guardrails. It was only a tragic accident."

"Then why weren't we going home when it happened, Leo?"

"Don't dwell on it, Delaney."

"I can't help it. We left the restaurant in Bedford at nine. It's a seven-minute drive from there to the estate. The police called in the crash at one a.m., and we were almost to the Hudson."

"There could be dozens of innocent explanations for the detour."

"Okay, name one."

"You could have decided to drop in on friends."

"Stanford wasn't impulsive. He ran his life like he ran his business, always on a schedule. And if we had visited someone, why haven't they come forward?"

"Perhaps it was a business acquaintance."

"That's stretching things, Leo. Where were we for four hours?"

"Getting coffee. Enjoying the scenery."

"It was cold and dark."

"There were plenty of holiday lights to admire."

She looked at her hands as she asked the question that haunted her the most. "Why was I driving?"

"Stanford could have been sleepy," Leo replied. "Or maybe he felt he'd had too much wine at dinner."

"He loved that Jag. He didn't want anyone else to drive it, even me."

"There's really no point speculating about this."

"You can be sure that Elizabeth has. She might know something I don't. It's frustrating."

"Many trauma victims never regain their memories of an accident. You could be better off not remembering."

She dropped the back of her head against the chair. "The doctors said the same thing, but I don't agree. Now it's more important than ever that I do remember. You have to admit all the unanswered questions make the accident seem suspicious. If I knew why I was behind the wheel and why we were on that road, at least we'd have a chance of gathering some corroborating evidence to prove my innocence. That would take the steam out of Elizabeth's lawsuit."

Leo touched her knee. "Delaney, I don't believe she expects to win. That's not her primary motivation for taking you to court."

"Then what is?"

"She wants a forum to air her grievances. She'll use rumor and innuendo to humiliate you publicly and destroy your reputation."

Leo's bluntness was one of the things she liked about him. But he wasn't saying anything she hadn't already thought of herself. "She wants to punish me for Stanford's death any way she can."

"Yes. She also wants to punish you for stealing her father and for beguiling him into making you his sole heir."

Beguiling. It was an old-fashioned word, yet Stanford had used it himself. He'd maintained that he'd fallen under her spell the first moment he'd seen her. "Elizabeth never believed that the money didn't matter to me."

"She doesn't know you."

"She didn't want to. I loved Stanford, which should have given me some common ground with his daughter, but she never believed that, either. She had trouble accepting the fact that we were happy."

"She made no secret of her opposition to your marriage. She was very vocal about it. I believe that's one of the main reasons Stanford changed his will in your favor. He needed to demonstrate who was in control."

"They were a lot alike. Neither of them would accept defeat; they were too proud. I don't believe he meant to cut her out for good, though." She sat forward. "Couldn't we make some kind of settlement to transfer a percentage of the estate to her? I've got more than enough for five lifetimes."

"I'd advise against it. Unless she drops her suit, it would appear as if you're attempting to silence her. That would help fuel her allegations. In fact, it would be wise to consider returning to Bedford. That would strengthen your position by reinforcing your claim to the house. It's been vacant for too long."

"The security company does regular checks."

"Yes, and the yard service is maintaining the grounds, but it can't remain unoccupied indefinitely."

The idea of going back to the place she'd shared with Stanford left her cold. She wasn't ready for that. Not yet. "What other suggestions do you have?"

Leo undid the clasp on the front of his briefcase, withdrew a sheaf of papers, and held them out to her. "We should come out on the offensive. Attack her credibility."

"What's this?"

"We're going to sue her for slander and harassment. There are several individuals at Grayecorp who have agreed to testify on your behalf."

"Why would they do that?"

"They're not entirely happy with Elizabeth's vision for the company. What's more, her recent behavior could be viewed as irrational. They'd like to see her out."

Rather than taking the papers, Delaney held up her palms. "No. I can't do that to her. Regardless of our personal issues, I happen to agree with her when it comes to Grayecorp. She's good for the company."

"Speaking as your attorney, I urge you to reconsider. In this instance, it's impossible to ignore what you call your personal issues. Her public criticisms of you reflect on the company."

"She's just lost her father. I'm not going to be responsible for her losing her position, too. Thanks to Stanford's will, it's the only thing she has left."

"She's far from destitute. She has a sizable trust fund."

"Yes, from her mother, but nothing from her father. Even I can see that's not fair. I want to stop her but not destroy her."

"Speaking as your friend now, I have to warn you that your sympathy for your stepdaughter is misplaced. You persist in seeing the good in people, Delaney. It's an admirable quality, but in this case it could hurt you."

"Leo—"

"Kindness isn't always returned for kindness. Neither is love. You've already been hurt enough."

"I appreciate your concern, but I still owe Stanford my loyalty. I won't deliberately ruin his daughter."

"You owe him nothing!"

The vehemence in Leo's voice surprised her. "He was my husband," she said.

He pursed his lips, as if debating whether or not to continue. "Forgive me, Delaney," he said finally. "I realize it's your decision. I only want what's best for you."

"I understand. You're a good friend."

His silence went on longer this time. "That's what I've always endeavored to be." He cleared his throat, then tapped the papers on end to line up the edges, placed them on the table, and closed his briefcase. "I'll leave these here in case you change your mind. As distasteful as you might find it, taking the offensive is our best option."

* * *

THE HOUSE HAD SETTLED IN FOR THE NIGHT. NO VOICES sounded through the walls; no pipes clanged. The last guest room toilet had been flushed more than an hour ago. All was silent, apart from the occasional whisper of rustling leaves in the maples and the monotonous croak of bullfrogs in the pond. The familiar chorus used to lull Delaney to sleep when she'd been a child. It wasn't working tonight.

Shrugging on her robe, she padded through the darkness to her bedroom window and drew the curtain aside. Mosquitoes hummed as they bumped against the screen, another sound from her childhood. The view had changed, though. The glow from the trailer park that used to brighten the sky beyond the woods was gone. Only a single light twinkled through the trees now. She looked down on the moonlit yard, then at the oak that had held her swing, and her thoughts drifted to her mother.

She didn't have many memories of Annalee Wainright, so what she did have were precious. Besides the rare occasions her mother had played outside or pushed her on the swing, Delaney remembered her mother's voice as she'd read to her. Annalee had loved books and had seldom been without one. Her fingers had been long and delicate as she'd smoothed her hand over the pages. Because she'd spent so much time indoors, her skin had been pale, nearly translucent. It had been her mother's face that Delaney had pictured whenever she'd listened to a story about a fairy princess.

Annalee had been in her freshman year at college, younger than Phoebe, when she'd become pregnant. Neither she nor Delaney's father had been in a financial position to support a child, and neither had planned on getting married at such an early age. They'd had a one-night stand, which wasn't enough to base a lifetime commitment on, so Annalee had continued to live at home. She arranged to leave the child-care duties to her parents while she went back to school to finish her degree, dreaming of eventually becoming a teacher. She'd planned to build an independent life for herself and her daughter, but she never got the chance. Less than a year after Delaney was born, Annalee was diagnosed with leukemia.

Delaney's grandparents had done a good job sheltering her from the situation. Rather than remembering her mother's illness, she remembered her love. It had been unconditional, always there, as much a part of her as her blonde hair or her laughter or her delicate hands. Even now, when Helen spoke of her daughter it was usually with a smile. Loss hadn't turned her bitter. It had made her cherish the living even more.

Delaney sighed. She and Elizabeth had both lost their mothers when they'd been children, and as a result they had both drawn closer to their fathers. She hadn't been entirely honest with Leo. It wasn't only her loyalty to Stanford that caused her to go easy on his daughter. She understood where Elizabeth was coming from. Delaney might not have behaved any better than her stepdaughter if she'd had to share her father's love with a stepmother, particularly if she'd believed the match was wrong for him.

The issue had never come up, though. Charles Cowan, Delaney's father, had never married. That hadn't stopped him from gaining custody of his natural daughter. At first Delaney had hated being wrenched from her grandparents and the only home she'd known, but once she got older she understood what an exceptional man her father had been. Many men in his position would have turned their back on an unplanned child. Not Charles. He'd tailored his life to make room for her. Though he hadn't been as emotionally demonstrative as Delaney's mother or grandparents, she'd been just as sure of his love.

That was important to a child, regardless of age. No matter how annoyed Stanford had been with Elizabeth, he shouldn't have changed his will to cut her out. She would have interpreted that as a rejection. Perhaps if Stanford had lived longer, Elizabeth would have come around. She was only a few years younger than Delaney, a fact that had strengthened her objections to the marriage, yet Delaney had hoped their close ages could have at least allowed them to be friends. From what she'd seen, Elizabeth was too immersed in her career to have many of those. That was another trait Stanford had shared with his daughter. Business had always been his first priority, too.

Most of the time, anyway. Except for their final night. He'd cut short a meeting so that he wouldn't be late for their dinner. At the restaurant, he'd turned off his phone completely instead of setting it to vibrate silently, which had been another exception. When her phone had rung on the way home, he'd insisted that she not answer it.

Delaney froze, not daring to move or even to breathe. The memory fragment hovered in front of her, tantalizingly close and so clear she could feel the hum of the engine through the soles of her boots as she leaned over to reach for her purse. Stanford took one hand from the wheel and caught her wrist, saying he wanted her all to himself . . .

The memory wavered, then slipped from her mind like mist through her fingers.

She exhaled carefully, her heart thudding. It hadn't been much, but it was something. Another moment of life with Stanford. A glimpse of truth to build on. This proved she was right; her memories weren't gone. All she had to do was unlock them. She leaned closer to the window and focused on the darkness, opening her mind to the past.

Moonlight spilled across the yard like snow. There had been a light dusting of it the night of the accident and snowbanks along the sides of the road from an earlier storm. She tried to picture the ride home. Had there been snow in the headlights? The road in her nightmare had been wet. It had turned to water and seaweed that had curled around her ankles to hold her down . . .

Delaney shuddered, then tried to take control of her memories the way she'd controlled her nightmare. The water was only dew. The fire was sunshine. There was nothing to be afraid of because Max would keep her safe.

A shadow moved in the center of the yard. It was in the same place where Max had appeared yesterday morning. The shape was shot full of moonlight, as if it weren't entirely there. As she watched, it darkened into the silhouette of a man. A tall man with broad shoulders and dark hair. A sensation of warmth and welcome settled over her. She knew who it was. "Max," she whispered.

It had happened again. She'd been seeking a memory and had found Max instead. Why? Was she crazy? Was she dreaming?

Did it matter?

She'd already decided it didn't. As long as he helped her

cope, she would use anything, even a figment of her imagination. "Hey, Max," she murmured. "Up here."

The hazy shape disappeared.

She peered at the spot where he'd been until her eyes watered and she had to blink, but the lawn remained empty. A cool breeze stole through the screen. She crossed her arms, rubbing her palms over her sleeves.

"You don't sleep much, do you?"

She jerked. That was Max's voice. He'd sounded annoyed, just as he had yesterday, as if she'd disturbed him and he didn't want to talk to her.

But the voice hadn't come exclusively from her head. It seemed to have come from the room behind her.

SIX

❧

DELANEY TURNED.

A man was standing beside her bed. He was part shadow and part moonlight, just as he'd been in the yard. She could see one of the bedposts and the pattern of the wallpaper behind him. *Through* him.

Yet the more she stared, the more the image solidified. Details emerged. There were loose folds in the pale shirt that draped his shoulders. It fell untucked over his hips. Faded, washed-soft denim molded to his long legs. His feet were braced apart. They were bare. His shirt wasn't only untucked, it was half-buttoned, as if he hadn't finished dressing. Or more likely, as if he'd been taking his clothes off.

She thought of the naked skin she'd glimpsed the night before. Awareness tickled down her spine like the brush of an electric current. She raised her gaze to his face.

A lock of dark hair fell across his forehead, partly obscuring his left eye. His lips were pressed in a firm line, deepening the shadows beneath his cheekbones. The features that had once been boyish had become too sharp to be handsome, as if a sculptor had chiseled them down to the quintessential mascu-line basics. To someone who didn't know him, he might appear harsh. To anyone else, he wouldn't even be here.

Yet he looked real to Delaney, as real as the boy who had been her playmate and best friend.

She deliberately dug her fingers into her arms. She felt the prick of her nails through the silk of her robe. She felt the floorboards beneath her feet and heard the insects and frogs outside the window. She couldn't explain the vision away this time. She was actually seeing . . . "Max," she breathed.

"Why do you sound surprised every time? You're the one who did this, not me."

"Did what?"

"Brought me here."

"I . . . didn't plan to. It just happened."

"And you figure we can just pick up where we left off, is that it?"

She bit her lip. She was still giving her imaginary friend an attitude. "Be nice, Max. You used to be happy to see me."

"I used to be a lot of things that I'm not anymore." He turned his head, as if he were looking around him. "Is this your old room?"

"That's right."

"It's changed. I didn't recognize it last night."

"Last . . ."

"When you brought me into your nightmare." He finished his survey and focused on her. "Do you get a lot of those, Deedee?"

"Nearly every night. Uh, thanks for helping me handle it."

He dismissed her thanks with a shrug. "You didn't give me much choice. I'd been asleep and didn't see you coming. Why did you call me this time? Did it come back again?"

"No. I didn't mean to call you. I was only trying to remember."

"Yeah, you mentioned that. Why?"

"It's important."

"Take it from me, there are a lot of things that are better off left buried."

"Like you, Max?"

"Exactly like me."

She shook her head. "Why are you acting this way? You used to be my best friend."

"That was more than twenty years ago, Deedee. You've been gone for a long time."

"Is that why you're acting so hostile? Because I left you? Max, I couldn't help it. I . . . grew up."

"I noticed."

His voice had roughened. The deep tones licked across her nerves, as cool as the breeze that wafted over the tops of her breasts. She drew the sides of her robe together and tightened the belt.

He arched one eyebrow.

She dropped her hands. It was ridiculous to feel modesty in front of a figment of her imagination. She'd thought him up. She'd given him the attitude. It must mean she wanted him to be that way.

What way? Brooding? Tough? Self-confident and sexy?

Sexy? That was ridiculous, too. Of all the issues she needed to deal with, sex wasn't even on the radar. "You might as well stop being difficult and help me. It's the reason you're here."

He walked toward her soundlessly. "Let's get one thing straight. I'm here to satisfy my curiosity, that's all. You disappeared last night before you answered my question." He cupped her right shoulder. As gently as a whisper, his thumb skimmed over the silk that hid one of the burns.

The sensation that followed his touch stunned her. The damaged skin tingled with life, as if the pleasure came from the inside. Even through her robe, the contact felt wonderful. No one had touched her injuries except for doctors. No one, besides Max, had even seen them. "Question?"

"Tell me how you got these."

It was odd that she needed to explain them to herself.

Odd? Could it be any odder than seeing him in the first place? Imagining him here? *Touching* her? "It was an accident," she replied rather than analyzing the apparition any further. "At least that's what the police said."

"A car accident?"

"That's right. Apparently, I drove a Jaguar XK into a utility pole."

"Then the nightmare was real."

"The crashing part was."

He slid the backs of his knuckles down the front of her robe, following the scar to her breast. "And the fire."

"Yes. All of it was real, except the water."

"That was real. The seaweed, the mud. You almost died then, too."

She swallowed. Imagining his touch was making it more difficult for her to think. She stepped back to break the contact and bumped into the window frame. "No, my subconscious probably put that in because I don't like water. That's what Dr. Bernhardt believes."

"Who's that, your shrink?"

"Yes." And he'd probably lock her up if he saw her now.

"So it's your shrink's idea for you to remember your childhood."

"No, you've got it wrong. I don't need help remembering that. It's the more recent past. I have a . . . mental block of the accident."

"From what I saw last night, that's something else that's better left buried."

"I'm not trying to remember the accident itself. It's the four hours before it that matter."

"Why?"

"I want to know the truth. I need to know what happened during my final evening with my husband."

"Your husband," he repeated. He held her gaze as he touched her jaw. "That's where the pain came from, isn't it?"

Somehow she knew he wasn't speaking only of the physical pain. She nodded, brushing her cheek across his fingertips. It felt so good. Right. As if he fit there, like a missing part of herself.

"You need to let this go, Deedee."

The way he said the childhood name was like another caress. "What?"

"The accident. Your husband."

"It's not that easy."

"It's the only way to get past the pain."

"No, *remembering* is how to get past it."

He withdrew his hand and placed it on the wall beside her head. "I'm giving you good advice, but you're as stubborn as you always were."

"It's just that this is important. I feel as if there's something I have to know but I don't. It's like . . . a tickle in the middle of my brain. And I really don't understand why you keep resisting the idea of cooperating with me."

"Simple. I've changed. I'm not the boy I used to be."

"Max . . ."

"That means I'm not into rescuing little girls or needy women anymore."

It took her a moment to process what he'd said. Her temper

stirred. "I am not a child, nor am I needy. I'm not asking you to rescue me, only to help me help myself. This bad-boy attitude of yours is getting irritating."

"If you don't like it, then stop barging into my head."

She frowned, tipping up her chin so she could look into his face. He'd been taller than her when she'd been a child, but she'd never thought much about the difference in their heights. She was aware of it now, though. She was also aware of the breeze, and the moonlight, and the intimacy of being alone in her bedroom with a large, partially dressed man.

Which was crazy, since he wasn't even here. "Maybe you've got a point. Maybe that's why you're being so unpleasant. It's forcing me to face the unpleasantness. That's something I tend to avoid. By creating you again, I'm already on the way to breaking through my block."

"Creating me?"

"It's a form of self-hypnosis," she said, deciding she needed to remind herself of that before her fantasy got out of hand. "I imagine I see you just as I did when I was young because you're a way for me to unlock my subconscious."

His eyebrows drew together, mirroring her frown. "I'll be damned. You don't believe I'm real."

This was getting complicated again. She tried to imagine Max the way she wanted him to be, smiling at her, patient with her, never saying a bad word, walking across the lawn near her swing . . .

His image wavered briefly. He slapped his other hand against the window frame, caging her between his arms. "No you don't. You're not breaking off this time until I'm ready to go. We're not done."

Her pulse stuttered. The illusion was getting so vivid, she imagined she could feel the heat from his body. A faint whiff of paint came from his sleeve, mixing with the musky scent of male skin. She held her hands up to his chest, meaning to push him away, even though part of her knew there was nothing to push in the first place . . .

Her palms touched soft cotton. The tip of her index finger brushed over a button. Beneath the shirt lay the firm contours of a man's chest. It rose and fell with his breathing. Like his touch on her skin, the impressions didn't come from outside, they came from inside, as if she *knew* them more than sensed them.

"I'm not who you think I am, Deedee."

"Yes, you are," she said. "You're Max. I know you as well as I know myself."

"That's not saying much. Your memory is full of holes."

"Stop being like that!"

"You know the solution."

"I can't let you go. I'll do whatever I have to, to remember."

"You don't need me for that."

"Oh, yes I do. I know you can help me, Max."

"Why? I'm not a shrink."

"Yes, but you're my friend."

He took his hand from the window frame and touched her hair. "I take it back. You didn't grow up. Only a kid would be naive enough to trust a man she hasn't seen in twenty-four years."

Her imaginary friend had become cynical. What did that say about her? "Go ahead and bluster. I don't care, because I have faith that somewhere in there"—she poked at his chest—"you're still the sweet, kind, and gentle little boy I used to love."

He didn't respond.

Her finger rested on his shirt, then slowly sank into the place where he stood. She could see the bed behind him. She reached for his arms but grasped only air. "Max, wait!"

The old Max would have stayed.

This one turned without another word and faded into the wall.

SEVEN

❦

MAX HELD THE PALETTE KNIFE ON EDGE, SCRAPING THE blade over the slab of glass where he mixed his colors. He slashed it across the canvas in one fluid motion, and another flame swirled to life. With a twist of his wrist, he dragged the knife tip through the wet paint to define the outer contour of the fire. Instead, he revealed the layer beneath. A core of pale white diluted what should have been red. He used the heel of the knife to repair the stroke, but that made it worse. Blue bled into the muted red, softening the entire area to a gentle smear of lilac.

He cleaned it off, wiped the knife on a rag, and tried again.

The same thing happened. The canvas seemed determined to reject the vision in his head.

Max let the vision fade, then stepped back from the easel and tossed the knife on the table. The daylight was waning. That explained why the colors weren't cooperating. How long had he been at this? He rolled his shoulders, only then becoming aware of the discomforts in his body. His right arm ached. His back was stiff. The low rumble in his stomach reminded him he hadn't eaten since noon. He'd agreed to put in an appearance at the opening of his show in New York tomorrow, so it was past time to call it a day.

He capped the paint tubes and cleaned his tools, then returned to regard the painting. He'd left his brushes in the jar for this one. Only his palette knives could have applied the pigment with enough force to suit him. The result was as violent as the concept he'd begun with. Flames licked in oily circles. The darkness surrounding them was crusted with monochrome ridges of blackened aquamarine, like terrors glimpsed on the limits of vision and only half-remembered. The image extended to the very edges where the canvas was stapled over the wooden frame, as if it fought its containment in two dimensions.

The accidental smear of pale white in the center didn't belong. It was a mistake, a contradiction. A core of softness, light inside darkness, hope inside horror, like the woman who had created this image in the first place.

He'd been trying to recapture Deedee's nightmare in this painting. The image had been haunting him almost as much as she had. Both had been impossible to get out of his mind.

She was a puzzle, a mass of contradictions with as many layers as the paint he'd applied to the canvas in front of him. Darkness inside light inside more darkness. Innocent. Sensual. Both woman and child. She didn't seem to realize the power of her mind. She wielded it as carelessly as a kid with a crayon.

Max shifted his gaze from the painting to the easel. He'd screwed two slats of wood on either side of the back leg to patch it together and had completely replaced one of the front ones to fix the damage he'd caused when he'd fallen into it. A faint outline of red still stained the floor. He hadn't been able to get all of the paint out of the wood planks any more than he could keep Delaney out of his thoughts.

That was three times she'd found him now. The panic that had sent him crashing into his painting the first time hadn't happened again, though. His fear had been unfounded. The ugly emotions he'd learned to control had remained locked away in spite of her repeated forays into his head.

But she wouldn't think about what her return was doing to his peace of mind. She didn't care how often she barged into his thoughts or how many demands she made. Why should she? She didn't believe he was real.

He should have figured it out earlier. She would have been too young to remember their first encounter, and she'd obviously blocked her memory of the way she'd almost drowned. She wouldn't have questioned their exceptional relationship, either. Kids accepted what happened to them, both the good and the bad, with no explanation, as if it was meant to be. Children had no choice. They were powerless to change anything. The best they could do was to pretend it wasn't there.

Delaney wouldn't have questioned leaving him behind, either. How could she have deserted someone she hadn't considered human? Max had opened his heart to her as well as his mind. He'd shown her parts of himself no one else had seen. When she left, he had felt her loss all the way to his soul, yet in her mind, she'd have packed him away with no more concern than boxing up an old doll.

Max moistened the corner of a fresh rag with turpentine and rubbed hard at the dried paint on his fingers. He'd been more of a fool than he'd thought. The closeness he and Delaney had shared couldn't have meant as much to her as it had to him. She'd used him to ease her loneliness and to amuse herself. Like a toy. Or a pet.

I know you can help me, Max.

She wanted to use him now, too. That was the only reason she'd broken her silence.

It was the wrong thing to ask him. No one called him Max anymore. He hadn't answered to that name for years. He was John Harrison, artist, ex-con, the monster mothers warned their children to keep away from. The last time he'd helped a woman, it had landed him in prison.

He twisted the rag between his hands as he walked to the window. He filled his lungs with fresh air, clearing out the taste of the solvent. The stink of confinement hadn't been as easy to shake off, that mixture of steel and concrete and recycled air that wasn't touched by the sun. It had lingered for years. Even now, he seldom closed his windows, regardless of the weather.

In spite of what he'd told the parole board, he had no remorse over what he'd done. He would have said practically anything to regain his freedom, so he'd told them what they'd wanted to hear. His only regret was that he hadn't managed to finish the job. Virgil Budge had needed killing. That fact had never been in doubt. Although he hadn't taken his belt to Max once he'd grown big enough to defend himself, the man had been incapable of change. He'd merely gotten craftier. He'd gone after Max's mother only when he'd been sure Max wasn't around, and he'd made sure the bruises he'd given her didn't show. She'd never said a word, because she'd known what her son would do if he found out, so she'd lied and pretended everything was fine.

The farce had ended the summer Max turned seventeen.

He'd been working construction, long, hot, and dusty days of framing houses. The trailer had been dark when he'd come home that night, but even before he'd reached for the door, he'd felt that something had been wrong. He'd found his mother on the bathroom floor, spitting up blood. Virgil had broken three of her ribs, and one of them had punctured her lung.

Hell, yes, the bastard had deserved to die, so Max had let the rage out. He'd unleashed a lifetime of anger. It had poured from his muscles and bones and memories in a blur of violence that had strengthened with each blow. It grew with each scream for mercy. It fed on every drop of blood that had spattered his hands and shirt and face. Damn, it had been easy. And it had felt good.

It had taken five cops to pull him off Virgil. Max had weighed less than he did now—he hadn't yet filled into his height—but swinging a hammer and carrying lumber all day had conditioned his body better than any prizefighter's training. Three of the cops had ended up in the hospital. They'd gotten out in time to testify, but they hadn't needed to. His mother's testimony alone had been enough to damn him.

She hadn't viewed what she'd said as a betrayal. The truth was, she hadn't wanted to be rescued.

You're still the sweet, kind, and gentle little boy I used to love.

Max snorted a laugh. Delaney was wrong on all counts. The boy was gone. His illusions had been scoured away by the only two people he'd allowed himself to love. The whole concept of love was a lie. It was as make-believe as the worlds he and Delaney had created. She hadn't loved him; she'd cared only about what he could do for her.

And she didn't believe he was real. Why couldn't he get past that? He should be pleased. It made the situation easier to handle. He might be unable to stop her from touching his mind, but there was no way he would let her touch his heart this time. No one did.

He leaned a shoulder against the window frame as he looked down on the yard. Dusk leached the color from the new grass that sprouted from the soil. He'd been trying for years to get it to grow. The site had been bulldozed down to the dirt when he'd bought the property. The trailers had been sold off and carted away well before that, but the bleakness seemed to have leached through the asphalt. He'd ripped down the chain-link fence that used to surround the place with his bare hands: it had reminded him of the fence around the exercise yard. The rusty train tracks that had once been on the embankment were gone, though it would take a few more years before the gravel rail bed sprouted anything more than weeds.

The trailer park where he'd grown up was unrecognizable now. The house he'd built bore no resemblance to the place he and his mother had shared with Virgil. It was nothing like the cell he'd been confined to, either. The structure was octagonal rather than square, so it had no tight corners. His studio stretched across most of the second story, as open and free as an aerie. It had been the first room he'd completed, and the one where he spent most of his time. The ground floor was almost as open, with walls only where they were structurally necessary. He had what he needed.

This was how Max dealt with the past. He got rid of it. What he couldn't bury, he conquered or transformed. He'd wiped out all the traces of the evil that had happened here. Virgil's taint would never return. Delaney was wrong to want to remember. That wasn't the way to find peace.

He lifted his gaze to the woods beyond the old rail bed. The trees were far taller than they'd been when he was a kid. The roof of the Wainright House was hidden behind the treetops, yet he could see the sparkle of lights through the branches. She must be there now. He could feel her on the edges of his mind, a distant tug on his consciousness.

He was tempted to confront her with the truth. It would be simple to do, now that he knew where to find her. The games she'd devised as a child had taken him into every corner of her grandparents' place. He knew his way to her bedroom. He even knew which floorboards creaked. He could cross the old rail bed, take the path through the woods, and be there within minutes. He could get into her room the regular way with no one else knowing, whenever he chose.

Sure, why not show her it was a real man she had pulled into her bed? A living being who had helped her conquer her nightmare, and who had touched her in the moonlight? He'd seen her eyes darken. She'd liked his caress, even if it hadn't been flesh on flesh. She was all grown-up, and he would enjoy discovering some new games to play.

He pictured the Wainright rose garden. The blooms were

furled for the night and already deep in the shadow of the cedar hedge. Light from the kitchen window spilled across the terrace. It was open, as it usually was during the summer. There had always been good smells in that kitchen, warm, homey scents of food and clean clothes. No beer. No sweat. No raised voices, either. Would Delaney be in there now?

Or would she be in her bedroom? Slipping off her clothes. Pulling on satin or silk that flowed over her body like the touch of his mind? He closed his eyes, probing the darkness.

Her thoughts brushed his, soft as butterfly wings. They held a smile he felt rather than saw. "Max?"

The invitation was as eager as it had always been, in spite of the way he'd left her the night before. She'd been right; he'd been deliberately harsh in an attempt to discourage her from seeking him. He'd tried to warn her, but she hadn't cared. She'd left her mind open like a child.

Her image began to coalesce in shades of pale lilac. She wasn't upstairs. He recognized the bay window at the back of the house in the room that used to be her mother's. It had been changed into a sitting room, with oak bookshelves lining the walls and armchairs upholstered in deep green. Delaney was nestled on the cushioned seat in the curve of the window. Lamplight glowed on her hair, gilding the short curls with highlights of gold. A long-sleeved blouse covered her arms and concealed all but the upper edge of the scar at her throat. She had curled her legs beneath a flowing, flowered skirt. A book lay open on her lap. Her fingers skimmed his arm, drawing him closer.

His body responded instantly to the thought of her touch. It had nothing to do with his heart. He had physical needs, like any other healthy male. He couldn't channel all of his passions into his paintings. She'd used him; why not use her? She still had no idea what she was dealing with. Sex would be a small step from the intimacy she'd already forced on him. She'd given him no choice when she'd slid into his head. He'd told her to stop, and she hadn't. She wouldn't be able to stop him from doing the same. Why not give her a taste of what it felt like to be helpless?

Pain knifed through his hand. He broke off from Delaney and glanced down.

His knuckles were white. His hand had cramped. He'd wound the paint rag around his fist as if it were a belt.

EIGHT

❧

"HANG ON, LEO. YOU'RE FADING OUT." DELANEY HELD HER
cell phone to her ear, walked past the edge of the terrace and
into the yard. The sky was overcast and it was still early, so
she wasn't worried about protecting her skin from sun damage.
Her sandals were no protection from the dew, though. Within
seconds her feet were soaked. She halted at the oak tree where
the signal was better. "I know it's early for me to be calling,"
she said, "but I'm eager to know what you've learned."

"About . . . ?"

"About my phone records."

"Ah, right. You'll have to excuse me. I'm only on my second
coffee."

"You have them, don't you?"

"Sorry, not yet. These things take time."

"I don't see why it should. All this information must be on
the phone company's computer somewhere; it's only a matter
of printing it out."

"I assure you, I'm doing everything I can." He paused. "But
don't place too much importance on this detail. Even if you
knew who called you the night of the accident, it could very
well turn out to mean nothing."

"Or it could be the key that unlocks the rest."

"Have you remembered anything else, Delaney?"

"No, not yet, but the rest will come. I'm sure of it now."

Brave words, she thought as she ended the call. So far she
had nothing to back them up. She slid the phone into her skirt
pocket and drummed her fingers on her thigh. It had been three

days since the memory of the phone call had surfaced. Nothing further had come back, no matter how hard she'd tried. That was the mistake she'd made before. She needed to relax and let the memories appear the same way she let Max appear.

Only, Max seemed to have deserted her. He might not have been much more help, anyway. His last visit had left her confused and frustrated. It was hard enough to fight her memory block without having to battle her subconscious at the same time.

This would have been so much simpler if she hadn't made him into a man. A boy would have been easier to deal with. The young Max might have enjoyed the challenge of delving into her head. They could have pretended it was a treasure hunt, with her memories as the prize.

"Max," she whispered. "Why can't we go back?"

A patch of air near the gate shimmered. She stared at the spot, waiting for a glimpse of dark hair and blue eyes. For an instant, she felt the brush of Max's presence.

But his image refused to form. It dissolved like a heat mirage, leaving nothing but emptiness between her and the back fence.

Was she trying too hard with him as well? Maybe this worked like her phone, and she should move around until she found a better signal. Or maybe she should start leaving the back gate open to make it easier for him to drop by.

The laugh that came from her throat scared her. It held no humor. It was too close to tears. She walked the rest of the way to the fence and curled her fingers over the top of the gate.

In its own way, the view from the back fence was as picturesque as the Wainright House's tended yard. A haze of mist hung over the tops of the trees that hid the pond. Dew darkened the leaves in the shadows. The colors and shapes were beautiful, like the kind of soft-edged painting one might find on a greeting card. It should have looked soothing and peaceful.

It didn't. This morning it looked ominous.

Her fingers tightened on the gate. Near the fence, the path to the pond was overgrown with weeds and long grass. It became more defined as it reached the trees. There it was bare dirt. Branches grew down on either side, close enough to form a tunnel for anyone who walked through. Delaney could almost feel the leaves and twigs whip against her face as she hurtled into the darkness . . .

This was the narrow road in her nightmare, the one she always saw before the crashing started.

Her first impulse was to turn and run back to the safety of the house. She forced herself to remain where she was. She had to face the unpleasantness, right? This wasn't what she was trying to remember, but the dream couldn't hurt her. It hadn't since Max had shown her how to take control.

Why would her subconscious include this place in her nightmare of the accident? She had seldom come to Willowbank with Stanford. Whenever they'd arranged to visit, some business emergency usually had cut the visit short. While they'd been here, they'd never taken a stroll to the pond. He hadn't been fond of the outdoors, and she disliked water. Her grandparents had lectured her about the dangers of wandering down that path so thoroughly, she had no desire to set foot on it.

Of course. This fit with what Dr. Bernhardt had said about her aversion to water. *That* was why the scene was incorporated into her nightmare. Her grandparents had warned her so often to keep away from the pond that she would have developed a dread of the path that led to it.

In light of that, it was odd that she often used to imagine Max appearing from this direction when she'd been a child.

Or maybe it wasn't that odd. She must have been using him as an emotional crutch even then. He could have been her way of facing what frightened her.

The shadows over the path wavered. They gathered into an oblong shape the size of a man, then flattened once more.

Without pausing to think, Delaney opened the gate and started down the path. "Max? Where are you?"

A flock of crows took flight in a flurry of squawks when she reached the trees. Water glinted through the undergrowth. The smell of mud settled in a lump at the back of her throat. She was almost to the pond when her legs began to feel heavy, as if something was holding them down. Water flowed over her feet and rose to her ankles and then to her knees. Seaweed curled around her thighs as her toes sank further into the muck . . .

She recognized the sensations as more pieces from her nightmare. There was a logical explanation for those, too. They must be more manifestations of her dislike of water. She wiped her palms on her skirt, trying to deflect her fear the way Max had shown her. The dampness on her palms was sweat. This time, the moisture on her feet actually *was* dew. She took a few deep breaths, put up her arm to push a branch aside, and followed the path around a birch tree.

The pond was suddenly in front of her. It was another greeting-card-peaceful scene. Boughs from the birch provided a natural frame. Twining fingers of mist curled among lily pads and their half-opened flowers. The surface of the water mirrored the clouds like polished silver. Something plopped within the patch of bulrushes that flanked the shore. The silver rippled. The lily pads bobbed.

Delaney shivered. She really didn't like water. Regardless of how much she tried to reason it away, the mere smell of the pond was turning her stomach.

Yet she couldn't leave. The sensation of Max's presence was much stronger here than it had been in the yard.

That didn't make sense. She wasn't relaxed. Hadn't she decided she needed to be relaxed in order to see him? She grasped the tree trunk, digging her nails into the papery bark. "Max? I know you're here. I can feel you."

A cicada whirred.

The noise made her jump. She moved around the tree, placing her back to its trunk so she faced away from the pond. Her pulse steadied once she could no longer see the water. "Please, Max. Why won't you answer me?"

A breeze came up, rustling the leaves overhead. The nape of her neck tingled. She glanced to the side.

And just like that, there he was, standing on a patch of moss in front of a willow on the other side of the path. The pattern of the bark showed through him, then gradually faded as his image strengthened.

Delaney smiled. The mere sight of him spread such a sense of . . . rightness, she could forget about the taste of mud in her throat. "Uh, hi."

The sharp angles of his face appeared more dramatic in daylight. His shirt was black silk that rippled against his chest and arms in the same breeze that stirred the leaves above him. He wore narrow black suspenders rather than a belt. Instead of jeans he wore tailored black pants that accentuated his narrow hips and long legs. He stood with one foot crossed over the other ankle in a negligently masculine pose while he cradled a thick, white crockery mug in his hands.

He lifted the mug to his lips. He regarded her over the rim in silence.

His perusal made her self-conscious. He was regarding her as a man who was interested in a woman.

But that was absurd. He had seen enough of her scars to know how ugly they were. Besides, she had no desire to interest any man. She was still mourning her husband.

Then why had she made Max so damn sexy?

Her pulse skipped. She told herself to ignore it. "Where have you been for the past three days?" she asked.

He swallowed and lowered the mug. "I was out of town."

"Okay. Where?"

"Manhattan."

Well, ask a stupid question . . . "I missed you."

"Do you still believe you made me up?"

"I hurt your feelings when I said that, didn't I?"

"How could you? You don't believe I'm real."

"You're real to me, Max. Don't you remember?"

His image blurred at the edges for a few seconds, then firmed once more. "How am I going to get through to you? I'm not who you think I am."

"Yes, you said that already. Fine. Then tell me who you are."

"I'm a man, not a boy."

"Obviously."

"And you should be careful about inviting me into your mind. Don't assume I've got a conscience or that I'm going to watch out for you."

"Why are you so determined to make out that you're bad?"

"You need to accept the fact that I've changed."

"You couldn't have changed that much, or you wouldn't be so concerned about warning me."

He frowned.

"Hah. Gotcha there, didn't I?"

"This isn't a game, Deedee."

"Whatever, I'm glad you decided to come back. I've been wanting to talk to you."

"Don't you have any real friends to talk to?"

She and Stanford had had dozens of friends. They'd had a very busy social life. She also knew scores of people through the fund-raising she'd done. She had Leo, too. Helen had invited her to confide in her many times.

But Delaney didn't want to burden her grandmother. There were personal things she wouldn't be comfortable discussing with Leo. She'd drifted apart from the other friends she'd known before she'd married Stanford. The rest were from his world, not hers. Many of them had shared Elizabeth's reservations about their marriage, although they had been too well-bred and probably too afraid of Stanford to show it while he'd been alive. That had changed after his death. Few had made the effort to visit her during her recovery, and the ones who did had seemed so uncomfortable she'd been relieved when they stopped coming.

The lump she felt in her throat had nothing to do with the smell of the mud, but she refused to give in to self-pity. She was alive while so many of the people she loved weren't. Her problems were nothing compared to that. "They're not like you, Max."

"Yeah, I bet they aren't."

"I don't have to pretend with you." She laughed shakily. "That sounds silly. All you and I ever did was play pretend."

"That was a long time ago."

"Yes, I know. And you've changed. I got the message. What I meant was that with you, I can be honest. I don't need to be brave. You see the real me. That's a rare and precious thing between friends, and I don't care whether you're a fantasy or a hallucination or an undigested piece of beef; we *are* friends, Max."

"Beef?"

"Dickens's *Christmas Carol*. The ghost of Marley."

His lips twitched. "I'm no ghost. It might be simpler if I was."

She had a crazy urge to fling herself across the path so she could feel his touch once again. She wished he *was* real. That must be why he kept bringing up the subject. "You said you didn't want to help me remember, but couldn't we just talk? What's the harm in that?"

He didn't reply. His image wavered, as if he were debating whether or not to stay. Finally, he drained the cup, then hooked his finger through the handle and crossed his arms. "If I were a real man, what would you talk about?"

If he were real, she would want to do more than talk. She would want to walk into the shelter of his arms and run her hands over his silk shirt and inhale the scent of his skin and . . .

"Deedee?"

She dropped her head back against the tree. "Good question. My social skills are a bit rusty. I haven't been out much lately."

"Yeah, I know how that is. Where have you been?"

"Hospitals. A rehab center. Until last week, I was at a private clinic."

"Is that where you saw the shrink?"

"Yes, but that wasn't why I was there. Not entirely, anyway." She twisted her wrists to show him her hands.

"Are those skin grafts?"

"Uh-huh. Most of the work doesn't show. It was a long process because some areas had to be rebuilt from the bones out. It's really quite amazing what the doctors were able to accomplish. These burns were . . ." She slid her hands into her pockets. "They were worse than the other ones."

"I know. I felt it. Have you had the nightmare again?"

"Not really. I've been able to deflect it, thanks to what you showed me."

"Don't thank me. I just wanted to get a full night's sleep. How are your hands now?"

"Fine, as long as I'm careful. My doctors had wanted me to remain at the clinic another few weeks, since there's still some risk of infection until the grafts completely heal, but I just couldn't stand the confinement anymore."

"I can understand that."

Another silence fell. When he spoke again, his tone was gentler. "Where were you living before the accident?"

"My husband and I have a house near Bedford. It's in Westchester County."

"Yeah, I've heard a lot of rich people live there. Do you have money?"

"More than I know what to do with, to be honest. Stanford was well-off."

"He'd have to be if he owned a Jag. What did he do?"

"He was a real estate developer. Ever heard of Grayecorp?"

"Can't say that I have."

No, of course he wouldn't have. That had been another silly question. Imaginary friends wouldn't subscribe to the *Wall Street Journal*. "Stanford and I met when he did some business with one of my clients."

"What kind of work did you do?"

"I was a Realtor." She paused. "I haven't sold anything for five years, though."

"Why not?"

"I gave it up when I married Stanford."

"I can't picture you as a Realtor, Deedee. You're too honest."

"That's a cynical thing to say. I'll have you know I did very well being honest. I loved helping people find the home that was right for them. Everyone deserves having a place where they belong."

"Yet you came to Willowbank when you got out of the clinic instead of going home to Westchester."

"This place was my first home."

"You used to want to be a gardener, didn't you?"

She had almost forgotten. He was right, she had loved the flowers in her grandmother's garden, and she used to dream of playing there forever. She could chase the bees or push her fingers into the soil and get her hands as dirty as she wanted. No one would tell her to wear a hat in the sun, or come in when it was dark, because she would be the grown-up.

"Or was it a cook?" he asked.

That was another aspect of her life here that she'd loved, the good smells in the kitchen, the neat lines of golden cookies cooling on racks, the sound of her grandmother humming as she worked. Somehow, everything had tasted better when she'd been young. "How did you know?"

"You mentioned it a few times."

"My career ambitions weren't very, ah, ambitious. I was seeing it from the perspective of a child."

He studied her. "How old are you now, anyway?"

She wasn't the only one with rusty social skills. Then again, an imaginary playmate wouldn't hesitate to ask a woman her age. "I just turned thirty. Your birthday's in the summer, too, isn't it?"

"Why do you say that?"

An image drifted through her mind. It was a warm day, like today, only sunny. A woman was singing "Happy Birthday" in a house with white curtains. There had been chocolate cake, and a black dog . . .

It disappeared in a flash. Where had that come from? "Forget it. Just a stray thought. You'd be in your mid-thirties now, wouldn't you?"

"I suppose. If I was real. Tell me more about your husband."

"Why?"

"Because I can't picture you married any more than I can see you selling real estate."

She pulled the collar of her blouse aside to reveal the edge of the largest burn. "I didn't always look like this."

He regarded her without blinking. "What's your point?"

"Stanford was determined to marry me. He wouldn't take no for an answer. He thought I was beautiful."

"You are."

"Thank you, Max, but only a figment of my imagination wouldn't be repulsed by way I look now."

"You told me you had lots of money."

"Well, yes."

"If you believe those scars are repulsive, then why didn't you get the plastic surgeons at that clinic to repair them the way they did your hands?"

"Why bother? No one's going to see them."

"I did."

"Sure, but you're not—"

"Real," he finished.

"I meant no one *else* is going to see them. It's no hardship for me to keep away from scoop necklines and sleeveless tops. Swimsuits won't be a problem since I don't sunbathe and I don't like the beach. The scar tissue doesn't hurt anymore and it doesn't hamper my movements, so there's no reason to put myself through more surgery simply for my appearance."

"Sounds as if you've thought it all out."

"I have."

Max crossed the path to stand in front of her. "And it sounds as if you actually believe that if a real man saw what's under your clothes, he wouldn't want you."

Her lips parted. Sexuality seemed to crackle around him. "Max . . ."

"Because if you do, if that's the reason you're hanging on to those scars, I'm telling you now it won't work."

"Whether it does or not is irrelevant, because the issue won't come up. I've just lost my husband. I have other priorities, as I've already told you."

"You mean remembering what happened."

"Yes. I owe it to Stanford. And to myself, for my own peace of mind."

"Remembering the past won't necessarily give you peace of mind. Sometimes there's no explanation for evil."

"Evil? That's getting overly dramatic, isn't it?"

"Call it what you want. Shit happens."

"I think I've read that on a T-shirt somewhere."

"Trying to make sense of it only makes it worse. You need to take control so it can't hurt you anymore."

"Take control? Like we did with my nightmare?"

"For starters."

"Getting my scars fixed won't necessarily fix my life."

"Does your life need fixing?"

She laughed. "Oh, no. Everything's just peachy. Why else would I be standing here talking to an imaginary playmate while we both take a stab at do-it-yourself psychology?"

Max took her chin in his hand.

She pressed harder against the tree. A piece of bark crackled beneath her back. She caught another whiff of the pond, but the smell of the mud didn't turn her stomach anymore. It was countered by the clean tang of Max's soap. Her flesh tingled where he touched her, even though she knew it wasn't really a touch. That made no difference to her pulse.

Max brought his face to hers. His eyes gleamed. "We don't have to talk."

She moistened her lips. "Uh, Max . . ."

"There are plenty of more interesting things we could try."

"Let's stick with talking."

"If I were a real man, I would kiss you."

"If you were real, you wouldn't want to."

He smiled and stroked his thumb across her lower lip. "Don't bet on it."

Pleasure shot through her body. Her legs shook. She locked her knees to keep herself upright.

Good God, how had she thought that he wasn't handsome? His smile took her breath away. It transformed his face, deepening the lines beside his mouth and etching tiny new ones at the corners of his eyes. The crooked front tooth she remembered had almost evened out, but not completely. There was still a trace of the little boy's grin in the man's smile.

And she wanted to kiss him. In this moment, she couldn't think of anything she wanted more. She yearned to feel his lips on hers and taste his breath on her tongue. *Really* feel him and taste him, not through her mind but directly through her senses.

A twig snapped. Someone was moving in the woods. Someone real. Voices drifted through the trees.

"We could get a pizza on the way."

"Sure, that's a good idea. When does the movie start?"

"Eight thirty."

"I'll meet you at seven, then."

Delaney recognized Phoebe's voice a second before she caught sight of her pink T-shirt through the trees. The other voice belonged to a young man. She glanced at Max.

He cocked his head and turned to look behind him. He appeared to have heard the voices, too.

Then why wasn't he going away? He seemed content to stay where he was, in spite of the couple that was rapidly approaching. He should go now, before they saw him. How would she be able to explain who he was and why he was standing so close to her . . . ?

The thought was too bizarre to pursue. So was the stab of guilt she felt for being caught with another man. He wasn't a man. And no one had caught her. And she had nothing to feel guilty for, because she would always love Stanford, regardless of stray physical urges that might occur.

Stray urges? Even in the early days of their marriage, Stanford had never made her knees shake with merely the thought of a kiss. He'd never looked at her the way Max did. No man had.

But Max wasn't real.

This had gone far enough. Delaney closed her eyes, willing him to go away.

His taunt whispered through her head. "Trying to get rid of me already, Deedee? You were the one who's been calling me."

"I'm sorry. I—" Now she was apologizing? "I must be going insane," she said through her teeth.

He laughed. *Laughed.* The sensation rumbled along her bones. He pressed the pad of his thumb to her chin.

No! She felt nothing. Her thoughts cracked out like mental finger snaps. *He isn't here.*

The sound of the footsteps halted. "Delaney?" Phoebe asked. "Are you all right?"

She opened her eyes fast.

Phoebe stood on the trail beside the big willow where Max had first appeared. A young redheaded man with the build of a football linebacker was behind her, his hand on her shoulder. It was Pete Pattimore, the handyman's nephew. They were both regarding her warily.

Their view of her was unobstructed. Max was gone.

Relief mixed with disappointment. Delaney extended her hand through the place he'd stood. The air seemed warmer there. The fresh scent of his soap still lingered. She started to spread her fingers, then realized what she was doing and shoved her hand back into her pocket. "Good morning."

Phoebe took a step forward. "Are you feeling okay?"

Sure, aside from the fact that I'm likely losing my mind. "Yes, thanks. I just decided to take a walk down the path." She stifled the compulsion to make excuses. This was her grandmother's property. She had every right to go anywhere she wanted. She peered past them. "What are you doing here?"

"Taking the shortcut," Phoebe replied.

"Shortcut?"

"This path goes all the way to the old train tracks," she said, pointing her thumb over her shoulder. "It's a lot faster than going around by the road. I live in the new subdivision near the lake," she added.

"Then I take it you're on your way to the house?"

"We both are."

Pete glanced at Phoebe, then fixed his gaze on a point past

Delaney's shoulder. "Maybe you should walk back with us, Mrs. Graye."

"No, you two go ahead. I'm fine."

"My uncle said someone's been hanging around these woods. It might not be a good idea to be down here by yourself."

Delaney started. "Edgar mentioned last week that someone had been in the garden shed. Has he seen anyone since then?" Like a tall, dark-haired man dressed in drop-dead-sexy black?

"No, but Phoebe did."

"I didn't really see him," she said. "I just heard someone moving around behind me. It creeped me out. I heard a woman got mugged at the restrooms beside the lake last week. That's why Pete started walking me to work."

"It's not the only reason," he said, taking her hand. "This way, I have you all to myself."

Phoebe smiled and bumped her shoulder into his chest.

I want you all to myself, Delaney.

The memory of Stanford's voice rose without warning. It was the same memory fragment Delaney had recalled three days ago, only this time, she saw more.

The car was moving around a corner as her phone rang. She bumped her head on the dashboard as she reached down for her purse.

"Don't answer it, Delaney."

He'd spoken sharply. She glanced up, surprised by his tone. "It could be Jenna Chamberlain. She said she'd get back to me about the dinner on Saturday."

"Let her leave a message."

"It'll only take a minute."

He took one hand from the wheel and grabbed her wrist. "Let's not spoil the evening. I want you all to myself."

She wiggled her arm to ease his grip.

He hung on until the phone stopped ringing, then returned his hand to the wheel. "Cancel the dinner."

"I thought you liked the Chamberlains."

"I like my wife more."

She smoothed her glove over her wrist. He couldn't have known that he'd been hurting her. "They might decide not to come anyway. She wasn't sure when Trevor would get back from L.A."

"Then there's no problem if we called it off. Tell them we're spending Christmas in Paris. We can leave tomorrow."

"What? Why?"

"Why not?"

"Isn't this rather sudden?"

"I wanted to surprise you. You've been the soul of patience lately over my schedule." He slowed as they approached the house and used the remote to open the gates. "We deserve more time together."

She remained silent as they went up the driveway. This wasn't like Stanford. He never did anything spontaneous. In spite of the Jag's heated leather seats and the wool coat that enveloped her, she shivered as they drew closer to the house. Something was wrong.

He stopped at the front portico and was rounding the hood to open her door when her phone began to ring again.

Some instinct propelled her to answer it. Before he could reach her, she pressed the phone to her ear.

The voice she heard didn't belong to Jenna, their neighbor, calling about her dinner invitation.

It was Elizabeth's.

NINE

❧

"Elizabeth?"

Delaney's voice hit Elizabeth like a slap. She lowered the phone, breathing slowly through her nose until the shock faded. The driver's gaze met hers in the rearview mirror. She carefully blanked her expression and raised the partition behind his seat. His salary was paid through Grayecorp, not her. Any number of people could be slipping him extra money in exchange for information.

"Hello?"

She returned the phone to her ear, reminding herself that she did have the upper hand. Seven days had passed since Delaney had been served. Was this to be a plea for mercy? "Delaney."

"I need to talk to you."

"If you have anything to say, you should say it through your lawyer."

"Wait, don't hang up! We do need to talk."

"I would think my lawsuit speaks for itself."

"This is all so unnecessary. We're both after the same thing."

"I sincerely doubt that."

"We both want the truth."

"Are you prepared to confess how you killed my father?"

"It was an accident. In your heart, you must know that."

"Nothing happens by accident. There are always reasons. Your own recklessness and gross negligence caused the crash, and I'll make sure the world knows about it. You're not going to skate through this with your helpless innocent act. You're not going to play the martyr and testify from your hospital bed as you did for the inquiry. You'll be in a courtroom, and you're going to pay."

"This antagonism is only hurting you. We've both lost someone we loved. We should be trying to heal together."

"I've heard this before. It sounds more absurd every time you say it."

"Elizabeth, please."

The sympathy in Delaney's voice was feigned. It was as phony as the overtures of affection she used to feel obliged to make to her. The first thing Delaney had done after returning from her triumphant honeymoon was to claim she wanted to be friends. Friends. How stupid did she think Elizabeth was? Obviously, she'd only been trying to lull her stepdaughter into dropping her guard while she cemented her position with her new husband. Not that it had done her any good. Stanford had always had his own agenda when it came to his new acquisitions.

She focused on the buildings sliding past the window. They would reach the site of the new condominium development in less than twenty minutes. This was *her* new acquisition, the first major project to be initiated by Grayecorp without her father at the helm. She'd put Alan in charge, but the construction was behind schedule, hence this visit to the site, regardless of offending his ego. If he thought their personal relationship gave him a free pass, she needed to set him straight.

No, Elizabeth wouldn't let anyone use emotions to manipulate her. She'd learned that particular skill from a master.

"Eyes on the prize, Bethie. Take your amusements where you can, because you've earned them, but people like us never forget what matters. That's why we always win."

"Elizabeth? Are you still there?"

"Unless you get to the point, I see no reason to continue this conversation."

"I need your help."

She laughed in disbelief. This was why Stanford had never wanted his wife near the business. She was incredibly naive. "My help? Why would I help you?"

"Tell me why you called that night."

"What?"

"You phoned me the night of the accident."

Her mind froze. For six months, Delaney had claimed amnesia. Her doctors had backed her up. With head trauma, there was often permanent physical damage to memory areas of the brain. In particular, the time period surrounding the trauma could be impossible to recall. Elizabeth had read everything she could find on the subject, and she'd concluded the doctors had been right when it came to Delaney's case. Otherwise, she wouldn't have resorted to the lawsuit.

No, this would have been her only recourse, regardless. Delaney had been living a lie for five years. She had even less reason to tell the truth now. "All this time, your amnesia was simply a charade."

"No. It's real, but it's starting to lift."

"How convenient."

"You did call me, Elizabeth. That particular memory came back to me a few days ago. I clearly remember hearing your voice on my phone. I want to know what we talked about."

"Why?"

"So I can remember the rest. We need to make peace with the past."

"You don't really expect me to swallow that, do you?"

"I've always been honest with you," she said quietly. "And I've always wanted peace between us. I think it would break Stanford's heart if he saw how miserable your anger is making you."

"Don't presume to speak for my father. He would be proud of what I'm doing."

"Then tell me what we spoke about. It might help me remember the rest."

"We talked about your divorce."

There was a silence. "I don't believe you," Delaney said finally. "Stanford loved me. We were making plans for a trip."

"We also talked about his new will. He was going to cut you off. He planned to right the wrong you'd caused him to do. I was his blood and you were only a passing fancy."

"No."

"You tried to poison his mind against me because you knew I recognized you for what you were. It was effective for a while, but he saw reason before he died."

"Elizabeth—"

"I was willing to compromise then, but I won't make that mistake again. You didn't want me to win. That's why you killed him."

"No!"

Elizabeth hit the disconnect and lowered her head between her knees. Her head was spinning. Her entire body was trembling from the emotion she fought to contain.

Strong feelings were counterproductive. They put a person at a disadvantage. Yet if she did choose to indulge herself enough to hate, she would have plenty of cause to hate Delaney. She would hate her for stealing everything that should have been hers. She would hate her for talking so easily about love and for making her believe, even for an instant, that love truly was possible.

But most of all, she would hate Delaney for the things she had caused her to do.

THE KETTLE SHRIEKED. HELEN SLID OFF HER STOOL BEFORE Delaney could stand. "I'll get it."

"I wish you wouldn't fuss."

"I have to. It's in my grandmother contract."

"How's that?"

"Making tea is part of my job description. So is fussing. I do both extremely well." She moved around the work island and lifted the kettle from the stove. "You wouldn't want me kicked out of the grandma union, would you?"

Delaney quirked her cheek into a one-sided smile. Helen's humor was so corny it was adorable. "If there were such a thing, you'd probably be running it."

Helen struck a thoughtful pose, as if considering the possibility, then shook her head and measured tea into the pot. "No, I wouldn't do well with all the meetings. My arthritis acts up if I have to sit still for too long."

Delaney slid off her stool and went to the cupboard to take out a pair of mugs. In spite of the warmth of the day, iced tea wouldn't do. Nothing was quite as comforting as a pot of warm tea. "You're amazing."

"Careful, or I'll ask for a raise."

She brushed a light kiss on Helen's cheek. "I love you, Grandma."

"Love you, too, Deedee. Now sit," she ordered, pointing to the breakfast nook beneath the back window. "And tell me what that brat said this morning to make you cry."

It had been two days since her flash of memory by the pond. She had delayed calling Elizabeth until today in the hopes that more details would have emerged, but nothing else had come. Asking for her stepdaughter's help had been a last resort. She would have preferred not to have this conversation with her grandmother either, but it had been unavoidable. Helen had come into the kitchen just as Delaney was hanging up the phone.

She bypassed the stools and carried the mugs to the table, then waited until Helen had slid onto the bench across from her. "It's not a big deal. I'm closer to tears these days than I used to be, that's all."

"Please, don't shut me out."

There had been a thread of hurt in her grandmother's voice. "That's not what I'm doing," Delaney said.

"You might not intend to, but it's how I feel. I've given in about letting you help me with the business, haven't I? How about allowing me to do the same? Let me help you."

"I'm sorry, Grandma. I just haven't felt right about burdening you with my problems."

"Don't assume all this white hair means I can't share your load. According to my doctor, weight training strengthens our bones, whatever our age. I'm stronger than I look." She poured the tea. "Talk to me, honey. You've been here over a week now. It's not healthy to keep everything inside."

I don't keep it inside. I talk to Max.

Delaney curled her hands around the mug Helen passed to her. It was delft blue, with tiny geese marching around the rim, unlike the plain white one she'd seen Max hold.

But both the man and the mug had been imaginary, she reminded herself. The very fact that she needed to remind herself was disturbing.

"Delaney?"

"Elizabeth wasn't what I'd call cooperative."

"Did you expect she would be? She is suing you."

"Sure, but I'd hoped she would have been pleased that my amnesia was beginning to lift. I thought she would have wanted to help me fill in the blanks."

"She must have said something."

"She claimed that Stanford was going to divorce me and change his will."

"And that's what you were upset about?"

"Why wouldn't I be? Stanford and I were happy. We had a good marriage."

Helen added a spoonful of sugar to her tea. She stirred it slowly, tapped the spoon twice against the sides of the mug, and set it down. "Okay."

"Elizabeth was being deliberately cruel."

"Oh, very likely."

"Stanford and I were happy."

"Yes, you've said that. Several times."

"And Elizabeth must have lied."

"All right."

Yes, she must have lied. Delaney should have dismissed her stepdaughter's claim as nothing more than spite.

Then why couldn't she?

She regarded the patchy skin over her knuckles. "Leo says that I try to see the good in people."

"You do. You always have."

"But that means I also have a habit of denying the bad. I go to great lengths to avoid looking at things that bother me."

"That's probably my fault, Delaney."

"You? Why?"

"When you lived with us, I wanted to protect you from the reality of Annalee's illness. I encouraged you to ignore what hurt you and pretend that everything was fine."

"Grandma, you did an awesome job. You stepped in to raise me when you were going through what no parent ever should. You can't blame yourself for my bad habits. I'm a grown woman."

"Then what is it that you think you might be denying?"

Pressure built behind Delaney's eyes. The tears *were* close to the surface these days. "I keep insisting that Stanford and I were happy. I hear myself doing it, and even to my ears it's starting to sound as if I'm protesting too much. Who am I trying to convince? Myself?"

Helen was quiet for a while. "I've been wondering about that, too. You feel it's disloyal to Stanford to remember anything negative, don't you?"

"More than disloyal. It would be petty and ungrateful. He was my husband."

"That doesn't mean you can't be realistic. When we love someone, we accept both the good and the bad. It's all part of the healing after a loss. Did I ever tell you how your grandpa used to grind his teeth in his sleep?"

"No, I don't think you did."

"He also had the ability to walk straight past his dirty socks and not see them. He was old-school when it came to what he thought of as women's work. It drove me crazy. So did the way he tried to talk over me when he got going on a subject that interested him. There were other things, too, where our personalities rubbed against each other. We used to have plenty of fights."

"But you two were a perfect pair."

"What makes you say that?"

"Because you were a team. You shared a life. You depended on each other."

"It's true, we did."

"You weren't clones, but you were equals. You were like two halves of a larger whole."

Helen nodded. "That's a description of a good marriage."

It was. It was what Delaney had hoped for when she'd said yes to Stanford. She'd wanted the stability of a loving relationship. She'd wanted a home, somewhere to belong, as if marriage had been a place. She'd still been recovering from the shock of her father's death and had never felt more vulnerable. The loneliness was like a thing that she was running from.

Stanford had stepped in to fill the void. During the months after the funeral, he'd become more and more important to her. His presence had spread to every aspect of her life. She hadn't been aware when her gratitude toward him had changed to love, or when his consolation had turned to romance. It had simply happened.

The age gap hadn't mattered to either of them. He'd made her feel needed. He'd given her the emotional security she'd craved. He'd made her feel as precious as the jewelry he gave her, because that was how he showed his love. He'd never expected her to pick up after him because they'd had staff for that. He rarely had talked over her either—he was generally too well-controlled to get carried away by enthusiasm when he spoke.

But they'd never been a team. She hadn't felt as if they were two halves of one whole. No, the only man she knew who seemed like a part of her was Max.

She gripped her mug more tightly. The mere thought of him steadied her, although he was as different from Stanford as two men could be. It wasn't only his physical appearance, though the contrast there was considerable. For one thing, Stanford had been only a few inches taller than her. He'd felt uncomfortable looking up at anyone, so she'd limited the height of her heels to two inches. He'd had his hair trimmed weekly—no stray lock would have dared to fall over his forehead. His eyes had been brown rather than sparkling blue, so they couldn't have gleamed quite the same way Max's did. He'd seldom quarreled with her, either. He wouldn't have touched her ugly hands or her scars, let alone argued that she was beautiful when she appeared as she did now.

But Max saw past her appearance because their connection arose from the inside. He was her friend. No one had ever made her feel as safe. He would never hold her wrist hard enough to hurt. Even when he blustered, in her heart she knew he did care . . .

What on earth was she thinking? Max was a fantasy. No flesh-and-blood man could measure up to that. It was fine to use him to jog her memory, but she needed to maintain her grip on reality.

No matter how unpleasant it was.

She flattened her hands on the table and looked squarely at Helen. "Stanford was tense about something the night of the accident. He hadn't wanted me to answer my phone. I think he had guessed that Elizabeth was calling me."

"Are you worried there was some truth to what she said?"

Delaney stopped before she could make the automatic

denial. She did want to remember. Cutting off her thoughts before they could fully form wasn't the way to do that.

She attempted to reason it through. "Logic says there wasn't. Stanford took pride in the fact we didn't sign a prenup. He would have viewed divorce as a failure, and that's something he never would admit to."

"I wasn't aware you didn't have a prenuptial agreement. Isn't that unusual for a man with his wealth?"

"It was at his insistence. He wanted a total commitment from both of us." She swallowed. "'Til death do us part.'"

Helen laid a hand gently over hers.

"So even without remembering what we talked about that final evening," Delaney said, "I don't see how it could have been divorce."

THE WEEKLONG REPRIEVE FROM THE NIGHTMARE WAS over. The moment Delaney succumbed to sleep that night, the horror returned with a vengeance. She hurtled down the path to the pond. Crimson razors of pain sliced through her hands. She watched her skin peel from her flesh, then saw the fire melt the flesh from her bones, but she had no breath left to scream. Water filled her lungs. Mud clogged her throat.

No. The flames were sunshine. The water was dew. Neither could hurt her.

But they did. Over and over. She curled into a ball in the center of the mattress. Slime twined around her ankles, holding her down as flames clawed at her breast. She kicked. It grabbed her arm. It wouldn't let her go. It wanted her all to itself.

No! She didn't want to die. Not again.

"Over here, Deedee."

Max's voice blended with the noise of twisting metal and breaking glass. She couldn't tell where he was. She spread her fingers.

A beam of light pierced the darkness, as if a door had swung open to sunshine.

She turned her head. Flames crackled up her hair.

"Reach! Use your mind."

Delaney kept her gaze on the light and strained toward the threshold.

"That's it." Max's silhouette appeared against the sunlight. He was holding out his hand. "Almost there."

She kicked free from the nightmare and ran through the doorway.

He caught her in his arms.

She was suddenly weightless. Warmth and comfort enveloped her, along with what she recognized as the familiar scent of his body. Breath rushed back into her lungs. "Max!"

"Take it easy. You're safe."

Yes, she was. She knew it with the same utter certainty that she'd known she was drowning in that blackened, muddy fire. She looped her arms around his neck and hung on, drawing from his strength to push the last of the horror away.

Gradually, the noises dimmed. The crashing stopped. Stanford's screams faded and broke apart like rustling leaves. Nothing remained, except for Max. He set her back on her feet and moved his hands to her waist.

Still, she hung on. "I was having the nightmare again."

"I know. I heard you calling me."

"I didn't mean to."

"You woke me up."

She rubbed her forehead on his shoulder. "I'm sorry. Don't get cranky."

"Cranky? I came, didn't I?"

"I tried to take control the way you showed me, but it wouldn't work."

"Don't underestimate yourself, Deedee. You remember more than you realize."

"I don't want to remember the accident."

"No, I meant this place."

She lifted her head and glanced around.

Her bed was gone. So was her room. A sky the vibrant blue of Max's eyes arched overhead while mist spiraled lazily around them. The ground beneath her feet was soft, like a pillow. Or maybe a cloud. "This is a dream, right?" she asked.

Max was studying their surroundings, too. "Sort of."

"Where are we?"

"You tell me. You're making it up."

The wayward lock of hair had fallen over his forehead again. Delaney stroked it back. Her fingers tingled from the contact, sending a jolt of pleasure along her nerves. She curled her toes into the cloud. Yes, it was a cloud. A breeze was blowing right through it. "How?"

"Think of something."

A butterfly appeared in the mist. Colors rippled over its wings like a moving rainbow. It fluttered toward her, hovered teasingly, then lighted on Max's shoulder.

She put out her finger. "Shh. Don't move."

"Me or the bug?"

"Oh, this is wonderful. Thank you, Max."

"Hey, it's your picture."

"Picture?"

"We used to do this when we were kids. Sometimes you'd build it; sometimes I would. It doesn't exist anywhere except in our minds."

The butterfly inched onto her finger. She smiled. Yes, she knew where they were. It was their special place, where nothing hurt and nothing bad happened. "This is like the yellow flower you showed me last week."

"I only started that. You did the rest."

"Whatever it is, it's better than the nightmare."

Max traced one of the grafts on the back of her hand. That didn't hurt any more than the butterfly's touch. "You used to like birds when you were little, too."

"Did I?"

"Try it."

The butterfly pumped its wings a few times. Between one pump and the next, they became covered with feathers. Suddenly, it was a hummingbird.

She laughed, startling it into taking flight. It buzzed past Max's head, so she smoothed his hair again. She sighed with pleasure as it slid between her fingers. It was soft and unexpectedly silky. Sensuous. "This is some dream."

"It's not really a dream, Deedee."

She dropped her hand to his shoulder. His skin was warm beneath her palm. He wasn't wearing a shirt, so there was no barrier to her touch. Or her gaze. His shoulders were broad and square, his chest beautifully tapered. She rubbed her fingertips across the swirls of hair in the center.

"You sure as hell never did that when you were little."

She lowered her gaze. It wasn't only his chest that was bare. Max was totally naked.

And, oh, he was magnificent. There was no other word to describe him. His body was like his face, honed down to the masculine basics, all angles and taut curves and blatant, unapologetic sexuality.

The desire that rushed through her body in response to the sight of him shocked every nerve to life. Her heart thudded. Her breath caught.

The shot of adrenaline was enough to wrench her back to full consciousness.

Delaney blinked. The cloud was gone. So were the mist and the blue sky. She was once again in the darkness of her room, curled on the center of the bed with the sheet tangled around her ankles. The familiar chorus of bullfrogs came through the window screen. A breeze tickled her bare feet. Somewhere in the front half of the house a toilet flushed.

It had been a dream.

Of course it had been a dream. Her subconscious had found a different way to banish the nightmare. A very effective way. Her pulse was racing from sexual arousal instead of fear. Any woman's would after she encountered a sight like Max in the nude.

But no other woman would have seen him. He existed only in Delaney's mind. He wasn't real.

Maybe not, but the physical effect he had on her was. Sweat dampened her forehead and her upper lip. Her nightgown clung to her skin. She kicked aside the sheet and rolled to her back. She took slow, measured breaths through her nose, trying to calm her pulse.

It was no use. She was tingling. Everywhere.

"Why'd you stop? It was just getting interesting."

She lifted her head.

Max was sitting at the foot of her bed, his back propped against a bedpost. The moon was behind him so he was in shadow, but there was no mistaking the fact that he was still naked.

TEN

❧

DELANEY REACHED FOR THE LAMP, THEN THOUGHT BETTER of it. It might be wiser to leave Max in shadow. Otherwise, she couldn't hope to have a coherent thought. There wasn't enough blood in her brain. It was still pumping into all the erogenous zones of her body.

He drew up one knee and draped his arm across it, settling more comfortably against the bedpost. "I thought you told me the nightmare wasn't bothering you anymore."

"It wasn't."

"Then what brought it on this time?"

She sat up and tugged the hem of her nightgown over her thighs. He sounded as if it were the most natural thing in the world to be here. As if there was nothing strange about an imaginary friend sharing her dream or materializing on her bed.

"Deedee?"

So much for keeping her grip on reality.

But this must be what she'd wanted, since her mind had reached out to him again. She retrieved the sheet and pulled it over her legs. "I remembered something the other morning by the pond. After you left."

"It triggered the nightmare tonight?"

"I suspect following up on it did."

"Why?"

"It made me think about certain things I didn't want to."

"Like what?"

Like whether she and Stanford had really been happy.

Whether her marriage had been as good as she wanted to believe.

She glanced at Max's foot. It was on top of the sheet and only a few inches from her toes. His ankle was sturdy and bony at the same time, as only a man's could be. Moonlight touched the rounded bulge of his calf muscle and gleamed from the skin of his thigh. His bent leg blocked her view of his groin, but she didn't believe he'd done that deliberately. He was too at ease with his nudity.

He had every reason to be. *God*, his body was amazing.

"See something you like?"

She jerked her gaze to his face. "This is awkward."

He smiled. "Why?"

"Well, you're . . ." She waved her hand.

"I told you, I was asleep when you called me."

"And you sleep in the nude."

"Uh-huh."

"How does this work? Do you show up straight from whatever you were doing, like a come-as-you-are party?"

"I could smell your flesh burning. I didn't think you'd care if I forgot about grabbing my pants first."

"I'm sorry. I don't mean to be a prude. I'm grateful for your help, Max."

"You weren't acting like a prude when you were rubbing my chest."

"I thought I was dreaming."

"I warned you that you weren't."

"I know, but I saw the butterfly and the bird and—"

"And you assumed you'd made me up, too?"

"That's because I did."

"Right. I'm not real. Glad you reminded me."

"Max . . ."

"I'm a figment of your imagination, so you wouldn't expect me to sleep at night. I'm at your beck and call. You wouldn't think twice about inviting me into your bed or getting me worked up because I'm not a real man."

"I told you, I didn't intend to invite you."

"You sure enjoyed touching me. You seem to like looking at me, too."

"That's because you're *not* real."

He thumped his head against the bedpost. The impact made no noise. "Damn, this is complicated."

"You have no idea how many times I've thought the same thing."

"Why don't you want a real man in your bed, Deedee?"

"I love my husband. I mean, I loved my husband."

"I wasn't talking about love, I was talking about sex. Don't you like it?"

Delaney couldn't reply. This was another one of those subjects that she preferred not to think about.

Yet her subconscious must want her to. Otherwise, she wouldn't be fantasizing about a naked man. She wouldn't have made Max so attractive in the first place. The feelings he'd stirred up in her dream hadn't faded. He was stimulating responses that had been dormant for months.

No, it had been much longer than that. It had been years since she had experienced true desire with Stanford, and it had never been as strong as the feelings that Max evoked. Whether he was sitting naked in her bed or standing beside a pond in broad daylight, he touched parts of her that no one else could.

She took a steadying breath. "I only want you to be my friend."

"Then why are your nipples puckered?"

She didn't need to glance down to verify what he'd said. She could feel the tingling prickle as they pushed against her nightgown. Knowing that *he* knew tightened them further. She pulled up her feet and wrapped her arms around her legs. Oddly enough, she didn't give a thought to hiding her scars. "Do you really need me to answer that?"

"Yeah, I do."

"Take a look in the mirror."

He laughed. Like all the words he'd spoken, the sound bypassed her senses and slipped straight into her mind, rumbling along her nerves in a formless caress. "Do you like the way I look?"

"Duh."

"I can't take credit for that since you believe you made me up."

"Quit teasing me, Max."

He slid his foot over the sheet until his toes nudged hers. "What did your husband look like?"

"Nothing like you. Stanford was sixty-eight when we got married."

"Sixty . . . ?"

"Eight." She paused. Even with the honesty they'd always shared, she hesitated to go further.

Yet as bizarre as these circumstances were, they *were* forcing her to face reality. The strength of her reaction to Max was indisputable. She plunged ahead. "It wasn't so much his age, it was the demands of his business that absorbed most of his energy. Our sex life wasn't . . . very active."

"Sixty-eight."

"You sound as if you're having trouble grasping that."

"Damn right. Now I really can't picture you married."

"He was seventy-three when he died."

"You spent five years of your life with a man who couldn't satisfy you?"

"I never said that. There's more to a relationship than sex. He was good to me in other ways. He doted on me. He treated me as if I were precious. We were happy . . ." She stopped. There was that word again. It came automatically whenever she thought of her marriage, as if she'd brainwashed herself into making the response, as if she were afraid to make any other.

"Why did you marry him, Deedee?"

"Because I loved him." That response had come automatically, too.

Max withdrew his foot. "You said he was rich."

"I know how it appeared, but I didn't marry him for his money."

"He was more than twice your age. You didn't marry him for his looks or his sex drive, either."

"Age is irrelevant. I feel disloyal to Stanford even thinking about this. I'm sorry now that I told you anything."

Max snorted.

"What was that for?"

"You were married, not sentenced."

"Care to explain that?"

"Just because a man's your husband doesn't mean you have to take what he dishes out. You had a choice. You weren't locked up. You still had control of your life."

"There's such a thing as loyalty."

"Not when it's blindness."

"You sound angry."

"It's a dangerous pattern, Deedee."

"I don't understand. What pattern?"

"Some women can be so afraid of being alone that they stay married to a monster."

"I'm not afraid of being alone."

"Then why do you keep calling me?"

"That's different."

He rubbed his face. "Right. Because I'm not real."

"And Stanford was *not* a monster. He was simply human, which meant he had flaws like the rest of us. When did you develop such a flair for the dramatic, Max?"

"Did he know you liked yellow roses?"

"What does that have to do with anything?"

"Did he hold you when you were scared? Did you show him your thoughts?"

"Max . . ."

"Did he have any idea how powerful your mind is?"

"Powerful?"

"How can you doubt that? Your mind is incredible. Otherwise I wouldn't be here."

"My imagination has nothing to do with the quality of a real-life relationship."

"You mean sex."

"All right, yes. That's what I thought I wanted to talk about, but I can see it was a mistake. You're deliberately confusing me. Sex doesn't mean anything without love."

"Yeah, right. Thought you'd outgrown your fairy tales."

"Don't you believe in love?"

Rather than replying, he shoved away from the bedpost and knelt on the mattress in front of her. "How many times have you woken up in a sweat after dreaming about him?"

Never. "Max . . ."

"Do you enjoy imagining him naked?"

She tried to keep her gaze on his face. She couldn't. There was simply too much more to admire. "That's not fair."

"Why not?"

"Because no one could compare to you, Max."

He framed her face in his hands.

In the one remaining rational corner of her mind, she realized he wasn't really touching her. The sensation was too muted, yet at the same time it was too deep for a touch. She didn't feel it on the surface, but she felt it in every quivering nerve, even the ones that should have been dead.

"Do you want to kiss me, Deedee?"

If she'd wanted to lie, her body wouldn't let her. Her lips parted as she focused on his mouth. *With all my heart, Max.*

But this was a fantasy. He wasn't truly here. What was wrong with her?

His silhouette wavered. "Don't."

She tipped her head into his caress. "Don't what?"

"Send me away. Not yet." He traced his thumb along her cheek. "One kiss. What's the harm in that?"

"What's the harm? You mean besides losing what's left of my grip on reality?"

He brought his lips to hers. Sweetly. Gently. Somehow, in spite of his bluster, the grown-up Max understood what she needed the same way he'd done as a boy.

Delaney closed her eyes and surrendered to the moment.

His tongue slid into her mouth as his thoughts pushed into her mind.

The reaction was instantaneous. Pleasure flashed from the inside out. She felt Max's kiss in every corner of her being as a wave of delight surged through her body. It was more intimate than a physical orgasm. More vivid than reality. It was more intense than anything she'd experienced in her life.

And it was so achingly, undisputedly genuine . . .

. . . that she was probably quite insane.

ELEVEN

MAX SLOWED TO A STOP AT THE STONE GATEPOSTS AND LET the engine idle. A red-haired teenager was mowing the grass with a lawn tractor. An old man in coveralls stood on a ladder to use a hedge trimmer on the cedars that bordered the property. Pots of purple and white petunias followed the curve of the driveway, and more flowers spilled from boxes that were attached to the veranda railing. The Wainright House was the same gleaming white he remembered, with its gingerbread trim hanging from the eaves like scrolls of icicles. A profusion of gables poked from the roof, along with a rounded spire on one corner. The house was as different from the home Max had built as a Jaguar was from the old Jeep he drove.

Deedee had said she was rich. From the appearance of the place, her grandmother wasn't hurting for money, either. A lot of women married for wealth. When there was an age gap of forty-three years, it was usually the major factor. He didn't believe it had been for Deedee. She wouldn't have sold herself for a checkbook. She was too honest with her emotions and too passionate. She must have believed that she'd loved the man she'd married. That was typical of her. In spite of the darkness that lurked in her nightmare, she still clung to the concept of love.

He wasn't sure why that bothered him, since her marriage wasn't any of his business. He knew better than to get involved on an emotional level. Hearing her talk about her dead husband shouldn't have made him jealous, either. He had no claim on her, nor did he want one.

So, what was he doing here?

Curiosity. Masochism. Or maybe he just wanted to take his time going downtown. He was a free man, and this was a public road. He didn't give a damn about the curious looks the old man with the hedge trimmer was giving him.

The front door of the house opened.

Max held his breath, his pulse kicking. *This* was the real reason he was here. To get the adrenaline push of a gambler's high. To have the decision taken out of his hands.

To tempt fate.

But it wasn't Deedee; it was a couple in matching Hawaiian-print shirts. They loaded two suitcases into the back of a station wagon and started down the driveway. Departing guests, he decided, watching as they drove past. According to the sign on one of the gateposts, the place had been turned into a bed-and-breakfast.

He exhaled hard and returned his gaze to the house. He couldn't see the window of Deedee's room from here, since it faced the backyard, but he knew his way there. Up the stairs with the curving oak banister, down the hall to the bump in the floor where the front half joined the original house, then through to the last door on the right. He pictured her bed, letting his thoughts float in search of her, probing for her presence.

He found her in the kitchen. Her hands were wrapped around a mug that was decorated with geese. A crumbled muffin was on a plate in front of her.

She lifted her head quickly, as if she sensed his approach.

But she didn't welcome him into her mind. A barrier of wariness surrounded her.

He pictured brushing his fingertips across her knuckles.

Coffee sloshed out of her mug. She crossed her arms, tucking her hands beneath them, as she shielded her thoughts from his touch. Her image wavered, then dissolved like windblown smoke.

Max fisted his hands on the wheel. She had deliberately refused the link. He was disturbed by how much her rejection stung. This was what he'd advised her to do from the start, wasn't it? For her own good, she had to be more careful about leaving herself open.

Yet he doubted whether her new caution was due to his warnings. It was because of their kiss.

He should have thought of it before. What better way to convince her he wasn't the boy she remembered than to act like the man he was?

Too bad that hadn't been what he'd been trying to prove. He'd been operating on instinct. He hadn't questioned the impulse to kiss her. Given the circumstances, the real question was how he'd managed to hold off so long.

It had been better than he could have anticipated. Their thoughts had been so in tune, they hadn't needed to physically touch to connect. The pleasure had been pure, undiluted sensation, like colors squeezed straight from the tube. Simply remembering it was sending blood to his groin. It was more tempting than ever to visit her in person.

Yet she'd let him kiss her only because she'd thought he wasn't real.

He regarded the driveway for a full minute, then jammed the Jeep into gear and drove past. Seeing her in the flesh would add complications he didn't need. He had no intention of starting a real-life relationship with her.

But if she thought she could keep him out of her head, he would enjoy proving her wrong.

DELANEY CONCENTRATED ON HER BREATHING. IN, OUT, in, out. Her lungs were working as they should. So were her senses. The coffee smelled delicious, but she suspected the rest of it would slop onto the table if she tried lifting the mug. Maybe Max would drop in again to steady her hand for her . . .

She held out as long as she could, then slid from the breakfast nook and stumbled toward the phone that hung on the kitchen wall. She dialed Dr. Bernhardt's number from memory, thankful that her memory functioned for this, anyway. Who could predict how the mind worked? Who could have guessed that a harmless imaginary childhood friend would get so out of control?

But he hadn't been truly out of control, since he'd done what she'd wanted him to do, even though she wouldn't have guessed that what he'd done was even possible . . .

She dropped her forehead against the wall. *Focus!*

The phone rang three times, then went to voice mail. According to his message, Dr. Bernhardt was on vacation.

"No," Delaney whispered.

He went on to give the number of another doctor who was covering for him in case of emergency. She grabbed the pen that hung from the notepad that was tacked up beside the phone. Did this qualify as an emergency? Or should she wait until reality disappeared altogether?

Describing her symptoms wasn't going to be easy. What exactly was her complaint? That she'd experienced too much pleasure in her fantasy? Some women might consider themselves lucky to have an imaginary lover who was too sexy for words and showed up naked at the drop of a thought and kissed as if he was making love to her mind.

All right, she'd enjoyed what had happened the night before. The depth of her enjoyment was what alarmed her. How could she have thought that sex wasn't an issue? Not on the radar, she'd told herself. Look what too much denial had done. It had conjured up—

She blanked her mind fast before she could think of his name. He was liable to come back, drifting into the room on the edge of her vision, bringing the scent of paint and freshly cut grass, then making her pulse leap with the lightest brush of his fingers.

Suppressing her discontent with her and Stanford's sex life must have led to the fantasy. She'd been in denial for years. To acknowledge this major flaw in their relationship would have been unpleasant. It would have contradicted what she'd wanted to believe, so she'd ignored it, as was her habit. Helen was right; it wasn't healthy to keep things inside. Bottled-up feelings found another route to the surface.

Dr. Bernhardt's recorded voice invited the caller to leave a message. Delaney realized she hadn't written down his replacement's phone number. "Dr. Bernhardt, this is Delaney Graye," she said quickly. "I'm sorry to interrupt your vacation, but would you please call me back? I'm . . ." She faltered on the word. "Worried," she continued. "I'm remembering things I . . ."

Again, she hesitated. The memories that were upsetting her

had nothing to do with the accident or her resulting amnesia. No, these were things she'd chosen to deny. She didn't need her doctor's help for those; she only needed the courage to face them. Max had told her that she had a powerful mind . . .

Couldn't she go two minutes without thinking about him? Dr. Bernhardt should be able to treat her for her delusion about an imaginary friend. Didn't they have antipsychotic drugs for problems like that? It could be as simple as taking a few pills. She could chemically banish him from her head.

No more nighttime visits. No impromptu chats. No sensations of belonging and comfort and warmth.

"Never mind, Dr. Bernhardt," she muttered. "It will keep." She hung up the receiver and pressed her back to the wall.

If she wasn't clinically insane, then she was absolutely pathetic. Was she that needy? Was she actually considering relinquishing sanity for the chance to feel Max's touch one more time?

Max. Wasn't. Real.

A deep, masculine chuckle whispered through her brain.

Delaney clapped her hands over her ears. "Go away!" she said aloud.

Something brushed across her mouth as softly as the butterfly that she'd held in her dream.

She reflexively parted her lips, then realized what she was doing and clenched her teeth. She pictured her mind as a closed hand, then snapped her thoughts hard the way she'd done the other day at the pond. *No!*

He left.

All right. It had worked. That meant she did still have a modicum of control over her mind. Maybe things weren't as bad as she feared.

"What are you afraid of, Delaney? I'll never leave you."

That hadn't been Max's voice; it had been Stanford's. When had he said that?

A fragment of memory teased the edges of her mind. She saw Stanford in their bedroom. He was wearing the same deep blue wool overcoat he'd worn to the restaurant. An off-white silk scarf draped over the lapels, and its fringe swayed as he spoke. There was an open suitcase on the padded bench that stretched along the foot of their bed.

A suitcase. Looking at it upset her. It was a symbol of a bridge that was about to be burned. She remembered rubbing her arms against a chill.

Stanford said he would never leave her.

Then why was there an open suitcase? For their trip?

She strained. She wanted to know. She *needed* to remember.

But as had happened before, the more she tried, the more the memory escaped her grasp. The fragment refused to expand. The bedroom she'd shared with Stanford faded. In its stead, she saw the four-poster in her room upstairs. She remembered Max's voice, not her husband's.

"Some women can be so afraid of being alone that they stay married to a monster."

She shivered, rubbing her arms as she'd done in her memory. As before, thoughts of one man had triggered thoughts of the other. They were as different as two men could be, yet they were connected somehow. It was as if opening her mind to Max allowed her to see what else was buried in there.

What he'd said about a monster was overly dramatic, though. No, *he* hadn't said it, *she* had, because Max was solely a product of her own imagination . . .

"Enough," she muttered, shoving herself away from the phone. Her reasoning was going in circles. It wasn't getting her anywhere. But then, she couldn't expect any better from a mind on the precipice of insanity.

DELANEY TOOK ONE CORNER OF THE SHEET AND PULLED it up the bed as Helen did the same on the other side. She was glad her grandmother had given up protesting about her help around the house. Preparing the rooms for new guests had become a welcome routine for her. Today, more than ever, she needed the comfort of these mundane tasks. They helped to ground her in reality.

This room used to be Helen's sewing room. She had redone it in a palette of cream and pale blue, colors that contrasted beautifully with the dark walnut sleigh bed and matching dresser. The accessories had been kept to a minimum—the dresser was bare aside from an African violet in an earthenware teapot and a shallow willow basket that held a collection of tourist brochures. The shades of the bedside lamps were trimmed with the same pale blue as the curtains. The overall effect was an impression of cool serenity. It gave the room a country feel without the busyness of patchwork or calico. Delaney smoothed the sheet across the mattress, inhaling appreciatively as the scents of sunshine and fresh air rose from the cotton. "If a fabric softener company could duplicate this smell, they'd make a fortune."

"I'm sure they've tried."

Phoebe dropped a dustcloth on the dresser and picked up the stack of fresh towels. "I think it's terrific how you dry everything outside, Mrs. W. It saves so much energy."

"My grandmother's ahead of the curve on this," Delaney said. "She was line drying long before environmentalism got trendy."

Helen chuckled. "Who would have thought that being old-fashioned would become fashionable?"

"I heard when they were building our subdivision," Phoebe said, "they tried to make it illegal to hang laundry outside because it looked bad. Isn't that insane?"

Delaney mumbled an affirmative as Phoebe ducked into the bathroom with the towels. There certainly were many ways to define insanity.

"You seem jittery today, Delaney," Helen said, tucking a pillow under her chin as she slipped on a fresh pillowcase. "Was it a rough night?"

Which part? The nightmare or the imaginary lover? "I probably had too much coffee," she replied. "I should cut back."

"I know what you mean. I have to be careful myself, but I do love the stuff."

"Funny how we can enjoy things we know aren't good for us."

"One of the mysteries of life." She shook out the pillow, put it in place, and helped Delaney spread out the duvet. "Speaking of which, the potato latkes were delicious. I think I gained four pounds just smelling them."

"Oh, come on, Grandma. You're in terrific shape."

"You're the one who needs to eat, not me."

"Not those. I know what I put into them. They're fattening."

Helen laughed. "Well, my guests loved them."

"Are you talking about those potato thingies?" Phoebe asked as she returned from the bathroom. She added the used towels to the pile of stripped sheets. "They were awesome. I wish I could cook like that, Delaney."

"It's not hard. All you need is a good cookbook. That's how I learned."

"I thought you had servants to do that." She stopped. "I'm sorry. That sounded rude."

"No, it's okay, Phoebe. My husband and I did have staff who took care of the household chores. That wasn't the case when I was growing up. I learned to cook out of necessity when I lived with my father."

"Do you think you could show me how you make your orange muffins? The ones with the dates?"

"I'd be happy to."

"Thanks. I gave one of the leftovers to Pete, and he loved it." She glanced quickly at Helen. "I hope you didn't mind that I did that, Mrs. Wainright."

"Certainly, I don't mind. I hate seeing anything go to waste."

Phoebe gathered the laundry into a bundle. "Is it okay if I take Friday off and work Sunday instead? Pete's band is playing at the festival."

Helen heaved an exaggerated sigh. "I suppose we could muddle along without you if we must."

"I'll stay late to make up for it."

"I'm just teasing, Phoebe. You go and have a good time."

"Thanks!"

Helen smiled as Phoebe's footsteps pounded down the stairs. "I wondered when she was going to ask me. Edgar's been bragging about his nephew's upcoming musical debut for days."

"What kind of band is he in?"

"He calls it country rock. The festival committee has made it a policy to showcase the local talent." She fluffed a tasseled throw pillow and arranged it on the bed. "We have quite a variety in Willowbank."

"It's at the park by the lake, right?"

"That's the only place big enough to hold it. They seem to add more events every year. Do you remember my friend Ada Ross? She has a quilt on display in the arts and crafts tent. She took second prize last year, but I'm positive this year she'll win."

"Good for her."

"It's really a work of art. They should forget about the craft category." She tilted her head as the bell in the downstairs hall sounded. "Oh, no. I hope the Walts aren't early."

Delaney turned to the dresser and picked up the dusting cloth Phoebe had dropped. "You go ahead. I'll finish up in here."

It pleased her that Helen left to see to her guests without an argument. At least she understood Delaney's need to keep busy. Stanford never had.

The mental blinders came up with the thought, but she forced them aside. That particular criticism of her husband wasn't new. His determination to put her on a pedestal had frustrated her, yet he'd insisted it was out of love. She wondered what Max would say about that. He'd told her she'd still had control of her life, yet she'd handed it to Stanford simply because they'd married.

No, it wasn't *Max* who had told her, she reminded herself. It was her own subconscious. Odd, though, that her subconscious would raise the subject of control, since it was her struggle to corral her own imagination that was posing the biggest challenge.

God, she had to stop obsessing about this. She should think about muffins, or latkes, or Ada Ross's quilt. She swiped the cloth vigorously across the dresser, then tipped up the willow basket to clean beneath it. One of the brochures it contained slid over the side to the floor. She retrieved it automatically and dropped it back in the basket when an image of Max flashed across her vision.

She gritted her teeth and turned to finish dusting the sleigh bed. At least she didn't feel his presence this time, and it had been only his face that she'd seen. A black-and-white face, as if it had been a photograph . . .

She paused. Her pulse did a quick thump. No, it was her

imagination. It must have been. That was the only way she could have seen him. She looked over her shoulder at the basket of brochures.

The one she'd dropped back inside had landed facedown on the pile. There was a photograph on the back. It was a black-and-white photo of a man's face. Even from a yard away she could see that the man seemed familiar.

She moved closer, her hand shaking as she reached out to retrieve the brochure. She flipped it to the front first, forcing herself to read the words printed there.

It was an advertisement for an art gallery in downtown Willowbank. There was a photo of a building with striped awnings over the entrance and the two front windows. The Mapleview Gallery. Open Tuesday to Saturday, 11 to 5. Sundays by appointment. The current display featured the work of famous local artist John Harrison.

John Harrison. She had never heard of him. She breathed deeply a few times, then turned it to the back.

The caption beneath the picture said John Harrison.

But the face belonged to Max.

Delaney slapped the brochure on the dresser and covered the picture with her palm.

No. This was impossible. Imaginary friends didn't pose for photographs. They didn't assume an alias and masquerade as real people. They weren't famous. They existed only in the mind of their creator.

Famous local artist John Harrison.

Artist.

Sometimes Max smelled like paint. Sometimes he smelled like turpentine.

Did John Harrison paint with oils?

She snatched the brochure and carried it to the window. Maybe she hadn't seen it clearly enough. Max was in her thoughts so often, she might have pictured his image in place of the real John Harrison. Maybe in stronger light . . .

Her fingers crumpled the edges of the paper. The light at the window was stronger. So was the resemblance, except for his hair. John Harrison wore his hair combed straight back from his face. No wayward, rebellious lock softened his broad forehead. There was no mistaking those lean cheeks or that sharp nose, though. The black-and-white photo didn't show the color of his eyes, but it was plain they weren't brown. He looked unsmiling into the camera lens, as if impatient with the necessity of having his picture taken . . . as if he didn't give a damn what other people thought.

That was what Max had told her. He didn't give a damn.

But Max was a fantasy.

Wasn't he?

Delaney folded the brochure into a square, creasing carefully so that the photograph remained flat. There had to be a logical explanation. Yes, there must be. She needed to calm down so she could think of it.

Max couldn't possibly be John Harrison. Having an imaginary friend pop into her thoughts was one thing. She knew what that felt like. She'd done it throughout her childhood, as plenty of children did. Believing she'd suddenly begun interacting with a total stranger in her head for no apparent reason was something else entirely. It was simply beyond any rational possibility. Max had shared her nightmare, for God's sake, and she hadn't told the details about that to anyone except Dr. Bernhardt. What was more, Max knew things about her past that no one else could.

Therefore, whoever, whatever, John Harrison was, he couldn't be Max. Believing he was would truly be insane.

Then why do they share a face?

"No, of course we don't mind if you check in early, Mrs. Walt." Helen's voice echoed from the staircase. "An afternoon nap is a necessity in your condition."

Delaney slipped the picture into her pocket and stepped into the hall.

Helen was leading a young couple up the stairs. The man, who looked to be in his mid-twenties, was carrying one suitcase in his hand and a smaller one tucked under his arm, leaving his other arm free to keep a steadying hand on the back of his wife's waist. Delaney assumed she was his wife, since she appeared to be at least eight months pregnant, which explained Helen's remark about the nap.

All this Delaney absorbed with a kind of numb detachment. She responded when Helen spoke to her and managed to say a polite welcome to the new guests, yet she wasn't sure how she reached the stairs. She gripped the banister and paused to steady her breathing. In, out, in, out, just as she'd done that morning. This was turning into a habit.

The vacuum cleaner hummed from the dining room when Delaney reached the ground floor. Phoebe bobbed her head as she worked, her ponytail swinging in time to the wires that trailed from her earphones. She looked so blessedly carefree that Delaney wanted to hug her. She hugged her arms over her chest instead and went past the doorway to the table beside the front entrance.

It held a crystal bowl filled with potpourri and a philodendron that trailed gracefully over one side. On the polished surface between the plant and the bowl lay an assortment of brochures like the ones in the basket upstairs. Delaney forced her brain to focus on those.

There were rational reasons for the tourist brochures. While Helen's primary goal was to encourage her visitors to spend more time in Willowbank, she also arranged for other local businesses to display her promotional material if she displayed theirs. It was a mutually beneficial arrangement, a trade, and all very logical.

Delaney spotted the gallery's brochure immediately. She picked it up carefully and checked the back to make sure it held the same photo. It did. John Harrison's resemblance to Max seemed even more striking the second time around. It was a wonder she hadn't noticed it sooner. She had done the polishing for Helen several times during the past week. She had moved around everything on this table in order to reach the surface. For all she knew, the photograph might have registered in her subconscious without her being aware of it . . .

She latched onto the idea like a lifeline. Of course! Not only had she polished and dusted, she had walked past this table countless times since she'd arrived in Willowbank. She could have seen the photograph of John Harrison every day in her peripheral vision. She would have seen it *before* her first encounter with Max in the backyard.

She continued to study the photo. The initial shock of seeing Max's face was wearing off. The face of John Harrison was definitely memorable. Masculine, sexy, and brooding. She could easily picture him being the kind of man who slept in the nude. In fact, she likely wasn't the only woman who might want to imagine him that way.

Was it possible that her subconscious had given John Harrison's face to the adult Max?

Her reasoning made sense. Actually, it made more sense than believing she had created the face of the adult Max out of thin air. No wonder he appeared so real. She'd based him on a real man.

In a way, the idea was comforting. At least this aspect of her delusion had a rational explanation.

The hum of the vacuum cleaner cut off. Phoebe appeared in the hall, dragging the appliance behind her. She plugged it into the outlet across from the table, then grimaced when she saw what Delaney was holding. She pulled out her earphones and sidled up to her. "He would make a good Heathcliff, don't you think?"

Delaney swallowed a relieved laugh. Well, this confirmed that Phoebe saw the same photo that she did, so she hadn't imagined John Harrison. "Do you know who he is?"

"Are you kidding? Harrison's practically a legend in Willowbank."

"The brochure said he was famous. Have you seen his art?"

"I've seen pictures of it. I don't like it that much; it's too intense, and it costs a fortune. But that's not his main claim to fame."

"Oh?"

"He learned to paint while he was in prison."

She thought of Max's face. No, John Harrison's. His go-to-hell attitude, the toughness he strove to project. No, that was Max's attitude. It didn't necessarily apply to the real man. "Do you know why he was there?"

Phoebe leaned closer and lowered her voice. "From what I heard, he tried to beat his mother to death with a belt."

The words bounced around in her head a few times before she could completely grasp them. When she did, she felt sick. Max wouldn't have done that. She was absolutely certain of it. He wasn't bad or mean or . . .

Stop! They weren't talking about Max. "That's horrible."

"I was a baby when it happened, but I remember how upset people were when he moved back here."

Delaney tamped down the urge to deny what Phoebe was saying. It was only the artist's resemblance to Max that made her want to defend him. "He's successful now, though. It seems to me as if he managed to turn his life around."

"Sure, but you wouldn't catch me walking past his place at night." She gave a theatrical shudder. "Geez, I wonder if he was the creepy guy in the woods."

Delaney started. She returned the brochure to the table and slid her hand into her pocket. Her fingers closed over the folded paper. It wasn't Max's face she touched, she reminded herself. It wasn't Max they were talking about, either. He had disappeared before Phoebe and Pete could have seen him. Not that anyone else would have seen him anyway *since he didn't exist.* "Why would John Harrison be in our woods?"

Phoebe grimaced again. "Sorry, I guess you didn't know he's your neighbor."

TWELVE

❧

"The lamb looks good. What do you think, Elizabeth?"

Elizabeth paused as if considering Alan's question, then gave her head a restrained shake and handed her menu to the waiter. "I'll have the grilled sole."

Alan took a hefty swallow of his scotch as the waiter left. "I thought you didn't like fish."

"I'm quite fond of the way they do it here."

"You only ordered it because you didn't want to go along with my suggestion."

He was right. On principle, she didn't let anyone make decisions for her, regardless of how minor. Enough minor concessions could quickly lead to a loss of control, but she was hardly going to admit that to him. "Don't sulk, Alan. It doesn't suit you."

"I'm not sulking, I'm pointing out a fact."

"This isn't about my menu choice, is it? You understand why I had to assign Tirza to assist you on the condo project, don't you?"

"My mood has nothing to do with business."

"I think it does." She reached across the white linen tablecloth to touch her fingertips to his knuckles. "The project was running over budget. We need to maintain the confidence of our investors, and Tirza has a proven track record. You could learn a lot from her."

"She's a ballbuster."

Elizabeth withdrew her hand to pick up her Perrier. "I wouldn't have expected a comment like that from you, Alan.

If Tirza had been a man, you would be extolling her business acumen rather than stooping to a locker-room slur."

He drained his drink and signaled the waiter for another. It was brought promptly, which seemed to mollify him.

Alan likely thought the attentiveness of the staff was due to his authoritative manner rather than the generous tips she signed for whenever she entertained here on the Grayecorp account. "In fact," she continued once the server had left, "I'm doubly disappointed, since what you say about Tirza could very well apply to me. Is that how you think of me, Alan? That I'm a ballbuster?"

"I don't know, Elizabeth. It's been a while since you had anything to do with my balls. Why don't we skip dinner and go back to my place so you can remind me how you handle them?"

"Is that supposed to be funny?"

He curled both hands around his glass and rolled the bottom along the tablecloth. "I don't know what it's supposed to be. I don't know what *we're* supposed to be."

This was dangerous ground. She needed to massage his ego but not inflate it. "I thought we were friends."

"I thought we were lovers."

She touched his hand again. By nature, she wasn't comfortable with this kind of casual physical contact. That was the way she'd been raised. Her nannies and later her governesses had been staff, and one never, never hugged staff. As for her mother, well, hugs would have wrinkled her clothes, and her father had more subtle ways of expressing his emotions. She knew it was important to Alan, though, because he wasn't the most subtle of men. "I understand how you might feel you're getting mixed signals. All I can hope is that you'll bear with me. For both our sakes, I can't afford to give anyone grounds to claim favoritism with respect to your role in the company. Especially not yet."

"Not yet?" he repeated.

"We're still in a period of readjustment." She stroked his wrist. "Losing my father has been difficult for me, both personally and professionally. I feel it's my duty to preserve the legacy he left."

"Grayecorp is a profitable legacy."

"Yes, as long as it continues to be guided by a steady hand."

"Yours?"

She didn't bother to reply to the question in his voice, since the answer was obvious to both of them. Otherwise, he wouldn't be with her. She leaned closer, as if she were about to impart a confidence, but her real purpose was to expose her cleavage to his view.

Predictably, his gaze dropped.

"It's a time of transition," she said. "Which makes it also a time of great opportunity for people who share my vision."

He was too busy studying her breasts to grasp her words immediately. She could pinpoint the moment when he did, though. His lips, which had been lax from the scotch and his pout, firmed to a flat line. He lifted his head. "What kind of opportunity, Elizabeth?"

"I can trust you, can't I, Alan?"

"You know you can."

"I would like to give you more responsibility. My father always thought you had great potential."

The dual lies had the desired effect. His gaze glinted with the first spark of genuine interest he'd displayed that evening. If she could see through the table to his lap, no doubt she'd find that his pants were tenting. Yes, nothing got Alan excited quite like the prospect of advancing his career. His ambitiousness was far too transparent. It made him easy to manipulate.

"Stanford was a brilliant man," he said.

Brilliant enough to understand why you tried to romance me in the first place, she thought. "Yes, he was. And he knew how to reward loyalty."

The word hung in the air between them. A muscle flickered in his cheek. "What have you heard, Elizabeth?"

"Very little, which is why I suspect there must be something that I *should* be hearing."

Alan lifted his drink. He took a moderate sip this time. He appeared to need time to think more than he needed the alcohol. "There is something."

She toyed with the pearls at her neck, drawing his gaze back to her chest. She didn't want him to think too much. She needed him to commit to aligning himself with her for the upcoming showdown with the board. And she knew there would be one. Every instinct told her it would be soon, too. "Yes?"

"A lawyer contacted me the week before last. He insisted on speaking with me outside the office."

"Whom did he represent?"

"He wouldn't say."

That made sense. Whoever was making the move wouldn't want to show their hand before they could be sure they held a winning one. "What did he want?"

"He asked about your behavior at the office, whether your grief over your father was impeding your business abilities, things like that."

"Excuse me?"

"I told him you were doing a great job."

"The last quarterly report could have told him that."

"It didn't sound as if he was taking a financial slant with his questions. It was more personal."

"This lawyer questioned you about my personal life?"

"I'd say it was more that he was questioning your mental competency."

"Do you remember his name?"

"Leo Throop."

She heard a faint, grinding squeak. It was the sound of pearls rubbing together. She released her grip on her necklace before she broke the string. "You're certain it was Throop?"

"Do you know him?"

"He works for my father's widow."

Alan's upper lip bulged as he ran his tongue over his teeth. It was a particularly unattractive habit. "That's interesting."

"Who else did he speak with?"

"As far as I know, everyone at the office."

"And what did they say?"

"I don't know that."

"Find out."

"Elizabeth . . ."

She banged her fist on the table. "I want details. Names. I need to know who's on my side. If that bitch thinks—" She broke off when she saw several nearby diners turn their heads.

Damn the woman. Elizabeth had expected an attempt to

oust her, but she hadn't expected Delaney would be behind it. She'd never demonstrated interest in the company when Stanford was alive. Wasn't it enough that she had stolen her childhood home and her father's fortune? She must be hoping to take away her career, too. Why else would she send her flunky to nose around Grayecorp, questioning Elizabeth's competence?

Alan passed her what remained of his whiskey. "I've never seen you so passionate, Elizabeth. I didn't know you had it in you."

She tipped the glass to her lips, enjoying the fire that burned her throat. "You'd be surprised what I'm capable of, Alan."

THIRTEEN

THE PAINTING WAS A DEPARTURE FROM MAX'S RECENT work. It lacked the violence of the nightmare piece, both in subject matter and in technique. The brushstrokes were gentle, feathering one area into the next to give the impression of dreamy inevitability. The glass palette that lay on the table beside him was dotted with pools of sienna and cerulean blue softened with heavy doses of titanium white. He blended them on the canvas, keeping his wrist supple as he followed the vision in his head.

Normally, he didn't do portraits anymore. That hadn't been the case when he'd started out. For the group shows where he'd first displayed his work, he'd stuck to easy-to-grasp, representative pieces like landscapes and portraits because there had been money in them. He'd been desperate to support his habit, so he'd done anything that would sell. The important paintings, the ones that were based on subjects only he could see, he'd kept private. He'd believed they were therapy, not art.

He'd been wrong about that. Following his instincts had propelled him to a level of success that he couldn't have conceived possible in his wildest dreams. The group shows had led to his first commissions, which had brought more exposure and opened the doors to more prestigious exhibitions. Within only a few years, his reputation had snowballed to the point that galleries were contacting him and not the other way around. Critics used words like *raw* and *primitive* to describe his paintings, and some had even mentioned genius. Not that he bought into the hype. He painted what he felt like and considered himself lucky every time he cashed a check. Fortunes could change in the blink of an eye, and he didn't take anything for granted.

He probably wouldn't sell this painting, though. Not right away. It would be a while before he finished it to his satisfaction.

He put the horsehair brush into a jar of water to keep it from drying out and picked up a sable. He stepped closer to the easel, using his left hand to steady his right as he defined the rim of Deedee's ear.

Her own imagination had served as her backdrop: her left side was in front of the white cloud where she'd called up the butterfly. The scarred side was in front of a smoldering fire. He was trying to capture the contradictions in her character, but he wasn't there yet. She wasn't the kind of woman he could portray in one sitting.

He lowered the brush to add a gleam to her shoulder. It was bare, apart from the thin strap of her satin nightgown. He'd posed her half-turned, so that she was looking toward him while her body was almost in profile. The burns that snaked across her right shoulder and curled around her arm didn't detract from her beauty. To him, the contrast only enhanced it. Everyone had scars on one level or another. He admired the way she had accepted hers. He dabbed another highlight on the ridged tissue above her elbow, then used his thumb to blend the paint over her breast.

The vision in his head jumped, as if she had felt his touch.

He frowned, concentrating on steadying the image he saw, but it continued to shift. The ivory nightgown gradually darkened until it was the color of ripe wheat. Satin became cotton that expanded to conceal her shoulders and arms. A flared chambray skirt covered her legs to the tops of her calves. She took a hesitant step toward him, then stopped and shoved her hands into her pockets. She was no longer standing on a cloud. She was on a weedy embankment in front of a backdrop of trees.

Max recognized the scene immediately. He dropped his brush into the water jar and strode to the north window.

A woman in a yellow drawstring blouse and blue chambray skirt stood on the old rail bed at the back of his property. She was too far away for him to see her face. A broad-brimmed sun hat hid most of her features anyway. But he *felt* it was Deedee.

Had he drawn her to him by concentrating on her image? Why hadn't he sensed her approach?

He knew the answer to the second question. He'd been caught up in his vision of her, so he'd already felt as if she was with him. He wouldn't have noticed that her presence had grown stronger. She wasn't reaching out to him, though. Her thoughts were drawn in like a pursed mouth.

She'd been that way for two days, ever since their mind-kiss. He'd assumed her caution would wear off, but it hadn't. He'd had to content himself with memories and canvas.

But she wasn't in his head, she was outside his home. The breeze rippled her skirt against her legs. She took one hand from her pocket to hold her hat on her head. She seemed to be studying the house.

He wiped his fingers on his T-shirt and went downstairs. The inside back door stood open to the deck. Through the screen door he could see she hadn't moved from her vantage point.

What the hell was she doing here? How could she have known where he lived? More to the point, how could she have known that he even existed? She still believed he was only a figment of her imagination, didn't she?

He braced his hands on either side of the doorframe. His palms were sweating and slid over the wood. He experienced the same adrenaline rush he felt when he drove past her house, only the stakes had been raised. This was more than tempting fate; she was actually here, in the flesh. His muscles tightened to the brink of pain.

Only, it wasn't just his muscles that ached. The bulk of the pain came from a deeper source, a place he hadn't tapped for decades. It was the eagerness of a boy who wouldn't have thought twice about racing across the yard to welcome her. A lonely boy who had been happy to invite his friend into his heart. A naive child who'd known no caution when it came to love.

A reckless, needy fool.

That wasn't him. Damn, it couldn't be.

Yet he couldn't look away. His pulse was roaring so hard it

sounded like the ocean. For the first time in almost twenty-eight years he was seeing Deedee with his own eyes, without the filter of their minds to dilute his vision. Only a few millimeters of screening and thirty yards of dirt that refused to grow a lawn stood between them.

Instead of thinking of the pain, he thought of how her eyes sparkled and how sweet her mind felt when he touched it and how for a few precious heartbeats during their kiss he'd no longer been alone.

She turned away.

Max pushed open the screen door and stepped onto the deck. "Deedee!"

She couldn't have heard him. At that moment, two boys on bicycles sped past her along the rail bed. They whooped at each other and stood on their pedals to go faster, their front wheels wobbling, the striped beach towels that they'd tied around their necks billowing behind them.

Max jumped off the deck and ran across the yard. "Deedee?"

She was already at the trees. The slope of the embankment hid all but the top of her sun hat from his view.

Pain stabbed through his left foot. He hopped on his right and twisted his leg to check his heel. A narrow shard of brown glass was embedded in his skin. It appeared to be from the bottom of a broken beer bottle. Blood welled from either side of the glass and dripped to the dirt.

He knew people tossed garbage as they passed his yard. Sometimes kids deliberately targeted his place, egging one another on to see what kind of reaction they'd get out of the big, bad ex-con, but like an idiot he'd run outside without putting on any shoes.

What the hell had he been thinking? He was nothing to her. She hadn't come to see him. Her mind had been closed. She'd probably just been taking a walk.

"Idiot," he muttered. "Goddamn moron." He yanked out the glass, hurled it into the nearest clump of weeds, and limped back into the house. He snorted when he saw the red smears he left on the floor. The footprints were real blood this time instead of paint, graphic reminders of the lesson he'd already learned. This was what happened when he forgot. It hurt.

He grabbed the first aid kit he kept with his tools and

doused the wound mercilessly with rubbing alcohol, then slapped on a bandage and wrapped it tightly in gauze. He left no trail when he retraced his steps as far as the deck. He didn't go any farther. For what he intended, he didn't need to.

This time, he called to her silently. *Deedee!*

Her image flickered across his brain. He saw the reflection of water beyond her. She was approaching the pond.

He concentrated on the willow where he used to hide from Virgil. The instant he felt her near it, he followed her thoughts into her head and placed himself on the path in front of her.

She stumbled to a halt. She appeared to study his features, then glanced at his hair before she spoke. "Max?"

He shoved his hair out of his eyes. "Who else would it be?"

The question seemed to disturb her. She extended one hand to touch his arm, as if testing whether he was actually there. Her other hand fisted in her pocket, making a hard lump beneath the soft chambray of her skirt. "Why would you ask me that? What do you mean?"

"Dammit, Deedee, how many imaginary friends do you have?"

She closed her eyes tightly and breathed deeply through her nose.

The woods around her started to blur. Max dug in mentally and folded his arms over his chest to wait her out. "Save your energy. I'm not going anywhere."

She blinked. "You're in a foul mood. Did I wake you up again?"

"How could you? You weren't looking for me."

"But you're here anyway." She paused. Her eyes widened. "You have paint all over your T-shirt."

"So?"

"Why? Were you painting?"

"Was I? You made me up. You tell me."

"I found you here before. You often seem to come from this direction. Why?"

"Only you can answer that, Deedee. I'm your fantasy."

She gritted her teeth and looked past him. "That's right. You're a fantasy. You wouldn't live in any particular place. I shouldn't even be talking to you."

"Why not? Don't you have any more use for me?"

"Max—"

"Did your memories all come back? Is that it? You don't need my help anymore, so away I go into the mental toy cupboard until the next time you find yourself short of friends."

Her mouth dropped open. She reached for his arm. "Max, no. I've hurt your feelings again. I didn't mean to. I was just trying to keep sane."

Heat sparked along his skin where she imagined touching him. "Sane?"

"I'm relying on you too much. This isn't normal."

"Says who?"

"I realize I was the one who brought you back into my life, but I think that was a mistake."

A week ago, he would have agreed. Hell, it was what he'd tried to tell her. The fact that he now wanted to argue proved what an idiot he was. He raised his hands to cup his palms around the image of her face. "I warned you not to stir up the past."

"You weren't *like* this in the past."

"I warned you about that, too, but you kept haunting me. Now it's my turn."

"What does that mean?"

"This imaginary friend shit works both ways. I don't exist merely for your convenience."

Her breathing grew shallow. "I should be concentrating on my husband. It's him I want to remember."

"I can't see why. Doesn't seem to me you have many good memories of him."

"That's not fair. I was married to Stanford. He was real. You're not even here."

"And that's the only reason you want to see me. It's why you allowed me into your bed, and why you're letting me touch you now."

"Max—"

"You don't want this to be a flesh-and-blood relationship any more than I do."

"Why are you saying this? I *know* you're only fantasy. That's the point I've been trying to make."

"And you're the one who brought me back, Deedee, just like you said. I'm not ready to be packed away yet. I can be wherever you are."

"But I have to focus on reality."

Max brought his mouth to where he saw hers. "Focus on this."

It was a kiss of frustration more than passion, and it wasn't gentle. He could feel her uncertainty as he probed their connection, but he didn't pause to temper his strength as he had before. If he had, his logic might reassert itself and stop him. This was only desire. Not love, not caring. And since this was the only bond he would allow himself to have with her, he was going to make the most of it.

Deedee was capable of pushing him away; she'd done it before. Yet instead of resisting, within seconds she joined in the image he was building, sliding her hands to his shoulders as she reached to meet him. She opened her mind with a soundless moan. In her thoughts, her tongue stroked his, searing her taste across his nerves.

The first ripple of pleasure swept aside any remaining caution. Damn, he should have thought of this sooner. Some mutual enjoyment wasn't going to hurt either of them. She didn't have to understand where it came from to feel it. She swayed where she stood, her body trembling with the same reaction she was arousing in him.

He knelt at the base of the tree and beckoned her downward. "Come with me."

She slid her back down the trunk. "I can't believe this is happening again. It's broad daylight. I've gone over the edge, haven't I?"

"No, Deedee. You're just doing what comes naturally." He waited until she sat on a patch of soft moss. "Close your eyes."

"What?"

"We'll make it real. You know how. See what I see."

Her eyelids fluttered shut. "Max?"

He pictured a garden of wildflowers around them. It widened to a meadow, with daisies and buttercups and chicory swaying in the warm breeze. Clouds scudded across the sky overhead. No trees blocked their view of it. Nothing else existed except the meadow and the sky. And the two of them.

"Max, where are we?"

"Do you like it?"

"It's beautiful, but—"

"Don't analyze, Deedee." He imagined undoing the drawstring at the front of her blouse and easing the neckline apart. "Just feel."

Her breath escaped on a strangled gasp. "Max!"

"That's it." He drew the fabric to one side to bare her good shoulder. He smiled when he discovered she wore a camisole instead of a bra. He slid the strap down her arm. "Feel the sunshine on your skin. Feel the breeze."

She arched her back. Her blouse and camisole melted away.

His smile widened. She'd done that, not him. He cupped her breasts. "Do you feel my fingers?"

"Oh, *God*. How are you doing this?"

"We both are, Deedee." The vision solidified as her mind added its power to his. He stretched out amid the wildflowers and drew her down on top of him. Her hat fell to the ground beside them. "Think of it as a new game."

"You're not angry anymore."

"I wasn't angry at you."

"You were."

"I was frustrated by the situation." He sifted his fingers through her hair. Though it was short, the fine strands were as sensuous as silk. "I didn't want to miss you, but I did. I can't stop thinking about the last time we kissed."

She tipped her head into his caress. "I can't, either. I didn't really want to keep you away; I just thought . . . it was sensible. The right thing to do."

"Doesn't this feel right?"

She ran her palms over his shoulders and down his arms. Her fingers curled around his biceps. "It feels wonderful. *You* feel wonderful."

He remembered how her nightgown had clung to her nipples, then pictured the tight bud between his fingers. He rubbed his thumb across it.

"Oh!"

Her pleasure intensified his. He rolled her to her back. The sunlight hid nothing. The burn scars were jagged pink blotches scattered with raised lines of white. He traced them with his lips, placing gentle kisses from her elbow to her shoulder and down to her breast. Then he lifted her breast in his palm and closed his mouth over the tip.

He couldn't name the colors that swirled through the air around them. He'd never seen any so pure. They were the embodiment of Deedee's passion. They swept him out of himself and into her.

It wasn't really sex. It was an intimacy that reached a deeper level. And if it lacked the physical release of a flesh-and-blood connection, that was a fair trade-off. Touching Deedee like this was still better than not touching her at all.

Her chest heaved with a sob.

He lifted his head. "What's wrong?"

"I've lost my mind."

"No, you haven't."

"I've admitted sex was an issue. I've faced the fact it wasn't good with Stanford. I didn't need another fantasy orgasm to prove it to myself. And we didn't even *have* sex. All you did was kiss me . . . but that wasn't actually a kiss because we don't touch and . . . this isn't me."

"It's the real you. The one you keep inside."

"How would you know?"

"Because I felt you, Deedee."

She draped her forearm across her eyes. "Delaney."

"What?"

"Call me Delaney. I'm grown-up. I'm not the little girl I used to be. I'm an adult."

He reached past her and snapped the blossom of a daisy from its stem. He stroked the petals along the underside of her arm and across her chest.

She moaned. "How can that feel so good? I know it's only my imagination."

"You're trying to analyze again."

"That's what adults do. Sane, rational adults."

"You're not insane, Delaney."

She lowered her arm. Moisture had pooled in her eyes. "That's a hell of an endorsement, coming from a fantasy. I can't wait to tell Dr. Bernhardt."

Max wasn't accustomed to feeling guilt. It was uncomfortable. He'd already worked this out. She was using him, so he had every right to use her. If she was distressed about what she called a fantasy, she'd brought it on herself, because she was the one who had chosen to believe he wasn't real . . .

No, that was bullshit, and he knew it. If he'd stopped to put on a pair of shoes, he could have settled her doubts about her mental stability twenty minutes ago.

The flower melted from his hand as the meadow dimmed. The vision was fading because she had stopped supporting it. Max let the image dissolve and squatted beside her. "Consider it a daydream."

She hiccuped. The willow appeared behind her. She was once again sitting on the moss, her blouse fastened, her skirt draped over her legs, just as she'd been the entire time. "Sure."

"There's nothing crazy about daydreams."

"If you say so." She picked up her hat and crammed it on her head, then looked past him. "We're at the pond."

"Yes."

"I don't like the water."

"Next time, I'll come to you when you're somewhere more private."

"Next time? I don't know what happened this time. I must be certifiable."

He placed his fingertip at the corner of her eye. He could sense the moisture from her tears, but he couldn't wipe it away. Not here. "Don't cry, Deedee."

Her lips trembled. She pressed them together and dropped her head back against the tree. "You know what's *really* crazy?"

"What?"

"This all feels familiar."

"What does?"

"The pond. The make-believe world you took me to." She shifted her gaze to his face. "You telling me not to cry. I remember . . ."

He waited, but she said nothing more. "What do you remember, Deedee?"

"My grandmother calling me. But I didn't want to go. I wanted to stay and play with you, Max."

The boy inside him, that pathetic fool who didn't know any better, lifted his head to smile with eagerness.

Max ignored him. He stroked her breast in the same place he'd smoothed the paint on the canvas. "I like our new game, Delaney."

She touched her tongue to her lips. "Uh, Max . . ."

"You seemed to enjoy it, too."

"A bit too much. That's what I'm afraid of."

"You're afraid of pleasure?"

"I don't deserve it. I created you to help recover my memories, not resurrect my sex drive or—" She broke off as a blue jay squawked from the woods. "But you are stirring up my memories. Almost every time I see you, something else floats to the surface."

"That's because you're letting go."

"Of my sanity."

"Of your shackles. Trust your mind, Deedee. You're stronger than you think."

"Shackles," she repeated. She tugged at the hem of her skirt, then brushed her hand over her ankles. She looked at the pond again. "It's strange that you used that word. At times I do feel as if the past is holding on to me."

"I prefer the present."

She didn't appear to be listening. Her face, normally pale, lost the rest of its color. "I hate the smell of mud. I remember how it sucked at my shoes and wouldn't let me go. In my nightmare I can't move my legs because the seaweed wraps around them. It holds me under the water."

Images flashed across his vision. Some were from her mind, some were from his own memories. "There's nothing to be afraid of, Deedee. You're okay now."

"You said that before. I remember your voice. You held me and said I was okay, but I was so cold and wet and I could taste the mud in my mouth and nose." She wrapped her arms around her legs and rocked back and forth. Her gaze was riveted on the water. "I was in there. It was black and slimy. I couldn't breathe. I couldn't move. I can remember the feelings, Max. They're too real for a nightmare."

"It *was* real."

"You said that last week. You said I almost drowned. I nearly died." She released her hold on her legs and suddenly stood. She walked straight to the edge of the pond.

Max followed. "Be careful. There's a drop-off."

"The water went over my head. It was so dark and I was so scared . . ." The soles of her sandals sank into the mud. Water lapped at her toes. Her entire body was shaking.

"Delaney!" Alarm gave extra force to his mental shout. Unlike the other time, he wouldn't be able to help her if she got into trouble now. Thoughts alone wouldn't pull her out of the water. "Stop!"

She backed up fast and turned to face him. "It did happen. My God, you were telling me the truth!"

"I usually do. Sometimes you choose not to hear it."

FOURTEEN

❧

DELANEY PLUCKED OFF A DEAD PETUNIA BLOOM AND tossed it into the plastic bucket she'd taken from the garden shed. The bottom was already covered with papery brown seed heads, and she'd done only half the flower boxes along the veranda. It took patience to find the spent blooms amid the spill of purple and white flowers. They were well camouflaged and not easy to spot, but it was worth the effort to remove them. Otherwise the plant's health would deteriorate and it would stop producing new flowers.

There was a lesson in that idea somewhere. The tangle of stems and leaves could represent her memories. Some needed to be exposed so that others could emerge. It took patience, but bit by bit the job would get done. And afterward . . .

What? Her mind would become a well-ordered planter box of peppery-smelling purple and white? Then where did Max fit into the picture? Was he the gardener? His presence had definitely helped her unlock the past. She'd made no progress at all during the time she'd tried to shut him out, so that had been a mistake. He must be a necessary part of her recovery. She should accept where her subconscious was leading her, no matter how . . . disturbing the side effects were.

Disturbing? That was an understatement. Max was one sexy gardener.

Remembering she had almost drowned had been a huge step forward. Because of that, she had decided not to let the pleasure she got from her encounters with Max send her into a panic. She wasn't going to try contacting Dr. Bernhardt again, either, because there was a logical explanation for those sexual fantasies. She probably needed to stir up her more primitive desires in order to stimulate her memories. It was a way to get rid of her shackles, as Max had said.

"That's looking better already, Delaney."

She straightened as Helen stepped onto the veranda. "I'm enjoying it. It reminds me of the planter that Dad and I had on the apartment balcony. We always had petunias, too."

"They're hardy plants, which is why I like them. Not very fancy, though."

"I think they're perfect. They suit the house."

"They do perk it up." She shielded her eyes to look toward the road, then started down the front steps. "It seems as if we got mail."

"I can get it for you," Delaney said.

"After that pecan loaf you made for breakfast, I need the exercise."

Delaney peeled off her gardening gloves and left them beside the bucket. "Then I'll walk to the mailbox with you. There's something I wanted to talk to you about, anyway."

Helen strolled along the path to the driveway at a sedate pace, despite her remark about exercise. "What's on your mind? Has Elizabeth been bothering you again?"

"No, this has nothing to do with her, or even with Stanford. It's about the years I lived here."

"All right, shoot."

Delaney hesitated. She wasn't sure how to lead into this topic. If her grandparents had known about her near-drowning, they had apparently covered it up. "I went for a walk past the pond yesterday."

"I wondered where you'd gotten to."

"Lately I've felt . . . drawn to it. I hadn't understood why before, but now I'm suspecting my subconscious was trying to give me a message, because while I was there, I remembered being in the water."

"Are you sure?"

"It was a very vivid memory. I remembered the sensations more than the facts. It felt as if I was drowning. Could I have fallen in when I was little?"

Helen walked a few paces in silence before she replied. "I

find it incredible that you would remember. You were only a toddler."

Delaney had known in her heart that the memory had been real, but it was good to hear it confirmed. At least some parts of her mind could still be trusted. "Then it is true?"

"That you fell in? From what we pieced together, you did." She pinched the bridge of her nose. "It seems easy to say now, but we were never so scared in our lives."

"How did it happen?"

"Your grandfather was watching you play in the backyard, but it was a hot day and he fell asleep in his chair. By the time he woke up, you were gone."

"Poor Grandpa. He must have been frantic."

"He wasn't at first. He'd assumed you had run back into the house to your mother's room. She'd been at the hospital for another round of chemo, but you liked to play under her bed sometimes, you pretended it was a castle, so we wasted time checking there first. We hadn't guessed you would have gone in the other direction."

"I'm sorry I worried you."

"It was our fault from start to finish. By the time we thought to check the woods, we were in a panic. We found you a few yards from the shore of the pond. You were soaking wet from head to toe and had pond slime all over your legs so it was plain you had fallen in. It was a miracle you managed to pull yourself out. The bottom drops off fast, and that water was so muddy, we never would have found you if—" Her voice broke. She halted and shook her head.

Delaney put her arm around Helen's shoulders. "I'm sorry, Grandma. I didn't mean to upset you by bringing this up."

"I haven't thought about it in years, but those feelings are still fresh. We could have lost you, and it would have been our fault."

"It wouldn't have been anyone's fault. Accidents happen." Even as she said the words, she heard an echo of Helen telling her the same thing about the accident that had killed Stanford. The words were easy to say. Believing them was harder.

"We had Edgar install the fence the next day. We should have done it sooner."

"I do remember you and Grandpa both cautioned me about

staying away from the pond. You made sure it wouldn't happen again."

"Oh, we did that, all right. We probably scared the bejesus out of you."

They had. She'd believed it was their strict warnings that had led her to develop an aversion to water. While the warnings had played a part, it appeared the root of her fear had been far more direct. "I deserved it."

"Nonsense, you were only being a child. It was our responsibility to ensure your safety, and we had failed."

"But nothing happened. Everything turned out fine. Please, don't feel bad, Grandma. It was a long time ago."

Helen made an erasing motion with her hands, then linked her arm with Delaney's as they resumed their progress toward the road. "You're right. It's been close to thirty years. I'm amazed that you remembered."

"So am I, actually."

"You didn't want to talk about it afterward, and you absolutely refused to tell us how you got out of the water. We didn't insist because we thought your mind had preferred to blank the whole incident out of self-defense."

"That's probably what happened. I did the same thing with my memories of the crash."

Helen glanced at her. "I suppose this is another example of how we encouraged you to ignore what hurt you and pretend everything was fine."

Although Delaney hastened to reassure her grandmother that they'd done the right thing, she didn't believe it. Forgetting about the incident at the pond had been the easy way out, and because it hadn't been dealt with, the memory had festered. It likely had established the pattern that she'd repeated later. Not that she could blame her grandparents. They'd done what they'd thought best.

This did explain one of the key elements of her nightmare. The answer had been staring her in the face for months, but she'd reasoned her way around it. Hopefully, now that she knew the truth, the other memories she'd suppressed would be able to come out as well. As Max had told her, both the fire and the water had been real. She'd dreamed about dying because she almost had. Both times.

No, she reminded herself. It hadn't been Max who had told her; it had been her own subconscious. The trauma of nearly drowning must have caused her mind to create her imaginary friend. That must be why he'd appeared so vividly to her when she'd been near the pond . . . and when he'd laid her down in the field of wildflowers.

She slid her hand into her skirt pocket to touch the photo of Max. Correction, John Harrison. She'd cut the picture out of the gallery brochure, and now the edges were already feeling worn from repeated handling. He'd been the real reason she'd braved the walk past the pond. She'd wanted to see for herself where he lived. She'd hoped that would put her fantasy in perspective, but it hadn't worked out that way.

The moment she'd seen the house, Max's presence had become almost tangible. It had seemed like a place he might live, if he'd been real. Unlike the fussy, Victorian-era houses in the old section of town, John Harrison's place had been an unadorned octagon of cedar shingles and glass. It gave the impression of strength without showiness, as if the structure had been honed to the basics the same way his face had. At first glance, it didn't appear inviting, yet the more she'd looked, the more she'd wanted to cross the yard and . . .

And what? Knock on a stranger's door and tell him she had given his face to her imaginary lover? It was a good thing she'd restrained herself, especially in light of the fantasy she'd experienced on her way home. Good Lord, what if she'd behaved that way in the presence of a real man?

"This one's for you," Helen said.

Delaney returned her attention to her grandmother. She had taken a stack of envelopes from the mailbox and was holding out a large, padded mailing envelope.

Someone honked a greeting as they drove past on the road. Helen handed her the mailer, then turned to wave at a couple in a blue sedan.

Delaney gave the envelope a cursory glance, saw it bore a New York postmark, and assumed Leo was sending her more legal documents. She couldn't think of anyone else from the city who would address mail here. Whatever he'd sent would keep until later, she decided, tucking the envelope against her side. She fell into step with Helen as they started back up the driveway.

"That was the Reids," Helen said. "I heard they bought a cottage on the east side of the lake."

"There'll be two less customers for you next summer."

"Not necessarily. Once they start telling their friends about the lake, there'll be more people than ever who'll need a place to stay in Willowbank."

"Edgar said there were a lot of new people moving in."

"The town's growing. I hope it doesn't grow to the stage that it loses its charm."

She fingered the photo in her pocket. Helen had just given her the perfect opening to raise the other topic she'd wanted to discuss. "Phoebe told me that you have a famous neighbor. An artist."

"Ah, you must mean John Harrison."

She nodded.

"He's not that close a neighbor. He built his house on the site of the old trailer park past the woods."

"I saw it on my walk yesterday. It's . . . intriguing. The second story is nearly all glass."

"Actually, it's Plexiglas. John had to replace the regular glass a few years ago after someone threw rocks through the windows one Halloween."

"That's awful."

"It's shameful behavior. The kids have made him into the local boogeyman." She glanced at Delaney. "I imagine Phoebe told you he'd been to prison?"

"She said he'd tried to kill his mother. Is that true?"

Her expression tightened. "Partly. It was his stepfather who got the worst of the beating when he tried to defend her. He was in a coma for months. I followed the story quite closely when John was arrested. It must be going on twenty years ago now. The crime shocked the entire town."

"It's hard to believe anything like that could have happened here."

"I found it hard to believe myself. He was only a teenager. We don't want to think that someone so young could be capable of such violence, but there was no mistake. His trial ended when he changed his plea to guilty."

Delaney had been hoping her grandmother would deny what Phoebe had said. Instead, she'd made it worse.

But they weren't talking about Max. It shouldn't matter. "What happened to his mother?"

"I don't know. Apparently, she and her husband moved away after he got out of the hospital. John was in prison by then. It was a real tragedy."

"You called him John," she said. "Have you met him?"

"Yes, we met a few times shortly after he moved in, but I don't know him well. He's a bit of a recluse, which is understandable, considering the opposition he faced when he decided to settle here. People can be such asses." She clicked her tongue. "Including me. I shouldn't be gossiping. What's this? Another Bible pamphlet. That's the third one this week. And will you look at all these bills?"

Helen shuffled the envelopes she was carrying and launched into a complaint about the latest tax levy. The subject of her notorious neighbor was obviously closed.

That was for the best, Delaney decided as they returned to the house. She wasn't sure why she was still carrying Harrison's picture around. She understood that his resemblance to Max was arbitrary—her subconscious could have snagged someone else's face just as easily as it had latched onto the artist's. If she was going to carry anyone's picture, it should be Stanford's. That was who she should be thinking about.

Delaney retrieved her plastic bucket with the spent petunias as the front door closed behind Helen. She was about to toss the envelope from Leo onto one of the wicker veranda chairs so she could get back to her gardening when the label on the front caught her eye. It bore only her name and address, no return address, unlike the standard mailing labels from Leo's law firm. She had assumed it was from him, but now that she considered it, it was odd that he would use the regular mail. When he'd sent documents to her in the past, he'd always sent them by courier.

Curious, she set the bucket down and opened the envelope.

It wasn't filled with papers as she'd expected. It contained glossy sheets that appeared to be enlarged photographs. Why would Leo send her photos? She pulled the lip of the envelope wider so that she could get a better look. The top picture seemed to be merely random blobs of black and dark red.

She drew out the photographs, and the blobs suddenly assumed the pattern of a face.

Or more accurately, a skull. Blackened lumps sat where the eyes should have been. Shriveled, ragged lips bared a death's-head's eerie grin. Shreds of charred skin and bloody flesh clung to the jawbone like the leftovers of a barbecued steak . . .

Delaney dropped the pictures and pressed her fingertips to her mouth.

No! I don't want to remember this part. Dear God, I can't see this again.

But the images she saw weren't in her nightmare.

They were in eight-by-ten glossy prints that fanned out around her feet.

FIFTEEN

❦

DELANEY TIGHTENED HER GRIP ON THE WHEEL AS SHE fixed her gaze on the car in front of her. The buildings that lined Willowbank's downtown streets had been constructed during the same era as the Wainright House. The facades had been zealously protected from development by the local historical committee, which meant the streets hadn't been widened past two lanes. As a result, midsummer traffic often moved at a crawl.

Leo adjusted his seat belt to give himself more slack across his stomach. In deference to the warmth of the afternoon, he'd replaced his trademark tweed jacket with a rumpled linen vest. Its sides didn't quite meet, so he'd left it unbuttoned. "You didn't have to do this, Delaney."

"Yes, I did, Leo."

"But this is difficult for you."

"My hands are much better than they were when I first came home, so there's no reason why I shouldn't go to the station in person."

"That's not what I meant. You could have let me drive."

"You don't know the town."

"I do follow directions."

Delaney slowed to a stop at a red light and dried her palms on her skirt. Since the night of the accident, she had rarely been behind the wheel of a vehicle, as Leo knew full well. For the first three months of the year, she'd been confined to hospital rooms. Once her body had mended enough for her to be ambulatory, her hands hadn't been in any shape to grip a wheel, so she'd been transferred from place to place by ambulance and later by limo. The car she'd leased when she'd come home hadn't seen much use so far because she'd had nowhere she'd wanted to go. And to be honest, she'd also kept her outings to a minimum because she'd been afraid that the act of driving could stir up her nightmare.

But evidently, someone else had wanted to do just that.

Not simply *someone*. Elizabeth. Although Delaney had no proof the envelope of photographs had come from her step-daughter, there was no one else who would have had a motive to torment her like this. Leo had agreed. In fact, he'd been so incensed when she'd phoned to tell him what had happened, he'd been barely coherent. If anyone else had heard his rant against Elizabeth, they certainly wouldn't be mistaking him for a mild-mannered college professor.

"I can't keep avoiding things just because they're unpleasant," she said. "But I appreciate your concern. You're really a good friend."

"It's what I endeavor to be," he replied, as he had the last time he'd come to Willowbank. "Of course, I will be adding this trip to your bill."

She was too tense to give him the laugh he expected. She eased the car forward as the light changed. "I'm not as emotionally fragile as people think, you know."

"I've never considered you fragile, Delaney."

"Elizabeth does. She must have expected me to fall apart."

"I'm not sure what she hoped to accomplish by sending those pictures. She must have known we would guess who did it. That doesn't seem to be the action of a rational mind."

Rather than reply, Delaney concentrated on her driving. She was the last person who should speculate about someone else's mental state. She waited for a break in the oncoming stream of cars, then turned onto a side street that would take them around the bottleneck. A few minutes later, she pulled into a vacant parking spot half a block from the police station.

The Willowbank police station was housed in a century-old redbrick building with a deep cornice running along the edge of the roof and tall, arched windows. Wrought iron railings flanked the staircase that rose to a set of imposing oak doors. Worn wooden floors inside the entrance gave off the smell of age. She and Leo were shown to a second-story room of old-fashioned frosted glass set into pale green half walls. It was the detectives' office, but there weren't many desks—the town wasn't large enough to merit more than a handful of detectives on the police force.

A middle-aged man stood when they entered. He had a tired face that was dominated by a nose that appeared to have been broken and flattened sometime in the past. Like the other men in the room, he wore a white shirt and a tie. A brown suit jacket was draped over the back of his chair. "I'm Detective Toffelmire," he said, gesturing them forward. "I understand you have a complaint?"

Leo stopped beside Toffelmire's desk and placed his briefcase on the edge to open it. He withdrew the paper bag where Delaney had put the photos and the envelope that had contained them. "My client received this in yesterday's mail."

Toffelmire pulled the edges of the bag apart and peered inside.

"Those are police photos of my late husband," Delaney said. She heard a tremor in her voice and cleared her throat. "They were taken at the scene of the accident that killed him."

The detective rolled one of the vacant chairs closer and indicated that she should sit, then resumed his own seat as Leo brought over a third chair. He tipped the bag to let the photos slide onto the desktop and studied them one by one, using the eraser end of a pencil to slide them apart. "Don't think me insensitive, Mrs. Graye, but there doesn't appear to be much to identify here."

"They're of my husband," she stated. "I'm positive of that."

"Whether they are or not is immaterial," Leo said. "They're disturbing photographs, and they were obviously sent to harass Mrs. Graye."

Toffelmire pushed them back into a pile and turned his attention to the envelope. "Was there anything else inside? A note?"

"Nothing," Delaney replied. "Only the pictures."

"Have you received other harassing mail? Any specific threats?"

"No."

"Threatening phone calls?"

"No."

"Perhaps these pictures were sent to you by mistake."

"Do you get many cases where people receive photos like these in error, Detective?" Leo demanded. "My client was clearly targeted."

"Do you suspect anyone in particular?"

"Elizabeth Graye, the daughter of Mrs. Graye's late husband."

"She's my stepdaughter," Delaney offered. "We have a . . . difficult relationship."

"Why would she want to send you such grisly photos of her own father?"

"She's currently suing me for the wrongful death of my husband. It's clear that she wants to hurt me."

Toffelmire pulled a spiral notepad from a drawer in the desk and turned to a fresh page. "I'm going to need more details."

Leo gave him a summary of the circumstances of the accident and the results of the recent inquiry. The detective jotted notes as he listened, then turned to question Delaney further on her relationship with her stepdaughter. She kept her replies as objective as possible. The interview wasn't as painful as she'd expected, since it was Elizabeth's behavior that was the issue, not the accident itself. Still, it was hard to admit how badly their relationship had deteriorated. She'd always wished things could have been different.

Leo took a folded sheet of paper from his briefcase. "I've listed Elizabeth Graye's home address and phone number here, as well as the address and phone number of Grayecorp. Her title there is vice president, although she has assumed the management of the company since her father's death."

"I'll make some inquiries," Toffelmire said. "For starters, I'd like to know who has access to these pictures."

"Miss Graye would, since her lawyer has copies of them," Leo said. "They would be evidence in her lawsuit."

"Do you have copies as well, Mr. Throop?"

Leo's chair creaked as he drew himself up. "I'm not sure I like what you're implying."

"I'm not implying anything; I'm simply trying to get all the facts. It's standard procedure."

"During the course of the accident inquiry I obtained copies of all the pertinent evidence, including those photos. That would be part of my standard procedure."

Toffelmire made a note and directed his next question to Delaney. "Is there anyone else who might have done this?"

"Not that I know of," she said.

"I trust you'll be processing those pictures for fingerprints?" Leo asked.

"If our lab has time, but I doubt whether there are useful prints. Anyone who watches TV these days knows enough to wear gloves."

"But you will speak with Miss Graye, yes?" Leo persisted.

"I'll follow every avenue of investigation. In the meantime, call me if there are any further developments." He handed each of them his business card, then stood, signaling that the interview was at an end.

They returned to the car. Delaney waited as Leo fidgeted with his seat belt, then started the engine and pulled onto the street. The traffic had thinned while they'd been in the police station. Nevertheless, she kept her attention on the road and a firm grip on the wheel. "Toffelmire didn't sound hopeful," she said.

"I didn't expect him to. Our primary aim today was to get an official record of this incident."

"And also to get those photos out of the house. I hadn't known you had copies, Leo."

"I saw no reason to upset you with that particular detail. I'll add the police report to the affidavits I've already gathered from the staff at Grayecorp."

"You can add my phone records that cover the night of the accident, too. It proves Elizabeth called me. You obtained them, didn't you?"

"It wouldn't support our harassment case, since there's no record of what you discussed. The affidavits should provide sufficient basis to get a restraining order against Elizabeth."

"Do we need to go that far?"

"I realize you weren't keen on taking the offensive the first time I raised the subject, but in light of what she's just done, it's the prudent course to pursue."

"All right. Do whatever you need to do." Two weeks ago, she had refused to consider bringing legal action against her stepdaughter. She'd tried to be patient, but Leo was right. It was the only reasonable course. Her loyalty to her husband didn't extend to allowing herself to be victimized . . .

The thought niggled at something in her mind. A memory stirred briefly, then subsided into the darkness.

In its place rose the image of Stanford's charred skull. She shivered.

"Delaney?" Leo touched her elbow.

The pressure on her sleeve set off an echo of panic. She yanked her arm free. The car swerved toward an oncoming delivery van.

Brakes screeched. The van's horn blared. Delaney wrenched the wheel to the right, barely avoiding sideswiping the vehicle.

Leo grunted as he was thrown into his seat belt. "What happened?"

She pulled into a vacant spot at the curb. It was in front of a fire hydrant, but she didn't care. She needed time to catch her breath. She flexed her fingers. "My hand must have slipped. I'm sorry. Are you okay?"

"I'm fine." He blotted his forehead against his sleeve. "I knew I shouldn't have let you drive."

"I don't need your permission," she snapped.

"That's not what I meant."

"You have no right to decide what I can or can't do. You—" She halted. Leo wasn't the one she wanted to say that to, just as it wasn't Leo's touch that she'd been trying to free herself from.

God. What *had* happened?

"I'm sorry," she repeated. "I thought I might have been remembering something, but it's gone now."

"About the accident? Delaney, you're not still attempting to push past your block, are you?"

"I'm making progress, Leo."

"At what cost?" he asked, waving one hand toward the traffic. "I've told you what I think about that idea. There's no need to torment yourself further. Wasn't seeing those photos of Stanford traumatic enough?"

Blackened eyeholes. Shreds of burned flesh. In her mind, she heard the screech of twisting metal and breaking glass and the liquid gurgle of her husband's agonized screams . . .

She tried to blank the nightmare image. "What if Elizabeth doesn't want me to remember, either?"

"Why would you say that?"

"It could be the real reason she sent me those pictures."

MAX PRESSED THE HEEL OF HIS HAND TO HIS FOREHEAD. The image of a corpse had flashed across his vision. Red and black, with patches of bone gleaming through the gore, like something out of one of Deedee's nightmares.

He closed his eyes, opening his mind as he listened for her, but she wasn't calling to him. His thoughts touched the edges of hers. He didn't sense the skin-peeling agony that accompanied her nightmares. She wasn't asleep; her mind was too alert. She stiffened, as if she recognized his presence.

He stroked her fingers and eased away without completing the link.

"Hey, Johnny, you holding out on me?"

The sound of Oz's voice brought him the rest of the way back with a snap. Max blinked and lowered his arm.

Lamont Osborne leaned against the support column at the edge of Max's kitchen, his arms crossed over his massive chest. Tattoos crowded his coffee-colored skin. He had the swelled-tight, no-neck build of a weightlifter, a product of years of free access to the exercise facilities at various penal institutions.

He'd been finishing up a stint for grand theft auto when he'd shared a cell with Max. Out of necessity, they'd fallen into the habit of watching each other's backs. Aside from that and a mutual determination never to get locked up again, they had little in common. This was only the second time he'd looked Max up since he'd gotten out. "You're high," Oz said. "What are you on?"

"I'm not on anything."

He narrowed his eyes. "Hell, are you still doing that spooky thing?"

"Depends what you mean."

"Zoning out. That used to scare the crap out of me."

Max laughed. One aspect of living in a cage was the complete lack of privacy. The first time Oz had seen Max "zone out," he'd thought he was having some kind of fit and had yelled for the guard. After that, he got accustomed to the occasional naps with open eyes that his cell mate took. Max opened the refrigerator, took out two cans of Coke, and tossed one to Oz. "Here."

His lips curled as he regarded the can. "Don't you have any beer?"

Max didn't have beer. He kept no liquor of any kind in his house because he never drank it. The smell made him nauseous. "If you want a drink, there's a roadhouse on the highway south of town," he said, popping open the Coke. "According to their sign, the band doesn't start until eight. If you leave here now, you won't need to pay the cover charge."

Oz shrugged and opened his can. "This'll do." He took a long swig, burped, and pushed away from the column. He wandered into the living area, his boots thudding on the floor. It was hardwood, like the rest of the house. A fireplace of fieldstone took up one wall. The furniture was large and upholstered in oxblood leather. Oz dwarfed it as he sat. "So, it looks like you're doing okay for yourself."

"I get by. What about you?"

"Can't complain." He used his chin to point to the painting that hung over the mantel. It was one of Max's earliest works, a depiction of a summer thunderhead. "Do people really buy this shit?"

"Nobody bought that one."

"I remember when you started messing with those paints. I thought you were just trying to suck up to the social workers."

"I was."

"It sure paid off. What kind of money would you charge for one this big?"

"I leave the pricing to the galleries. They've got a better idea of what their clients are willing to pay."

"Ten grand? Twenty?"

"Why? You looking to invest in art?"

Oz laughed. A diamond stud flashed from his earlobe. "No way. If I can't wear it or drive it, it won't impress the ladies. What good is that?"

Max thought about the Mustang he'd seen Oz park behind his Jeep. It was cherry red and probably hot. "What happened to your girlfriend? Luanne, wasn't it?"

"Her? She's long gone. Hooked up with a dude who runs a diner."

"That's too bad."

"Yeah. She packed on at least a hundred pounds."

"I thought you liked a woman with meat on her bones."

"Not if she's liable to crush me if she rolled over." He drained his Coke, pancaked the can between his hands, and held it up to illustrate his point. "Nope, the cook can have her."

"Where are you living these days?"

"I move around."

"How's the car business?"

"Why? You looking to buy one?"

They went around like that for almost an hour, talking about nothing as they felt each other out. Max took the empty cans and dropped them into the recycle bin. Oz made a crack about what a good citizen he had turned into. It wasn't until they'd moved out to the back deck so Oz could have a smoke that he worked his way to the reason he'd come. He propped one hip against the railing as he drew on his cigarette. "You keep in touch with anyone else from inside, Johnny?"

Max shook his head. "Haven't heard from anyone besides you."

"That's right." He blew a smoke ring toward the yard. "You kept to yourself. I wasn't the only one who thought you were weird."

"Works for me, Oz."

"Then you didn't hear he's dying."

"Who?"

"That guy you tried to kill. Budge."

The breeze that had been wafting across the deck suddenly dropped. The birds in the woods went silent. Or so it seemed as time crawled to a halt. Max braced his hands on the railing. He couldn't feel the wood. An insulating distance was settling around him. "What's wrong with him?"

"Liver cancer. A friend of mine was doing time at the Ohio state pen, got out last month. He told me about Budge, said they're shooting him up with a bunch of drugs at the medical center, but it's a waste of time. They say he's only got six months, maybe a year."

"Couldn't happen soon enough."

"Yeah, figured you'd say that."

"The bastard doesn't have the right to draw even one more breath."

"Some preacher's been going to bat for him. Said he got religion and is a changed man."

"He snowed him like he snowed the judge. He would never change."

"That's why I thought you'd want to know he's on the way out." Oz flicked his cigarette butt toward a patch of dirt. "Just in case you've got a mind to party."

Max remained where he was long after Oz had left. Clouds rolled in to cause an early dusk. The nightly chorus of bullfrogs started up. The wood beneath Max's fingers was beginning to splinter from the force of his grip on the railing, but he couldn't risk letting go. Not until the rage was back under control.

He should have killed Virgil himself. He should have looped that belt around his throat and finished him instead of enjoying the sound of his screams and the slick heat of his blood.

It was right here, on this very spot, that he'd last seen him. The deck had been built over the place where there had once been a cement foundation block that had served as the trailer's front step. Virgil had crawled through the doorway and slid over the step to the dirt when he'd heard the sirens, the only time in his life he'd been eager to see the police. They'd taken a while getting out of their cars so Max had still had the opportunity to end it. He could have slammed the bastard's head against the cement block and split his skull open before the cops could reach them. Or he could have driven the steel-reinforced sole of his construction boot into his throat and crushed his windpipe, but that would have been too easy. He'd wanted him to suffer and bleed and whimper the way Mommy always did . . .

Max realized he was on his knees. He hadn't been aware of dropping. His legs had simply given out on him. He shoved the heels of his hands against his forehead, the same way he'd done when the skull from Deedee's nightmare had slipped into his mind, only this wasn't her past; it was his.

His mother had been the one to call the cops. She'd lied even then. She'd never once stepped in to protect her son or herself, but she'd committed perjury to protect her husband, and all in the name of love.

He pushed himself to his feet. Violence bubbled within him like a living thing. He'd believed he'd buried the past. He'd wiped out every trace of the evil that had happened here, but all it took was the thought of Virgil, and the beast he'd once released was eager for one last chance. He didn't want to leave Virgil's death to fate. He still wanted to do it himself.

He lifted his gaze to the light that shone through the trees. He thought of Deedee.

And the violence shifted to something equally primitive.

SIXTEEN

❧

THE RAIN FELL STRAIGHT DOWN, PATTERING ON THE
leaves outside Delaney's bedroom window and filling the air
with the sharp scent of moisture. Water gurgled quietly as it
ran from the eaves to the downspout. It was a soothing, timeless
sound. Apart from that, the house was silent, yet she was too
wound up to sleep.

She concentrated on the suitcase that sat open on her bed.
It was identical to the one she had glimpsed in her memory a
few days ago. It was black, with a pearl white lining and criss-
crossing elastics to hold the layers of clothing in place. There
was nothing in it now, nor was she planning to pack anything.
That wasn't why she'd brought it out.

This was an exercise in facing what had upset her. She was
hoping the sight of the luggage would jog something loose in
her memory in the same way that being behind the wheel had.
She slid the suitcase toward the foot of the bed. There was no
bench in this room, so she aligned it along the edge of the
mattress between the bedposts, trying to come as close as she
could to duplicating the scene she remembered. She stepped
back and thought of her and Stanford's bedroom, picturing him
in his dark blue overcoat and silk scarf.

Instead, she saw the gleam of bone beneath patches of gore,
the skull that had once been his face.

She shuddered. This was what had happened in the car
today, too. If Elizabeth had indeed sent those pictures to keep
her from remembering, the strategy was proving effective. The
fact that her stepdaughter didn't want her to recover her

memories meant there must be something significant she should know. In spite of Leo's opinion, Delaney believed it was more imperative than ever to discover the truth.

She returned her attention to the suitcase. She and Stanford each had matched sets of the same luggage, although she had used far more pieces of hers than he ever did of his. When they'd traveled together, she had made sure to bring every possible item she might need to put together any outfit that might be necessary. Depending on their schedule, it could be anything from a chic linen suit for a lunch date to a floor-length evening gown. That meant the right lingerie, the coordinating shoes, and the appropriate makeup and jewelry. It had been important to look nice for Stanford, because that had been important to him.

Her gaze drifted to the mirror above her dresser. Even apart from her scars, Stanford wouldn't like the way she looked now. She hadn't worn makeup in over half a year. She hadn't been to her manicurist—considering the state of her hands, worrying about her nails had seemed ludicrous. She hadn't had her hair streaked, either. Large sections of it had been burned to the scalp in the accident, and she'd had the rest trimmed. It was still too short to do much with, so she styled it with her fingers and let it dry on its own. She'd been wearing comfortable skirts with loose tunics or cotton blouses and flat-heeled sandals since she'd come to Willowbank. She hadn't brought anything tailored or formal. What would be the point? The accident had freed her from the obligation of being beautiful.

Delaney moved around the bed to the dresser and regarded her reflection critically. The satin nightgowns she slept in since she'd come to stay with her grandmother were holdovers from her pre-accident days. She had kept them not because they were pretty but because they were comfortable. The fabric was slippery enough not to catch on her scars while she slept. Same with the silk robe. It didn't bind anywhere, and its light weight was perfect for these warm summer evenings. The lack of a collar exposed the upper edge of the scar at the base of her neck. A few of her blouses failed to cover it completely, too. That wasn't a consideration for her, and it hadn't appeared to have drawn much attention from other people, *real* people, who had seen it, but she was certain Stanford would have been repulsed by even that slight trace of her disfigurement.

She slipped the robe off her right shoulder and drew down the strap of her nightgown, baring her breast and upper arm. The light from the bedside lamp cast shadows that accentuated the ripples in her scarred flesh. It was far from pleasant to view, so she made a point of studying it. She'd told Max that she hadn't wanted to go through additional surgery to have the scars on her body repaired, but that hadn't been entirely accurate. They could have been dealt with at the same time as her hands. The doctors had encouraged it. Given the kind of life she'd led before the accident, everyone had expected that her appearance would have been one of her first priorities.

Dr. Bernhardt had spoken of survivor's guilt. He'd been concerned she viewed her scars as her penance, but that was way off base. They were her liberation. They guaranteed she would never again fall into the role she'd filled for Stanford.

It had taken a lot of time and energy to maintain her appearance, but then, what else did she have to do? Because of Stanford, she'd quit her job. Because of him, she'd lost touch with her old friends. She'd taken up charity work because she couldn't stand being idle, but there had been only so many fund-raisers she could organize without cutting into the time she and Stanford had together.

His work had taken precedence over hers, and she'd given in about that, too. He controlled a multibillion-dollar business. Next to that, her volunteer fund-raising couldn't count as a real job. He viewed it as a diversion, not a career, but it had been important to her. There were countless other things that she'd given in about, too. It had been easier that way. Stanford had been so pleasant and attentive whenever they did have time together that she would feel guilty if she cut it short.

She lifted her hand to her right breast, fitting her fingers to the scar that reached toward the tip. Sex wasn't the only aspect of her marriage that had been less than satisfying. The changes in her life because of the accident had been enormous. Not all of them were unwelcome.

Two weeks ago, that thought would have triggered an automatic denial. Not now, though. That had to mean she was making progress. As Helen had told her, she needed to accept the bad as well as the good if she was going to get past her loss.

"Planning a trip?"

She started at the sound of Max's voice in her head. She shouldn't have been surprised. As had happened so often already, thoughts of one man tended to lead to thoughts of the other. She hitched her nightgown and robe back into place and turned. "Hello, Max."

He was standing beside the dieffenbachia plant, his hands hooked into the front pockets of his jeans. His feet were bare. His short-sleeved shirt hung open, baring the center of his chest from his throat to his navel. Lamplight gleamed on his taut skin, etching the contours of his muscled arms and abdomen. He looked sexier than humanly possible. And he was perusing her body with a frank hunger he didn't try to hide.

Her blood warmed in response. He seemed different tonight, edgier, as if his passions were roiling closer to the surface. Her nerves tingled with echoes of how he'd made her feel in the meadow. How did he manage to arouse her so easily? All he'd done was show up.

Yet she wasn't going to fight this reaction. She'd already figured it out. Stirring up her desire helped to loosen her memories, so there was no reason to feel guilty about it, either. She braced her hands against the edge of the dresser behind her. "I'm glad you're here. I hope you can help me."

"That depends on what you want me to do."

Kiss me again. Hold me, make me feel as if you care, as if I belong, as if I'm loved . . .

He nodded toward the suitcase. "You're not leaving on my account, are you?"

"Why would I?"

"You didn't seem too happy about our last meeting."

"I've . . . come to terms with it, Max."

"So you no longer think you're nuts?"

"Let's just say I'm reserving judgment. There must be a good reason why I keep imagining you."

"Then you're not leaving."

"Not yet. I can't keep avoiding what upsets me. I need to face it."

"Do I upset you, Deedee?"

She thought about that. "It's not you, Max. It's my reaction to you. You make me feel things that force me to reassess what I've believed about myself."

"Damn, that sounds way too complicated." He moved to the bed.

A flash of white caught her gaze. A strip of what appeared to be gauze was wrapped around his left foot. She pointed. "What's that?"

"What's it look like?"

"A bandage."

He shrugged. "Then I guess that's what it is."

"Why? Did you hurt yourself?"

"You tell me. I'm your fantasy."

She understood why she imagined Max with paint at times—her subconscious apparently had given him John Harrison's profession along with his face—but why would she picture a strip of gauze around his foot? She would never want to see Max hurt in any way. Still, the bandage made him seem oddly vulnerable. And even more real.

Was that why? Because she wanted him to be real?

"What's the suitcase for?" he asked.

"I'm trying to stimulate my memory."

"Ah, more do-it-yourself psychology?"

"You could call it that."

He ran his fingertip down the curved surface of the wooden bedpost and smiled. "Let's stimulate something else."

Sensation tickled beneath her skin, as if he'd stroked her instead of the wood, a teasing reminder of the pleasure he could generate. The urge to lose herself in it was nearly overwhelming, but she firmed her grip on the dresser and stayed where she was. "I'm trying to think of my husband."

At the mention of Stanford, his smile faded. "Like I said before, it doesn't seem to me that you've got good memories of your husband."

"He wasn't perfect, but he loved me."

"Uh-huh. Just not often."

"I was talking about love, not sex. Why are you so fixated on that?"

"Because love's a myth." He left the bed and came to stand in front of her. "Sex, on the other hand, is as honest as you can get, Deedee."

Heat seemed to radiate from his image. It was hard to keep her train of thought. "Delaney," she corrected.

His gaze dropped to her breasts. "Right. You're grown-up. Which makes for some interesting new games."

Her nipples tightened instantly. Judging by the gleam in his eyes, the fact hadn't escaped his notice.

Well, naturally he would notice. She had made him sexy, and she was the one who was making him act this way, because she did enjoy what happened when she fantasized about kissing him. If she could overlook the crazy aspect of it, that was.

He lowered his head. The air beside her ear stirred, as if she could feel his breath. "Don't think about the past. It's gone. Let it stay buried."

"That doesn't work. It needs to come out."

"Enjoy the moment. Try thinking about how good we can make each other feel."

"Believe me, I haven't forgotten that."

His smile returned. "Open for me, Delaney. Let me slide into your mind the way I did before."

His tone was as suggestive as his words, as seductive as his smile. "Max . . ."

"I need to feel you pull me inside." His voice sank through her nerves to her bones, forming a caress of its own. "Wrap your thoughts around mine and hold me so tight that you tremble."

She couldn't help it; she swayed toward him.

"I want to see the color of your passion again. Taste you in my head if not on my tongue."

The edges of the room grew hazy. His image was gaining substance.

"That's it, Deedee. Come with me."

"Stay with me, Delaney."

That had been Stanford's voice, not Max's. She blinked hard and looked past him to the suitcase.

An image from the past surged into her mind, melding with the one she actually saw. The suitcase was no longer empty.

"What are you afraid of, Delaney? I'll never leave you. How could you believe Elizabeth over me?"

"Why would she lie?"

"Because she's jealous of how happy we are. It pains me to admit it, but the failure of her romance with Alan has made her bitter."

"*Alan doesn't love her. She was right to break it off.*"

"*That's immaterial. All she understands is that she failed. She's trying to poison your mind against me out of spite.*"

Delaney scooped a handful of underwear from one of the drawers in her dressing room and carried it to the suitcase. It was filled with her clothes, not Stanford's. Sweaters tangled with plain blouses and pants. They were the kind of comfortable outfits she would wear around the house, not on a trip to Paris. They were the clothes her husband didn't like.

He reached for her arm. "*It's late, darling. I can't let you do this.*"

She twisted out of his grip and snapped the suitcase closed. "*I don't need your permission.*"

"*Please, don't be angry. I can't bear it when you're angry with me.*"

"*I have a right to my feelings.*"

"*You know how much I love you.*"

"*You're the one who slept with my friend, our neighbor. You can't claim Elizabeth lied about that, because Jenna just confirmed it.*"

A muscle in his cheek jumped as he glanced at the phone beside the bed. "*I wish you hadn't called her. It's going to make the situation awkward.*"

"*I'm the one making things awkward? You play golf with her husband. I had invited the Chamberlains to dinner this weekend. You were willing to make a fool out of me.*"

"*The affair meant nothing. I've been trying to break it off because she couldn't possibly compare to you. You're everything to me; you know that.*"

"*Elizabeth said there were others. How many have there been, Stanford?*"

He turned up his palms. It wasn't a gesture of supplication; it was closer to dismissal. "*Don't condemn me for having needs, Delaney.*"

"*Don't our marriage vows mean anything to you?*"

"*It's you who should be reminded of our vows. I don't ask much from you, only your love. I didn't want to turn to someone else, but you gave me no choice. I'm only human. You've been too involved in your own activities to see how lost I've felt without you.*"

"How dare you blame your infidelity on me?"

"Everything you do affects me; you know that. Right now you're distraught and you're overreacting. I know in my heart that you don't mean to hurt me like this. Give me the chance to make this right."

She almost wavered. The urge to apologize, to smooth things over, to look the other way, rose to tangle with her anger. It was what she'd done for five years. Just one more concession, one more piece of herself, a fair trade for the love she longed for, wasn't it?

Yet the pieces she had given him added up. The balance she'd tried so desperately to shore up had finally tipped. This argument was about far more than an affair, and tonight, the anger was going to win. She dragged the suitcase off the bench and strode from the bedroom.

He followed her down the staircase. "After all I've done for you, everything I've given you, is this how you repay my love? I was there for you during the worst time of your life, Delaney. Are you so cold that you can turn your back on me when I need you the most?"

His barbs were well-placed. Every word he spoke sank its hooks into her emotions. He was good at that. She increased her pace before her resolve could weaken. Her boot heels echoed on the marble floor as she crossed to the front door. Why had she never realized how empty the sound was? She picked up the purse she'd left on the foyer table.

Stanford took it from her grasp. "This has gone far enough. You're obviously not yourself tonight. For your own good, I can't let you leave."

She held out her hand. "I need my keys."

"You're in no state to drive."

"You have no right to stop me."

"If you were thinking clearly, darling, you would realize that I do have the right. They're not your keys; they're mine. The car that I permit you to use is registered in my name. And if you're contemplating using the spare key, think again. I'll report the car stolen rather than allow you to leave in this condition."

"Fine. I'll call a taxi."

"And how will you pay the fare? With my cash? With the

credit cards I pay for?" He tossed her purse to the floor behind him and grabbed her suitcase. *"I won't permit you to take this, either. I signed the bills for those clothes you packed as well as the ones you're wearing."*

She backed away. "You can't force me to stay."

"Wrong again. I own everything in this house, including you." He caught her arm to stop her from retreating. *"You're mine, Delaney. I'll never let you go."*

SEVENTEEN

❧

THE LAMP DIMMED. MAX FELT HIS SENSES RETURNING TO the darkness of his own bedroom and struggled to maintain the connection with Deedee. Something was very wrong. She was trembling, and it clearly wasn't from desire.

She pushed away from the dresser and moved past him. Through him. He had no more substance than what she gave him, and her thoughts were someplace else. "Deedee?"

She stood at the foot of the bed and steepled her fingertips on the suitcase. "I remember."

The words were as faint as her image. He strove to hang on to both. "Tell me what's wrong."

"I was leaving him. That's where I was going the night . . ." She swallowed. "The night of the accident. I was trying to get away."

He grasped her emotions first. Hurt. Fear. Helplessness. They tapped his own buried memories even before he processed her words. "You were leaving your husband?"

She turned. Tears glistened on her cheeks. "We had a fight."

Rage flooded his mind, giving him the power to strengthen his presence. He thought of blood and hidden bruises. God, no. Not Deedee. That particular form of evil couldn't have touched her, could it? He clenched his fists. "Did he hit you?"

"Hit . . ." She shook her head quickly. "No. He tried to stop me, that's all."

The room steadied. Max crossed the floor. "What happened?"

"He took my keys and my money. He grabbed my suitcase.

I ran." Her eyes widened. "That's why I was driving his Jaguar. It was still in front of the house. The keys were in the ignition. I remember sliding behind the wheel and starting it up."

"You must have had a good reason to leave."

"He was cheating on me."

"The man was an idiot."

"He said it was my fault. I neglected him." She wiped her cheeks with the back of her hand. "He turned it all around and tried to make *me* feel guilty."

"So you left."

"The car skidded when I braked to buzz open the gates. I was driving too fast, but I just wanted to get away before he could change my mind, before the hurt wore off." Her words tumbled over one another, as if a dam had opened. "It was the last straw. I was always the one who gave in. I made allowances, I smoothed things over. He was an expert at pushing my buttons."

"He must have been. You stayed with him for five years."

"I was a fool. I still am. I've been denying the truth because it was ugly. I've been blocking this entire memory because it didn't fit with the way I wanted to see my marriage." She closed the suitcase and smacked her palms against the lid, then sank to her knees on the floor. "I'm good at blocking memories I don't want. I've done it all my life. It's how I cope. I should have listened to you. You saw what I didn't."

"Don't give me too much credit. I don't believe in marriage. Not just yours, anyone's."

"My cynical subconscious. Why couldn't you have come back to me five years ago?"

"Deedee—"

"Why didn't you warn me what would happen? Tell me what an idiot I was being back then?"

"Knowing you, you would have been too stubborn to listen to me anyway."

"You're right. I wanted to believe he loved me and we were happy. I ignored anything that didn't fit. I brainwashed myself into making excuses." She turned, placing her back against the footboard as she drew her knees to her chest. A tear trickled into her mouth. She licked it away. "I even made excuses about our sex life. I assumed it was because of his age and the stress of his career when all along there was a much simpler explanation. He had no energy or desire left for me because he was spreading it around with everyone else. That was another one of those answers that had been staring me in the face."

Max knelt on the floor beside her. "It's over, Deedee. Don't cry."

"It hurts. I did love him."

"You believed you did."

"I wanted to love him."

"Why?"

"Because I was afraid of being alone. You were right about that, too. I stayed with him because I wanted to be loved. And he'd been so kind and thoughtful and sweet throughout the funeral—"

"Whose funeral?"

"My father's. He died of a heart attack. It was sudden. I was devastated, but Stanford was like a rock. He was good to me. I had been feeling so lost and then so happy when he proposed, it was like a . . ." She laughed without humor. "A fairy-tale ending."

"He took advantage of you."

"No, I went to him willingly."

"And you're still making excuses."

"Maybe I am."

"I'm glad you decided to leave him."

"I was coming here to Willowbank, to my grandmother. That's why I was on the highway. I hadn't cared if I had to drive all night. It was my first impulse because this is the place I always felt safe."

"It's your home."

"It must be the reason I came here after I was discharged from the clinic. Even without remembering why, I knew I didn't want to return to Bedford." She stopped suddenly. "Max, I was leaving him, I wanted to get away, so how did he end up in the car?"

"You don't remember that?"

"No. The last thing I remember is going through the gates and driving past our neighbor's house and wondering how I could have been so blind to what she was doing with my husband. I couldn't have changed my mind and gone back to talk to him, could I?"

"It doesn't matter now."

"Yes, it does. I need to know it all. I won't be free until I do."

"You've got it wrong, Deedee. It's forgetting that gives you freedom." He glanced at the bed. It still held the suitcase. He couldn't physically remove it, so he would have to take her someplace else. He pushed at her consciousness, painting a picture of a birch grove. Pale trunks gleamed through mist tinted gold by sunrise. He used the sound of the rain outside her window, turning it into the drip of moisture from the sheltering boughs. Peace. Serenity. He stepped into it first, then held out his hand. "Come with me. Nothing will hurt you here."

There was no hesitation, she needed no coaxing. Her thoughts latched onto the image immediately, strengthening what he'd created and adding details that were entirely hers. The ground beneath the trees sprouted tiny blue flowers. Birds twittered in the mist. Her fingers were firm and warm as she laced them with his and stepped to his side.

He used their joined hands to wipe away her tears. "I hate seeing you cry."

She rubbed her cheek against his knuckles. "Kiss me, Max."

The bald request surprised him. That was why he'd decided to seek her out tonight. He'd planned to enjoy the pleasure of their mental connection. It was all he wanted from their relationship. He'd had no intention of getting involved in the other aspects of her life, yet he'd created this birch grove with the idea of giving comfort, not pleasure.

She lifted her face. Tears brimmed in her eyes. "Max, please."

But what did he know about giving comfort? He leaned closer to bring his lips to hers.

Their minds touched, twined, and meshed. Her passion didn't stir.

She clutched his shoulders, molding her breasts against his chest. "Again."

Max nuzzled the skin beneath her ear. This time, a tendril of heat curled between them. He focused on it, nurturing it, letting it build.

"That's it." She arched her back to fit their bodies together. "Help me."

"There's no rush."

"Do what you talked about before. Come into my mind. Join our thoughts."

"Our thoughts are already joined. That's why you can feel me."

She tunneled her fingers into his hair. "Yes, I feel you, but not deep enough. Not hard enough."

It was the same for him. The pleasure he should have been getting from imagining her touch was too thin, as if it was diluted. Too much of her mind remained apart. He kissed her nose. "Take off your robe."

He'd barely finished forming the thought when ivory silk drifted to the ground. Mist dampened her nightgown. He drew back, wanting to admire how the fabric clung to her curves, how much she looked like her portrait, but he didn't get the chance. She pulled his face to hers, her hands shaking.

The tension that swirled from her was due to anxiety, not eagerness. Max enclosed her hands between his. "Relax." He flicked the tip of his tongue across her fingertips. "We've got as long as we want."

"No, we need to do it now while the memories are still fresh. Help me see the rest."

"The rest?"

"Why Stanford was in the car. Where we were going. What happened. You already helped me loosen the block tonight, and we hadn't even kissed."

"What are you talking about?"

"You. It's the reason I brought you back. You unlock all the thoughts that I've buried. It took me a while to figure it out, but I've realized you're the key to my subconscious, Max. You do tell me the truth. That's why when you help me let go, I remember it."

"Let go of what?"

"My inhibitions, my reason. You cut straight through to my emotions."

"That's why you asked me to kiss you."

"That's right."

"And that's why you were so agreeable when I showed up tonight. You're using me to remember your husband."

The answer was in her eyes. They shone with tears and with

the passion he hadn't been able to stir himself. "I'll use anything that works."

He wished he could laugh. It would ease the tightness in his chest.

She didn't care about him. She only wanted to use him. He'd been aware of that from the start, but he'd needed this reminder of just what he meant to her. The husband who had abused her trust was still her priority. Max should have remembered that pattern. Would he never learn?

He looked at the birch grove where they stood, at the gentle mist and the golden sunrise he'd dreamed up for Delaney's benefit. This was the kind of thing the boy he used to be would have done. He'd wanted to please her, to give her tenderness. He would have been content to simply hold her.

The hell with that.

A sudden gust of wind rattled the branches above them, knocking loose a shower of moisture from the leaves. The dawn faded as clouds rolled over the sun. Lightning strobed stark white, searing away the softness. Thunder vibrated through the soles of his bare feet.

"Max, what's happening?"

He clamped his hands at her waist, lifted her from the ground, and pressed her back to the nearest tree trunk. "I'm giving you what you asked for."

"But—"

"You want to feel passion?"

"Yes."

"You want to let go?"

The mist became rain. The leaves overhead dissolved from the onslaught, leaving no shelter from the storm. Water dripped from her hair and gleamed on her face and shoulders. Her nightgown clung like a second skin to her body, revealing every curve and dip. She didn't seem to notice. She kept her gaze on him. "Yes!"

"Open your mouth. Taste the rain on your tongue." He rubbed his mouth over hers. "Taste me."

She turned her head to follow his movement. Her pleasure flowed across him like the rain. It wasn't gentle or cool but warm. Demanding. Driving. Her mood had switched, adding power to the storm faster than he did.

He licked her lower lip. "That's it. Think of what you like. Think of me inside you. Deep. Hard."

Thunder crashed, closer than before. The wind whipped the bottom of her nightgown against his legs. He reached for the hem, gathered the wet satin in his fist, and pulled it to her waist.

He would give her what she asked for, but he'd be damned if he left any room in her head for thoughts of another man.

She whimpered as the first shudders of pleasure rippled through her mind. The colors were pure enough to burn tracks across his vision.

Max dropped to his knees and stroked the insides of her thighs until she eased them apart. She'd asked him to kiss her. He could tell by the catch in her breathing that she hadn't expected him to kiss her in such an intimate spot. It made no difference. He could have imagined touching her anywhere. Her mouth, her breasts, the dip of her elbow, the base of her throat; anyplace that gave her pleasure could have served to focus their passion. It was just an illusion anyway.

She grasped his shoulders. A bolt of pure sensation fused his thoughts to hers so tightly that tears filled his eyes. For an instant, he felt as if they were one heartbeat, one soul, closer than real lovers could ever hope to be.

But he needed no reminder that love was the biggest illusion of all.

EIGHTEEN

THE RAIN THAT HAD BEGUN ON FRIDAY CONTINUED OFF
and on throughout the first weekend of Willowbank's annual
Waterfront Festival. Although there were a good number of
visitors, it wasn't the crowd the organizers would have hoped
for. Only a few dozen music fans clad in plastic rain ponchos
braved the drizzle on Sunday afternoon to gather on the
benches in front of the band shell. Undeterred, a group of folk
musicians were taking their turn onstage, scraping out a tune
on their mandolins and fiddles. The rides of the midway that
had been set up near the lakeshore twinkled with more lights
than customers. Most people had gravitated to the central food
tent and the open-sided beer tent.

"They can plan for everything except the weather," Helen
muttered. She closed her umbrella, put the tip on the ground,
and twirled it back and forth to knock off the water. "Hardly
anyone's here."

Delaney shook out her compact umbrella and collapsed it.
They had paused at the entrance to the arts and crafts tent,
which had been pitched between the food tent and the band
shell. The smell of mustard and hot grease wafted through the
rain, blending with the pungent odor of damp canvas. She
glanced back to the roped-off area of the lawn where she'd left
her car. Normally there were so many visitors that the closer
parking spots were packed solid by this time of the day. "True,
but it was easy to find a parking space."

Helen tsked. "We should have parked on the gravel lot and

done the walk. The grass is going to be a mud bog by the time we leave."

"Sorry."

"Oh, don't mind me. The rain makes my joints ache, so I'm a bit grumpy today."

"Only a bit?"

Helen laughed and pointed her umbrella at her. "Cheeky girl. I'm off to see Ada's quilt."

Delaney slipped the strap of her umbrella over her wrist and trailed behind Helen. The large, wooden racks that held the quilts had been set up in rows along the back wall of the tent. Several local artisans had erected booths along the center aisle. One table held a collection of waterbirds carved from wood; another had an array of framed collages of pressed wildflowers. Quirky, feathers-and-beads jewelry was displayed next to hand-painted glazed pottery that wouldn't have been out of place in an art gallery.

Delaney stopped to admire a table of stained glass ornaments. A miniature blue butterfly caught her eye.

The middle-aged woman behind the table smiled. "That's one of my favorites," she said. "Although, I shouldn't admit that. It's like saying I have a favorite child."

"It's lovely." She leaned down to take a closer look at the ornament. "And so delicate."

"Go ahead and pick it up."

"Are you sure?"

She laughed. "The floor's grass, isn't it? You'd have to try hard to break it."

Delaney set the butterfly on her palm. It was heavier than it appeared. Sturdier, too. For some reason that disappointed her. Had she been expecting it to be as weightless as the one she'd imagined in her fantasy last week? The one that had alighted on Max's shoulder?

She understood the difference between fantasy and reality. She knew perfectly well that the pleasure she experienced in any of her make-believe scenarios wouldn't be possible in the real world.

Her wet umbrella swung against her side, sending a trickle of water down her bare calf. She saw an image of birch trees.

Dark clouds. Rain. Max's wet hair plastered tight against his head as he pressed his face between her legs and—

"I did one in violet, too. Would you like to see it?"

Delaney blinked, stunned by how vivid the recollection had been. She *did* know the difference, didn't she? She cleared her throat. "I'd like this one," she said, handing the butterfly to the woman. "Do you have a box for it?"

"Sorry, no, but I'll wrap it in tissue. Is that okay?"

"The paper's fine." She paid for the ornament and slipped it into her purse, then went to look for Helen.

Initially, she hadn't planned on attending the festival, but she'd jumped at the chance when her grandmother had asked her to come along today. First of all, the idea of being near the lake didn't bother her as much as it used to. Learning the reason behind her aversion to water was helping to deflate it. And secondly, she needed to make the effort to get out more. She needed to be around people, *real* people.

That fantasy in the storm had been incredible, but it hadn't triggered more memories. Her thoughts had been too filled with Max. It was just as well. She should take a break from her memory hunt until she came to terms with the bombshell she'd already remembered.

Although, what remained to come to terms with? She'd been leaving Stanford. In her heart, she must have known that all along—it had likely been the source of the itch in her mind—but she'd had to work through her own mental blocks before she could face it. Her subconscious in the form of Max had guided her. He'd consistently told her the truth. Two weeks with him had accomplished more than six months with Dr. Bernhardt.

It was odd to think that Elizabeth had actually told her the truth, too. Part of it, anyway. Delaney remembered the phone call the night of the accident vividly now. Elizabeth had revealed Stanford's affair with Jenna, and she'd been eager to bring up the topic of a possible divorce. The issue of Stanford's will had never arisen, though. There hadn't been time, since their conversation had lasted less than a minute.

Helen hadn't seemed surprised in the least when Delaney had told her what had happened. That in itself spoke volumes. The age difference alone had given her grandmother concern about her marriage to Stanford, but she had kept her doubts to herself because Delaney had appeared happy. Then again, they both had a history of sweeping unpleasantness under the carpet.

Stanford's infidelity hadn't been the only problem with the marriage. It had been a symptom of his complete disregard for her as a person. The proof of that was he'd felt no remorse over betraying their intimacy. There must have been rumors about his wanderings. That helped explain why so few of her and Stanford's circle had kept in touch with her after the accident. Jenna couldn't have been the only one of Delaney's so-called friends who had slept with her husband, which would have made it awkward to console his grieving and apparently oblivious widow.

God, she had been a fool. How relieved Jenna must have been to hear that she couldn't remember the night of the accident.

Max never encouraged her to remember, did he? He maintained she should let the past stay buried. That was a contradiction, since being with him had the opposite effect.

Something twitched inside her mind. Warmth whispered across her hand as his presence drifted through her consciousness. He seemed so nearby, she glanced over her shoulder to see if he was there.

A group of people stood inside the entrance to the tent. They appeared to be in the midst of a spirited discussion as they peeled off rain ponchos and furled umbrellas. One waved to the woman at the table of glass ornaments as the others hurried over to the wood carvings.

Delaney gave herself a mental shake and kept walking. So far, Max came to her only when she was alone. She wasn't going to imagine him here, of all places. That would really be nuts.

She found Helen beside a large quilt done in an interlocking log-cabin pattern. It was dominated by eye-popping shades of orange and red that were difficult to look at for more than a few seconds.

"What do you think?" Helen asked. "Would you want to sleep under this one?"

"Maybe the sight of it would help a person wake up in the morning."

Helen laughed. "Exactly what I thought. Let me show you Ada's," she said, hooking her hand through Delaney's elbow. She guided her to the next row of frames and stopped in front of another quilt. The colors were all earth tones, soft greens, creams, and browns. Fabrics that ranged from corduroy to chintz had been expertly pieced into a jagged starburst.

"That's incredible," Delaney said. "It looks like springtime."

"As far as I'm concerned, it's a work of art," Helen said proudly. She pointed to the sign on one side of the frame. "Did you see the best part?"

A blue ribbon rosette had been fixed to the label that bore Ada Ross's name. "First prize!" Delaney read. "That's terrific."

"She deserves it. I'd hang this on my wall before I put it on a bed." She looked past Delaney and smiled. "Ada! There you are. Why didn't you tell me you won?"

A tiny, white-haired wren of a woman hurried over to hug Helen. What Ada Ross lacked in height she made up for in energy. She grinned, practically dancing in place as if she couldn't contain her excitement. "I just found out myself," she said.

"Congratulations," Delaney said. "That's fabulous news."

Ada nodded. "When I heard who the judges were, I thought I didn't have a chance. Moira Nolan has had it in for me since Bruno dug up her hydrangea."

"Bruno is Ada's dog," Helen explained with a laugh.

"Moira does understand quilting, though, I'll give her that," Ada continued. "She's got the tiniest stitches; I'm sure she must work with a magnifying glass. But what would a real artist know about it? That's what worried me. You know what he said? It was an easy decision. He says I have artistic vision. *Me*." She fluttered her hands in front of her. "John Harrison thinks I'm talented. That's worth more to me than the ribbon."

Delaney stiffened. "John Harrison?"

Ada's smile faded at her tone. "I don't care what people say about him. You can't argue with success. He's a good artist."

"Yes, I'm sure he is," Delaney said quickly. "I was just, ah, surprised."

"I told her John keeps to himself," Helen put in.

"That's true. I heard we were lucky he could fit this into his schedule. It's such a shame. He seems decent enough. If people saw more of him, maybe they would go easier on him." She dug into the handbag that she held hooked on her arm. "Look what he gave me," she said, holding out a white business card. "It's the phone number of a gallery owner he knows who deals with fabric art."

"Good for him," Helen said. "I was just saying to Delaney that your quilt belongs on a wall."

The name and number had been written across the back of the card in a bold, masculine scrawl. John Harrison had done that, Delaney thought. She had a mad urge to touch it the same way she touched his photograph. She could almost imagine the strength of his hand.

Ada tucked the card away. "I always viewed it as just a hobby, but he told me people regard it differently if they have to pay for it. It got me thinking."

"A new career?" Helen asked.

"Why not? My youth isn't going to last forever."

This brought on a round of laughter from Ada and Helen. Delaney started to join in when the nape of her neck tingled. Her pulse lurched. Awareness stroked across her skin and spread through her mind.

She took a few deep breaths and turned.

A tall, broad-shouldered man was moving in her direction along the center aisle of the tent. He was dressed all in black, from his tailored pants to the silk shirt that stretched across his chest. A black raincoat was draped over one arm. His dark hair was damp and combed straight back from his face, revealing the features that Delaney knew by heart: the bold nose, the lean cheeks and sharp jaw, the grooves beside his mouth that deepened when he smiled.

But he was no figment of her imagination. An officious-looking woman in a beige business suit walked beside him, gesturing to the metal clipboard she held. He bent his head toward her as she spoke. A young couple detoured around both of them in order to reach the booth with the bead-and-feather jewelry. He wasn't hazy around the edges. There was no hint of transparency to his image. He was indisputably there. His leather shoes connected solidly with the worn-down grass of the aisle with each step he took. Water beaded on his raincoat just as it had gleamed on his face when he'd knelt at Delaney's feet and moved her thighs apart . . .

No! It wasn't this man who had kissed her. He'd never touched her scars or shared her most personal secrets. That had been Max. Only Max. This man didn't know her. She should stop staring at him.

He lifted his head slowly, as if he sensed her regard. Blue eyes met hers.

Logic be damned, she wanted to run to him, yank aside the beige woman and her clipboard, and fling herself into his arms, take him to the meadow of wildflowers or the cloud or her bed and taste his skin and his mouth and his love because dear God wouldn't it be wonderful if her friend could be real.

He continued to regard her, his expression shuttered. He didn't look like the kind of man who had ever been a child, let alone a boy who had made imaginary mud pies with her or slid down a banister or run along the drive with his arms stretched out like airplane wings. He didn't look like a man who would share his thoughts, either. There was a self-contained stillness around him. A wariness.

She smiled and opened her mind, putting all the strength she had into a silent shout. *Max!*

There was no response. No teasing laugh rumbling along her bones. No phantom caress on her cheek or her breast. Not even a cranky order to stop bothering him. There was no trace of passion in his gaze, only caution and a hint of . . . puzzlement.

Her vision blurred. Good God, of course he would seem puzzled. He probably thought she was hitting on him. She turned away before she could make a complete fool of herself. Mercifully, he would have no way of knowing what was going on in her head.

Get a grip, she ordered. *He's not Max.*

Right. He was John Harrison. Famous painter. Infamous ex-con. Helen's neighbor and apparently a judge of the arts and crafts displays at the Willowbank Waterfront Festival. A real man. A total stranger . . .

. . . who had just happened to appear naked in her fantasies.

Helen touched her arm. "Is something wrong?"

She jumped. "Sorry, I—"

"You look like you've seen a ghost," Ada said.

"You only picked at your lunch," Helen said. "You really need to eat more, Deedee."

"I'm fine, Grandma." Delaney forced a smile. "I was just looking around. Your quilt is truly in a class by itself, Ada. How long did it take to complete?"

Ada exchanged a glance with Helen but accepted Delaney's change of subject. It took little prodding to get her started on a description of her craft. Delaney admired her enthusiasm, and she tried to pay attention, yet it was difficult to focus on the conversation.

Awareness continued to chase across her nerves. It was different from before, because there was nothing imaginary about the male presence she sensed. John Harrison was a physically compelling man. It was why she'd given his face to Max. He was tall, dark, and had the edgy, bad-boy aura that many women would find irresistible.

Not Delaney, though. She'd never been attracted to that type of man. Except for Max. And she'd made Max that way because he was Stanford's opposite. He was pure, unvarnished emotion. He could get her excited with merely a look, a touch, a thought . . .

But she couldn't analyze this now, not when the living embodiment of her sexual fantasies was less than thirty feet away. This was too embarrassing for words. How could she even think about sex? She was standing in front of her grandmother while her friend discussed the merits of polished cotton thread.

She couldn't hear any footsteps on the ground that separated them, yet some instinct told her when he drew nearer. It wasn't her mind that felt his proximity, it was her body. Her nerves hummed, her senses sharpened. Although Helen and Ada were still talking, she had no trouble picking out the conversation that was going on behind her.

"John, we need to make a decision on the handicrafts category."

"I told you my choices, Moira."

Delaney bit her lip. It was Max's voice, yet not Max's. It wasn't as deep, and the tone was rougher. The differences were subtle, like hearing a recording of her own voice compared to how she sounded in her head.

"But you gave me three names. We need one."

"I told you the category is too broad. It should be broken down."

"All right. We'll keep that in mind when we make the rules for next year's festival."

"You want a decision that's fair, you change the rules now. Three winners. Bill me for the extra two ribbons."

John Harrison's voice might sound different from Max's, but those words were exactly like something her friend would have said. He never failed to speak his mind.

Images jumbled through her head. Her bedroom, the pond, the oak that used to hold her swing. She closed her eyes. In spite of what she knew to be real, to be sane, she opened her mind to their connection one last time.

There was no response.

Because, of course, he wasn't Max. She dropped her hand to her purse, cupping the bulge the paper-wrapped butterfly made against the leather. She did know the difference, she reminded herself. As she'd already realized, no real man could measure up to the fantasy she'd created.

The voices grew fainter. They must have changed direction. Only through a supreme effort of will did Delaney stop herself from turning to watch him go.

"Honey, are you sure you're all right?"

Delaney blinked. "I'm fine, Grandma. Really."

"It's the dampness, if you ask me," Ada said. "It sucks all the heat out of your body. Makes my joints ache, too."

"Tell me about it." Helen rubbed her hands over her arms. "Though with all the goodies my granddaughter's been baking, you'd think I'd have enough padding for insulation."

"I left an extra sweater in the car," Delaney said. "I'll get it for you."

"Oh, don't bother."

She slid the strap of her umbrella from her wrist, fumbling it in her eagerness. "It would be my pleasure, Grandma. I could use some air."

It was a flimsy excuse, but it got her out of the tent and away from John Harrison before she could do something completely ridiculous. Granted, she'd told herself she was going to face what bothered her, but there were limits, especially in public.

Not every man would be as understanding as Max when it came to explaining the workings of her subconscious. That was because Max *was* her subconscious. God, could this get any more confusing?

The folk musicians who had been playing in the band shell when she and Helen had arrived were packing up their instruments as she passed by the stage. The audience that had gathered on the benches had mostly dispersed, some going toward the refreshment tents, some toward the parking area. Engines revved as headlights shone through the gloom.

Delaney held her umbrella close to her shoulders as the drizzle increased to rain. Although it was coming straight down, it struck the ground hard enough to splash. Her ankles and the hem of her skirt were soaked by the time she reached her car. The feel of the water didn't bother her, though, any more than the sight of the lake did. Her wet skin didn't remind her of her nightmare; it reminded her of the pleasure of kissing Max in the storm . . .

Damn, she had to try harder to focus. She angled the umbrella over the door as she opened it and reached into the backseat for her sweater.

A shiver went down her spine, as if someone was watching her. She held the sweater to her chest and straightened quickly.

A pickup truck went past, its windshield wipers beating against the rain. A couple was loading a group of children into a station wagon a few rows away. No one appeared to be paying any attention to her.

She closed the door and locked the car, then walked between the cars to the lawn.

The black sedan seemed to come out of nowhere. It fishtailed on the wet grass, spraying arcs of water behind it, then straightened and accelerated toward her. Disbelief kept her rooted to the spot for a critical instant.

"Watch out!"

The shout went through her head a split second before a large body collided with hers. Her umbrella flew out of her hand as she was knocked off her feet. There was a dull thud behind her. She hit the ground hard enough to jar the air from her lungs. Gasping, she rolled to her knees and lifted her head.

The car didn't stop. It didn't waver or slow down. Its brake lights didn't shine once as it sped past a garbage bin and onto the road.

A woman screamed. Someone else was shouting to call 9-1-1. People ran toward her and to the large, dark figure that lay motionless on the ground.

Delaney shoved herself to her feet and stumbled across the tracks the car had torn through the grass. The man had pushed her out of the way. He must have been struck instead. He lay on his back, his black raincoat spread like wings beneath him. His black shirt was plastered tight to his chest. She couldn't see whether or not he was breathing.

But she could see his face.

Her knees gave out. She sank to the ground beside his head. "Max," she breathed.

Yet she knew his name wasn't Max. It was John.

NINETEEN

꧁꘎꧂

THE BEEPING WOKE HIM. NEXT CAME THE PAIN. MAX
gritted his teeth. His head was killing him. So was his arm. The
rest of his body felt like one big bruise. He hadn't felt this bad
since the days when Virgil used to go after him with his belt.

That thought snapped him completely awake. He opened
his eyes.

He was in a hospital room. An IV tube snaked into one arm.
The other was immobilized against his chest. The beeping was
coming from a monitor on one side of the bed. On the other
side, a woman sat in a chair, her arms crossed on the metal bed
rail, her head pillowed on her forearms. He couldn't see her
face, yet he recognized her short hair, her grass-stained blouse,
the slope of her back, the curve of her shoulders . . .

The pain receded on a wave of joy. Deedee! She was here.
He'd reached her in time. He lifted his hand, his palm hovering
above her hair.

His movement rattled the IV tube against its metal stand.
Before he could touch her, Delaney jerked her head up.

Her gaze was springtime. Life. Calm and sweet and impossible to capture on canvas. Real. *Here.*

He touched her sleeve. Nothing except cotton separated him
from her skin. Her warmth seeped through the fabric to his
fingertips. The impact crashed through his senses. The monitor
accelerated along with his pulse.

Her chin trembled. "I'm so sorry."

"Why?"

"You're hurt because of me."

"I've had worse." And he had. The morning he'd met her—the only other time he'd actually touched her—the pain in his back had been worse than the bruises he felt now. She had helped him escape it. She had countered the effects of Virgil's evil because she'd been everything bright and good. "Your hands. They're okay?"

"They're fine. I landed on my side." Her eyes shone. "What you did was very courageous, Mr. Harrison. You probably saved my life. I don't know how I can thank you."

He'd saved her life twenty-eight years ago, too. Afterward, she hadn't thanked him. Instead, she'd curled into his arms and slipped into the place he'd opened in his mind.

That was when it struck him. He was hearing her voice, not sensing it. She was talking aloud to him. She hadn't called him Max.

He clamped his fingers around the bed rail and levered himself up on his elbow. "You know who I am."

It was both a question and a challenge. It appeared to unsettle her. She pressed the controls at the side of the bed to raise the mattress beneath his head. She stopped when he was sitting at a forty-five-degree angle. "Is that better?"

"Sure."

"I know my way around hospital beds," she said. "I spent way too much time in them. Do you want some water?" she asked, springing to her feet.

"I'm fine. *Do* you know me?"

She fiddled with the plastic pitcher beside the bed, picking it up, putting it down. "I knew who you were when I saw you at the festival. I . . ." She cleared her throat. "I recognized you from your picture."

"My picture?"

"It's in the brochure from the Mapleview Gallery. My grandmother keeps them for her customers. I'm Delaney Graye, Helen Wainright's granddaughter. I'm sorry," she said, turning toward the door. "I was supposed to tell the doctor as soon as you woke up."

She thanked him again, said good-bye, and left.

Max dropped his head back against the pillow, then swore at the fresh burst of pain the movement sent through his skull. It made it tough to think, but he had to. What the hell was going on?

She hadn't acknowledged him, she hadn't tried to reach his mind; she was treating him like a stranger.

Yet she knew his name because she'd seen his picture . . .

Okay, now her reaction at the festival made sense. No wonder she hadn't freaked out when she'd seen him in person. She'd seemed surprised, yes, but not as shocked as he would have expected. She had backed off when he'd refused her mental overture. She'd already known there was a John Harrison.

And considering Deedee's habit of rationalizing away what didn't fit her view of reality, she'd probably found some convoluted psychological explanation for his resemblance to her imaginary friend.

Lucky, wasn't it? He'd already decided against revealing the truth. He'd reasoned it all through when he'd seen her outside his house last week. He didn't want a flesh-and-blood relationship; he didn't want to get close or to care. The last time he'd gone to her, she'd admitted flat out she was using him. Her dead bastard of a husband was still her priority. As long as she believed Max was imaginary, he could keep her safely out of his life and his heart.

Sure, that was what he'd told himself, but he'd followed her out of the tent anyway. There had been no logical reason for it; he simply hadn't been able to keep away. How could he expect to maintain a grip on his logic when she was close enough to touch, really touch?

This time, it hadn't been a broken beer bottle that had stopped him; it had been a car.

Yeah, real lucky.

"Mr. Harrison." A woman in a white coat bustled in. "I'm Dr. Yarrow. How are you feeling?"

"Like I got hit by a car. What's the damage?"

She took a penlight from her breast pocket and checked his eyes. "In spite of the pain you undoubtedly are experiencing, you got off rather easily. You have extensive bruising but no broken bones, likely due to the fact you landed on grass. The laceration on your forehead was too shallow to require stitches. Unfortunately, you did sustain a concussion."

He touched his forehead and found a wide bandage taped just below his hairline. He wiggled the fingers of his bound arm. "What about this?"

"Your wrist is only sprained. However, I'd like to keep the

arm immobilized for a few days to minimize the strain on the bones while the joint heals. The X-rays showed several healed fractures in both your arm and your wrist." She hesitated. "Were you an accident-prone child, Mr. Harrison?"

The question was thirty years too late. So was the sympathy in her eyes—no doubt she'd also seen the other souvenirs from Virgil. "My arm's fine."

"We can give you medication to dull the pain."

"No drugs. I can handle it."

It appeared as if she wanted to say more.

He hardened his jaw.

"All right, then. Let one of the nurses know if you change your mind." She finished her brief examination and made a note on the chart at the foot of his bed.

He glanced around. "This isn't the ER."

"Mrs. Graye insisted on paying for a private room."

"Not much point, since I'm not staying."

"Your other injuries may be minor, but your concussion concerns me. You were unconscious for a significant period of time, so I'd like to keep you overnight for observation."

"Where are my clothes?"

"Mr. Harrison," she began.

She didn't have the chance to finish. A man in a brown suit coat appeared in the doorway. "Is he up to answering some questions?"

A cop, Max decided. The room immediately seemed to shrink. He had to remind himself it wasn't a cell. He knew his rights, and regardless of what the doctor had said, he was free to leave. "Did you get the driver?" he demanded.

"Not yet."

Dr. Yarrow moved to the door. "You can have five minutes," she told the man. "But then he needs to rest."

"I'll keep it brief." He pulled a notebook from his pocket as he walked to the side of the bed. "I'm Detective Toffelmire, Mr. Harrison. Can you tell us anything about the vehicle that struck you?"

"It was a black car."

"Make? Model?"

"Some kind of sedan. Could have been high-end, like a Caddy."

"What about a license number? Were they New York plates?"

"I didn't see them."

"The driver?"

"Didn't see that, either. The car had tinted glass, and it was raining hard."

"Hard enough for the driver not to notice you or Mrs. Graye?"

"Only if he was blind. There must have been a dozen witnesses. Didn't any of them get a license number?"

"Unfortunately, no." Toffelmire consulted his notebook. "Did you observe whether or not the driver made any attempt to avoid the collision?"

"Not that I saw."

"Was there anyone else in his path, other than Mrs. Graye?"

Max considered it. "Besides me, no. You sound as if you think it was deliberate."

"These are routine questions."

"Why would anyone want to hurt her?"

"Do you have reason to believe someone attempted to?"

Typical police word games, answering a question with a question. "I wouldn't know," Max said.

"Are you acquainted with Mrs. Graye?"

"We just met."

Toffelmire studied his face. "What were you doing in the parking lot, Mr. Harrison?"

Max regarded him in turn. The cop seemed familiar, and not simply because of the hostile glint in his eyes. That expression was common to all cops Max had dealt with. "Going to my car."

"You drive a '94 Jeep TJ, is that right?"

"Did you get that from the insurance slip in my wallet?"

"The paramedics removed your wallet in order to verify your identity. They shared all the information with me."

"So?"

"The Jeep was parked at the opposite end of the lot from where the accident occurred."

"What does that have to do with anything?"

"What is your relationship to Mrs. Graye?"

"Besides shoving her out of the path of a drunk driver?"

"Why do you assume the driver was drunk?"

"Beer tent. Rainy day. You do the math."

"It was a lucky coincidence that you happened to be there."

The beeps from the monitor accelerated again. Max reached beneath his hospital gown and yanked the contacts off his chest, then gripped the bed rail to haul himself upright. "Don't you think you're getting off track here? Instead of hassling me, go find the bastard who used the park for a drag strip. There were kids there, too. He could have hit one of them."

"Several people mentioned you appeared to be following Mrs. Graye."

"So were they. We were all heading in the same direction. Have you got a problem with that, Detective Toffelmire?"

"Should I, Mr. Harrison?"

"You got something to say, then say it."

"You don't remember me, do you?"

Max scrutinized his face.

Toffelmire stroked his nose. It was mashed sideways. He'd obviously run into someone's fist sometime in the past . . .

Shit. Now he recognized him. Toffelmire had been one of the cops who had tried to pull him off Virgil. He'd testified at the start of the trial. He'd been in uniform then. Max hadn't made the connection at first because the man had gained weight and lost half of his hair. He also appeared a lot different without the bulky white bandages that had crisscrossed his face.

Was he expecting an apology for the nose? No way. Max had served his time. He'd more than paid for what he'd done, and he hadn't gotten so much as a parking ticket since he'd come back to Willowbank. That made no difference in some people's minds. "Yeah, I remember you. You haven't changed a bit. You're still going after the wrong guy."

A nurse rushed in, probably alerted by the dead monitor. Max waved her away when she moved to reattach it. "Get this needle out of my arm."

"Sir—"

"If you don't, I will."

Dr. Yarrow returned. She ordered Toffelmire out as well as the nurse, then came to Max's side and laid her hand on his injured wrist. "Calm down. We can remove the IV. It was only a routine precaution."

"Fine. Do it."

She eased off the tape that held the needle in place, pulled it out, and pressed a cotton ball against his arm. "You need to rest, Mr. Harrison."

"I'll get more rest at home."

"I can't in good conscience discharge you."

"I'll sign a waiver. Whatever you want. Just give me the bill." He slid down the bed until he was past the railing and swung his legs over the side of the mattress. He sucked in his breath at the pain the movement caused, then flicked his mind away until it eased. He'd had plenty of experience handling pain. He hadn't needed to do it for decades, but it was just like riding a bike.

"Mr. Harrison . . ."

"Where the hell are my pants?"

"Did they get the guy yet?" Phoebe asked, folding the edge of a pillowcase over the clothesline.

"Not that I know." Delaney handed her a clothespin. "Detective Toffelmire promised he'd call me if he learned anything."

"Last year some guy got drunk enough to put his car in the lake. It was a slow-motion disaster, like a clip from one of those home video shows, and we all laughed at him, but what happened to you wasn't funny." She shook her finger in a gesture reminiscent of something Helen might have done. "You know what? Maybe at next year's festival they should make people hand over their car keys before they can get a beer. They don't get them back unless they can prove they're sober or they have a designated driver."

"That is an excellent suggestion."

"Really? You think they'd go for it?"

"It's worth a try. Willowbank could set a new trend."

"Sure, why not? It was horrible luck, though. I mean, of all the people in the park, why you? After the car crash you've already gone through—" She stopped. "Sorry, that was a dumb thing to say."

"Why? It's true."

Phoebe leaned across the wicker laundry basket at her feet to give Delaney a quick hug, then gasped and jumped back. "Ohmigosh. Did that hurt?"

It had, but only a little. Compared to the battering her body had taken six months ago, the few bruises on her hip and shoulder that she'd sustained yesterday were nothing. The aches were already fading. It was fortunate she hadn't landed on her hands, though. That might have undone months of healing. She picked up another clothespin. "The hug was worth it."

"I can't believe how well you're taking it all. You're so brave."

"Me? Hardly. It's John Harrison who was brave."

"I still can't believe that part, either. He *rescued* you. Wow. Who would have thought?"

"People should do more thinking where he's concerned. What he did was completely selfless. Even heroic."

"That's what I mean. From what I've heard, he's more the type to do the hit-and-run than to push someone out of the way."

As much as Delaney was growing to love Phoebe, she had a sudden urge to shake her. "Then you've heard wrong."

"Sorry." She twisted her lips into an exaggerated grimace. "It's kind of hard to think of him as a good guy. My friends and I used to scare each other with stories about him when we were kids."

"Like the boogeyman in the woods?"

She reached into the basket for a sheet. She concentrated on aligning the corners together before she spoke again. "It probably wasn't fair, but that's how kids are."

"I know. You likely picked up on the attitudes of your parents."

"Maybe. But he did go to prison for beating up his mother. We didn't make that up."

"People can change."

"I guess."

"He was very kind to my grandmother's friend Ada."

"Oh?"

"He also volunteered his time to help support the town's summer festival. That doesn't sound like boogeyman behavior to me."

Phoebe laughed. "Okay, okay. I won't let my little brothers soap his windows this Halloween."

"Good."

She clipped the sheet to the line. "But I still say he'd make a good Heathcliffe."

Delaney rolled her eyes. "He's just a man, Phoebe, and I owe him my gratitude."

HALF AN HOUR LATER, DELANEY STOOD ON THE EMBANK-ment behind John Harrison's house and reminded herself of what she'd told Phoebe. John Harrison was just a man, not a figment of her imagination or the embodiment of her fantasies. He lived in a real building. There was nothing mysterious about sensing that he was at home; she could see the evidence of it: his windows were open, and a patch of daylight showed through the screen door that overlooked the deck, so the interior door must have been left open as well. Apparently, he enjoyed the warmth of sunshine and the freedom of fresh air.

Part of her couldn't believe she was here. Less than a day ago she'd been trying to get as far away from this man as she could. He was still a veritable stranger.

Yes, but he'd saved her life, she reminded herself. She owed him some courtesy, didn't she? If he'd been anyone else, she wouldn't be hesitating to call on him. She wouldn't have fled his hospital room yesterday, either. Not that she could begin to explain her behavior to him. She couldn't very well admit it wasn't his reputation that had bothered her, it was his resemblance to her dream lover.

Before she could change her mind, she found a path down the embankment and crossed the yard to the house, picking her way around the puddles that remained from the weekend's rain. As she was trying to decide whether or not to go around the house to look for a front door, a large figure moved behind the screen door.

Well, there was no turning back now. He'd obviously seen her coming. She walked toward the stairs that led to the deck.

John pushed open the door and regarded her in silence.

He was dressed in blue jeans and a plain white shirt that he wore untucked. A navy blue sling supported his forearm horizontally across his waist. The bandage that was taped to his forehead was almost hidden by the lock of hair that had fallen across it.

Her steps faltered. She knew it was impossible, but he looked so much like Max, she called to him anyway. *Max!*

Not a flicker of reaction crossed his face. He seemed to be studying her as intently as she studied him.

"Good morning," she said aloud. "I hope I'm not visiting too early. How are you feeling?"

"I'm fine. Why are you here?"

His attitude was as much like Max's as his appearance. "I phoned the hospital to see how you were, and they told me you'd left," she said.

"Couldn't see the point of staying."

"I'd be the last person who would want to spend any more time in a hospital, so I understand why you wouldn't want to stay. I just thought I'd make sure you were okay."

"I'm fine," he repeated. "I settled the bill myself. You didn't need to pay."

"It doesn't come close to what you did for me."

"Thanks, but I don't need your gratitude."

"And besides, we're neighbors." She held out the towel-wrapped loaf that she carried. "I bake for my grandmother's guests. I made some extra banana bread today, so I brought it over. I realize it can't repay you for your quick thinking yesterday, but I hope it makes up for the hospital food you're missing."

The lines beside his mouth deepened briefly. She couldn't tell whether he was clenching his jaw because he was annoyed or because he was suppressing a smile. A day's growth of beard stubble bristled from his skin. Along with the bandage on his forehead, it gave him a faintly piratical appearance. "Banana bread?"

"It has fruit, eggs, and whole wheat, three major food groups, so you can call it breakfast if you want. Or have you already eaten?"

He wiggled the fingers that poked above his sling. "Haven't gotten around to it today."

An image stole through her mind. Max leaning against a willow tree, his fingers hooked through the handle of a coffee mug. "Then let me fix breakfast for you," she said.

"Why?"

"It's the least I can do, since your arm's in that sling because of me. I shouldn't be keeping you standing around like this to talk to me, either. You should probably be in bed."

He lifted one eyebrow, as if her suggestion had been an invitation.

That reminded her of Max, too. So did the flutter of her pulse. "I don't mean to intrude, but I know how frustrating it is not to have the full use of your hands. Please, let me help you, Mr. Harrison."

"Most people call me John."

She smiled. "John."

He focused on her mouth.

She started. She could have sworn she'd felt a touch on her lips. *Max?*

John held the door open and motioned her inside.

Delaney took care not to brush against him as she walked past. He had a sprained wrist, and his bruises were likely ten times more painful than hers. The compulsion she felt to lean on his chest and press her face to his shoulder was completely irrational.

The interior of his house was a surprise. Apart from some scattered pillars, the ground floor appeared to be all one room. Sunlight poured through long, deep windows and reflected from the wood floors. Two sleek, reddish brown leather sofas stood in front of a stone fireplace that stretched across one wall while floor-to-ceiling bookshelves flanked the windows of another. Only the placement of the furniture and a few low cabinets defined the separate areas of use, so it all flowed together, as unimpeded as the sunshine. The effect was airy and inviting. She wouldn't have expected that, considering how inhospitable John was being.

Still, no one would be in the mood to socialize less than a day after being struck by a car. It had been more than six months since her own accident, and she hadn't yet had any desire to resume her social life. Not the one she'd had, anyway.

Her gaze returned to the fireplace. The painting above was the only one she could see. Even from a distance, it was impressive. Phoebe had called his work intense, and she could understand why. The storm on the canvas seemed poised to stretch past its frame. She would have liked to study it more closely, but he led her in the opposite direction, past a spiral staircase and a door she guessed led to a bathroom until they reached the kitchen area.

A counter of amber-colored polished stone nestled in the angle between two of the outside walls. It extended beneath a window, where it formed a small bar. A glass half-filled with orange juice rested on the bar in front of a padded stool. She placed the loaf beside it. "You have a lovely home."

He grasped the edge of the bar for support and lowered himself to sit on the stool. It was the first sign he gave that his injuries affected him. The pain that clouded his gaze was quickly extinguished. "You've been here before," he said.

"What? No, I—"

"Out there," he said, nodding out the window. It overlooked the deck, giving a clear view of the embankment and the trees beyond it. "You were on the old track bed last week. I saw you from my studio upstairs."

She took a few moments to unwrap the loaf. Great. He'd seen her spying on him. Added to the way he'd caught her staring at him yesterday, was it any wonder he'd hesitated to let her inside? "Yes, I was going for a walk when I noticed this house."

He studied her again, as if he were waiting for her to say more.

"I used to work in real estate, and I can appreciate the craftsmanship that went into this home. The design is unique."

"Should be. I built it."

"Really? I should have recognized it had an artist's touch. It's beautiful, especially the interior. Walking inside is like taking a deep breath."

"Why didn't you come in last week?"

"What?"

"You knew who I was then, didn't you?"

"I, uh, wouldn't presume—"

"Or is that why you didn't come in, because you did know who I was?"

There was a challenge beneath his words. She wasn't sure how to respond. "I, uh, couldn't. I was meeting someone later."

His jaw flexed. This time she was almost certain he was suppressing a smile.

"I'd better get busy," she said. "Would you like something besides that banana bread? Do you have any eggs? I make a mean omelet."

"What you brought is plenty. You'll share it, right?"

"Thanks. Where do you keep your coffee?"

The question was unnecessary. The cabinets that ranged along the wall above the counter were glass-fronted. She got the coffee started, found a cutting board, and took one of the knives from a wooden holder to slice the banana bread. She took out some plates and reached back into the cupboard for the mugs.

They were plain white crockery, exactly like the one she had seen Max hold.

Her hand jerked. She fumbled with the mugs to keep them from dropping, then set them on the counter and looked at John.

Raw hunger flashed in his gaze. It was veiled so fast she suspected she must have imagined it in the first place.

"You mentioned you've been in hospitals," he said. "What happened?"

"I was in an accident last winter. It seems as if I haven't had good luck where cars are concerned. I'm really sorry that you got hurt."

"I'm a free man. What I did was my choice."

"Well, it was very selfless. You . . ." She halted, struck by a detail she hadn't considered before. "You asked me how my hands were."

"What?"

"When you first woke up. Why would you ask me about my hands? How did you know they were my main concern?"

"You just said you knew what it was like to be without the use of your hands."

"That was today. How did you know yesterday?"

"You had your arms on the rail of my bed. I saw what looked like skin grafts over your knuckles."

She glanced down. The lines had faded substantially in the last few weeks and were barely visible. "You're very observant."

"I'm an artist. I notice things."

"Oh."

"How else would I know? We'd only just met."

How else? Max knew. She'd told him all about it the same

morning she'd seen him use that coffee mug . . . but that was crazy.

John broke off a chunk from a piece of banana bread and popped it in his mouth. His eyes half closed as his expression softened with pleasure.

It was exactly how Max looked whenever he cupped her breasts.

But he couldn't be Max. In addition to the whole impossibility of having a psychic bond with a total stranger, the idea made no sense. Because if for some reason she could wrap her head around the notion that Max was real, why would he pretend not to know her?

"This stuff's good." He licked a crumb from the corner of his mouth. "Ever thought of going professional?"

"Funny you should mention that. It was one of my earliest career ambitions." She filled the mugs—the plain, white crockery mugs that were probably sold by the thousands—with coffee and slid one along the counter toward him. She didn't bother looking for cream or sugar, because Max drank his coffee black. Evidently John did, too, since he accepted it without hesitation. Keeping her gaze on his face, she pulled a second stool from beneath the bar and sat. "You remind me of someone," she said.

"Who?"

"A friend of mine. We were children together."

"Uh-huh?"

"We lost touch for years, but I met him again recently."

He ate another chunk of banana bread.

"We're very close."

"Good for you."

"Yes, it is good. Everyone should have a friend they can rely on and be totally honest with. Did you ever have anyone like that, John?"

"Sure, and then I grew up." He hooked his finger through the handle of the coffee mug. "Was that who you were thinking of when you smiled at me?"

"When?"

"In the arts and crafts tent yesterday. You damn near singed my toes."

"I, uh . . ."

"I figure there had to be more behind that smile than just recognizing me from my picture."

"That's right. That's what happened. I was thinking of him."

"Lucky guy. Where is he?"

"I wish I knew. He comes and goes."

"Some men are like that." He shifted on the stool, hooking his heel over a rung. His knee bumped her leg. "Did you know that I followed you?"

Her leg tingled from the glancing contact. She thought of rain and the feel of his mouth on her skin. "Uh, followed me?"

"To the parking lot."

His admission didn't surprise her. On some level, she must have realized it. How else would he have gotten to her side in time to save her? "Why?"

"It's what any man would do when a beautiful woman gave him a smile like the one you gave me. Too bad I hadn't known it was for someone else."

He'd called her beautiful. He wouldn't if he knew what was under her clothes.

Yet he was regarding her as if he knew exactly what her blouse concealed. She could almost imagine the sensation of his fingers slipping beneath the cotton to stroke across her skin.

This time she was the one who shifted on her stool. She pressed her knees together and smoothed her skirt over her thighs. "Well, I'm fortunate you were there, whatever the reason. You risked your life to save mine. Detective Toffelmire should be recommending you for a citizen's award."

He laughed. It was short and sharp and entirely without humor. "Don't hold your breath."

"Why are you dismissing what you did?"

"Have you talked to Toffelmire today?"

"No, not yet, but I already told him everything at the hospital."

"Did he warn you about me?"

"No. Why should he?"

"I gave him that nose."

"It must have been a long time ago."

"He's got a long memory. What about your grandmother? She told you about me, right?"

"I won't lie and pretend I haven't heard about the troubles in your past, John. Willowbank's a small town."

"Troubles, huh?" His lip curled. "Never heard it put like that before. Then you know I've been to prison."

"Yes, but we all make mistakes. I wouldn't presume to pass judgment on anyone."

"You should listen to what they say. Just because I've got one arm in a sling doesn't mean I'm harmless."

"Are you deliberately trying to make me uncomfortable?"

"Is that what you feel, Delaney?"

She choked down a wild laugh. Her mind spun with confusion while her body was humming with a purely physical reaction to his proximity. No, having one arm in a sling didn't put a dent in his appeal. He radiated virility. Discomfort was the least of the feelings that were rolling around inside her. She stood. "You must be tired. I've intruded long enough."

He reached for her wrist. The movement didn't alarm her because it seemed perfectly natural. He paused a scant inch before he made contact and frowned at his outstretched fingers. A second passed. Then two. The air between them warmed. The edges of her vision began to shimmer.

She locked her knees to keep from swaying toward him. She remembered stroking his chest and fitting her hands to the curves of his biceps . . . "I'd better go," she murmured.

"Yeah." His voice tingled across her skin like an extension of the touch that hadn't happened. He lifted his gaze to hers. "Maybe you better."

It was more than hunger that flashed in his eyes this time; it was yearning. Despite his beard stubble, despite his harsh features and the strength that was so obvious in the set of his shoulders and his outstretched hand, for an instant she saw a lost boy, searching for a home.

Or was that her imagination, too? She bit her lip. *Max? For God's sake, if that's you, why don't you answer me?*

The shutters came down on John's gaze even faster this time. The child disappeared. He closed his fingers into his palm and dropped his hand. "Thanks for breakfast."

"Thanks for saving my life."

"Anytime."

TWENTY

THE WHINE OF ELECTRIC SAWS REACHED HER THE MOMENT Elizabeth stepped off the elevator. She headed for the noise. "What's the repair estimate?"

Alan fell into step beside her. "I can't give you a dollar number until we determine the source of the leak."

"The water should have been shut off immediately. That would have confined the damage to the twentieth floor."

"There was a miscommunication. The drywallers had been backed up waiting for the plumbers to finish. We had to bring in a new crew over the weekend to keep to the schedule Tirza set."

"And the new crew didn't understand how to turn off a valve?"

"They were working on the eighteenth. They weren't aware of the problem on the twentieth until the water seeped through."

"Need I remind you these units have to be finished by the end of the month, Alan? The ads have been booked. The sales team is already taking advance offers. The success of this condominium project is crucial to the smooth transition of the company."

"I'm aware of that, Elizabeth."

The noise of the saw cut off. She pulled in front of him in order to move around a series of crates. More plumbing fixtures waiting to be installed. She stepped through the roughed-in doorway of what was slated to become one of the model suites and came to a dead stop.

The destruction was worse than she'd anticipated. Large

pools of water dotted the floor. The hardwood hadn't yet been sealed and was visibly buckling. Huge holes had been cut into the drywall to reveal lines of copper piping. Two men were shining flashlights into the holes as the remainder of the crew stood gawking with their hands in their pockets.

She strove to hang on to her temper. "Alan, perhaps you could find something else to keep these men busy."

He stepped around the water and crossed the floor to issue orders, sending half the crew to one of the other floors and putting the rest on cleanup. By the time they dispersed, one of the plumbers had pinpointed the source of the water.

"A join between two pipes was improperly soldered," Alan told her when he returned. "I'd say it was a result of this schedule."

"It is a result of shoddy workmanship and lack of supervision."

"It was Tirza's weekend to babysit. The men don't like her pushing so hard. If you ask me, she's part of the problem."

Before Elizabeth could respond, she spotted the site foreman in the doorway. He was pointing her out to a middle-aged, balding man in a shoddy sport coat. Like Alan and her, the man wore a white visitor's hard hat. He moved purposefully across the floor. "Miss Elizabeth Graye?" he asked as he neared.

Judging by his attire, he wasn't a banker or a buyer—his crooked nose lent him the appearance of a thug—but since the foreman had escorted him up, he must have a valid reason for seeking her. She gave him a gracious but I'm-very-busy smile. "Yes?"

"I'm Detective Toffelmire of the Willowbank police." He held out his credentials. "I'd like to ask you a few questions."

It took her an instant to change mental gears. The condo project, the delay, the consequences of failing to bring in the job on budget withdrew from her mind like a receding wave, leaving a hollowness in its wake. How had Delaney known?

But she could ride this out. They had no proof of anything, she reminded herself. She excused herself from Alan and guided the policeman back through the doorway. "I'm afraid we're in the midst of a crisis here, so I can only spare you a few minutes. You're from Willowbank, you said?"

"That's correct. Are you familiar with it?"

"Only so far as my late father's wife came from Willow-bank."

"How would you describe your relationship with Delaney Graye?"

The corridor was empty of people. Once she passed the crates of plumbing fixtures, she stopped and turned to face him. "I don't think either of us wants to waste time, Detective, so I won't do so. It's no secret that I never approved of my father's marriage to that woman. She was the trophy wife of an aging, extremely wealthy man. She has inherited his entire estate. The situation is intolerable."

"I understand you're currently suing her for his wrongful death."

"That's correct. And if you know that, then you also must know that her lawyer has just retaliated by filing a restraining order against me in the most vindictive way possible."

"Mrs. Graye received some disturbing material in the mail several days ago. Would you know anything about that?"

She kept her gaze steady on his, aware he was likely paying more attention to her body language than to her words. She shouldn't have brought up the restraining order. The thought of it enraged her. "I have no idea what you're talking about."

"Photographs, Miss Graye. Very graphic ones of your late father taken at the accident scene."

Bile rose in her throat. She restrained herself from swallowing because he would be sure to see it. "That's shocking, but I fail to see how it concerns me. Now, if you don't mind, I have other matters that really can't wait."

"Just a few more routine questions, Miss Graye. You own a black Mercedes sedan, is that correct?"

"Yes, I do."

"Did you drive it here today?"

"No, it's at the repair shop."

"Mechanical problems?"

"It was damaged at a parking garage last week. Apparently some skateboarder ran into it."

"How did you get here?"

"I usually use the company car and driver when I'm on business."

"Would you mind if I took a look at your car?"

"For what reason?"

"I'd rather you agree voluntarily, but if you refuse to cooperate, I can get a court order."

"Then I'm afraid that's what you'll need to do, Detective. That's not being uncooperative; that's being prudent. It seems as if you're accusing me of something."

"Where were you on Sunday afternoon between four and six?"

"Excuse me?"

"Is there some reason you don't want to answer the question?"

"I was at home."

"Here in Manhattan?"

"Yes, at my apartment."

"Can anyone verify that?"

A bead of sweat trickled from her armpit and over her ribs. She had no cause to feel guilty. Her crime was negligible compared to what Delaney had done. She strove to keep her face expressionless. "Perhaps it's time for me to call my lawyer."

"Miss Graye was with me."

Elizabeth started at the sound of Alan's voice. She hadn't heard him approach.

He moved to her side and thrust his right hand toward Toffelmire. "Alan Rashotte," he said. "I'm Miss Graye's fiancé."

The lies left her speechless. She listened in silence as Alan fielded Toffelmire's questions with an aplomb she might have admired under other circumstances but instead found disturbing, as if a pet had suddenly learned how to operate a can opener. He placed his palm at the small of her back, a familiarity obviously meant to reinforce his lies. It made her flesh crawl. Somehow, she managed to remain impassive, aware the detective was scrutinizing them both.

The minute the elevator doors closed behind Toffelmire, Elizabeth spun to face Alan. "What on earth was that for?"

He smiled. "I could see you were in trouble, and I wanted to help."

"I didn't need your help."

"You weren't home yesterday. You weren't there for the entire weekend. I know that because I tried to get in touch with you several times, and I also dropped by your apartment. You hadn't even told your personal assistant how to reach you." His smile turned calculating. "And now the police want to know your whereabouts. It makes me wonder: where *were* you, Elizabeth?"

"I took some private time."

"Why would a detective from Willowbank be so interested in your car? Is that where you went?"

"No. Obviously he's made a mistake. Alan, what possessed you to claim we were engaged?"

"It gave more weight to your alibi."

She managed a laugh. "Alibi? You've obviously been watching too many crime shows."

"Should I call him back and tell him what I know?"

"There's nothing to know. All you've done is add a needless complication, since he probably didn't believe you."

"What I've done is prove you can trust me." He stroked her cheek with the backs of his knuckles. "And you did mention something about rewarding loyalty, didn't you?"

She tipped her head away from his caress. Her nails dug painfully into her palms. This couldn't be happening. She was the one in charge. She was the one using him. The power was supposed to be hers. How could it have turned around so quickly?

This was Delaney's fault. If it hadn't been for her, Elizabeth would have had nothing to hide.

DELANEY GRIPPED THE PHONE HARD AND LEANED HER shoulder against the wall. Through the back window, she could see Helen taking down the laundry while Phoebe held the basket for her. Late-afternoon shadows were stealing across the yard. The kitchen was filled with the aroma of the lemon chicken she was cooking for supper. Everything seemed so ordinary, it was hard to grasp what Toffelmire was telling her. "You must have made a mistake," she said slowly. "I'm positive Elizabeth's car is white. It's a BMW."

"Not anymore. She's the registered owner of a black Mercedes. She purchased it three months ago."

That would have been while Delaney was in the hospital. "There must be thousands of black sedans in New York. Tens of thousands."

"I found it has front-end damage consistent with striking a heavy object."

A heavy object. Like Max. No, John.

Still, Elizabeth? Cold-bloodedly running anyone down? No, she didn't want to believe it. "I thought you had assumed the accident was a case of drunk driving."

"Drunks seldom drive straight. All the witnesses at the scene agreed that this driver didn't swerve."

"But—"

"Mrs. Graye, I wouldn't normally be discussing the details of an ongoing investigation with you because I need to be careful about treading on a suspect's rights. I'm making an exception in this case because I'm concerned for your safety."

Delaney automatically reached for a denial. "I find it hard to believe that Elizabeth's grief could have taken her that far. Bringing a lawsuit was understandable. In a way, so was sending the photographs. My stepdaughter is much more emotional than she likes to admit. But harassment is a huge leap away from trying to physically harm me."

"You just said she was emotional."

"Yes, but she's not . . ." She paused as she searched for the word. "Evil," she said finally.

"It's true that she has no record of violent behavior, but that's no guarantee. It's been my experience that given the right circumstances, anyone can be capable of violence."

"But you have no proof."

"Correct. At this stage I'm still checking into the facts and can't justify giving you police protection. It's up to you to take precautions. Be aware of your surroundings when you go out in public. Since there is already a restraining order in place against your stepdaughter, we can have her arrested if she approaches you."

Matters were escalating too fast. Every instinct told her Elizabeth couldn't have had anything to do with the hit-and-run, but her instincts hadn't proved all that reliable. She'd also once believed that her husband had loved her. She struggled to think logically. "Wait. Elizabeth couldn't have known I was at the festival in the first place. No one did. I decided at the last minute to accompany my grandmother."

"Would you have noticed if someone had followed you from the house?"

No, she wouldn't have noticed. It had been raining, and she'd had no reason to be suspicious. Besides, she'd been thinking about Stanford, not his daughter, and about what she'd remembered.

"Mrs. Graye?"

"You believe there's a link between the photographs and the hit-and-run. Elizabeth isn't the only one who might have sent me those pictures."

"Please explain."

"I should have told you about this earlier, but I think that those photographs weren't meant to simply hurt me; they were to discourage me from recovering my memories." She cleared her throat. "My husband had been having an affair with one of my friends. There had been other women, too. I don't remember whether or not I learned who they were. Any one of them might not want that information made public. And for all I know, there could be something else altogether about the night my husband died that I should remember but I don't."

There was a pause. A movement outside the window caught her eye. A gust of wind billowed the loose corner of a sheet, sending it above Helen's head. Phoebe laughed and hauled it down. Delaney hoped Toffelmire would tell her she was wrong, that she was only being paranoid, that he had overreacted and no one would really be trying to hurt her. Because if she truly was at risk, that would mean the people around her weren't safe, either. They could get in the way as John had.

"Let's start with your friend's name. And in the future," he said, "be sure to tell me immediately if you remember anything else."

FIRE STREAKED ACROSS MAX'S BACK. IT BURROWED through his skin to the place where the other pain was buried. It was the belt. Virgil had returned. It was starting all over again . . .

Max jerked awake. The stink of burning flesh hung over the bed. Flames curled up the posts at the corners, painting the wood orange and red. This wasn't his bed, it was Delaney's. She lay beside him, facing away, her nightgown twisted around her legs, her arms locked around her knees. He grabbed her shoulder. "Deedee!"

She was shaking. Despite the fire, her teeth were chattering. "Max! Help me!"

He slid against her back, spooning his body behind hers to shelter her from the flames. "It's okay. You're safe."

"I'm not. No one is." A canopy of fire arched overhead. From it came the din of crunching metal. "Max!"

He looped his good arm around her to grasp her hand. "Hang on to me. We'll go together."

She twined her fingers with his, her grip fierce. "Where?"

"Hilltop. Pine trees."

"The smoke—"

"It's only mist. It's blowing past us. Smell the pine."

"It burns."

"No, that's only the sunset. It's orange and red. I painted the sky for you. Look."

"I want to. The water's pulling me. The mud won't let me go. I can't breathe."

"There's no mud, only the bed." He rubbed his nose against her hair. "Soft. So soft."

"He's screaming. Again. Don't you hear him?"

"It's the breeze in the pines. The boughs are creaking and whispering."

"Max!"

"Let go of the nightmare, Deedee. Hang on to me."

She curled their joined hands to her mouth, pressing his arm to her breasts as she molded herself to his angles. Her mind opened.

This time the transition wasn't gradual. She knew how to build their private world and fused her strength with his. Their thoughts fitted together as closely as he imagined fitting their bodies.

The scene burst full-blown in his head. They were still in the bed, but it was on top of a rounded hill. A massive pine tree rose above them, its branches silhouetted against a sky streaked with sunset colors. Dusk hid the valley below in gentle shades of lavender. Mist blurred the horizon.

The nightmare was gone, yet Delaney continued to tremble. Max concentrated on the sensation of holding her, using his thoughts to reinforce his embrace. "It's okay. It's over."

She kissed his knuckles. A tear fell on his thumb.

"Hey." He stroked her cheek. "The nightmare's gone. It can't hurt you. Nothing hurts here."

"I know."

"Don't cry."

"I tried to deflect it. I understand why I dream about drowning and burning, but it still happens. I hate this. I wish it would stop."

"You're safe now, Deedee."

"I'm always safe with you." She hugged his arm more tightly. Her shudders tapered off as her body relaxed. For a while, it seemed as if she might slip back into sleep, yet he could tell she was awake because the world they'd created remained vivid. "Max?"

"Yeah?"

"Why haven't you answered me? Why did you keep away?"

Aw, hell. He'd resisted the temptation for days. He'd almost convinced himself he could stay away from her, but the instant he'd sensed she needed him, the decision had been out of his hands; he'd already been here. "It doesn't matter. It's late. Go back to sleep."

"I'd rather stay with you."

"Deedee—"

"I've missed you, Max."

"You mean you've missed what I can do for you."

"Haven't you missed me?"

"Sure." He withdrew his arm from her grasp and rolled to his back. "Who wouldn't enjoy getting woken up from a sound sleep to get fried in someone else's nightmare?"

"Yet you came anyway."

"I never claimed I was smart."

The mattress creaked softly as she turned over to face him. She lifted her hand to stroke his hair from his forehead and trace the edge of the bandage. She made no attempt to hide her confusion.

He should have gotten rid of the bandage. He should have lost the elastic cloth that wrapped his wrist, too. It would have been as easy as creating the hill and the pine tree. Only, she'd been responsible for imagining this scene as much as he was. *She* wanted to see him this way.

"Does it hurt?" she asked, tapping the bandage.

"Not now. Nothing hurts when we're in this place."

"How did it happen?"

"You made me up. You tell me."

She continued her inspection, studying the bruising on his shoulder, touching his wrapped wrist. She got to his waist and inhaled sharply. Her gaze returned to his.

He stretched out and crossed his ankles. "I could imagine some pants, but you've seen it all before."

"And you've seen me." She touched the spot where the scar on her breast disappeared beneath the edge of her nightgown. "Max, did I really make you up?"

"Why are you asking me that? I thought you had it all figured out."

"So did I."

He ran his forefinger along her nightgown strap. "The last time I saw you, you asked me to kiss you."

Her breath hitched. "Max . . ."

"Did you like how it felt?"

"You know I did."

He traced her neckline to the shadow between her breasts. "Where do you want me to kiss you this time, Deedee?"

"Max, stop. I don't want sex."

"We don't really have sex. We just think about it."

She caught his hand. "Are you John?"

His pulse leapt. He should have expected the question. In fact, he'd half wanted it after the dance they'd done around the truth when she'd come to his house. "Who?"

"He's a real man. He has a sprained wrist and a scraped forehead and he looks exactly like you."

"Poor guy."

"Yes, he is."

"You sound as if you feel sorry for him."

"He's so alone. I don't think he really wants to be."

"Oh, yeah?"

"It's my guess that he's been given a hard time by so many people that he's decided he'd rather push them away than give them a chance."

"What's this? You finished psychoanalyzing yourself and you've decided to start working on him?"

She sat up and swung her legs off the bed. She walked to the pine tree and braced her palm against the trunk. "I'm a long way from being finished, Max. The fact that I needed my imaginary friend to pull me out of my nightmare again proves it."

The boughs above her blurred as the sky began to dim. So did the sensation of the mattress beneath his back. He nudged his thoughts closer to hers until the scene regained its substance, then went to stand behind her. He slid his arms around her waist. "What brought on the nightmare this time?"

"Insanity."

"I told you, Deedee. There's nothing wrong with having a powerful mind."

"No, I mean the world. People I thought I knew, I didn't know at all."

He rested his chin on her shoulder. "You're talking about your husband."

"Him and Elizabeth and Jenna." She touched his swollen wrist. "That's probably why I gave you John's injuries. The hit-and-run was my fault. He was hurt because of me."

"Don't beat yourself up. Shit happens."

She shook her head. "It might not have been an accident."

"What?"

"The detective who's investigating suspects my stepdaughter tried to run me down."

"Why the hell would anyone think that?"

"Why do you need to ask? You're my subconscious. You should already know."

"Humor me."

She related what Toffelmire had told her. Max listened in growing alarm. The cop might be a pain in the ass, but it sounded as if he was right to issue a warning. Max's arms tightened reflexively, though he knew that he wasn't actually holding her. His thoughts alone couldn't shelter her from perils in the real world. He'd have to be here in the flesh to do that. "Damn, how could anyone want to hurt you?"

"The answer has to be in my memory." She thumped the heel of her hand against her temple. "But I'm still blocking it."

"The cops should arrest your stepdaughter."

"They don't have enough evidence, and she's not the only one who might have done it." She turned in his embrace. Her eyes shone. "I need to remember. The nightmare won't end until I do."

"Deedee—"

"I was wrong." She ran her palms across his chest. "I do want sex."

"Let me guess. To help break your mental block, right?"

"Yes."

"You don't need me for that."

"Yes I do!"

"Did you remember anything the last time?"

"No, but it's helped before."

"And you'll use whatever works."

"Kiss me, Max."

He should be angry. They'd been through this already. She saw him as a tool, a key, not a man.

Yet that was his own choice, wasn't it? She was right; he'd rather be alone than risk the consequences of a real-life relationship. He was the one who wouldn't end the charade.

She slid her hands to his groin. "Please."

Instinct took over. It made no difference why she wanted this. He was enough of a bastard to oblige.

TWENTY-ONE

DELANEY CARRIED THE STAINLESS STEEL BOWL OF ORANGE peels, coffee grounds, and eggshells toward the compost bin behind the garden shed. For as long as she could remember, Helen had been composting her kitchen scraps, not only for the sake of the environment but because the compost was good for her roses. It was part of the daily routine. Delaney had done it dozens of times since she'd come home and thought nothing of it.

Only this morning, the door of the garden shed was open.

She focused on the shadowed interior, her steps slowing. She didn't like being afraid. She resented it. Edgar had told her it had probably been kids who had been in the shed before. There was a chance the process server had been watching the house from there before he'd snuck into the house. She couldn't picture Elizabeth hiding amid the garden tools and the cobwebs, though, waiting to pounce. She couldn't see any of Stanford's lovers doing so, either. He'd been too fastidious. He wouldn't have had an affair with the type of woman who would skulk in garden sheds.

So there was no reason to feel nervous, she told herself, firming her grip on the bowl. She stopped at the shed and poked her head inside.

No one was there. Of course, no one was there, only the lawn mower, some bags of fertilizer, and the garden tools. Nothing more threatening than some rakes and a few shovels that hung from the wall. She was being paranoid, likely due to lack of sleep.

Or did a fantasy count as sleep? After all, she'd been on a bed.

No, there had been nothing restful about last night's fantasy. Max had managed to stimulate every nerve in her body and every synapse in her brain. He'd wrung one climax after another from her mind with nothing but kisses. Imaginary kisses. Yet this morning she was exhausted and aching as if she'd spent the entire night having sex.

We don't really have sex. We just think about it.

And now she couldn't stop thinking about it. What was wrong with her?

But she hadn't been seeking pleasure; she'd been seeking memories.

There. See? She'd had a perfectly rational reason for the fantasy sex. A logical reason. Unfortunately, in spite of Max's best efforts, she hadn't remembered a thing. Drat.

She went to the compost bin, lifted the lid, and banged the bowl hard on the edge. A wasp buzzed past her hand. The scent of rotting vegetables and old grass clippings hit her like a slap of reality. She replaced the lid fast, pressing her lips tight against a desire to laugh.

It wasn't funny; it was pathetic. The years of being married to Stanford must have left her starved for affection. Either that, or she was finding a new avenue for denial. Sure, why worry about whether someone was trying to harm her? That was definitely unpleasant. It was much better to channel her energy into the arms of a make-believe lover.

The hair on her arms tingled beneath her blouse. She glanced over her shoulder toward the back gate.

A tall, dark-haired man was coming up the path that led to the pond.

Good God, she must have conjured him up by thinking of him. "Max?"

His right arm was in the sling across his waist. He placed his left hand on the gate and lifted his face. Blue eyes met hers.

And she remembered how his eyes had glowed as he'd rubbed his teeth over her hip bone.

The bowl slipped from her fingers and bounced on the grass. She wiped her palms on her skirt. "Max, I didn't mean to call you."

The gate creaked loudly as he pulled it open.

"This isn't a good time . . ." She stopped. The gate had creaked. He'd swung it on its hinges.

Max couldn't move things. His touch felt real in her fantasies, but he had no physical presence except in her mind. What happened in the world they created was merely an extension of her imagination. She understood that. So she couldn't have just seen him open an iron gate.

He stepped onto the lawn and strode toward her. His shoes connected firmly with the ground. His shirt was pearl gray and had the liquid drape of fine cotton. The breeze rippled the fabric against his chest and arms. The bandage on his forehead was stark white in the sunshine. No stray lock of hair covered it this morning. His hair was combed straight back from his face.

It wasn't Max; it was John Harrison.

Then why was he watching her as if he knew she was picturing him naked?

Maybe because she was staring at him with her mouth open and her cheeks burning. God, she would have thought she was too old to blush.

She left the bowl where it had fallen and walked forward. "Good morning, John," she called. She paused to wait for him in the shade cast by the big oak. "This is a surprise. How are you today? You must be feeling better if you decided to take a walk. At least, I hope you are. But I suppose there are plenty of activities you can do with a sprained wrist." She heard herself babbling and cringed inwardly. Wasn't the blush bad enough?

"Yeah," he said. "You'd be surprised what I can do."

The injuries she'd imagined Max having hadn't hampered him much, either. His arms had felt as strong as always. He'd seemed to enjoy it when she'd kissed his bruises. She thought of the discolored flesh on John's shoulder, the broad chest, the line of soft, dark hair that led past his navel . . .

"See something you like?"

She jerked her gaze away from his pants. They were similar to the pleated pair he'd worn at the festival. They were almost identical to the ones Max had worn the first time she'd met him at the pond. He hadn't worn a belt then, either.

And his question was word-for-word what Max had asked her the first time she'd seen him naked.

This had to be more than coincidence. How could two men be so much alike? Her instincts were screaming with recognition, regardless of how insane the idea was.

What if it *was* possible? What if there really was such a thing as a psychic connection between two complete strangers?

What if her deepest wish had come true, and Max actually existed?

No, it was crazy. Impossible. She had to get a grip.

Yet now that she'd allowed herself to think it, the idea wouldn't go away. Her heart pounded so hard it stole her breath. What if? What if?

"I brought back your towel," John said.

What if she was simply punchy from lack of sleep?

He reached into his sling with his left hand and brought out the linen tea towel that she'd wrapped around the banana bread she'd taken to him. It had been folded into a square and appeared to have been washed. "Thought you might want it."

"Oh. Thanks."

"You're a good cook."

"Thanks."

"Were you thinking about him?"

"Who?"

"The friend I remind you of."

"When?" She had to stop speaking in monosyllables.

"When you were staring at my crotch."

She took the towel from his hand. "Do you enjoy trying to make me uncomfortable?"

"What would you like me to make you feel, Delaney?"

"I suspect that depends on you, John."

"Why?"

"I have to wonder why you want to shock me."

"Shock you? You were the one ogling my pants."

"Okay, fine. I was thinking about him."

"Then he must be good in the sack."

"He's a fabulous lover. Everything I could dream of. More than that, he's the very best friend I've ever had. I've loved him from the moment we met."

He snorted. Just as Max did whenever she mentioned love. "That doesn't mean much. You said you were a kid when you met."

"Children are capable of all the feelings adults have, only they're less complicated."

"Sure. They don't have choices. They don't know any better."

"My friend often pretends to be cynical, too."

"Pretends?"

"I know in his heart he's the same boy I remember."

"He told you this?"

"No, he's been showing me. He might snarl and posture sometimes to show he's tough, but he's always there when I need him."

He shoved his hand into his pants pocket. "Sounds like you need a cocker spaniel, not a man."

"Max."

He lifted one eyebrow.

"That's his name," she said.

"You want me to be honest?"

"I'd like nothing better."

"I didn't come here to listen to you talk about another man."

"He's so much like you, I get confused."

"You don't know me. We only met two days ago."

"But I feel as if I do know you, John. You snarl and posture just like Max, but you can't hide who you really are."

"And who do you think I am, Delaney?"

"You're a good person."

He laughed. "You must have hit your head harder than I did. Didn't anyone at the hospital check you out for a concussion?"

"I'm not wrong. Otherwise, you wouldn't have risked your life to push a stranger out of the way of a car. You wouldn't have the sensitivity to be able to design such a beautiful house. You wouldn't have encouraged a sweet little old lady to pursue a career in fabric art, and you wouldn't have worried about judging the crafts category fairly at the festival. That's what I've seen in two days." She searched his expression, watching for a glimpse of Max, wishing that her brain could confirm what her heart was telling her. "I do know you."

"Okay, honey. Next time you drop by my place, I'll unzip and you can know me a hell of a lot better."

"Don't be hateful."

"Hateful? You wouldn't recognize hate if it bit you in the

butt. You'd probably make some excuse and deny anything hurt."

"How can you say that if you claim you don't know me?"

"I'll tell you what I've seen in two days. I've seen you flit around like a butterfly, brushing your smiles over anyone who crosses your path as if the world is basically good, playing Betty Crocker for an ex-con as if warm banana bread and ten minutes of being neighborly can change who I am."

He hadn't raised his voice throughout his outburst. His words had all the more impact because of his control.

And for some reason, it made her throat ache. He *was* lonely. He *was* pushing her away.

She laid her fingers on the sling where it covered his forearm. "You weren't listening. I don't want to change who you are."

"Sure, you do. You're looking for a stand-in for this friend of yours. You figure I'll do, so you'll use me until you get what you need, and then you'll flit off without a backward glance."

"If you think so little of me, why did you come here this morning?"

"Mainly, I wanted to volunteer my services." He glanced at where she touched him. "But now I'm thinking there are a whole lot of services I could offer you."

She dropped her arm to her side. "What did you have in mind?"

"If you need to go out, give me a call, and I'll ride shotgun."

It was the last thing she would have expected, especially after the turn the conversation had taken. "I don't understand. Why in the world would you do that?"

"My schedule's flexible. Someone should keep an eye on you in case that hit-and-run wasn't an accident."

"How would you know it might not have been an accident?"

"Sounds like you don't believe it was, either."

"Toffelmire suspects it could have been deliberate. Did he tell you that, too?"

"He didn't have to. I got to thinking about the way he slanted his questions at the hospital, and it wasn't hard to figure out."

"Thank you, but I can take care of myself."

"Hate to break it to you, Delaney, but you're not batting a thousand when it comes to self-preservation."

"Then you wouldn't mind if I pointed out that you're not in any condition to act as someone's bodyguard."

"You want references? My old cell mate can tell you I know how to watch someone's back. Besides, saving your ass could get to be a habit."

"While I appreciate your concern, if the situation does get to the point where I need protection, I'll hire a security service. You don't need to feel responsible for my safety. I'm already far too much in your debt."

"Yeah, that's true." His eyes gleamed. "How about posing nude for me, and we'll call it even?"

"You're trying to make me uncomfortable again. Why? Is it to hide the fact that you offered to do something nice?"

"I'm not hiding anything. I'm an artist. I appreciate beauty, and I'd like to see more of yours."

It wasn't an invitation, it was another push. Was she merely seeing what she wanted to see again? So desperate not to be alone that she was making excuses for John's behavior? Logic told her his offer to protect her probably wasn't sincere. It could be another attempt to unsettle her. "That's not going to happen," she said.

"Too bad." He looked at her breasts. "I would have made sure you enjoyed yourself."

She crossed her arms. "Good-bye, John."

"See you around, Delaney."

She watched him go. He swung the gate closed behind him without glancing back. His image didn't fade or grow hazy; he walked away like regular people did until the woods hid him from her view, because he was a real man.

Sighing, she turned back to the house. She squinted at a flash of sunlight from the stainless steel bowl she'd dropped on the lawn. She peered at the light in the distance as her phone began to ring . . .

What light? And she didn't have her phone with her. It was in her bedroom.

The sound of the phone startled her. She'd assumed it was in her purse, along with her money and her credit cards. She'd forgotten she'd dropped it on the floor of the car before she'd gone into the house with Stanford.

Delaney's pulse was already elevated from her encounter

with John. She sucked in a deep breath, striving for calm. She wouldn't reach for the memory this time. She couldn't force it. That never worked. She had to let go and trust herself, believe that the rest would come.

Slowly and deliberately, she lowered herself to the lawn. She was still near enough to the oak tree to be within its pool of shade. The grass was cool beneath her legs. The heated seat warmed her back while more warmth from the dashboard heater blew over her feet. She twisted the dish towel in her hand as she turned the steering wheel to the right.

The pavement was slick with melted snow. It gleamed in her headlights as she rounded the bend. In the distance the lighted sign of a gas station glowed in the darkness. The highway was deserted; she felt more alone than ever in her life. The sound of her phone was like another light in the darkness. She pulled to a stop on the shoulder so she could answer it.

For the second time that night, the voice she heard was Elizabeth's.

"He called the police, Delaney. You won't get far."

"I'm not stealing the car!"

"Technically, you are, which is why he didn't hesitate to enlist the police. If you don't know what my father is capable of by now, then you obviously should never have married him."

"Did you call to gloat?"

"No, I called to help."

"Why should you help me?"

"Because you're leaving my father, and that's what I've wanted from the day you married him. Tell me where to meet you, and I'll take you wherever you say."

Delaney's eyes filled. For five years she'd tried to be friends with Elizabeth. She would have given anything to hear the earnestness in her voice that she heard now. She would have loved to win her cooperation. How ironic that this was the price.

She blinked away the tears and focused on the gas station. The lights above the pumps were off and the building was dark—it appeared to be closed for the night. Her stepdaughter was right. Whether or not Stanford had reported his car stolen, she wouldn't get far in it. There wasn't enough gas in the tank to make it all the way to Willowbank, and even if the station up ahead had been open, she had no means to buy more. "You would really do this for me?"

"Not for you, Delaney. What I'm doing, I do for me."

She didn't want to trust her, yet she couldn't think of a reason why Elizabeth would be lying. It was she who had triggered the events of the evening, so she had plenty of motivation to help them through to their conclusion.

"What's going on?"

Delaney tightened her grip on the towel. And it was once again a towel, not a steering wheel or a phone. She glanced up.

John had returned and was standing in front of her.

She waved him away and squeezed her eyes shut. She pictured the Jaguar, the winter night.

His knee bumped her thigh as he knelt beside her. "Delaney?"

Headlights flashed in her rearview mirror. The white BMW pulled into the gas station and came to a stop behind the Jaguar. Delaney unlocked her door and stepped out before she realized that Elizabeth wasn't alone.

"Where are you?" It was John's voice again, cutting through the memories, pulling her back to the yard.

She put her hands over her ears. "Go away!"

"Hey, I thought you needed my help."

"You said you'd help me, Elizabeth!" Delaney slapped her palm against the driver's side window of the BMW. "You said you wanted me to leave."

Elizabeth kept her hands on the wheel. She spoke through the glass. "I made a deal with my father."

"Elizabeth!"

She threw the car into reverse and backed away. Her wheels spun on the wet pavement as she accelerated onto the highway.

Stanford caught Delaney's arm. "Don't blame her, darling. I can be very persuasive."

"You're two of a kind. I was a fool to trust either one of you."

"You must have known I was the one who asked her to call you. Deep down you wanted the chance to sort this out."

She broke away. "We had five years to talk."

"Which is why we can't end it like this." He put his hands in his pockets and hunched his shoulders. The light at the entrance of the gas station shone full on his face, draining it of color. The self-assurance he normally draped himself with was gone. He appeared every day of his seventy-three years. "Please, Delaney. I'm begging you. Give me an hour, that's all I ask."

"Stanford—"

"One hour. If you still want to leave, I won't stop you."

Elizabeth's taillights had disappeared. The highway was once again black. Delaney was in the middle of nowhere. She had no money and was almost out of gas. Unless she decided to walk to Willowbank, she had no option but to believe him.

"It's cold," he said, his voice quavering. "Let's talk in the car."

She shivered as the memory faded.

Warmth flowed over her hands. She opened her eyes.

John had taken his arm from his sling and had enclosed her hands with both of his.

The contact with his skin was electric. Tingles chased through her nerves, just as when Max touched her, yet the sensation was more intense than anything her imagination could have created. This was living flesh against living flesh, and the connection was so powerful it made her head spin.

John leaned closer. "What happened?"

"I know how Stanford got in the car. Elizabeth set it up. She'd claimed he'd called the police but she lied to me. So did he. I should have kept going, even if I'd needed to walk, but I felt sorry for him because he looked so old and sad, and damn it, she knew all this. She could have told me months ago. I don't understand—"

"Who the hell is Stanford?"

She stopped. Max knew. John wouldn't. God, this was too confusing. "Stanford was my husband."

"The old and sad guy."

"He wasn't—"

"Who's Elizabeth?"

"My stepdaughter. She might have been the one who hit you."

"And I thought my family was dysfunctional."

Without thinking, she slipped her hands from his grasp to cradle his face.

He appeared as startled by the caress as she was. "Delaney?"

The square edges of his jaw fit into her palms the same way Max's did. The scent that rose from his skin was the same as Max's. His nostrils flared, his eyes darkened, like Max's, yet there was no distance, no disconnect between her thoughts and the man in front of her. He was *real*.

She wasn't conscious of making a decision. Her instincts took over. His muttered curse puffed across her lips a heartbeat before her mouth touched his.

It wasn't Max's kiss. It didn't bypass her senses. It was a kiss of the here and now, of reality, of firm, male lips and the taste of coffee and toothpaste, of soft grass beneath her legs and warm skin under her fingers. No phantom pleasure burst through her mind, because her mind wasn't involved. Only her body. The connection was purely physical. Man to woman, with a need as simple as the desire to eat or to breathe.

Yet she was certain she'd felt his mouth before, not in her imagination but in her memory. His lips had been cool as he'd fitted them to hers. She'd felt his breath before, too. It had been warm, like his arms, and like his fingers as he'd wiped her tears.

The whirling in her head got worse. She pulled away and sat back on her heels. "I'm sorry. I don't know what came over me. I . . ." She swallowed. "I was thinking of someone else."

The breeze tossed his hair over his forehead. The boughs overhead swayed, sending dapples of sunlight that softened his face. He seemed younger, like the lost boy she'd thought she'd glimpsed the day before. "No problem," he rasped. He gripped her thigh, bunching her skirt under his hand. His jaw worked, as if he fought the urge to say more. In the end, he exhaled slowly, met her gaze, and smiled. "Anytime."

This was the first time she had seen John smile. It deepened the lines beside his mouth and crinkled the corners of his eyes. It fully revealed the crooked front tooth that she knew so well, the one that had straightened since his childhood but not completely, leaving indisputable evidence of the boy he used to be in the man he was now.

John Harrison hadn't been smiling in the photograph that had been taken for the Mapleview Gallery brochure. There was no possible way she could have guessed that he had a crooked front tooth.

Yet she'd always known he did, because this *wasn't* the first time she'd seen him smile. No, the first time he'd smiled for her, she'd been lying flat on her back at the shore of the pond, and he'd been kneeling beside her, his hair stuck to his head with water. His white T-shirt and the jeans that were too big for him were plastered to his skinny frame with mud and bits of seaweed and . . .

And he'd wiped her tears and told her not to cry and said his name was Max.

TWENTY-TWO

❧

MAX DROPPED A FISTFUL OF ICE INTO A GLASS AND regretted having no alcohol to offer. Delaney appeared as if she could use some. He topped up the ice with water and carried the glass to the sitting area in front of the fireplace.

She hadn't moved from the leather couch where he'd left her. She'd barely spoken during the walk to his house, though thankfully some of the color had returned to her face. She was working things through, but he could tell by the stiffness in her body that she hadn't yet lost the battle with her logic.

He'd given up his own battle already. Otherwise, he would have phoned her this morning instead of going to see her in person. He wouldn't have returned to the yard when he'd sensed her distress, either. He wouldn't have given in to his craving and touched her skin, and he sure as hell wouldn't have let her kiss him.

This wasn't smart. He didn't need this girl from his past, stirring up his memories, messing with his head, slipping into his thoughts. He didn't need the complications or the pain.

But it was too late for denial or for more games. In truth, this moment had been inevitable. The only wonder was that it had taken this long.

She took the glass from his hand mechanically and drank without looking at it. "It's all so unbelievable." She spoke aloud, as they had been doing since she'd recognized him. "I don't know where to begin."

"Okay, I'll start. Why did you kiss me?"

She pressed her lips into a tight line.

"You knew who I was."

"Maybe in here," she said, tapping her chest with her free hand. She moved her hand to her temple. "But not here. It was too twilight zone. Maybe I've gone right around the bend, and I'm imagining everything that's happening now."

He sat beside her and laced their fingers together. They had twined their thoughts far more intimately. He'd almost convinced himself that was enough, yet it couldn't compare to the simple joining of their hands. Hearing her words in his head didn't include the impact of her voice in the air around him. Sensing her presence was a pale reflection of having the warmth of her body next to his. "This is real, Deedee."

"Why did you lie?"

"I didn't."

"You said your name was Max."

"It is. John Maxwell Harrison. I'll show you my driver's license if you don't believe me."

"But—"

"I was seven years old when I met you. Only my teachers and the cops called me John in those days. My mother called me Max, that's how I thought of myself, so that was the name I told you."

"Are you some kind of psychic? Do you talk to everybody in their heads?"

"No, just you."

"Why? How?"

"It started the day you almost drowned. You weren't breathing when I pulled you out of the water. I figure something happened in our minds when I resuscitated you. We formed a link."

"You're so calm about all this. You almost make it sound reasonable."

"I've had more time than you to accept it. I use the power of my mind every day in my art."

She set her glass down on the table beside the couch. Her head bowed, she studied their joined hands. "You gave me cake that day. You let me pet your dog. Your mother sang 'Happy Birthday.' "

"I never had a dog or a birthday cake. It was a fantasy. I thought of it as painting pictures in my head. Somehow, you saw them, too."

"It's still incredible. You were only seven, yet you saved my life. Didn't anyone know?"

"The pond was on your grandfather's property; I was trespassing, so I ran away when I heard them coming. I didn't want anyone else to see me."

She squeezed his fingers. "Oh, Max."

"I used to live here then, too. I built this house where our trailer used to be."

"Then you really did come to play with me in the yard and at my grandparents' house."

"No, I never came back. After that first time, we only saw each other in our minds."

"I thought you were make-believe."

"I hadn't realized that then."

"But you were aware of it now. Why didn't you tell me?"

"I tried. You didn't want to listen."

"You could have tried harder."

"What difference would it have made?"

She lifted her head. "What difference? Don't you think I had the right to know?"

"You wanted to use me. I let you. You seemed happy enough the way things were."

"Happy? I thought I was going insane!"

"Sure, but you enjoyed yourself, didn't you? What did you call it? Fantasy orgasms?"

She yanked her hand from his. "You came to my bedroom. You made love to my mind."

"I'm a man, not a boy. What did you expect me to do? Make mud pies?"

"That's not fair."

"I warned you."

"You knew I didn't believe you."

"You weren't ready to believe me, or else you wouldn't have concocted all those screwy excuses to explain me away."

"You took advantage of me."

"No, Delaney. Our fantasies only work if we both power them. You were an equal participant. You came to me of your own free will."

"You're the one making excuses now. We met in person

three days ago. You had plenty of opportunities since then to tell me the truth."

"Why should I? Neither of us wants a real relationship. You were clear about that the first time you saw me naked. Your priority has always been your scumbag of a dead husband. You're obsessed with remembering him."

"You're purposely twisting things. It's what led to his death that I need to remember."

"What's the difference? You still wanted to use me."

"So instead of acknowledging me when I called to you as Max, you toyed with me. You played word games. You teased me with little clues that you knew would confuse me. Did you have a good laugh?"

"It wasn't like that."

"Then how was it?"

"I thought we were better off leaving things the way they were."

"You knew damn well that if I'd understood you were real, I never would have done what we did last night."

"Yeah, I knew."

Her eyes widened.

"You're not the only one who's been enjoying our fantasy orgasms, Deedee."

"You bastard."

"Exactly."

She drew back her arm.

Max had had plenty of experience reading violence on a person's face. He knew the way the jaw flexed, the nostrils flattened, and the chin thrust forward. He'd learned to watch for those signs out of self-preservation. At first, he'd used the split-second head start so he could cower or run. Later, he'd gotten even faster at raising his own fists. He hadn't allowed himself to be struck in more than twenty years.

This time, he left his hand on his thigh and braced himself for the blow.

Because this time, he deserved it.

Yet the blow didn't come. Delaney stopped with her hand poised in midair. She remained motionless until her arm began to tremble, then she curled her fingers into her palm and lowered her arm. "No," she said finally. "That's what you want. You're trying to provoke me into severing our bond."

"What I want is another taste of your mouth, but I doubt if you're in the mood."

"You just said you didn't want a real relationship."

"That's right, I didn't, but seeing as how the truth is out, we might as well make the most of it. Have some fun. Aren't you curious to find out what would happen if we did sex the old-fashioned way?"

"You're saying this to push me away."

"Make up your mind. You just reamed me out for not pushing you away."

She got to her feet. She walked as far as the fireplace and stopped. She spoke without turning. "You might have been playing games, but I wasn't. I meant what I said, Max. I've loved you from the moment we met."

"Wrong, Deedee. You loved what you believed was a figment of your imagination, not a real boy or a real man."

"Then give me the chance to know the real man."

"I already offered to unzip."

"Stop being crude, Max. This isn't you."

"Seems to me that nothing has really changed. You're still pretending."

"And you're still trying to run away before anyone else sees you. What are you so afraid of? How can you be so reckless with this connection we share? I used to think our friendship was rare and precious, but that doesn't even begin to describe the potential of what's between us. I don't understand why you're so determined to diminish it."

"Hey, you want more, just say the word. What was it you told me? I'm a fabulous lover? Everything you could dream of?"

"Don't mock me."

"I don't want to mock you, Deedee, I just want to fuck you."

Her shoulders hunched, as if he'd physically hit her. She grasped the edge of the mantel to steady herself. *And I just want to love you, Max.*

The words tore through his head. He clung to the contact, wrapping her in his thoughts, opening his own to hers. He wasn't conscious of crossing the floor. He didn't realize his body had mirrored his mental impulse until he felt the silk of her hair on his fingers. He slid his hand to her nape, tipped her face toward his, and kissed her.

That was all he did. A simple kiss. No groping, no tongue. He didn't trick her mind into a climax or build a picture to enhance their surroundings. The pleasure that seized him came from something else altogether. A dumb chickenshit's hunger to be loved.

He wished she had slapped him after all. It would have hurt less.

TWENTY-THREE

❧

AT FIRST GLANCE, THE PAINTING APPEARED TO BE A peaceful scene from the countryside around Willowbank. A grove of apple trees, their blossoms just past their peak, dominated the foreground. Beyond them stretched the fresh green of a hayfield in early spring. Yet the longer Delaney studied it, the more she realized the peace was an illusion. Clouds billowed purple and black on the horizon, trailing shadows that swallowed the sunlight. Ragged pieces of a split-rail fence clawed at the tender shoots in the field. The trunks of the trees strained and stretched as if they were being drawn back into the ground. Between the ridges of their roots, drifts of fallen petals curled in brown-edged death. This was no idyllic landscape. It was a powerful depiction of fragility and passion and the struggle to survive.

Then again, she was no art critic. She might be reading more into it than the artist had intended. Seeing a sensitivity that wasn't there. Attributing insight where there was only cynicism. Looking for love and tenderness in a heart that was sealed shut.

She swallowed, annoyed to feel the lump had returned to her throat. She was getting weary of this need to cry. She should be concentrating on the positive. In spite of the fact that she was being sued by her stepdaughter, despite the possibility that someone might be intent on harming her, at least she wasn't insane. That was definitely a plus. There was no need to call Dr. Bernhardt or to keep making up screwy excuses, as Max had called them. Her subconscious wasn't out of control. She wasn't responsible for her friend's attitude or his behavior. She'd wished Max was real, and he was.

The signature at the lower right corner of the canvas read J. M. Harrison. He had used his middle initial. If she'd come to the gallery when she'd first seen his photograph, she would have stumbled on the truth a week ago.

She moved to the next painting. According to the card that had been fixed to the wall beside it, it was titled *Inside Deedee*.

If she'd needed more proof, this was it. He'd painted her nightmare. Flames swirled across the canvas in bold, brutal swaths. Mud sucked at their edges. The tangle of agony that wove through the brushstrokes made her scars throb in remembered pain, until her gaze moved to the center, where a beacon of pure white spread calm amid the chaos. It was another depiction of contrast and struggle. Good and evil. It wasn't clear which would win.

"Disturbing, isn't it?"

She started at the voice. She turned to find a tall woman in a striking red suit at her elbow. "It's . . ." She searched for a word. "Very dramatic."

"You could say that about all of John Harrison's work." She smiled. "I'm Shirley Flindall. My husband and I own the Mapleview Gallery."

Delaney introduced herself in turn. "I'm Helen Wainright's granddaughter," she added. "I've seen your brochures at the house."

"Of course. How is Helen?"

"Feisty as always."

"She must be busy. We've noticed an increase in our number of visitors this summer. We plan to expand into the space next door once things slow down in the winter."

"Congratulations."

"It's our policy to promote local talent, so we need more room. We have several very promising area artists."

"Yes, I noticed there's quite a variety here."

"If you do decide you'd like one of John's paintings, better not wait too long."

"They sell well?"

"Yes, and we're lucky to be able to offer what we do."

"I'm not sure I understand."

"He has an arrangement with a gallery in New York City that handles the bulk of his work. We couldn't hope to reach such a large market here."

"Is the gallery in Manhattan?"

"Yes. How did you know?"

That was where Max had claimed he'd gone once when she'd asked him where he'd been. He'd told her the truth about that, too, only she hadn't been ready to believe it. "A friend mentioned it."

"In spite of his success, he hasn't forgotten how difficult it is to build a reputation," Shirley continued. "He drops off a few pieces every now and then to help draw in customers for our others artists."

"I see. That's . . . nice of him."

The bell over the front entrance tinkled. Shirley glanced past her and blinked. "John, what a pleasant surprise. We were just talking about you."

Delaney didn't turn around. She didn't need to. She'd been feeling Max's presence since she'd walked into the gallery. Now it burst across her back like sunshine.

"Should I be worried?" he asked, drawing closer.

Shirley laughed. "We were both admiring the piece you brought in last week."

His footsteps stopped behind her. "Hello, Delaney."

She found herself debating what to call him. She settled on the truth. "John Maxwell."

"Do you like the painting?"

"I'm surprised you did it."

"Why?"

"I would have thought you had enough material in your own imagination without stealing from someone else."

His arm brushed her shoulder as he moved beside her. "I didn't steal; I was invited to share."

"Invited? You complained about being disturbed from a sound sleep."

"Uh-huh. Seems fair to me I should make some money off it."

"Well, I'm happy I could be of use to you. It's interesting that you would criticize me for doing the same."

Shirley looked from one to the other. "I hadn't realized you two were acquainted."

"We're neighbors," Delaney said.

"Oh, I see. Is there a problem with *Inside Deedee*? It sounded to me as if you were questioning its authenticity."

"Not at all," Delaney said. "There's no one else in the world who could have done this except J. M. Harrison. That fact is staring me in the face."

Shirley chatted with them for a few more minutes. She appeared aware of the strain between them and stuck to innocuous subjects in an attempt to defuse it. When the bell over the door announced another customer, she excused herself with obvious relief and went to greet the new arrival.

Delaney finally looked at Max.

She'd had more than twenty-four hours to get accustomed to the fact that he was real. It couldn't have completely sunk in. Her pulse leapt at the sight of him. She found it hard to catch her breath. She'd once thought that she'd been the one who had made him sexy. No matter how powerful her imagination was, she should have realized she never could have created a man as attractive as this one.

He wore what she was coming to think of as his going-out clothes: polished leather shoes, tailored pants, and a silk shirt, all in black today. As usual, he wore no tie or belt or any jewelry for adornment. His features were arresting enough on their own. He'd replaced the white gauze bandage on his forehead with a smaller, flesh-toned one. Though his right wrist was still wrapped, he'd discarded his sling altogether. There was no sign of discomfort in his stance. She hoped it meant the aches from his bruises were easing. She'd felt his pain when he'd kissed her.

But she didn't want to think about that kiss, or she was liable to start pretending again. He was watching her as if he was as starved for their connection as she was. Not the physical one he'd claimed he wanted but the bond of mind and emotion.

Or was she seeing what she wanted to see? She'd come to the gallery hoping to gain some insight into the adult Max through his paintings. All she'd learned so far was that there was much more she had yet to learn. "Why are you here?" she asked.

"I volunteered to watch your ass when you went out, remember?"

"I didn't think you'd meant it."

"Like I said, it's a habit."

"Under the circumstances, I would have expected you to change your mind."

He shrugged. "I'm partial to your ass."

"How did you even know where I was? Did you follow me?"

"I followed your thoughts. I recognized your surroundings."

She rubbed her eyes. That must have been the reason she'd felt his presence. She'd assumed it was because she'd been looking at his work. "I find this awkward."

"Why? I've got clothes on this time."

"Things have changed, Max. You don't have the right to dip into my thoughts whenever you please."

"I didn't dip, I just looked. I don't need permission for that. It's the difference between looking at your mouth and pushing my tongue into it."

Her lips warmed. She pressed them together.

He ran his fingertip over her shoulder and down to the edge of the scar that curled around her upper arm. Though her blouse hid it from sight, he accurately traced its outline with his knuckles.

The repercussions of Max being real continued to mount. He was the only person besides her doctors who was fully aware of the disfigurement of her body. He'd seen her scars exposed in full sunlight—he'd even imagined kissing them— yet he continued to want to touch her.

No, he didn't just want to touch her, he wanted to *fuck* her.

It still hurt. She didn't want to believe that her Max could be bad or mean. His crudeness had been a warning snarl. He didn't want to admit he might need her emotionally, so he'd tried to reduce the bond they shared to its lowest level.

And she was continuing to make excuses.

She gestured toward the canvas, breaking the contact with his hand. "What does the white in the center mean, Max?"

"It means my palette knife slipped."

"Would you like to know what I think?"

"Sure, why not?"

"I believe it means hope. You recognized that ugliness doesn't have to win, no matter how terrible the odds appear.

There's a core of goodness inside us that has the potential to triumph."

"And you got all that from a few smears of paint?"

"You did the same thing with that orchard," she said, moving back to stand in front of the other painting. "The blossoms die, but new ones will take their places. The trees will still be trees; they won't change their nature, no matter how many storms batter them or how much they strain to escape the earth."

"You could have a career writing blurbs for art catalogues."

"Why did you come back to Willowbank, Max?"

"I liked the climate."

"Why build your house on the site of the old trailer park?"

"The property wasn't scenic and didn't have waterfront, so it was cheap."

"I have told you the most personal things about my marriage and about my life. I've never held back. Don't you think you could drop the tough-guy act long enough to give me an honest answer?"

He didn't respond.

"All right, I'll tell you what I think about that, too."

"This should be good."

"You knew you wouldn't be welcomed here. You deliberately chose the hardest path in order to punish yourself."

"Your do-it-yourself psychology is way off base with that one."

"Then correct me."

"I came here to bury my past. I built my house where I did to obliterate the memories of the place I grew up. You said that walking inside my house was like taking a deep breath, and that's a good description. It's freedom. That's all I need."

"You need love, too, Max."

"Love is a myth."

"Yes, you've said that before, but the boy I knew was capable of it. I loved him, and he loved me."

"Deedee—"

"Neither of us had any agenda then. We weren't using each other. We trusted each other. We were true friends."

"Are you still harping on that? We were *kids*."

"You know what happened to me. Tell me what happened

to turn the boy I knew into the man who would create paintings like these."

"It's no secret. I was arrested for two counts of attempted murder. I pled guilty to aggravated assault. I decided to learn a trade while I was serving time, and now I'm able to throw some paint at a canvas and con a bunch of gullible art collectors into giving me money. End of story."

"You are a very frustrating person, Max."

He lifted his hand and pushed her collar aside to touch the scar on the side of her neck. His forearm brushed her breast. "If you're frustrated, I could remedy that."

She was tempted to call his bluff, though she wasn't sure why she thought he wanted more from her than sex. Maybe it was because she'd seen the emotions in his paintings.

Or maybe she was repeating the pattern of her life, clinging to the good and denying the bad. She turned away. "I need some air."

He followed her to the sidewalk. When she started walking, he fell into step beside her, placing himself between her and the curb. "I do like the climate here," he said. "I enjoy the contrasts in the cycle of the seasons."

She shouldn't be as pleased as she was. He was only talking about the weather. It wasn't much of an olive branch. Still, it was a start. "You use it as an element in your paintings."

"It's part of the fabric of a scene. Most of it isn't visual, unless it's obvious like sunshine or rain. I use it to set the tone and give a sense of place. It's one of those background things that shapes our lives and half the time we don't realize it."

"We take it for granted."

"Sure, because we can't change it."

They paused at the corner of the block. The parking lot where she'd left her car was on the street to her right. She decided to go straight instead, toward the center of town. "What else do you believe shapes our lives?"

"You're going to start getting all analytical again, aren't you?"

"Possibly."

"That could turn into a nasty habit."

"Do you believe in fate, Max?"

"I used to."

"Tell me about it. Why did you stop?"

He rested his palm at the small of her back as they moved around a couple with a baby stroller. With any other man, the contact would have been casual, but there was nothing casual about Max's touch. He rubbed his thumb along her backbone, sending echoes of the same pressure around her ribs and down to her thighs as if he was reaching beneath her clothes . . .

She glanced at him sharply. "Max."

"Mmm?"

"You're doing that to avoid my question."

"You won't like my answer."

"You haven't been happy with a lot of the things I've told you, either."

He withdrew the mental caress, slid his arm around her waist, and guided her across the road where a small park bisected the block. Though the far side bordered the main street, raised beds of colorful annuals bordered by low yew hedges helped absorb the noise of the traffic. He waited until they'd found a vacant bench in the shade of a huge sycamore before he replied. "I used to think it was my destiny to kill my stepfather."

There were other people in the park, families with children, an old couple leaning on each other as they walked arm in arm along the paved pathway. A dog barked as it chased a Frisbee. It was a beautiful day. It took a moment for his words to penetrate.

He was right. She didn't like this answer and had to tamp down the reflexive urge to deny it.

Yet this was what she'd asked for, wasn't it? To know what had happened to him?

"I grew up imagining how I'd do it," he said. "I fantasized about seeing him bleed and hearing him scream. When I finally had the chance to kill him, I failed. I didn't finish him off."

"Why?"

"I was enjoying watching him suffer."

No, she didn't like this answer, either. "I meant why did you want to kill him?"

He fisted one hand on his knee. "Virgil was one of those things like the weather. Always there. Impossible to change. I was lucky they reduced the charges to assault. I lied through my teeth when I said I was sorry. The only thing I'm sorry about was that he was still breathing when the cops pulled me off him."

She covered his fist with her hand. The tension that flowed from the contact gave her goose bumps.

"I heard that liver cancer's doing what I couldn't. He could be dead now, for all I know. How's that for destiny?"

"You must have really hated him."

"The word doesn't come close, Deedee. He was . . ."

"Evil," she finished.

He lifted his shoulders. The gesture would have been a shrug if his body weren't so stiff.

"That's what I saw in your paintings," she said. "The struggle against evil, against forces that can't be controlled." And children were defenseless against the worst forms of evil. She squeezed his fist. "What did he do to you, Max?"

"He murdered my mother."

To say she was relieved with the reply wasn't right. Rather, she was less horrified than she'd feared she might have been. "I don't understand. I thought she was—"

"She was alive when I went to prison? Yeah, she was. She didn't die until a month before I was due to get out, but he'd started killing her long before that."

"What happened?"

"They moved to Cleveland after he got out of the hospital, probably because nobody knew them there so he figured he'd keep getting away with it. It worked for a while. She took what he dished out and never fought back. She never thought of leaving. She claimed she loved him."

A piece from one of their earlier conversations clicked into place. "You once told me that some women are so afraid of being alone that they stay married to a monster."

"He was that, all right. The night he killed her, he had broken both her arms first. She couldn't fight him even if she'd chosen to. She couldn't have screamed, either, because one of his blows had split the inside of her cheek and knocked out four of her teeth. She was choking on her own blood. That probably would have done it, but he couldn't wait. He used his belt to strangle her."

Bright spots blurred her vision, as if she'd looked straight into the sun. It was the spillover from Max's emotions. They were seeping into her own mind. She clasped his hand more firmly, wishing there was something she could say, but no words would be adequate. "I'm so sorry, Max."

"So am I. I should have killed him when I'd had the chance. If I had, she'd still be alive."

Another piece clicked. Phoebe had said John had beaten his mother with a belt. Delaney had never wanted to believe that, even before she'd known he was Max. Now she was certain it wasn't true. "You were innocent. You never should have gone to prison. You didn't assault her; he did."

A ghost of a smile touched his lips. "There you go again, wanting to believe the good."

"I know I'm right. You never would have hurt her. You would have tried to protect her."

"Not everyone wants to be rescued."

"Why didn't you tell anyone the truth? Why did you plead guilty?"

"I tried to tell the truth, but she testified against me. She said I beat up Virgil because he tried to stop me from beating her. She was damn convincing, too. I realized I would serve less time if I took a plea bargain."

"Your mother lied?"

A couple on a nearby bench turned toward them. Delaney lowered her voice. She was shaking with outrage. "How could she lie? Why?"

"She loved him."

"That wasn't love; that was an abused woman's dependence on her abuser." Like her love for Stanford? Though his abuse hadn't been physical, on a smaller scale the effects would have been similar: the denials, the compulsion to make excuses, the desperate attempts to please and to maintain the relationship at all costs.

The ramifications of what Max was telling her were too complex to sort through here. She would save that for later, when she had more time. Her only concern now was Max. "There must have been some way to prove the truth. Someone else must have known. Willowbank's a small town."

"I had a juvenile record because I used to get into fights; that's what the town knew. Besides, trailer park trash don't get fancy lawyers. The guy Legal Aid assigned didn't look much older than me. He seemed more scared of the judge than I was. The plea bargain was the best he could do."

"What about now? It's not too late to set the record straight."

"There's no point. The law got it right with Virgil eventually. He got convicted of second-degree murder. He roughed up a guard a few years back and got extra time tacked onto his sentence. He's going to die behind bars in the Ohio state pen while I have my freedom. Thanks to my time in prison, I've also got my art. That's all I need. I like my life the way it is."

"Let me help you. We can get your case reopened. We can—"

"What? Change me? Pretend I'm someone else?"

"The way people treat you isn't fair."

"Most of what they say about me is true, Deedee. I was innocent of only half the charges. For the rest I was guilty as hell."

"There were extenuating circumstances."

"I don't need your sympathy or your pity. I was getting along fine before you came, and I'll be fine when you leave."

"If you didn't want me to care, then why did you tell me all of this?"

He opened his fist and turned his hand over to clasp hers. "Because I figured you wouldn't have sex with me unless I did."

By now she should be accustomed to his penchant for flipping conversations when they became too emotional. Advance and retreat. He'd done it countless times. "Don't be afraid of getting close to me, Max. I would never hurt you."

"But I do want to get close, Delaney." He curled his middle finger to tickle the center of her palm. A similar sensation curled between her legs.

Her chin trembled. The sob she'd managed to suppress until now finally broke free. Not for the tragedy Max had been unable to prevent or the injustice of what he'd endured, but for the rare and precious connection that he was refusing to accept now. Calling what they could have between them *sex* was like focusing on a single raindrop and ignoring the rainbow. He was afraid of emotional closeness, and who could blame him? She opened her mind, drawing in his anger, absorbing his pain into her warmth, imagining her love like arms to shelter him.

"Well, well, I hardly recognized you, Delaney." A woman stopped in front of them. "You certainly appear to have recovered from your grief."

Max broke the contact, both the physical and the imaginary. He rose to his feet. Delaney looked past his shoulder.

Elizabeth Graye stood on the grass beside the pathway. Her blonde hair was coiled into her trademark French twist, and a tasteful string of pearls circled her neck. Her leather clutch purse, taupe linen suit, and matching pumps projected understated elegance. Her expression projected pure distaste. She glanced at Max. "My, he's a big one. Did you use my father's money to hire yourself a new toy?"

TWENTY-FOUR

❧

THE WAITRESS WAS CHEWING GUM. SHE SHIFTED IT TO ONE cheek as she put the glasses on the table. The name tag on her pink uniform said her name was Mary Lou. "Are you sure I can't get you girls something else? We've got a sour cream apple pie that's to die for."

Elizabeth refused the offer without bothering to look at Delaney, then used her fingertips to slide her glass of club soda to one side. She couldn't recall being in a place where straws came in paper wrappers and the only napkins provided were more paper and fastened around the cutlery with a strip of tape. Country music warbled from speakers on the walls, as if they were in Oklahoma instead of upstate New York. This would have been the kind of dining establishment Delaney would have frequented before she'd married Stanford.

It was as fitting a place for this meeting as any. Their conversation wouldn't carry far over the atrocious music, and because it was midafternoon, the restaurant was almost empty. A group of teenage girls sat in a booth beside the front window. A few tables to their left, a young couple was valiantly feeding dishes of ice cream to a pair of squealing toddlers. Although Delaney had asked her companion to give them privacy, he had gone only as far as the next table. He sat slouched in his chair, his long legs stretched in front of him and his arms crossed over his chest. The relaxed pose didn't fool Elizabeth. He was as alert as a hungry watchdog.

John Harrison had been a surprise. She wouldn't have expected her Pollyanna stepmother to have gone for a man like that. His attire might be civilized, but his demeanor was far from it. Elizabeth was accustomed to dealing with powerful men. Her father had been one of them. The aura of power around John was different, though. Much of it was sexual, to be sure, yet there was an edginess about him, a current of danger that fascinated as well as repelled. Judging by the giggles and furtive stares being cast his way, the teenagers beside the window had noticed it as well.

Leave it to Delaney not to waste any time. So much for her supposed devotion to her late husband. She and John had made holding hands on a park bench look like foreplay. Elizabeth had been on her way from the airport through town to the Wainright House when she'd spotted her stepmother in the park. The couple had been so completely absorbed in each other, they'd had a circle of stillness around them that had caught her eye even from the street. At least ten feet of space separated Delaney from John now, yet the connection between them was almost palpable.

Why was it always so easy for Delaney? What was it about her that drew men in? She never had to work for it. She never had to prove herself. She was weak and useless, the antithesis of everything Elizabeth had been raised to value, yet she managed to come out on top.

It wasn't fair.

"Why are you in Willowbank, Elizabeth? You realize there's a restraining order against you, don't you?"

"I'm fully aware of your latest salvo, Delaney. Your lawyer saw to it that I would be informed in the most public way possible to ensure maximum humiliation and damage to my reputation."

Her eyes widened. "What do you mean? What happened?"

"Save the innocent act for someone who would buy it."

"It's no act. Tell me. What did Leo do?"

"Besides spreading rumors about my mental competency among not only my staff but my clients?"

"He questioned people about your slander against me. He didn't spread rumors."

Either she was lying, or she was totally oblivious of Throop's actions. Neither possibility reflected well on her. "You can't dispute the fact that he brought an armed police escort with him to interrupt a meeting with the Grayecorp board and inform me my movements have been restricted like a criminal's. There was no cause to put on a show like that. As far as I'm concerned, that qualifies as harassment, yet you have the audacity to accuse me of the same."

"Audacity? You sent me accident scene photographs of your own father."

"I did nothing of the kind!"

John was on his feet the instant she raised her voice. He put his hand on the back of her chair. That was all. He didn't say anything. His presence was message enough.

She strove to hang on to her temper. Getting into a shouting match was beneath her dignity. She had to control her emotions better than this. She smoothed a wrinkle from her sleeve, then clasped her hands on the table. "I did not send you any photographs," she said. "It was obviously a clumsy attempt to incriminate me."

"Did you try to run me down?"

"Don't be absurd."

"Then how did your car get damaged?"

"It was a parking lot mishap. Apart from the fact that I wouldn't stoop to such thuggish tactics, it's ridiculous for anyone to assume I would drive all the way to Willowbank. My time is far too valuable for that."

"I want to believe you, Elizabeth, I really do. I hate to think you're this troubled."

"Unlike you, Delaney, I am fully capable of recognizing the truth. All I want is what's rightfully mine."

"No, that's not all. You also want to hurt me."

Elizabeth could feel the vibrations travel from her seat to her spine as John tightened his grasp on her chair. She twisted to look at him. "Your lurking is getting tiresome."

He studied her, his gaze probing hers.

She curled her toes in her shoes in an effort to remain motionless. It was difficult to maintain eye contact, but she was loath to show weakness by being the first to break it. "If you believe glowering will intimidate me, you're sorely mistaken."

"Your father was a real son of a bitch," he said. "Persecuting Delaney isn't going to change that. Save your anger for him."

The jab stunned her. It was astoundingly accurate and was

the last thing she would have expected from a piece of eye candy. She swallowed her pride and glanced away before he could look any deeper. "For a total stranger, he presumes to know a great deal about me. What carnival did you find him in, Delaney?"

John slid into the chair beside Delaney. Though he didn't touch her, she seemed to draw support from his presence. A look passed between them that shut Elizabeth out entirely. It was almost as intense as what she'd seen on the park bench.

She envied their obvious closeness, and she resented the fact that she envied it. He undoubtedly had an agenda, as all men did. He was likely after Delaney's fortune the same way Alan hoped to further his career by inveigling his way into Elizabeth's life.

The thought of Alan wrenched her back on track. She drummed her nails against the Formica table to recapture Delaney's attention. "My father didn't raise a fool. Although he taught me to use any means necessary to achieve my goal, he also taught me to keep my personal feelings out of business decisions. As much as I despise you, I would not stoop to causing you physical harm. It wouldn't be remotely as satisfying as ruining you. If you persist in flinging groundless accusations against me, I won't hesitate to sue *you* for slander."

"It isn't slander if it's true."

"Which is why you can't win."

"I've remembered more of what happened, Elizabeth," she said. "I've realized how Stanford used my need to be loved to manipulate me. I also know that he manipulated you into helping him. That's why you tricked me into meeting him that final night."

"Your so-called amnesia is too convenient for anyone to believe. I don't suppose you've also remembered my father was changing his will?" She paused. "No? What a surprise."

"Your goal was to break up our marriage. That's why you told me about his affair with Jenna. That's why I believed you when you'd said you would help me leave him."

"You have so little imagination. My goal wasn't to break up your marriage. You were leverage, that's all."

"What do you mean by leverage?"

"I threatened to reveal my father's adultery unless he agreed to a public reconciliation and amended his will. He was so confident of his hold over you that he called my bluff. *That's* why I told you about Jenna."

"My God," she said slowly. "You tried to blackmail your own father."

She picked up her glass, wiped the rim, and took a sip of the soda she didn't really want, buying time to steady her nerves. "I didn't merely try; I succeeded. Your ensuing temper tantrum provided the advantage I needed. We reopened our negotiations. I won. He agreed to all my demands. In return, I gave him the opportunity to recover one of his prized possessions."

"You really are two of a kind."

"It was just business. You're the one who made it personal when you drove his car into that utility pole before he could meet with his lawyer."

"How many times do I need to tell you that it was an accident? I didn't—"

"You didn't help him. You left him to burn in the wreckage while you saved yourself. *That* was no accident."

She regarded her hands. Her fingers trembled. "Why did you come here today, Elizabeth? What did you hope to gain?"

"I came to give you a warning."

John stiffened.

She ignored him and kept her gaze on Delaney. "I brought my lawsuit because it was the only recourse left to me after you refused to abide by my father's wishes. Until now, I've been willing to restrict our fight to the courts, but your attempt to take away Grayecorp has crossed the line."

"That's not what I'm doing. In spite of our differences, I've always valued your role in the company."

Elizabeth knew that Delaney didn't even understand her role in the company. She was a brainless trophy wife whose only accomplishment had been outliving her husband. "Don't insult my intelligence. Your lawyer's actions speak for themselves. It's unwise to start a war with me, Delaney. Grayecorp is mine, and I'll do whatever it takes to keep it."

"If this is only about the money, I'll gladly give you a share of Stanford's estate."

The glass slipped before Elizabeth could set it down. It

banged on the table, sloshing club soda on the bundle of napkin-wrapped cutlery and sending a stream across the table toward her. She took a tissue from her purse to stem the flow before it could drip on her lap. "What game are you playing now?"

"No game. I never wanted Stanford's wealth. I don't want the house, either. What I do want is to stop this antagonism before it escalates out of control. Stanford shouldn't have cut you out of his will in the first place. It was hurtful."

It had been more than hurtful; it had been a public rejection of his only child. It had negated a lifetime of devotion and sacrifice and hope. He'd hit her where he'd known it would cause the most pain.

But the situation was already spiraling out of control. Even if she managed to hold on to her position at Grayecorp, she had Alan and his ambitions to contend with. She mashed her fingertips into the sodden tissue. "Why the sudden change of heart?"

"It's not sudden, Elizabeth. I used to hope we could be friends, but your need for revenge is turning you into someone I don't recognize."

That must be how she did it, Elizabeth thought. That was how Delaney managed to charm otherwise canny people. She zeroed in on their weaknesses almost as skillfully as Stanford used to. It was a form of emotional judo: analyzing an opponent's center of balance, applying pressure to the precise spot that would tip it, and using their own momentum to defeat them.

Friendship. Love. The concepts belonged in children's stories. The real world didn't work that way, regardless of how fervently a person might wish it could.

She turned her mind back to business. The question remained: what did Delaney hope to gain with this offer? "You're afraid of what will come out in court, aren't you? That's why you want to settle. You've known all along it was your fault that he died."

"No, Elizabeth. I just want the nightmare to end."

TWENTY-FIVE

❧

IT BEGAN AS IT ALWAYS DID. DELANEY SAW THE ROAD through the tunnel of her headlights. It was slick and shiny and seemed to go on forever, but all too soon it narrowed. She was going too fast. The branches tore at her face and her clothes as she hurtled forward.

A weight settled on the bed behind her.

Even through her panic, she knew who it was. Max had come. He would keep her safe.

The fireball glowed in the distance. Mud spread beneath it, curling its tentacles toward the bed.

"It's okay, Deedee."

"Help me. Make it stop!"

He slid his arm around her waist and touched her hand. "Hang on to me. We'll go together."

She laced her fingers with his and tried to pull him back from the inferno. The fire was clawing toward him as well as her. She didn't want him to be hurt again. This was her fault. "It's coming. Can't you smell it?"

"We'll take a detour."

"How?"

"This time, we're going past the pond, okay?"

The path became a black ribbon, reflecting the flames as they writhed overhead. It held her feet fast. Her legs wouldn't move. "Max!"

"We're going past the car wreck, too," he said. His breath warmed her cheek. "He can't keep you anymore. You left him behind."

"The mud—"

"I already saved you from it, remember?"

"I can't breathe!"

The mattress shifted, as if he had pushed himself up. He leaned over her and took her chin in his hand. "Then I'd better help you again."

The kiss was like sunrise. It sent air to her lungs and streams of light through the darkness, just as it had the first time his mouth had touched hers. The water receded. The mud shrank away. Next to the brightness of her link with Max, the flames paled to nothingness.

No metal crashed. No bones broke like celery. No screams clawed at her heart. Her toes sank into cool moss. A blue jay squawked overhead. They had gone past the car wreck and the pond and were standing beneath the drooping boughs of a willow.

The scope of the change stunned her. Max hadn't merely pulled her out of the nightmare; he'd managed to avert it.

He kissed her cheek. "Better?"

She nodded, turning her head to follow his mouth.

A laugh tickled her lips. "I take it that's a yes."

"Thank you, Max."

He swept her up in his arms and carried her deeper into the woods. The trees opened up to a familiar field of wildflowers. "Don't be too grateful. You did most of it yourself."

"How?"

"You left him. You broke his hold over you."

He meant Stanford. God, she hoped it was true. "Is he really gone?"

Max laid her on a patch of sun-warmed grass and curled behind her once more. He fit his chest to her back and his thighs beneath hers. "We're the only two around, aren't we?"

She relaxed within the shelter of his presence, content for the moment to let her mind drift with his. She'd lost track of the number of times he had appeared to her in her dreams. This was the first time he'd done it since she'd known he was real. "I'm glad you're here, Max."

He kissed the nape of her neck. "Good. Hold that thought."

Their mental bond was strengthening now that she was consciously exercising it as well. That must be why his embrace felt so vivid.

That was her last thought before sleep blanketed her once more. It was approaching dawn when she surfaced again. She was back in her bedroom, warm and safe in her bed. She yawned and arched her back in a sleepy stretch.

Max's presence hadn't dimmed. It still surrounded her. It suffused her with a sensation of well-being and rightness. She closed her eyes to enjoy the feelings as long as she could.

Was the nightmare truly over? It seemed too easy. She'd lived with it for more than half a year.

Yet as Max had told her, she was breaking Stanford's hold, wasn't she? Settling with Elizabeth would go a long way toward that, as would facing the truth about her own mistakes. Like her fear of the water, knowledge was the key to overcoming it.

So was Max. He wasn't her subconscious, but in some ways, he knew her better than she knew herself. She was finally beginning to know him, too. Yes, there were issues between them that they hadn't even begun to deal with. In spite of that, he'd come to her when she'd needed him. His heart couldn't be as hardened as he wanted her to believe.

Even now that she was awake, she could sense the firmness of his body behind hers. The illusion was so strong, she felt the rise and fall of his chest against her back and the tickle of his breath across her ear. His weight was compressing the mattress, forming a dip beside the place where she lay. His fingers were toying with the hem of her nightgown.

She blinked and looked down.

The light that filtered through the bedroom window was too weak to define colors. It was too dim to dispel the shadows in the corners of the room, but enough spilled across the bed to reveal Max's hand on her thigh. His wrist rested along her hip. His arm flexed as he crumpled her nightgown in his fingers.

He had physically moved the satin.

"Good morning, Deedee."

And his whisper hadn't been in her head.

She broke free of his grasp and turned over.

Max was stretched out on his side, his head propped on his bent arm. His hair was even messier than usual, falling over his forehead as well as sticking up around his head in sleep-tangled tufts. A night's worth of beard stubble darkened his jaw and cheeks. His pale shirt was partially unbuttoned. The sides hung loosely against his chest. Faded, washed-soft jeans hugged his hips and molded his legs.

He smiled. "It's about time you woke up."

He was no fantasy. She doubted whether she would have been able to create one to match what she was seeing now. "Max!"

He placed his finger against her lips. "Shh. The walls in this old place are thick, but not that thick. Getting interrupted by a curious grandmother would kill the mood."

"What are you doing here?" she whispered furiously.

"Funny how you're always asking me that."

"It's not funny. How did you get in?" She glanced past him to the door. It was closed. Had he *materialized*?

He laughed softly. "I don't need to be in your head to see what you're thinking. No, Deedee, if I was able to get here through the power of my mind, I wouldn't have bothered putting on clothes."

"Then how . . ."

"I walked here."

"You walked here? In the middle of the night?"

"I had insomnia."

"And you just happened to wander inside and up to my room?"

He slid his hand across her cheek. "I know this house as well as you do. You took me over every square foot when we were kids. I know the quickest way to your room. I remember which boards creak. I also remembered how your grandmother used to leave the window at the back of the kitchen open all summer." He stroked the curve of her ear. "I locked it after me, just in case Toffelmire was right about your stepdaughter."

"Don't tell me this is your idea of protecting me."

"Hell no. Nothing noble like that."

"Then what?"

"You were due for the nightmare. I decided I would wait for it here."

"I still don't understand."

"I thought that meeting up with Elizabeth yesterday would trigger it. Seems to me that she often does."

"You guessed right."

"Uh-huh. I got here in the nick of time, too." He trailed his knuckles along the side of her neck and down to the slope of her breast. He slipped one finger beneath the satin. "I figured if I was going to get yanked out of a sound sleep to help you, I might as well get something more out of it than a painting."

She shuddered. Their thoughts weren't joined, yet she could feel his touch throughout her body. "You just said you had insomnia."

"That's because I was thinking about the other times you brought me naked to your bed." He pulled back his hand and unfastened another button on his shirt. "Which reminds me . . ."

"Max!" she hissed.

He continued working his way down the shirt. "What's wrong? You've seen everything before."

"I know, but this is different."

"Damn right." He pushed the ends of his shirt aside so he could unsnap the stud at the waistband of his jeans. "There's a big difference between thinking about it and doing it."

It was true, she had seen him naked, but that couldn't compare to the impact of so much virile male, clothed or not, mere inches away. As the rest of the house still slept, her dream lover had come to life. Her sexual fantasy was here in the flesh.

She pressed her fingers to her lips, torn between a laugh and a groan. "You're outrageous."

"Just doing what comes naturally." He sat up and pulled her to her knees in front of him. Before she realized what he intended, he grasped the bottom of her nightgown and skimmed it over her head.

Her laughter froze. She grabbed for the sheet.

"Come on, Deedee." He dropped her nightgown on the floor. "I've seen you before, too."

She held the sheet over her breasts. "I know, but—"

"You weren't shy the last time I was here."

"I didn't realize you were real." She pulled the sheet to her neck and tucked it over the edge of the largest scar.

"Don't hide them. You're beautiful."

"I'm not, Max."

"*You're* beautiful," he repeated. "Not just the packaging. I've seen what's inside you."

"That's because we were in a fantasy."

"For you, yeah, but I've always known you were real." He cupped her right breast through the sheet. His nostrils flared. "All those nights you brought me here, do you have any idea how hard it was for me to touch you and yet not touch? To hold you in my arms, but know you weren't there?" He leaned over. His breath warmed her skin as his beard stubble rasped against the cotton that covered the largest scar. The sound alone made her breasts tingle.

She slid her free hand into his hair. "You told me you enjoyed it."

"Sure. It was better than nothing, but not as good as this." He rubbed his thumb across her nipple, then turned his head and drew it, sheet and all, into his mouth.

She bit her lip to keep from crying out. The walls of the house were indeed thick. Only one of the guest rooms was occupied tonight, and her grandmother's bedroom was downstairs, but the night was still, and a scream was bound to carry. She didn't want to risk an interruption. Not now. She arched her back, channeling her passion to her mind. *Max!*

He lifted his head. "No tricks this time, Deedee."

Damp cotton clung to her breast. Fresh pleasure zinged through the already sensitized skin as it cooled. "Mmm?"

"No head games, no pretending, just you and me on a four-poster bed." He slipped his hand into his pocket, pulled out a handful of condom packets, and leaned over to set them on the bedside table.

Her gaze went to the condoms. More than anything he'd said, they brought home the fact that this was no dream. Max was a real man, and he wanted intercourse, not an imaginary orgasm. She pictured him entering her, physically joining her, going deep, hard . . .

Her body responded with painful swiftness. She swallowed a moan. "I still can't believe this."

He peeled off his shirt and tossed it behind him. Though dark bruises marred his skin, his movements were fluid. The swelling around his shoulder was gone. He didn't appear to feel any discomfort. "Don't let the speed of those make-believe orgasms fool you. I plan to take my time."

She skimmed her fingers across his chest. She was already familiar with the swirls of dark hair and the contours of his muscles. Or so she'd thought. Yet the mind-picture she held of him was a mere shadow. This man was solid. Her touch connected outside and in. He was actually in her bed this time. Here. With her. Close enough for her to feel the heat from his body and smell the musk from his skin. "I meant I can't believe you really came to my room."

"I've thought about that a lot, too. It's been hell, knowing where you lived. I've seen your light through the trees and imagined coming to you here."

"Then why didn't you?"

He slid his hand beneath the sheet to her leg. "It would have been complicated."

"And this isn't? We haven't settled anything. We need to talk. You can't just show up out of the blue and expect to make love with me."

"We're going to have sex, that's all. Genuine sex. Skin to skin. My body inside yours."

"Max . . ."

He traced the crease at the top of her thigh. "I'll make it good for you."

Oh, she had no doubts about that. His thoughts alone had made it good. Making love with the entire man would be . . . "Love. It would be love, Max."

He covered her mons with his palm as he fitted his lips to hers.

The kiss took away her breath and then gave it back, just as it had in her dream. He already knew the perfect angle and the right amount of pressure, the subtle shift and the gentle suction that worked best. When she opened her mouth, he slid his tongue inside gently. That was all, just his tongue. He didn't use his mind, even though hers was wide-open.

She twined her thoughts around his.

He wedged two fingers between her legs.

Her body tumbled to the brink of a climax. And remained trembling. There was no mental push to send her over. *Max, please!*

He withdrew his hand. His zipper rasped.

She put her hand over his. To stop him? To help him? *Let me love you, Max.*

He lifted her hand to his mouth, kissed her fingers, and

returned it to his lap. He pushed down his briefs. His erection butted against her palm. "I've told you what I'm offering, Delaney. If it's not enough for you, you'd better send me away now."

The light had strengthened. It tinted his face with orange gold. Desire was plain to see in his clenched jaw and the muscle that jumped in his cheek. Tension sparked from his body. Her fingers curled around him reflexively. He was a large, very aroused man, and yet . . .

And yet there was a tremor at the corners of his mouth that reminded her of a boy. Defiance in the lift of his chin. His gaze was naked with a yearning that reached past her mind and her body and went straight to her heart.

He didn't want her love, but he needed it. He might never admit that he did, because that would leave him as vulnerable as he'd been as a child. Yet she loved the man as much as she had loved the boy. She couldn't send him away now, no matter what he said or did. If this was the only connection he would accept, then she would make the most of it.

She dropped her sheet and helped him take off the rest of his clothes.

There was no room for more thought, only feeling. He drew her to her feet and pressed her back to one of the bedposts. With their fingers laced together, he raised her arms over her head to clasp their hands against the wood.

At first she tugged against his grip. She wanted to explore him with her fingers as she'd already learned him with her mind. She lifted her chin to seek his kiss.

He pulled back his head and rubbed his body against hers. It was a kiss that used everything except their lips, and it was more erotic than she could have dreamed. Slowly, thoroughly, he caressed her with his chest and his thighs, with the sides of his knees and the firm ridges of his hips. Crisp hair teased her breasts. The length of his erection dragged across her stomach, slick, silky, pulsing with life.

Delight sparked from every point where they touched. There was no need for a fantasy to augment the pleasure. Her senses heightened until merely drawing breath made her quiver. She lifted on her toes and hooked one leg around him, opening herself to his caress. Just when she was sure she couldn't take any more, he let go of her hands and used his mouth as well as his body.

Release exploded through every stretched-taut nerve. Colors she couldn't name flashed across her vision. The instant the peak began to ebb, he was already pushing her toward another.

They fell across the bed in a tangle of arms and legs, of heated skin and mingled sweat. Real sex, like real life, was messy. There were packages to open, hairs that tugged when they got caught, and weight on her chest that crushed her lungs. The need for silence made her bite her lip to swallow her moans. By the time the sun rose, she was sodden, aching, and so physically satiated her bones had turned to mush.

Max held her in his arms as she drifted back to sleep. When she awoke again, she was alone.

She spread her fingers over the dip his head had left on the pillow. His warmth was gone, yet the aroma of what they'd done still hung in the air. It had been incredible, beyond anything in her experience or her imagination.

But it was no use pretending that what he'd given her had been enough.

TWENTY-SIX

❦

DELANEY WAITED AT THE TOP OF THE FRONT STEPS AS LEO hoisted himself out of the taxi. A bumblebee droned from the petunias in one of the planter boxes. Helen stood on the driveway with her departing guests, giving directions to the lake to a plump woman in Bermuda shorts while the woman's husband loaded a suitcase into their car. Edgar's red truck was parked beside the hedge near the gatepost. He was applying mortar to replace a missing stone. From the backyard came the noise of the riding lawn mower where Pete was cutting the grass.

And on the other side of the fence, past the woods and the pond and the old train track embankment, Max was upstairs in his studio, squeezing colors onto his glass palette. Delaney caught the whiff of oil paints as he mixed a bright swirl of yellow and white. The corner of his mouth lifted in a one-sided smile, as if he were aware of her presence.

"You told me it was urgent," Leo said as he climbed the steps to the veranda.

At the sound of her lawyer's voice, Delaney pulled her thoughts back from Max. She'd only looked, not touched, yet even that fleeting contact had energized her. She was disturbed by how powerless she was to resist her attraction to him. She was only now realizing the extent of how bad her marriage had been. It would be foolhardy to dive into another relationship so soon, especially when the rest of her life was in such a state of flux.

But calling what she shared with Max a "relationship" was

like calling . . . She couldn't think of a comparison. Their bond could very well be unique in the world.

She knew how Max would label it, though. At least he'd restrained himself from repeating aloud the crude term for what they'd done on her bed.

"It's not too late to have Elizabeth arrested," Leo continued. "From what you related to me, she knowingly broke the restraining order."

"That's not what I had in mind." She led Leo into the house, past the staircase to the book-lined room at the back that had once been her mother's bedroom. It served as a sitting room and Helen's office now, and would ensure them privacy. Once they were settled in a pair of wing chairs, she filled in the details of her conversation with Elizabeth the previous day, then outlined what she wanted him to do.

He pursed his lips, his cheeks twitching as he digested what she'd said. He shook his head violently. "This is a mistake, Delaney. I implore you, take more time to think it over."

"I have thought it over, Leo. It's what I want."

"I've told you that Elizabeth has no case. There is no evidence of any wrongdoing or negligence."

"It doesn't matter."

"Doesn't matter? You deserve that money. You earned it."

"I *earned* it? What does that mean?"

"I meant no offense. You were a good wife to Stanford, better than he deserved. You've been loyal to a fault. You don't owe him anything, and you most certainly don't owe his daughter."

"You mentioned that before."

"Excuse me?"

"That I don't owe him anything. Leo, did you know about his affairs?"

He took off his glasses and polished them with the end of his tie. "Let's not talk about that."

"No, I think we need to. You knew, didn't you? That's why you were so adamant that I not compromise with respect to his estate."

"Delaney . . ."

"Why didn't you tell me? You're my lawyer. You're also supposed to be my friend."

"It's because I'm your friend that I remained silent. I was protecting you. I didn't want you to be hurt."

"You must have known the truth would come out."

"Your own mind suppressed the memories. There was a reason for that. I warned you to let them be."

"Yes, you did warn me. You've discouraged me from remembering anything. Is that why?"

"I believed it was for the best."

"You had no right to decide—" She stopped. "Leo, how did you know that I'd learned Stanford had been unfaithful?"

"I assumed you had realized it because even I had heard the rumors. When you spoke about Stanford in such glowing terms after the accident, I believed you were happier not remembering." He resettled his glasses on the bridge of his nose. "This has no bearing on the matter at hand. Elizabeth is unbalanced. Trying to appease her is a serious error. She belongs in jail."

"She claims she didn't send the photographs or try to hurt me."

"Naturally, she'd deny it. You're far too trusting, Delaney."

"She also claims that you've been undermining her position at Grayecorp. Is that true?"

"Everything I've done is in your defense."

"Is it true?" she repeated.

"Some people may interpret it that way; however, it will give us leverage to fight her lawsuit."

Leverage, like Elizabeth had used against Stanford. He would probably have been proud of how single-minded his daughter had become. She was as calculating as he'd been. How empty it must feel to go through life not trusting anyone.

Like Max?

Her gaze strayed to the bay window and to the woods beyond the back fence. Max scorned the very concept of love, just like Elizabeth. On the surface, they had been raised in completely different environments, yet a parent's income bracket was no guarantee of a good home. Elizabeth had learned to be as wary of emotions as Max. They'd both had loveless childhoods, too, although Max did have a best friend who had loved him . . .

How simplistic that was. The love of one self-centered,

blindly innocent child couldn't have counteracted the horrendous situation in which Max had been raised. Declarations of love and a few rounds of sex wouldn't negate the betrayal that had sent him to prison. It was a testament to the strength of his character that he'd been able to show her any tenderness at all.

She returned her attention to Leo. "This fighting is getting out of hand. It has to stop before it escalates further. We have to break the pattern."

"We can't back down when we're gaining the advantage."

"I've made my decision. I'm giving Elizabeth the Bedford house as well as half her father's estate. I'd like you to get the necessary documents started."

"Delaney, please! Consider the value of what you're giving up."

"If it's the price of peace, I'll gladly pay it."

"At least make the deal contingent on her dropping her lawsuit."

"Yes, of course. The whole idea is to end this antagonism. She's taken a suite downtown at the Riverview Hotel. Her lawyer should be arriving in town this afternoon, and I've invited them both to meet with me here. I'd like you to be present as well, Leo."

"What time?"

"Three o'clock."

"Fine. Perhaps by then you will come to your senses."

"I assure you, I already have."

"I don't understand how you can overlook the crimes Elizabeth has committed."

"There's no more proof that she's guilty of trying to hurt me than there is proof that I'm guilty of causing Stanford's death."

"Your naïveté has always been charming, but in this case it could prove dangerous."

"Don't patronize me, Leo. I have a right to my opinion, and I don't appreciate having it belittled. If I had followed my instincts when Elizabeth initiated the lawsuit instead of listening to you, all of this strife might have been prevented."

"I was only thinking of your best interests."

"I'm not blaming you; I blame myself for giving in. I've done that far too often during my life. That has to change."

He took a handkerchief from his pocket and blotted his face, then sighed deeply enough to make his chair creak. "Are you truly prepared to relinquish the Graye house?"

"Absolutely. It was never my home. I want none of the furnishings, either."

"Delaney, no! The piano alone is worth half a million."

She held up her hand.

He sighed again. "Where will you live?"

The answer sprang full-blown into her head, as if it had been there for months. Six months, in fact. "I'm going to stay in Willowbank."

"What will you do?"

"I'm not sure. Maybe I'll be a gardener or a cook."

"You can't be serious."

"I don't need a job to support myself. Even with only half of Stanford's estate, I'll still have more money than one person could ever need."

He rocked forward and caught her hand. The motion surprised her, and she jerked reflexively. He clamped his other hand on top to keep her from pulling away. "You have a brilliant mind, Delaney, and you deserve a brilliant career. I've always admired you, and it pained me to see how much you gave up for your marriage."

She wasn't sure how to respond. "Leo . . ."

"Why don't you come back to the city? You could return to real estate. With your current resources, you could establish your own company."

Light reflected from the lenses of his glasses, hiding his eyes. Although he was seated, his head was considerably higher than hers, reminding her of what a large man he was. His grasp was making her hand ache. She tugged free and flexed her fingers. "I could do the same here. The town's growing. There would be plenty of opportunity for a Realtor."

"It would be a waste of your talent. You have an excellent network of contacts among Stanford's crowd, and you could have the backing of Grayecorp. I could help you with the legal work free of charge. A favor between friends."

"That's a generous offer, Leo, but I'm not going to rush into anything."

"Yet you're giving away billions of dollars on a whim."

"It's not a whim. It's the right thing to do."

"You're not giving credence to Elizabeth's claim that her father wanted to change his will, are you?"

"It's possible. She's been far more honest than I would have expected. Once I remember the rest—"

"No!" He reached for her hand again. When she flinched, he braced his palms on his knees instead. "Delaney, I'm begging you, leave well enough alone. Your mind blanked those final hours for a reason."

"Leo . . ."

"You won't like what you find."

She stared at him. "You think she's right, don't you? That's why you've been so zealous about fighting her. That's why you've never wanted me to remember. You believe the accident was my fault. You think I did cause Stanford's death."

He tipped his head. The reflection on his glasses disappeared, revealing the truth of what he thought in his eyes.

Delaney felt the lick of fire against her fingers.

The nightmare wasn't through with her yet.

MAX CLAMPED HIS HAND AROUND THE DECK RAILING AS he peered into the gathering dusk. There was a saying he'd heard as a child. Something about mentioning the devil and he was sure to appear. He'd thought it was stupid, right up there with step on a crack, break your mother's back. Avoiding cracks was useless. There had been no mystery to the cause of his mother's pain, because there was nothing superstitious about Virgil's belt or fists. Speaking a name out loud had no power, either.

Yet the skin between Max's shoulder blades was prickling. He could feel Virgil's presence in the atmosphere that surrounded him, like the dull throb he got behind his forehead before a thunderstorm.

Telling Delaney about his stepfather had gotten him into her bed, just as he'd said it would. He couldn't be sorry for that, but sharing that particular piece of himself had also stirred up the past. It had breathed life back into the things he'd taken years to bury . . .

"No." His voice was swallowed by the sunset sounds of insects and bullfrogs. He moved to the stairs. The thud of his shoes on the thick planks was reassuringly solid. He crossed the yard, climbed the embankment, and headed for the lights that twinkled through the dusk.

No, he repeated silently. The past was dead, as was the boy he used to be. Slowly, the shadows on his vision receded. He no longer felt Virgil's presence; he felt Delaney's.

She was sitting on the window seat in her mother's old bedroom, her feet tucked beneath her skirt and a sheaf of legal-sized papers on her lap. She wasn't reading them. The colors of her thoughts were muted, shifting silver and gray. She sighed and turned her mind toward his.

He wished she was already in bed. It was easier to communicate with her body. More satisfying, too, without all the words getting in the way. If he kissed her, he wouldn't have to put up with her relentless poking and prodding at his psyche. If he pulled the blind over the window to shut out the light, he wouldn't need to deal with that look in her eyes, either, her little-kid faith that had almost made him feel as if things could be different, as if love wasn't just a fairy-tale concept, as if trust wasn't a bludgeon.

Yet that was how she was wired. She tried to see the best in everyone. She wanted life to be fair. Didn't she realize how defenseless that left her?

He pulled his mind away from hers and walked the rest of the way to the Wainright House alone. He had just gone through the back gate when he saw her step off the terrace. She walked to meet him. Warmth brushed across his thoughts, as soft as the remnants of sunshine that lingered on the undersides of the clouds. "Hello, Max."

It was a small thing, hearing her say his name aloud. He still wasn't used to it. His pulse kicked every time. "Hello, Delaney. How'd the meeting go?"

"It never happened."

"Did you change your mind?"

"What? No, of course not. Giving Elizabeth part of the estate is the right thing to do."

He nodded. He hadn't expected anything else. That was vintage Deedee. "So what happened?"

"Her lawyer couldn't get here today. We postponed the meeting until tomorrow. I did learn something interesting, though. It seems Elizabeth has been spending the odd weekend at the Bedford house."

"Why?"

"She wouldn't say. She only admitted to trespassing. It was a minor crime, but it's encouraging that she wants to clear the air. She could be right about the damage our conflict is doing to her position at Grayecorp. Leo's been more . . . zealous than I'd realized."

"From what I saw of Stanford Graye's daughter, you can save your concern. The woman's a shark. She thrives on confrontation."

"She's more sensitive than she lets on. She's been under a lot of emotional stress and—oh!"

He kissed her. He'd intended only a quick one, but the taste of her mouth drew him back for more. That was something else that he hadn't gotten used to yet: the physical sensation of her lips beneath his. The pleasure didn't reach as deep as when she put her mind into it, so it was simpler. He slid his hands around her waist. "I was right about you."

"Why?"

"You're making excuses for Elizabeth, too. You really don't recognize hate if it bites you in the butt."

"Like you don't recognize love?"

He nibbled her earlobe. "Does every conversation with you have to turn into psychological analysis?"

"What do you want to talk about?"

"Getting naked."

She sputtered a laugh. "Max, I've got papers to go over."

"Lawyer stuff, huh?"

"That's right. Leo drew up drafts for the property transfer agreements."

"Sounds boring."

"Not really."

"No, it must be. You look ready to fall asleep. You should be in bed."

"It's too early."

"Then let's take a walk."

"Where?"

"Back to my place."

"Why?"

"Because there are too many mosquitoes for us to get naked out here."

"You've got a one-track mind."

He firmed his grasp on her waist, pivoted away from the house, and moved her backward toward the gate. "I've also got a king-sized bed and a fresh carton of condoms."

She placed her hands on his shoulders and let him guide her, as if they were dance partners. "One night and you're already taking me for granted."

"No, Deedee, it's the other way around. I don't take anything for granted." He slowed to a stop. "That's why I want to bring you home with me. We should enjoy what we've got while we can."

"And what do we have, Max?"

"This." He slid his hands to her buttocks and tilted her pelvis into his. "I've been thinking about you all day."

"I know. I felt it."

He dropped his face to the side of her neck. "I couldn't stop thinking about last night, either."

"Neither could I. It was . . . special."

"Best you've ever had?"

"I've always known that no one could compare to you, Max. There's no need for you to get a swelled head."

"You're the one who makes everything swell." He licked the edge of her jaw. "I'm sorry now that we wasted as much time as we did playing pretend."

"It wasn't wasted time. We were getting to know each other."

"Yeah." He nuzzled past her collar and inhaled. "I know your skin smells like roses."

"Sometimes yours smells like turpentine."

"Hazard of my profession. What about now?"

"Just soap and you."

"I didn't shower when I got home this morning. I waited until tonight because I liked carrying your scent on me."

"I didn't change my sheets for the same reason." She slid her hands to his chest. "Do I really smell like roses? I don't use rose-scented perfume."

"It's your essence. Delicate, sweet. But your body's got more variety than that." He turned his head toward her arm. "The inside of your elbow is more like apples."

Her breath warmed his ear. "Apples?"

"Sweet, ripe apples. Same with the backs of your knees."

"I had no idea."

He rubbed his knee against her thigh. "Want me to tell you where you smell like honey?"

"I think I can guess."

"Will you let me have another taste?"

"You know I love you, don't you?"

Damn, why did she have to say that? She should have given up by now. He pictured the silky folds of skin between her legs, remembering her moisture on his tongue and the way her thighs had shuddered against his cheeks.

Her knees buckled. "Max!"

It was too far to his house. They wouldn't make it to her bedroom, either. He hauled her to the back fence, pressed her against the iron gate, and aligned her hips with his.

He'd told himself he wouldn't use tricks, he'd wanted to keep it simple, yet just this once wouldn't hurt. He opened his mind.

She wrapped herself around his thoughts. The gate softened, becoming the edge of a thick feather mattress. Streamers of mist curtained the bed. She didn't imagine a kiss; she imagined lowering his zipper, pulling up her skirt, and welcoming him into her body.

Pleasure flooded his brain, along with the memory of her legs locking around his waist as she rode his thrusts. He played it back for her, smiling as she trembled both in his arms and in his thoughts.

A scream tore through his head.

His reflexes were sluggish. It took him a few beats before he realized the scream hadn't been hers.

A dog barked from the direction of the front yard. There was a second scream.

The mist disappeared. The bed reverted to a gate. Delaney was once again standing on her feet. Her clothes were in place. Only her face bore any hint of what had been happening in their minds. She blinked groggily, then shoved away from the fence and raced toward the house.

He caught up to her as she passed the terrace. Floodlights set high on the corners of the house switched on to illuminate the grounds. He spotted a woman standing beside the cedar hedge near the front gatepost. She cradled a white poodle in her arms.

Helen burst through the front door as Max and Delaney reached the veranda. "What on earth is going on?" she asked, hurrying down the steps. "Mrs. Leach? Is that you?"

Max recognized the woman and her dog. They lived a few houses up the road from Helen. She turned as they approached. Her voice was high-pitched and too fast. "I hadn't seen her there. I walked right by. I thought Jasmine was chasing a cat. Is she dead? She's not dead, is she?"

The floodlights from the house didn't penetrate the darkness at the base of the hedge. All he could see at first was a high-heeled shoe. Then he saw the pale curve of an arm and blonde hair matted with blood. A woman lay facedown beneath the cedar boughs.

He grabbed Delaney before she could go farther. "Take Helen and Mrs. Leach back to the house," he said. "Call an ambulance."

She clung to his arm. "Oh, my God!"

In the shadows, from the back, the woman could have been mistaken for Delaney. She was a similar size, and her hair color was nearly identical. He steeled himself against a flood of completely irrational panic.

Delaney was safe; she was standing right next to him.

The woman on the ground was Elizabeth.

TWENTY-SEVEN

❖

DELANEY ROSE TO HER FEET AS SOON AS DR. MCFADDEN pushed through the swinging doors to the waiting room. This wasn't the doctor who had been on call when Max had been brought to the hospital a week ago. That doctor had been a woman, and she'd had a pleasant smile on her face when she'd come out to speak with Delaney because she'd had good news.

Dr. McFadden wasn't smiling. The lines around his mouth were tight with tension, and his eyes appeared tired. Delaney felt Max move behind her, and she reached for his hand. "How is she?"

"Miss Graye is out of surgery and has been moved to recovery," McFadden said.

"Will she be all right?"

"I'm afraid she suffered serious head trauma."

Delaney recalled Elizabeth's face as she'd been loaded into the ambulance. Her left eye had been purpled and swollen. Her skin had been streaked with dirt and dried blood. More blood had soaked into her hair. It had come from a gash on the back of her skull. There had been blood on one of the stone gateposts, too.

The injuries couldn't have been accidental. She'd been attacked, knocked into the gatepost with enough force to crack her skull, then stuffed under Helen's cedar hedge and left to die.

Please, this couldn't be happening. This was Willowbank, not the big city. Let it be another nightmare.

The bloody face faded into an image of a baby bird. A tiny, fluffy swallow. It wobbled like a lopsided ball on top of a wooden railing. Beyond it, a yard of patchy grass stretched to a ridge of gravel and a line of trees . . .

Delaney's chin trembled as she recognized the scene. The bird was on Max's back deck. He had given her the image to counteract the other one.

She squeezed his hand and returned her attention to the doctor. "How serious is it?"

"We've done what we could to relieve the pressure on her brain. There was a great deal of swelling within her skull."

"What's her prognosis?" Max asked.

"It's too soon to make predictions. We'll have a better idea in another forty-eight hours."

"Is she awake?" Delaney asked. "Has she told you what happened?"

Dr. McFadden regarded her with sympathy. "At the moment, we're concentrating our efforts on keeping her alive. Whether or not she will regain consciousness is another matter. It might be wise to prepare yourself for the possibility that she won't."

The words rolled past her. She didn't want to grasp them.

"You told me she's your stepdaughter, Mrs. Graye?"

"That's right. Her father was my husband."

"Does she have any other relatives we could contact?"

"None that I'm aware of."

"I realize this is a difficult question, but would you know whether or not she signed an organ donor card?"

Delaney closed her eyes. No, this couldn't be happening.

Max slipped his arm around her back to steady her. "Aren't you jumping the gun, Doctor?" he asked. "You said it's too soon to make a prognosis."

"I apologize," McFadden said. "My job doesn't always allow me the luxury of diplomacy. My first priority always has to be the welfare of my patient. All of my patients."

"When can we see her?" Delaney asked.

"We're monitoring her closely and aren't allowing any visitors at this stage. It could be a long night, so I'd advise you to go home and get some rest. I'll have someone call if there's any change."

Max took his wallet from his pocket, withdrew one of his business cards, and passed it to the doctor. "Here's my number. You can reach Mrs. Graye there."

They drove past her grandmother's place on the way to Max's. The Wainright House was once again dark. The police cars that had arrived with the ambulance were gone. Yellow crime-scene tape cordoned off the area between the hedge and the nearest gatepost—the area would be examined more thoroughly once it was daylight. Though Max offered to stop, Delaney shook her head. Helen had been exhausted and about to go to bed the last time she had called from the hospital to check on her. The bad news about Elizabeth would keep.

Max parked his Jeep beside his front door and led her inside. She hadn't questioned his assumption that she would be staying with him. In truth, there wasn't anywhere else she would rather be.

His house looked different at night. Without the sunshine streaming across the floor to meld the separate areas, the living room was an island of soft lamplight, rounded fieldstones, and oversized furniture. It was as inviting as it had been in daylight, though in a more intimate way. She went to the empty fireplace, drawn once again to the painting of the storm.

Keys rattled into a ceramic dish. Max's footsteps moved toward her. "We'll to need to talk to the cops first thing in the morning."

"Yes, they'll want our statements." She turned to face him. "It's horrible to think the neighborhood isn't safe."

"The neighborhood isn't the problem. We have to make sure Toffelmire is told what happened. That couldn't have been a random mugging."

"Why not? Elizabeth's purse was missing. Phoebe told me that a woman was mugged down by the lake a few weeks ago, and she was sure she heard someone lurking in my grandmother's woods."

"She probably did. Kids use the woods for a shortcut. Teenagers go there to drink. There were stories about a boogeyman in the bushes even when I was a kid."

"What if it's real this time? Both Helen and Edgar said there are new people moving to Willowbank. There are always strangers in town during the summer. Who knows what kind of criminals might be in the area?"

"Besides me?"

She frowned. "You know that's not what I meant."

He took her by the shoulders. "I'm not saying there isn't crime in Willowbank. It's got its share of muggings and break-ins like any other town. I just think with everything else that's happened lately, it's too much of a coincidence that Elizabeth would be attacked when she's on her way to see you."

"You're right about one thing; she must have been coming to see me. It's the only reason she would have been at the house. But why would she do that? She knew the meeting had been postponed."

"She probably wanted to catch you when you were alone. She sure wasn't pleased to have me hanging around the last time."

"Then where was her car? She rented one at the airport. We saw it yesterday."

"She could have taken a taxi. Or she might have wanted some exercise and decided to walk there."

"Not in those heels. That wouldn't be something Elizabeth would do, anyway. Walking isn't an efficient enough exercise for her. She works out on a Bowflex so she can get maximum results for her time. Maybe she was carjacked. Whoever hit her could have stolen her car. It still could have been random."

"Sure, it's possible, but it's more likely that she was targeted."

She rubbed her arms against a sudden chill, then pulled away from him and went to sit on one of the leather couches. "First the hit-and-run, then this. Why?"

"Well, we can be sure she wasn't the one responsible this time."

"No, but maybe I am."

The cushion creaked softly as he sat next to her. He laid his arm across the back of the couch behind her shoulders. "Just because your life would be easier without her doesn't mean you brought this on."

As usual, he zeroed in on what she'd avoided facing herself. Having Elizabeth out of the way would definitely make her life easier. And that did make her feel guilty. "I never wished her any harm. I just wanted her to stop."

"Sure. She was being a pain."

"My grandmother called her a spoiled brat, but she was wrong. Elizabeth wasn't indulged; she was neglected."

"Poor little rich kid, huh?"

"You think I'm crazy for sympathizing with her, but she made herself tough in order to survive. Inside, she's not that way at all."

He stroked her hair.

"She did want to make peace. I saw it on her face at the restaurant."

He traced her ear.

"And now this happens before she can resolve anything. It's just not fair."

"Newsflash, Delaney. Life isn't fair."

She turned her head to kiss his fingers. "There you go again, being the cynic. We're quite the pair."

"Uh-huh."

"Like two halves of one whole."

He dropped his hand to the front of her blouse. "Sounds sexy. Want to go to bed?"

The laugh surprised her. After the previous several hours, she wouldn't have thought herself capable of it. "Thanks for your help tonight, Max."

He tapped the top of her breast. "I intend to get rewarded."

"Did you make up the baby swallow you showed me?"

"No, that was a memory. There was a nest under the eaves last summer. A few fell on the deck when their mother pushed them out. One sat there for a few hours, trying to get up the nerve to fly."

She smiled, thinking of this unquestionably virile man watching baby birds. "It was very cute. Did he finally do it?"

"Mmm?" He slipped open her top button.

"Fly."

"Yeah."

"It's sweet that you kept track of them. The image was very vivid."

Two more buttons slid from their holes. He fingered the edge of her camisole. "That's because I used it."

"How?"

"For a painting. They looked different by the time I put them on canvas."

"I'll bet. They probably were straining to launch themselves into the sky, in spite of the approaching wind that could break their wings to smithereens."

"Something like that."

"I'd like to see it, Max. Is it in your studio?"

"It's already sold."

"Oh."

"But there's something else upstairs you'll enjoy."

She sighed. They both knew this was where they'd been heading this evening before they'd been interrupted, and yet . . .

"Don't overthink it, Deedee."

"It doesn't seem right to enjoy myself, with Elizabeth in the hospital. I realize she despises me, but I'm her only family."

"We'll worry about it tomorrow. Picture the bird."

She leaned her head on his shoulder. The lopsided ball of beak and feathers stole back into her mind.

"Flying's a natural urge. It wants to fly, whatever the weather throws at it. Doesn't matter how long it sits there to think about it, either; the outcome's going to be the same. So it decides, what the hell, might as well let go and enjoy itself while it can."

"You're a philosopher as well as a cynic."

"Nothing that complicated." He turned her so that she was half lying across his lap. "I'm just a man who's doing his damnedest to get naked with you."

She lifted her hand to his cheek. "You're a lot more than that, Max."

He turned his head to nibble her fingertips, then tongued her index finger into his mouth. He drew on it gently. An identical sensation seized her nipple.

She shifted her legs on the cushion to fit herself more fully into his embrace. The familiar tang of his soap mixed with the scent of the leather couch.

The car smelled like leather from the heater within the seats. Stanford's lime aftershave hung thick in the air, making it difficult for her to breathe. Delaney lowered the window a crack, filled her lungs with fresh air, and returned her hand to the wheel.

Delaney jerked away from Max. She hugged her arms to her chest.

He held up his palms. "All right, I said no tricks, but I slipped, okay?"

Stanford grabbed her forearm. She cried out as the car swerved.

The memory disappeared as quickly as it had arisen. Delaney pushed herself backward along the couch until she squeezed into the corner. She tucked her legs beneath her, brushing at her arm, trying to erase the feel of Stanford's grasp.

Max knelt in front of her. He searched her gaze. "What's wrong?"

"I was in the car."

"You remembered your husband."

She rubbed her eyes. Her fingers shook. "It was only a fragment. It must be because of what you did."

"I don't see how. They're your memories; I can't put them in your head."

"You triggered my memories even when I thought you were John. With everything else that's happened, I haven't attempted pushing through the block since that morning in the backyard. I should have. If I had, maybe Elizabeth wouldn't have been hurt."

He eased her hands from her face. "Delaney, what happened to her wasn't your fault."

"We both know it has something to do with me. The answer must be in my head, and I have to get it out. How many more people around me are going to get hurt before I do? I have to remember."

"If you needed to, you would. The memories seem to come when you're ready for them."

"You're still the key, Max."

He released her hands and sat back on his heels. "This is sounding familiar."

She leaned forward, speaking quickly. "We could work together to unlock my memories. We don't have to leave it to chance. If we consciously combine the power of our minds, who knows what we could accomplish? We've only begun to explore what's possible between us."

"Nothing's changed, has it?"

His tone was a dash of ice water. She searched his expression. It was carefully shuttered. "What do you mean?" she asked.

"You get all misty when you talk about what you call our special bond, but when it comes right down to it, you still want to use me."

"That's not fair."

He lifted one eyebrow. "Do I need to repeat the newsflash?"

"Stop acting so cynical. I know that isn't really you."

"You don't want to recognize the real me. You went to a hell of a lot of trouble so you wouldn't."

"Max, please."

"I've been up-front about what I want from you. You were at the beginning, too, only I lost sight of that. The first thing you told me when you came back was that you wanted me to help you remember."

"You refused."

"Not when you asked for mind sex. I thought I was damn cooperative about getting rid of your inhibitions."

She swung her legs to the floor and stood. She didn't speak again until she had put the length of the couch between them. "That was before I understood you were real. We already talked about that."

"Right." He pushed himself to his feet. "You're big on talking. I went along with you on that, too, because it was the only way to get into your pants."

"This isn't you, either. You're a sensitive, kind man. That's why you gave me the baby swallow. That's why you opened up about your past. You've got a deep well of love inside you, Max, only you're afraid to let anyone see it. You show how you care in a hundred little ways but you're afraid to admit it."

He closed the distance between them in two strides. "Wrong. What I've got is a hard-on, and the only thing I want to open is a carton of condoms."

She stood her ground, even though every muscle was twitching to retreat. She focused on a vein that pulsed in the side of his neck. His heart was beating as fast as hers. "I understand why you try to push me away by talking like this. It's difficult for you to trust emotions. You're snarling because you expect to be hurt. I can only hope you'll eventually believe that I would never betray you. I love you."

"Just as long as I'm useful."

"All right, since it's such a sore point with you, forget about helping me. Maybe you're right. Maybe you've got nothing to do with the way my memories return. Maybe it's a coincidence that it only happens when I've been around you."

"Oh, no you don't." He caught her chin. "You're not backing out now."

"What do you mean?"

He tipped her face to his. "I didn't say I wouldn't try to help you."

"Then what was all this about?"

"I just want us to be clear where we stand. I'll give you what you asked for as long as you do the same for me."

"Which means?"

"An even trade. A *fair* trade. You can use my mind the way you wanted in the first place. In return I get to use your body."

"But I was willing to give you that without a bargain, Max."

"No, Deedee, you expected more. I felt the truth last night. I see it in your eyes now. You're going to keep digging at me because you won't accept reality. You're still seeing me as a stand-in for the friend you made up."

"That's what this argument is really about. It's the same one we had here a week ago. You're worried that we're already too close. Now that I know who you are, you don't want to let me in, so you're scrambling to set up new boundaries. You're afraid of what will happen if we truly do combine our minds, aren't you?"

The moment stretched. Her challenge hung in the air between them and was reflected back at her from his thoughts. Emotions she couldn't name flashed in his gaze until one rose to conquer the rest. Hunger. He ran his thumb over her lower lip. The caress was as gentle as his words had been harsh.

Damn. All it took was one touch to dissolve her pride and her common sense.

Was she doing it again? Was her need to be loved making her blind to this man's true character? Was she making excuses for Max the same way she'd done for Stanford?

He stepped back and held out his hand. "I don't want to argue anymore, do you?"

No, she never wanted to argue. She always tried to make peace. Even now, regardless of how coarsely he spoke of it or how determined he was to demean it, she wanted nothing more than to lose herself in the simple bliss of making love with Max.

THE WINDOWS IN THE UPPER STORY WERE TALLER THAN the ones in the ground floor. Max hadn't switched on a light when he'd guided Delaney up the spiral staircase to the bedroom the night before; the moon had provided illumination enough. With the sunrise, she got a better look at her surroundings. There was no door on the bedroom, just an open archway that led to the landing of the staircase and the huge studio beyond it. The bathroom was angled behind a partition for privacy but it had no door, either. Obviously, Max didn't like being closed in. The walls that had appeared silver in the dark were revealed to be pristine, unadorned white. The windows themselves provided dramatic rectangles of color, as if the sky was a series of framed paintings.

Aside from the king-sized bed that dominated the space, the only other pieces of furniture in the room were a small table with a lamp and a white enameled wardrobe. The maple plank floor was bare of carpets. The effect wasn't bleak, though. It was clean and spacious and as peaceful as a blank canvas.

The simplicity made sense. For a man with a mind as powerful as Max's, he would need to have surroundings like these to enable him to sleep.

Not that they'd done much of that. It had been nearing dawn by the time they'd been too physically spent to stay awake.

She shifted to her side. Though Max's sheets were luxuriously smooth cotton, the friction from her movement was enough to send a lazy curl of pleasure across her skin. She propped her head on her hand.

Max lay sprawled on his stomach, his cheek flattened to the mattress. One arm dangled over the side of the bed while the other was bent toward his chin. His lips were parted and his jaw was lax with sleep. His eyelids were motionless—he'd told her he seldom dreamed. She knew he wasn't dreaming now, either, because no whisper of his thoughts touched hers.

He had frequently complained about being woken up by her nightmares. She could see why. He slept like the dead. Still, she had every right to disturb him now, because they'd made a bargain, and he had yet to fulfill his half.

Yet she didn't want to invite Stanford into this bed. Call it selfish or cowardly or just plain greedy, she didn't want the past to intrude on the pleasure of the moment. Max had always maintained that burying the past was the only way to be free of it. That must work to some extent. No nightmare troubled his sleep.

Unable to resist touching him, she stroked his hair from his forehead.

His eyebrows drew together in a brief frown, then smoothed out once more.

If she woke him with a kiss, she wouldn't have to put up with his keep-off growls and his cynicism. Their bodies had no trouble communicating, even without the benefit of joining their minds. She was happy there were no blinds to block the light from his windows. She loved being able to look her fill without their words getting in the way.

Considering the number of occasions they'd been intimate, both in their minds and in the flesh, it was odd that this was the first time she was seeing him naked in full daylight. His physique was truly magnificent. His arms were leanly muscled. The yellowing bruises on his shoulder didn't detract from his appeal; they made her more aware of his strength. Her gaze skimmed over his back to the tan line at his waist. The edge of the sheet lay low on his buttocks, revealing tiny scratches on the pale skin.

She pushed herself up to regard the marks more closely. The scratches were regularly spaced crescents that could only have been made by her nails.

Her lips twitched with a rush of purely female satisfaction. She had marked him. Never before in her life had she been that carried away by passion. Then again, as she'd already told Max, no lover could compare to him. She regarded his back. No red marred the skin there. Instead, it was crossed by lines of white.

White. Her smile vanished. She focused more closely.

They weren't scratches; they were scars.

Her own back contracted with agony. It lasted less than a heartbeat. It left her shaking.

"Oh, Max," she whispered. She lifted her hand, letting her palm hover above his skin as if she could draw out his pain, but the physical pain would be long gone.

She knew about scars, and these weren't recent. It took years for scar tissue to whiten completely, decades for it to smooth out to the extent these scars had. Some were mere threads of white a few inches long. Others were narrow ribbons where wounds had pulled apart before they had healed. Aside from a short, raised ridge beneath his shoulder blade, they lay flat, almost completely incorporated into the plane of his skin. These must be from wounds he'd received in his childhood.

Why hadn't she noticed them before?

Because it had been dark when he'd been naked. Because he'd kept his shirt on when there had been light. And mostly because she'd been too caught up in her own pleasure, too focused on her own hang-ups and neuroses and needs, to take a really good look at the man she claimed she knew.

But she should have guessed. An abuser as vicious as Virgil Budge wouldn't have limited himself to one victim.

She leaned over to kiss the raised scar on his shoulder blade. A parallel scar lay below it. A few of the other lines were in pairs, too, as if they'd been inflicted by . . . She closed her eyes as her mind filled in the rest. He'd said his mother had been strangled with a belt.

Oh, Max.

He stirred beneath her at the same time his thoughts responded to hers. He rolled over, looped his arm around her back, and pulled her sleepily to his chest.

She crawled on top of him, spreading her arms and legs as if she could shield him with her body. His mother had lied at his trial, but her betrayal had begun far earlier than that. She hadn't protected her child from a monster. Delaney pictured the boy he used to be, his eager smile, his patience and kindness and generosity . . . and his too-big clothes that had covered the brutality he kept secret even now.

Her lungs heaved. *Max!*

"You're way ahead of me," he murmured. He grasped her hips and moved her in a slow circle, angling himself to meet her. "Give me a minute to catch up."

"I saw what he did."

"Hell, you're not remembering stuff now, are you?"

"I'm not talking about Stanford. I meant your stepfather." She kissed his neck. "He's the one who gave you those scars, isn't he?"

He went still.

"You must have known I would see them. Why didn't you tell me all of it?"

"It doesn't matter."

"Doesn't matter? I'd say it's a major factor when you're talking about your life."

"That part of it is over."

"I'm sorry, Max. I'm so sorry. You were right. I've been too obsessed with remembering my own past when I should have been thinking of yours."

"This is why I didn't tell you. I don't want to remember mine. And I don't want your pity."

"I don't pity you. I admire you."

"There's nothing admirable about being a drunk's whipping boy. It didn't require any special talent."

"You don't realize how exceptional you are. The more I learn about you, the more I understand why I love you so much."

He slid her off his body, got out of bed, and scooped his jeans from the floor. He dressed without looking at her.

She wasn't sure what more she could say. She already knew that words alone wouldn't turn back the clock or undo the hurt that Max had suffered. His emotional wounds went deeper than she could have conceived. He had every reason to mistrust the concept of love. She could be driving him farther away each time she declared her feelings. She swung her legs off the bed.

Damn, she wished this wasn't so complicated.

The noise of slamming car doors came through the open windows. Moments later, knocking resounded through the house.

"Willowbank Police. Open the door, Harrison."

Max swore and headed for the staircase. Delaney pulled the sheet around herself as she moved next to the nearest window.

Three patrol cars were angled in the driveway and across the yard to block off Max's Jeep. Two uniformed officers, their hands on their holstered sidearms, jogged around the house toward the back. Two more policeman stood in the driveway.

The pounding resumed. Delaney stepped closer to the window so she had a view of the front steps. Though she only saw him from above, she recognized the balding man at the door. It was Toffelmire.

TWENTY-EIGHT

❧

THE TRAFFIC LIGHT TURNED AMBER AS DELANEY NEARED
the intersection. She pressed the accelerator to the floor and
sped through.

Leo clutched the dashboard. "Delaney, slow down!"

"It's been more than four hours."

"For heaven's sake, they're only questioning him, not exe-
cuting him."

"Don't joke about it, Leo. He shouldn't have to go through
this alone."

"John Harrison is no stranger to police procedure. He should
be able to cope."

She shot him a glance. "Then you already knew about him
before I called you."

"I thought it wise to do a thorough check on his background
after his heroic rescue of you last week. I know the details of
his criminal record."

"Good, then you understand what we're up against."

"You've always had a soft heart, Delaney, but don't you
think you're taking your gratitude too far?"

The tires squealed as she braked behind a slow-moving station
wagon. She pounded the horn as it crept forward. Unlike the other
time Leo had accompanied her to the police station, she felt no
uneasiness about driving. There was no room for it. It wasn't her
nightmare she was worried about stirring; it was Max's.

Toffelmire hadn't needed the show of force that he'd brought
to the house. Max had offered no resistance when they'd asked
him to accompany them downtown, even though it was obvious

to her that he was being railroaded. "My personal feelings are immaterial. The police are singling him out unfairly because of his reputation. He's done nothing wrong."

"As far as you know."

"What does that mean?"

"He has a history of serious violence, he was in close proximity to the crime scene, and who else would have had a motive to attack Elizabeth?"

She spun the wheel to turn onto a side street. "That 'history' doesn't tell the whole story, and it certainly doesn't explain why he would want to hurt her."

"It could have been retaliation. She hit him with her car."

"First of all, he wouldn't do that. Second, it's far from certain that she had anything to do with the hit-and-run that injured him."

Leo clutched his shoulder belt as she took another corner. "The police must have some reason to suspect Harrison. Detective Toffelmire struck me as competent enough, though somewhat averse to going beyond the minimum required for his job."

"He has an old grudge against Max. He's not being objective."

"And you are? Frankly, Delaney, I'm worried the stress of the situation has affected you. All this concern for a veritable stranger . . ." He paused. "Why did you call him Max?"

"That's his middle name."

"Yes, but why would you use it?"

She replied with complete honesty. "Because that's what he asked me to call him when we met. We're friends."

"This friendship developed rather quickly, didn't it?"

"Not really. In fact, on some level I feel as if I've known him all of my life." She spotted an empty parking space on the opposite side of the road, pulled a U-turn at the next intersection, and maneuvered the car to the curb. She shut off the engine and turned to Leo. "And it's because we're friends, I want to help him. That's what friends do, isn't it?"

"Of course." He opened his seat belt. He kept his gaze on the buckle. "Harrison's appearance is quite striking, isn't it?"

"What?"

"I saw his photograph on the Internet while I was checking his background."

"There's much more to him than meets the eye, Leo."

"I suppose I'll have to take your word for that."

"I hope you do." She touched his sleeve. "Despite what you must have read about him, he's a good man, and he deserves a good defense. Thank you for agreeing to represent him."

"It's only temporary. I expect he'll want to retain counsel of his own as matters progress further."

"I understand, but I'm hoping with your intervention, things won't go further."

"I'll do what I can."

"I appreciate it more than I can say. It's a terrible imposition for me to ask you to extend your stay here. I realize you have other clients."

"None are as important to me as you are." He squeezed her fingers against his arm. "You must know I would do anything for you, Delaney."

His tone made her uncomfortable. So did his grasp.

Would he really do anything for her? He'd made no secret of his antagonism toward Elizabeth and was vehemently opposed to the idea of settling with her. He'd known where Elizabeth was staying and could have followed her. He even was aware of Max's record of assault and could have guessed the police would have a convenient scapegoat . . .

The direction of her thoughts sickened her. She didn't want to believe she could be that wrong about her friend. Leo might be overzealous at times, but she couldn't picture him resorting to physical violence any more than she could picture Elizabeth committing a hit-and-run. Anxiety and lack of sleep were making her paranoid. She withdrew her hand. "Thanks, Leo."

He cleared his throat and leaned forward to retrieve his briefcase from between his feet. "I will, of course, be adding this to your bill."

THE ROOM HAD BEEN PAINTED GREEN SINCE THE LAST TIME Max had been interrogated here. It was a sickly color, sloping more toward the yellow end of the spectrum than the blue. The fluorescent bulbs in the overhead fixture killed any life there might have been in it. The digital tape recorder was new, but the table appeared to be the same, a small square of gray steel that was bolted to the floor next to the wall. There was only space for two chairs. His was facing the door. It was a small mercy. It helped him to hold the claustrophobia at bay.

"Why did you do it?" Toffelmire asked. "You just can't resist beating up women, is that it?"

"I didn't touch Elizabeth Graye." It was the same reply he'd given at least a dozen times.

"You were there when she was found."

"She was found by an old lady walking a poodle. Did you roust them out of bed to question them, too?"

"That's some coincidence you happened to be nearby."

"I was taking a walk. You saw where I live."

"You were visiting Delaney Graye, weren't you?"

There was no point lying. She hadn't tried to hide herself when Toffelmire had shown up at daybreak. Instead, she'd made no secret of her support for Max. Her presence seemed to have fueled the cop's suspicions. "Yes, I went to see her."

"You claimed a week ago that you didn't know her. Why did you lie?"

"I didn't lie. I told you that we'd just met, and we had."

"Then you worked fast. Mrs. Graye is an attractive woman. Her husband left her extremely well-off."

That hadn't been a question, so he remained silent.

"Recent widows can be lonely. Easy prey for a man with no sense of morals."

Max kept a tight grip on his temper. Toffelmire was baiting him, hoping to provoke a reaction he could twist against him later.

"Elizabeth Graye was suing her stepmother. She was threatening to take away her fortune. I wonder how far a man would go to protect a meal ticket as promising as Delaney Graye."

"You're chasing the wrong rabbit with that, Detective. I've got plenty of money."

"That remains to be seen. I'm in the process of getting a court order to inspect your accounts."

"Be my guest."

"I also have men searching your house as we speak."

His gut clenched at the thought of a bunch of cops violating his home. It was his sanctuary. Every square foot of the place was the way he wanted it to be. "Make sure they wipe their feet. I hate cleaning those floors."

"Aren't you worried about what they'll find?"

"No, I'm not. I've got nothing to hide. That's why I agreed to this interview in the first place. The sooner you get this stupidity out of your system, the sooner you can get on with a real investigation. You thought Delaney was the target of the hit-and-run last week. Didn't you notice her resemblance to her stepdaughter?"

Toffelmire scowled. "What are you getting at?"

"Did it never occur to you someone is still targeting Delaney? They could have attacked her stepdaughter by mistake."

"Is that what you did?"

"Do you have any idea how idiotic you're sounding?"

"How long have you been having an affair with Mrs. Graye?"

"I see no point to that question."

"Oh, there's a point, Mr. Harrison. A man looking to protect his potential meal ticket would have a good motive to attack Elizabeth Graye. A man protecting his lover has an even better motive." He paused. "Or was it a lovers' quarrel? Was it too dark to tell them apart? Is that why you hit her?"

Max ground his teeth. His cooperation was getting him nowhere. He would have more luck talking to the wall. He focused on Toffelmire's mashed nose. "Get much sinus trouble, Detective?"

Toffelmire switched off the recorder, braced his forearms on the table, and leaned forward. "You got off easy last time because of your age. Your sentence was a joke. Instead of being grateful for the break you got, you transformed yourself into some grand *artiste* and came back to town to rub your success in our faces. You might have fooled some people, but I knew you'd slip up sooner or later."

"I haven't done anything. If you could see past your nose, you'd know that."

Toffelmire smiled. "No, I've got you this time, Harrison. You got cocky and signed your work."

"What the hell does that mean?"

The door swung open. Another cop stood on the threshold. Behind him was a large man with the rumpled appearance of a college professor.

Toffelmire twisted in his chair. "What is it, Frank?"

"This guy says he's Harrison's lawyer."

"I'm Leo Throop," the rumpled man said. "Unless Mr. Harrison has been charged with a crime, you have no right to detain him."

Max recognized the name. This was Delaney's lawyer. That figured. He should have known she wouldn't be sensible enough to keep out of this.

"Then allow me to correct the oversight," Toffelmire said. His chair scraped across the floor as he got to his feet. "John Maxwell Harrison, you're under arrest for the attempted murder of Elizabeth Graye. You have the right to remain silent. You have the right . . ."

Metal rattled. Max glanced down just as Toffelmire snapped a handcuff around his wrist.

His flesh shrank. Despite the open door, there wasn't enough air in the room to fill his lungs. The past wasn't staying buried. It rose to embrace him like a rotting corpse.

FOR THE FIRST TIME SINCE SHE HAD INHERITED HER husband's fortune, Delaney was grateful to have the money. Because of it, she'd had no difficulty posting Max's bail.

Leo wasn't certain he was innocent. Delaney had seen it in his face, and she was sure Max couldn't have missed it, either. Leo's personal opinion hadn't prevented him from doing his professional best, though. He'd used every means available to ensure Max wouldn't spend the night in jail. Delaney was grateful for that, too. The effect that only eight hours behind bars had had on him was heartbreaking.

She stole a glance at his profile. A band of illumination slid over his chin as they passed a streetlight. He could have been a marble statue, except a sculptor would have given him more expression. She kept her hands on the wheel and slipped him a mental caress.

There was no response. His mind was closed tight, as it had been throughout the day. It was different from the blank she'd sensed when he'd been sleeping. There was no lack of activity in his head; it was the other way around. Emotions were seething inside him. Every now and then a spark escaped to burn a bright spot on her vision, but it was quickly doused. He was channeling all his energy into control.

She slowed as they approached the lane to Max's property. "I'm staying with you."

"Good."

His ready agreement surprised her. She'd been prepared for resistance.

"You'll be safer with me at night," he said. "Your grandmother's place is too easy to break into."

She started up his driveway. "Do you think I'm in danger?"

"Yes."

"Is that the only reason you want me to stay?"

"No. We made a bargain."

She dropped her hand on his thigh. "I don't care about the bargain, Max. My only concern is you."

"Watch out!"

Delaney braked hard. Broken glass glittered in the headlights. The pieces were thick and brown, like the glass from a beer bottle.

Max threw open the door and got out. She locked up the car and followed, picking her way through the scattered shards to where he stood beside his Jeep.

It sat lower than it should. All four tires had been slashed to the rims. A message had been scratched into the paint on the side: "BURN IN HELL."

Delaney groped inside her purse for her phone.

"Who are you calling?"

"The police."

"Save your breath. They're not going to do anything."

"We need to report it."

"This isn't the first time my place has been vandalized." He aimed a kick at one of the larger chunks of glass. It arced into the shadows. "I just hadn't thought it would happen so soon. Word must have traveled fast."

Another bottle had been smashed against his front door. There was a splintered dent in the wood and more glass lay on the steps. He cleared them aside with the edge of his shoe. The windows she could see from here appeared to be intact. Helen had mentioned he'd replaced them with Plexiglas. Wasn't that fortunate? Delaney fought back the need to cry.

She lost the battle as soon as he opened the door.

His beautiful house was in shambles. Every cabinet in the kitchen had been emptied. The bookshelves were bare. The living room furniture had been upended and cushions strewn across the floor. Even the painting of the storm over the fireplace had been taken down.

But the front door had been locked. The police themselves had been responsible for the condition of the interior. They'd had a legal search warrant.

Delaney reached for her phone again, not to call anyone but to use its camera to take pictures. This had been more than a search; it had been a vindictive invasion of an innocent man's home. She wanted to make a record of what had been done. Toffelmire and his cronies shouldn't get away with this. Leo could file a complaint. Too bad her hands were shaking so badly she couldn't steady the phone.

She gave up and dropped her purse on an empty cabinet. She walked to where Max stood beside the couch.

He held one of the cushions, but he made no move to put it back in place. He remained motionless, his shoulders squared and his feet apart, as if he was bracing himself against the kind of weather he often depicted in his art. His attention was on the painting that lay on the floor. It bore the imprint of someone's shoe.

She blotted her eyes on her sleeve and moved behind him. "I'm sorry."

Like the heat from an opened oven door, rage gusted from his mind to hers. It cut off just as quickly. He dipped his chin in a stiff nod.

She slid her arms around his waist, pressing her cheek to his back. She sent her thoughts around his the same way. *This isn't fair.*

He laughed sharply. "Yeah."

"What on earth were they looking for? Could they have thought you had Elizabeth's purse?"

"Sure, why not? They might have even thought I stashed her car in here somewhere."

"They had no right to be so destructive. They didn't have grounds to arrest you in the first place."

He flung the cushion toward the couch. It bounced when it hit, flipped in the air, and landed sideways against the arm. "Since when does what's right make any difference? Welcome to reality, Delaney. *My* reality."

"You're not without resources this time, Max. If Leo can't help you, I'll hire someone who will."

"I can't take any more of your money. I'll pay you back for the bond you posted and for Leo's fee. First thing tomorrow I'll contact a security company. As soon as we set up protection, you should get as far away from me as you can before the stink rubs off on you."

She locked her hands over his stomach. "I'm not going anywhere."

His control continued to slip. He could no longer rein in his anger completely. It surrounded him in a charged haze. "I believed the past was over. I built this house to bury it. I learned to paint so I could leave it behind." His body jerked against her arms as he kicked the ruined canvas. It skidded across the floor and hit the stone fireplace with enough force to crack the frame. "I was deluding myself. It was all as phony as the worlds we used to make."

A fresh spurt of tears blurred her vision. They spilled down her cheeks to soak into his shirt. She imagined spreading herself over his back, shielding him with her body and her mind. "No, Max. You did leave your past behind. You're much more than the helpless child you once were. You've made yourself into a man anyone would be proud to call their friend."

He reached back to grab her wrist. He spun her to face him. More emotions leaked into hers. Along with the anger, there was pain. "I should have kept away from you. I never wanted the ugliness to touch you."

She stroked his cheek. "This is all a mistake. Elizabeth will tell them as soon as she wakes up."

"And if she doesn't?"

There had been no change in Elizabeth's condition when

Delaney had visited the hospital that afternoon. The doctor hadn't given her much hope, either. "Then we'll find some other way to beat this. Toffelmire can't prove that you're guilty just because he doesn't like you."

"Cops can lie. They can manufacture evidence. People you thought you knew can lie, too." He stopped. "We're wasting time. You need to uncover the rest of your memories."

"You still believe the attack on Elizabeth was connected to me."

"It must be." He took her hands in his. "You were right before. We have to combine our minds."

"But you said they're my memories. You can't put them in there."

"I could try helping you find them. I can make the pictures more vivid."

"It might not work. We're both upset. This can wait until we're thinking more clearly."

"Toffelmire could come up with some excuse to get my bail revoked tomorrow. If there's a chance your memories can explain what's happening, we need to take it. It's the best way to keep you safe."

This was what she'd wanted for weeks, yet she hesitated. If they joined their minds when he was in a state like this, it would be nothing like the controlled fantasies they'd shared before. She knew instinctively their union wouldn't be gentle.

"Please, Deedee." His voice roughened. "I can't help you if I'm in prison. Don't make that part of my past come back, too."

It was the first time she'd heard him say please. It moved her, even as it held her motionless. Tension arced from every point where their bodies touched. It was too late to resist where this was leading; they were halfway there already. Delaney inhaled unsteadily, dropped her forehead against his shoulder, and put her trust in Max.

The connection didn't begin with an image this time. He wasn't giving her a picture; he was giving himself. The emotions he'd been struggling to contain flowed crimson and white across her skin and behind her eyes. Power flared, raw and breathtaking. Her feet remained on the floor, yet she was swept along by the flood. She grasped his shoulders to keep her balance.

Her hands closed over bare skin. His fingers dug into the backs of her thighs. She was naked and weightless, held suspended in the swirl of a shared memory. Before she could fully open herself to absorb it, his mind meshed with hers.

Her legs gave out. In the part of her brain still conscious of reality, she felt Max lift her in his arms. He carried her up the stairs to the bedroom. It had received the same treatment as the rest of the house. The mattress had been flipped and lay askew on the bed, so he sank to his knees on the floor.

The moonlit room filled with colors. Some streaked as pure as the pleasure he'd first shown her weeks ago. Others were a tangled, earthy blend evoking what they'd experienced in the flesh. Her senses wove into his, reflecting every nuance of thought and passion, building and multiplying until the fullness verged on agony.

They didn't stop to question their actions. Though they'd spoken only of joining their minds, what happened next was inevitable. Fabric ripped. Buttons popped. Her fingers shook as she helped Max rid themselves of the remaining physical barriers between them. When they were finally as naked in fact as they were in their thoughts, the urgency dimmed. They were already joined. How could they possibly get closer?

They did. They came together in one smooth stroke as their bodies meshed as thoroughly as their minds. She felt the cool of polished wood beneath her back at the same time she felt it beneath Max's knees. She felt his chest hair abrade her nipples, and she learned how the hard nubs felt to him as he relaxed into her embrace. She wrapped her legs around his hips and perceived the slide of her own skin cradling his.

This was more than either of them had bargained for, more than she could have dreamed. Their breath mingled. Boundaries dissolved. Images exploded in a dizzying collage.

She saw herself as a child at the shore of the pond, her hair straggling like seaweed and muddy water streaking her chin. Then she was in the trailer and her mother was crying. The air stank of beer. Delaney reached to help her and felt pain lash across her back.

No. Not mine. Look for yours.

She tried to picture Stanford, the car, the accident.

Instead, she saw Max stick a twig in the middle of her

imaginary mud pie. He laughed as she tried to blow it out. Afterward, he took her hand to lead her through the rose garden while her father loaded her new pink suitcase into his car. Tears brimmed from her eyes as she waved good-bye through the back windshield. She felt them trickle over Max's cheeks as he watched her drive away.

We're too far back. Think of your husband.

She felt the weight of her wedding dress. It was covered with beads that glinted and rustled as she moved, like something that belonged to a fairy-tale princess. She walked toward the front of the church, her steps slowing as her feet grew heavy and the dress became shackles. The prison bus reeked of metal and spit. Whistles and catcalls pummeled her ears as she walked through the cell block.

Max laced his fingers with hers and held their joined hands to the floor on either side of her head. He was breathing hard. Her lungs felt scoured bare.

The memories continued to cascade, his mixing with hers until she couldn't tell where his ended and hers started. Time lost its meaning. She didn't know whether seconds or hours had passed before the first rush subsided and they learned how to direct the wave.

She saw herself in her satin nightgown, her scars vivid white and pink against her skin. Max stood in front of her, a paintbrush in his hand. He stroked a cloud to life behind her left shoulder, but the other side was on fire. Flames screamed and licked at her hair as they tightened their grasp.

She crossed her ankles behind his legs as her teeth began to chatter.

The heater whirred. The engine revved.

"*Let go!*"

"*I told you to turn around.*"

She braked hard. The car skidded to the shoulder. She unbuckled her seat belt and reached for the door handle.

Stanford lunged across the console to hold the door shut. "*We're not finished.*"

She pushed at his arm. "*You've had more than the hour you asked for, but you obviously lied about that, too. I don't care if I have to walk all the way to Willowbank from here.*"

"*Don't say that. Not after what it's cost me to keep you.*"

"*You're so obsessed with your wealth and with winning, you don't recognize what you could have had. You're pathetic, Stanford.*"

"*This isn't over.*"

"*Wrong. We're done.*" She twisted to jam the sole of her boot against the door and shoved. He lost his grip on the handle, and the door flew open. She had one foot on the ground when the car jerked forward. Stanford had angled himself onto the edge of her seat to reach the gas pedal. She screamed and grabbed the doorframe to keep from falling out.

Stanford caught her by the hair and yanked her back inside. "*I won't be made a laughingstock by a nobody like you. You're nothing without me.*"

They were accelerating. She fumbled for the ignition switch, but he struck her hand aside. She kicked at his leg but couldn't dislodge it, so she slammed her foot on the brake. "*Stanford, stop! This is insane.*"

The car swerved across the highway.

Stanford wrenched the wheel to the right to center the car on the road. "*You see, Delaney? I never lose. You should—*"

She cried out a warning. He'd steered too far. The car wouldn't make the curve. She fought to take the wheel. Through the open door came the sound of tires skidding on wet pavement and the noise of a V8 shrieking as it overpowered the brakes.

Then came the sound of crashing. Of metal screeching as it buckled, glass singing as it burst. Fire whooshed and crackled, but it didn't touch her. It was in the distance, and she was cold. Freezing. She couldn't feel her hands.

Max brought their joined hands to his mouth. He warmed her skin with his breath. *That's enough.*

She didn't want to see the rest. She wanted it to stop, but she knew it wasn't over. The worst was yet to come. She had to see it all, or she would never be free. She rolled her head back and forth against the floor and looked past him.

She was in a snowbank. That was why she was cold. She had been thrown clear when the car hit the pole, but Stanford was still inside, and he was screaming. Pain sliced through her leg when she tried to stand, so she crawled. By the time she reached the car, flames were billowing through the rear windshield.

Stanford was crushed against the console between the deflated air bags. His knees were pinned beneath the dashboard. She stretched her arms through the open door to grasp his wrist, but she couldn't move him and his legs were on fire and oh, God, that stench. It was the smell of her husband's flesh burning.

He was dying. Through the glaze of pain, the knowledge was there in his eyes.

She shook his arm. "Stanford! Don't give up. Hang on!"

He fastened one hand in her hair and the other on her sleeve. His face contorted as he bared his teeth. Every muscle contracted with his efforts. But he wasn't trying to pull himself out; he was pulling her in.

The flames gnawed her fingers. Her sleeve caught fire, then her blouse, then her arm. It clawed from her breast to her neck and her hair. Even her lungs were burning. She couldn't breathe. Tendrils of seaweed combined with the flames. She was drowning in the midst of the fire.

"You're mine, Delaney!" Stanford's voice crackled through her head. "I'll never let you go."

No, NO! She tried to move, but her legs were caught by the mud. Her mouth filled with silt. She was sinking deeper. In a flash of awareness she remembered the other time. She saw the long-forgotten void where death had claimed her before . . .

And then she remembered the skinny little blue-eyed boy who had fought for her life.

Power washed through her body, giving her the strength to fight for herself. She barely felt the sizzle of flesh as she grabbed the metal doorframe for leverage. She smashed her elbow into her husband's throat again and again until she heard bone crunch like celery. His hold slackened. She fell to the ground and crawled back to the sheltering snow.

Delaney didn't realize she had been screaming until she felt the ringing in her ears.

She tore her mind free. The image shattered.

And the past lost its grip.

TWENTY-NINE

❦

THE COPS HAD GONE EASY ON THE STUDIO. THEY HAD probably exhausted themselves by the time they'd reached it. Apart from a stack of canvases that had been spread on the floor like a deck of cards and the shelf of paints that had been emptied, it had been left relatively untouched. It took less than ten minutes for Max to restore order to the room. Restoring order to his thoughts would take longer.

He cranked open the windows as far as they would go. While the breeze cleared out the last traces of the cops' intrusion, he retrieved the painting of Deedee from the floor and placed it on his easel. It still wasn't finished. After the connection they'd forged the night before, he should be able to spot what was missing.

Then again, maybe not. There were still layers of colors and textures they hadn't had the chance to share. It would take more than one night to experience them all. Maybe more than one lifetime.

"So it was real."

He turned toward Delaney's voice. She walked from the bedroom to the studio. She had wrapped a sheet around her shoulders like a cape so only her bare feet and one arm were exposed. They'd pulled the mattress back onto the bed before they'd gone to sleep, and she'd been snoring softly when he'd left her. She appeared as if she'd just woken up. Her eyelids were puffy, and a pink sleep wrinkle creased her cheek. He made a mental snapshot of the image. He decided he would paint her like this someday. "What was real?"

"The portrait. I saw it through your eyes in our minds." She stopped beside him and regarded the painting. "When did you do that?"

"I started it weeks ago."

She extended her hand through the gap in the sheet to touch the painted scars. "I don't know how you managed it, but they don't look ugly."

"I told you they weren't."

She shifted her hand to his back. "Neither are yours, Max."

It was another one of those small things that he wasn't accustomed to yet. Each time Delaney touched his scars, he felt the stretching itch of healing beneath his skin.

He leaned down to kiss her.

Afterimages of memories flashed through his head. A jumble of emotions followed. Sympathy, sadness, longing, loneliness.

No, the loneliness belonged with the memories. After last night, there was no going back. Whether he wanted it or not, she was a part of him now. Like the touch of her hand, he felt her presence right down to his bones. The ease with which their minds had fused made him suspect she had never left him. She'd been there all along, in the secret corner of his heart that he'd given to Deedee on the day he'd turned seven.

Was this what she called love? It was more than sex, that was for sure. It was more than their mental link, too. Each on its own had packed a wallop, yet combining the two had united them in a way that would take him a while longer to come to grips with. She'd told him he was afraid to love anyone. It must be true, because what he felt right now scared the hell out of him.

She turned her head aside to smother a yawn against his shoulder.

The sound of his laugh startled him. What did he have to laugh about? Nothing had really changed. The life that he'd built was unraveling. He was only a cop's whim away from getting tossed back in jail. Their efforts to delve into Delaney's memories had strengthened their bond and had severed her last tie with her husband but had yielded nothing that shed any light on who was behind the recent violence. He had no right to feel happy.

"What's so funny?"

"Yawning after a kiss is hard on a man's ego."

"Your ego needs no encouragement," she said. "If you weren't so insatiable I wouldn't be yawning." She nipped his shoulder. "I'm surprised you're up this early."

"I needed to make some phone calls."

She stepped back. "If you're still planning to arrange security for me so I can leave, forget it. I'm staying with you, Max."

The pleasure that followed her declaration was scary, too. For her sake, he should be tossing her out on her ass. He couldn't use their bargain to justify keeping her here, either. It had been fulfilled. "You should think about what you're getting into. I've been charged with attempted murder. I know the drill. The arrest was only the start. Things are going to get a lot worse."

Her thoughts wound a caress around his. "I'm sorry," she said. "I had honestly believed once I remembered what happened with Stanford, everything would become clear. It didn't help at all. The only person we know who had wanted to hurt me is already dead."

He sensed a curl of old panic deep beneath her words. He sent a stroke of calmness to smooth it out.

"The pain must have made him crazy," she said. "He wasn't an evil man. He was possessive and stubborn, that's all. And proud. He couldn't deal with failure."

"You're still making excuses."

"I need to make excuses for myself, too. Elizabeth was right. I did kill my husband. You saw it."

He'd done more than that; he'd experienced it with her. He'd felt her arm connect with Stanford's throat. The crunch they'd heard had likely been the cartilage of his windpipe breaking. He might have choked to death before the fire finished him, just like . . .

Like Max's mother had been choking on her own blood before Virgil had strangled her. The parallel was eerie. The outcome had been worlds apart. "It was self-defense. You had no choice if you wanted to live."

"You helped me then, too, Max. You were the key to my memories because you were at the heart of them. It was the memory of how you saved me from drowning that let me save myself from Stanford."

Above everything else their minds had shared, that particular detail remained the most vivid. The boy he'd once been hadn't always been a dumb chickenshit. He hadn't failed completely. Even though he hadn't known it, he had managed to protect one woman he loved from a monster.

Love. Damn. There was that word again.

"But none of this helps you," she said. "We still don't have a clue who attacked Elizabeth."

"It did help me, Delaney. It showed me that burying the past doesn't work. Not if it isn't dead first."

"It sounds as if you've done some thinking."

"Yeah. Your bad habits are contagious." The sound of slamming car doors came from the front of the house. He fought down a jab of panic, his own this time instead of hers. She'd had the courage to face her nightmare. He could do no less. "That's probably the cops."

She whirled toward the stairs. "Oh, God. Now what?"

"It's okay. I called them."

"Why?"

"I changed my mind and reported the vandalism. I want whatever snot-nosed punk who broke those bottles and trashed my Jeep tracked down and nailed to the wall, even if I have to pick up every piece of glass myself and have it dusted for prints. I'm going to file a complaint about the condition Toffelmire's crew left my house in, too. Someone's going to pay for that painting they stomped. I'm through taking this kind of shit."

Her smile was dazzling. So bright, in fact, it made his eyes water.

He cleared his throat. "Don't look at me like that."

"Like what?"

"Like you're about to get going on one of your do-it-yourself psychology kicks. It's not that big a deal. I pay my taxes. I recycle. I'm an upstanding citizen now, not some dumb teenager from the trailer park."

Delaney hiccupped on a sob. "Oh, Max."

"I served my time for what I did to Virgil, and I'll be damned if I'm going to keep taking the blame for what he did."

"Does this mean you're going to get your case reopened?"

"Sure, why not? Give the professor something else to do. He might give me a half-decent defense if he finds out I'm innocent. Of part of it, anyway."

"You're what I've always said you were. You're a good man."

Max wanted more than anything to believe she was right, but it was hard to hope. It went against the lessons of a lifetime. It made something stretch and itch deep inside, and it *hurt* . . .

. . . as healing often did.

THE WAINRIGHT HOUSE WAS UNCHARACTERISTICALLY empty as Delaney lugged her suitcase down the stairs. No vacuum cleaner hummed in the dining room. Phoebe hadn't come in today. The couple who had been staying here the night Elizabeth had been attacked had checked out early and gone home as soon as the police had finished questioning them. Helen had canceled the rest of her bookings for the next two weeks. Having violence essentially at her doorstep had disturbed her, and she was concerned about the safety of Phoebe and her guests. Above all, she worried about her granddaughter.

Delaney left her suitcase by the front door and went through the house to the kitchen.

The noise of a drill came from the backyard where Edgar was installing a lock on the garden shed. Metal rattled as his nephew propped an extension ladder against the oak to prune a dead limb. Max had spoken to them both before he'd agreed to leave her here to pack. Although it was broad daylight and he was only going as far as the gallery, he'd wanted their assurance they'd keep an eye on the place.

Helen was sitting in the breakfast nook beneath the window. A teapot rested on the table beside her elbow, and her hands were curled around one of the blue mugs with the marching geese. Her mouth was pursed tight when she glanced at Delaney.

Delaney slid onto the bench across from her. "Don't be mad at me."

"I'm not mad; I'm concerned. I wish you would reconsider your plan to move in with John."

"I love him, Grandma."

She added a spoonful of sugar to her tea and stirred vigorously. "It's because I love you that I'm going to speak bluntly, Deedee. I'm not sure you know what you're doing. You've been home for less than a month. You're still recovering from a terrible accident and from losing your husband. You've only just learned the truth about your marriage. This isn't the time to rush into another relationship."

"Believe me, I've told myself all of this already."

"Then don't go."

"He'll be picking me up as soon as he's finished at the gallery."

Helen clinked her spoon against her cup.

"I lent him my car so he could take the painting the police ruined to have it officially appraised," she went on. "He deserves to be reimbursed for its value. It's not the money; it's a matter of principle."

"It's fine to sympathize with his situation, Delaney, but don't confuse—"

"I don't just sympathize with him. I love him."

"How could that be? You just met."

This wasn't the time to explain her history with Max. Helen might not believe how they first met. She certainly wouldn't believe the other aspects of their relationship. Who would? "I feel it in here," she said, tapping her forefinger over her heart. "It's not anything like what I read about in fairy tales or what I talked myself into believing about Stanford. It's not sweet. A lot of the time it hurts, and the strength of what's between us is so totally encompassing that it can be frightening to regard head-on. He's a complex man. It's going to take me years to fully understand him. All I'm certain of is that we become more when we're together than when we're apart. What we have is . . . real."

"It sounds as if you do feel deeply about him. That only makes me more worried."

"Grandma . . ."

"Ada's granddaughter works in the emergency ward at the hospital. She's a nurse."

The change of topic startled her. "Oh?"

"She was on duty the night Elizabeth was brought in. She wasn't supposed to talk about this because it's evidence in the police investigation, but she did tell her grandmother because Ada had been singing John's praises since the festival, and she felt it was her duty to warn her."

"What is it you're trying to say, Grandma?"

"There was a welt on Elizabeth's back. It might have been from the edge of the gatepost, but the police think she was hit with something like a belt after she fell."

"And that's why they assume John is guilty? That's ridiculous. Ada's granddaughter shouldn't be spreading rumors, either. That's exactly the kind of attitude that encourages vandalism."

"If it turns out that he is guilty—"

"He isn't. Trust me, John Harrison would be the last man on earth who would strike a woman. Ever."

"He assaulted his mother."

There was no need to go into this, either. If Leo did his job—and she intended to make sure he did—the truth would come out soon enough. "Grandma, you said you followed the case. You're a good judge of character. Do you really believe he got a fair trial?"

Helen looked away.

It was a fitting response. How different would Max's and his mother's life have been if people hadn't looked away?

"I only want you to be happy, Deedee. I can't help feeling that you're making a mistake."

Her grandmother could be right. Trusting Max could be the biggest mistake of her life. Not because he might be guilty— that was simply inconceivable—yet she did have a poor record when it came to recognizing love. She and Max hadn't spoken of their future—they hadn't even spoken of tomorrow—yet she was already regarding this move as permanent. Maybe it was only sympathy she was feeling. Maybe he did want her only for sex. It was possible their relationship would fizzle as soon as the novelty wore off and life got back to normal.

Was it *normal* to experience sex from the inside out? Would she ever regard meshing their minds as routine? She closed her eyes and sought him. She sensed people around him, rectangles of color against a white wall and striped awnings outside a square window. He was still at the gallery. She trailed her fingertips down his arm. He responded with a quick squeeze. Pleasure as light as cattail seeds gusted across her mind.

"Are you all right?"

She pulled her thoughts back from Max's, reached across

the table, and took Helen's hands. "You must have asked me that a hundred times since I came home. You've been more patient with me than I deserve. You're the best grandmother in the world."

Her lips trembled. "Watch it. I'm liable to ask for a raise."

There was a knock on the back door. Delaney glanced past Helen to see Edgar through the window. She expected him to step inside before she remembered Helen had been keeping the door locked since the attack on Elizabeth. She went to let him in.

He pulled off his baseball cap as he stepped over the threshold. He held a stack of what appeared to be pamphlets in his other hand. "Found these in the shed," he said.

Helen rose from the table. She frowned when she saw what he held. "Are those more Bible pamphlets? I've been finding one in my mailbox practically every day. Who would leave them in the shed?"

"Same joker who's been leaving the empties, if you ask me." He dropped the pamphlets in the blue bin beside the door. "Just as well you wanted me to put on a lock. Looks like someone helped themselves to a few of the tools—"

There was a yell from the backyard. Metal clattered as the ladder Pete had been using crashed to the ground.

Edgar was the first to run outside. Delaney followed with Helen on her heels. Pete lay beneath one end of the ladder. The pruning saw glinted from the grass beyond him. They were all focused on Pete. No one noticed the man who was standing behind the tree. They didn't see him step forward, either. Edgar was kneeling beside his nephew when the blade of a shovel struck the back of his head.

It happened so quickly, shock kept them immobile for a crucial second. Then Helen screamed. Delaney grabbed her arm, spun her toward the house, and started running with her. She didn't have the chance to take more than two steps before the shovel connected with the backs of her calves and she fell.

Instead of running away, Helen flew at the man. He knocked her aside like a gnat and drew the shovel back to take another swing at Delaney.

Horror blurred her vision. Pain slowed her reflexes. She had no time to do more than raise her arm to shield her head from the blow. In the split second before it hit, the image of her attacker seared across her brain.

This made no sense. He was a complete stranger. A pale, sickly man with thinning hair and drooping jowls. His eyes were lifeless black that glittered with the kind of madness she'd seen in her dying husband.

Yet that wasn't the only reason he seemed familiar.

THIRTY

❧

DELANEY WOKE TO THE SMELL OF PAINT. SHE WAS LYING on her side on a hard surface. Her arms were angled so far behind her back, her shoulders burned. Her wrists were bound. She couldn't feel her hands.

In spite of all that, relief crashed through her mind. The force of it stole her breath. She inhaled frantically, but the air she drew in was ripe with turpentine fumes that singed her nose and the back of her throat.

The relief was followed by a flash of white-hot fury. *I'm sorry, Deedee.*

It was Max. Those had been his feelings that had flooded her head. She reached to absorb his thoughts. Tenderness engulfed her. The pain in her shoulders eased. So did the aches in her arm and the backs of her legs.

An image of the shovel descending replayed across her mind, along with a burst of something too deep to be called simply pain. Max reined in both fast and trembled another apology across her thoughts. *Where are you?*

She opened her eyes to a blur of color. Her head throbbed. She blinked, and the blur resolved into painted canvases that were stacked against a white wall. The wooden legs of an easel stood less than a yard from her face. Her sight confirmed what her other senses had already told her: she was lying on the floor of Max's studio.

Hang on, I'm coming.
Did you see?
I saw everything.

The throb in her head got worse. She saw the face of her attacker once more, the sagging jowls, the pale skin . . .

Other images superimposed themselves over the first. The man's undershirt was splotched with stains. It stretched tight across his belly. The sickly sweet, yeasty smell of beer hung on his breath and oozed from his pores . . .

Blood pulsed from his nose. She felt her knuckles crack and satisfaction race through her veins as she punched him again and again . . .

His hair was thinner. The belly had wasted to only a drooping pouch. The ravages of cancer had hollowed his cheeks and carved circles beneath his eyes.

Yet Delaney knew exactly who he was. The outside might have changed, but not the essence. She recognized that part from what she'd experienced in Max's memories.

Virgil Budge wasn't in prison. He wasn't dead. He had returned to Willowbank.

Scattered details moved into place. Phoebe's creepy guy in the woods. The open door of the garden shed, the gate left ajar. How long had he been here? What else had he done?

She thought of her grandmother. Edgar and Pete.

In reply, Max sent her an image of the Wainright House as it had been when he'd arrived there moments ago. His desperation tinted the scene orange and blurred the edges, yet she was able to see it. An ambulance was parked in the side yard. Helen was on her hands and knees in the backyard beside Edgar. Her hair had come loose from its pouf, but otherwise she seemed unharmed. She was yelling at Pete to keep still as paramedics lifted the ladder from him. One of his legs was broken—bone protruded from the skin—but he was trying to drag himself toward his uncle. Helen staggered upright when she saw Max. She told him someone had taken Delaney.

But he'd already known. Virgil's face had flashed across his mind at the same moment it had seared across Delaney's. It was why he'd driven back from the gallery when he'd lost contact with her. It was why he'd felt as if his heart had stopped beating until he'd found her presence once more. She knew all this instantaneously as his thoughts wove into hers. The connection between them was wide-open.

More rage spilled from Max's mind, along with waves of

fear that were both remembered and happening now. She clung to him as she saw the path through the woods unwind in front of him. She felt branches slap against his shins and brush his face as he ran. She'd traveled this path countless times in her nightmare. Now he was living it. He pushed his body for more speed, and her lungs ached with the effort.

Max broke free of the woods and sprinted across the embankment. Even from there he could see that the back door of his house gaped open. It hung crookedly from the splintered doorframe by one hinge. The garden shovel Virgil had used as a weapon lay on the deck with its handle snapped in two.

The splash of liquid brought Delaney back into her surroundings. She twisted her neck to look behind her.

Virgil stood near one of the shelves that held Max's painting supplies. He was pouring a can of turpentine on a roll of blank canvas. Another open can lay on the floor in a gleaming pool of liquid.

Max, he's here! She pulled her legs to her chest, shifting her weight to one side in an attempt to sit up.

Virgil looked at her.

The impact of his gaze made her gag. She'd been wrong; it wasn't like Stanford's. This man's gaze was pure evil.

He set the can on Max's worktable, crossed the floor, and grabbed her by the back of her blouse.

Fresh pain knotted her shoulders. Max's rage drowned it out. She threw herself to the side.

Virgil twisted the fabric in his fist and yanked her backward. "You're not going anywhere, whore. Not after the trouble I went to, to get you."

"Why?" She coughed. Her throat was clogged. "Why are you doing this?"

" 'Vengeance is mine, saith the Lord.' "

"You're insane." It wasn't merely an insult. Attacking four people in broad daylight wasn't the act of a rational man. He had to realize he wouldn't be able to fade back into wherever he'd been hiding now. "You know you can't get away with this."

He laughed. "I don't have to. I'll be dead before I get to trial."

She strained against his grasp but couldn't break it. He had the appearance of a sick man, yet he had the strength of a madman. It couldn't last for long. Or so she prayed.

"Now scream." He dragged her on her rear along the floor through the puddle of turpentine. "I like it when they scream."

She clenched her jaw.

He cuffed her across the shoulders.

The cry she heard wasn't hers; it was Max's. It was deep, rough, and primal, ripping through her head and her ears just as his footsteps pounded up the stairs.

Virgil jerked her toward the windows and pulled a lighter from the pocket of his pants.

Her scars stung. Her heart froze. Not again. Oh, God, she couldn't go through this a second time, or she would surely lose her sanity.

Max took in the scene in an instant. She saw it through his eyes: the fluid soaking into her skirt, the lighter, Virgil's sneer as he held her helpless. The panic that seized her was nothing compared to the terror that coursed through him. He held up his palms and stepped forward. "Let her go, Virgil."

"Stop!" He flicked the lighter. Flame sparked to life. He waved it over Delaney once in warning, then took his thumb from the flint wheel and let it subside. "Don't come any closer."

Max halted. "It's me you want to hurt, not her. She's done nothing."

"She's yours, isn't she? I've got the right one this time. I've been watching you, boy."

"What did you do? Break out of the pen just to spy on me?"

"Didn't have to break out. I'm dying. They opened the door and let me go."

"You should have kept going. You don't belong here."

"This used to be my home, you little prick. Look what you did to it."

"Yeah. It took years to get rid of your stench. Why'd you come back?"

"I'm on the Lord's business. I'm here to make sure you pay for your sins."

"Which ones? I've lost count."

"You turned my woman against me. It's your fault she died. It's your fault I'm sick. My insides never healed right after what you did to me."

"My mother's dead because you murdered her. You got liver cancer because you're a drunk. If I'd killed you when I'd had the chance, those things wouldn't have happened, so it's true it's my fault. Your problem's with me. Let her go."

"Sure. First, you pick that up." He nodded to the can he'd left on the table. "There's still plenty in the bottom."

Delaney kept her gaze on Max so that she couldn't see the lighter, but she began to tremble anyway. She knew how fast skin and hair ignited. Her throat was swelling from the solvent fumes. It was hard to draw breath.

Max skimmed his thoughts over her midriff and the tightness in her lungs eased. *Hang on, Deedee. The cops are on their way. I won't let him hurt you. I promise.*

"Go on, you chickenshit," Virgil said. "Do what I say, or I'll light her now."

Max snatched the can off the table. "Fire's not your style, Virgil. I didn't think a shovel was, either. Why don't you use your belt?"

"This is better. You deserve to burn in hell. Was damned handy you had all this turpentine."

"What's better than the feel of that belt? You like to beat defenseless women and children. That's easier than taking on a man."

"Quit stalling. Pour the rest of that stuff on your clothes."

"Remember how good it was? All that power in your hand?"

"I've got power now." He waved the lighter back and forth in front of Delaney's face. His thumb was poised on the wheel. "Go on."

Max tipped the can toward his chest. Turpentine flowed down his shirt. "That belt whistled before it hit. That's how I knew when it would happen. It made a noise like a snap when it hit the middle of my back and a crack when it hit my shoulder."

"More," Virgil ordered. "Douse yourself like your girl-friend."

"The noise was duller when you drew blood." Max upended the can over his shoulder. The liquid spread down his arm and dripped from his fingers to his pants. "Was that why you didn't do it every time? It wasn't loud enough?"

"You had it coming, just like your mother."

"You squealed like a pig when I did the same to you. Do you remember that, Virgil?"

Delaney heard the scuff of a footstep on the stairs. She

coughed again, hoping to mask it. Virgil didn't react. He didn't seem to notice that Max was moving closer, either.

Max shook out the last drops from the can and flung it aside. "I do remember. That's why I don't own a belt. I liked it too much."

"You caught me when my back was turned. I could've taken you."

"A fair fight's not your style either, Virgil. Where'd you steal the car you used at the park?"

Virgil laughed. "I didn't need to steal it. I borrowed it from the preacher who got me out of the pen. He knows I'm doing God's work."

"You still can't drive worth shit."

"You got lucky." He tightened his grip on Delaney's blouse. "It was because of *her*."

She tensed, gathering her feet beneath her, expecting the flames to start clawing her at any second.

Max squeezed her fingers. She felt it even though her hands were numb. *Almost there.*

"This is better than running you down," Virgil said. "I get to see your face when you lose it all. An eye for an eye."

Uniformed figures rushed from the staircase. "Police! Freeze!"

Virgil jerked. He flicked the lighter. Sparks danced off the flint.

Before they could ignite, Max launched himself at his stepfather. With a cry that sliced through her mind even before she heard it, he snatched the lighter from Virgil's hand and drove his fist into his stomach.

The force of the blow lifted Virgil from his feet and propelled him toward the open window. The backs of his legs struck the sill. He flailed to regain his balance, but his momentum carried him through the screen. There was a cry, followed by a thud.

Max didn't even glance outside. He was already on the floor beside Delaney. His mind was still open. Emotions too huge to name tumbled into hers. *Are you all right?*

Feel for yourself.

He tossed the lighter to one of the policemen and untied the rag that bound her wrists so he could check her skin for damage. The grafts were still whole. He followed her thoughts to probe gently through her body, found the aches he'd missed earlier, and drew them into himself. *He was after me, not you. I should have guessed it.*

You couldn't have known. We were both looking in the wrong direction.

When I saw that face . . .

A remnant of despair drifted into her mind from Max's. It was so deep it brought tears to her eyes. *It's all right. It's over.*

I can't imagine my life without you in it. I can't lose you, Deedee.

You won't, Max. I'm here to stay.

"The ambulance should be here soon. Do you folks need some assistance?"

The policeman's voice cut through their haze. More voices came from outside. A siren wailed in the distance. Max shoved himself back to his feet and helped Delaney to stand. Two more officers stood at the window Virgil had gone through. One spoke on his radio. The crackled response was a blur until one phrase floated free from the rest.

"Budge is dead."

Max jerked. His chest heaved as it had when he'd been running here, as if he couldn't draw enough air into his lungs. She curled her thoughts around his to steady him.

"Better wait for the paramedics, Frank. The drop wasn't that far."

"No, he's dead, all right. He hit the edge of the deck and snapped his neck."

"Well, I'll be damned," Max said hoarsely. "I finally did it."

The policeman lowered his radio. "We all saw what happened, Harrison. It was accidental."

"That's right. I wasn't trying to kill him. I was trying to save—" His voice broke. A long-forgotten thought rose from his memories.

On the very day he had decided to take a life, his destiny had been to save one.

Max folded Delaney into his arms. Images streamed from his mind to hers. The pond where he'd first seen her. The cement block step in front of the trailer where he'd last seen

Virgil. The fire from six months ago, and the fire that Max had stopped from happening today. Something shifted into place, like a puzzle, like two halves at last fitting together to form a whole, like . . .

Like destiny fulfilled.

EPILOGUE

❦

"THE SWELLING WITHIN MISS GRAYE'S SKULL HAS GONE down." Dr. McFadden made a note in the chart he held as he spoke. "Her body is healing well, due in part to her excellent physical condition."

Delaney stepped around the extra shelf they'd placed in the room to accommodate all the flowers Elizabeth had received. Cards and gifts had been pouring in from the Grayecorp staff, although so far only one friend had come to Willowbank to visit her. Edgar and Pete, on the other hand, had been swamped with well-wishers. They were both expected to make a full recovery from Virgil's attack. "Has she shown any signs of waking up?"

"No, I'm afraid not. She continues to be unresponsive."

Max squeezed Delaney's shoulder. "Go ahead and talk to her. Sometimes people in comas can hear what's going on around them."

"That's been true in rare cases," McFadden said. "However, whether it's true in Miss Graye's case or not, she might benefit from sensory stimulation of any kind."

"There's still hope, then?"

"There's always hope, Mrs. Graye."

Delaney moved to her stepdaughter's side as the doctor left the room. She took her hand. It was completely flaccid, proof of her condition, because she would have yanked it away if she'd been capable of it. With her hair loose around her shoulders and her face bare of makeup, she appeared softer, younger, nothing like the driven executive she'd been a week ago. "I wish I could reach her mind the way I can reach yours, Max."

"Doesn't work that way, does it?"

"No, but think of how much we could help her if it did."

"You're incredible."

"Why?"

"You're just so . . . good."

She smiled. "Sometimes it pays to look on the bright side, you know. I was right about her. She didn't try to run me down. All she did was try to be her father's daughter." She massaged Elizabeth's limp hand. "I'm sorry this happened to you, Bethie. I want you to know that the man who did this to you is dead. He was the one responsible for the hit-and-run you were suspected of, although I never did want to believe you would want to hurt me that much. It turns out he wasn't aiming for me anyway; he was aiming for Max. I mean John."

"Yeah," Max said. "Too bad I hadn't seen it."

"A very good friend of mine once told me there's no explanation for evil."

He trailed a kiss across her mind. It was a taste of what would come later.

Five days had passed since Virgil's death. It was wrong to say the event had changed Max. He was the same man he'd always been, as she'd often said. The only difference was that he was learning to recognize it.

No, that wasn't the only difference, she thought as he continued the mental caress. The nights since the first time they'd united themselves completely had brought one discovery after another. They'd only begun to explore the potential of their special bond. Max had been applying himself to the pleasurable aspects of it with impressive enthusiasm.

Her lips quirked. There were advantages to having a lover with a vivid imagination.

"Delaney, John. I'm glad I caught you."

At Leo's voice, she returned Elizabeth's hand to the blanket and turned toward the doorway.

Leo bustled in, his ever-present briefcase tucked beneath his arm. "Congratulations, John. You're officially a free man. The police have dropped the attempted murder charge."

Max snorted. "Took them long enough."

"That's wonderful, Leo," Delaney said.

"Detective Toffelmire insisted on processing the evidence first. It was overwhelming. The imprint of the belt that was taken from Mr. Budge's body matched the mark on Miss Graye's back perfectly. The police had been hoping to find that belt and her purse during their search."

"Idiots," Max muttered.

"Her rental car was found abandoned near the lake, along with her purse. Mr. Budge's fingerprints were on both. They believe he did attack her on the assumption she was you, Delaney."

"It still doesn't make complete sense to me," she said. "He wanted revenge against Max. Why go after anyone else?"

"He liked to hit women," Max said.

"Actually, there could be more involved," Leo said. "The preliminary autopsy reports indicate Mr. Budge's cancer had spread to his brain. He may not have been completely sane."

"He never was."

"Budge's fingerprints were also found on a fragment of glass that was collected from your driveway, John. He was responsible for the vandalism."

"Yeah, I kind of figured that out."

"Unfortunately, Detective Toffelmire is remaining firm in his stance that the damage to the interior of your home during its search was accidental."

"Naturally."

"Do you think it might help if I offered to pay for the surgery to have his nose fixed?" Delaney asked.

Max laughed, but Leo shook his head. "Some things are better left alone."

"Not always," she said. "The past needs to be dealt with before we can move forward."

Leo glanced past her to Elizabeth and cleared his throat. "About that . . ."

She waited, but he seemed hesitant to continue. "Leo, what is it?"

"I hope you will understand that I've always had your best interests at heart, Delaney. While my methods may have been harsh, everything I've done, I've done in the name of friendship."

"Yes, I know. You've been—"

"Wait, please let me finish. I've admired your courage during your long climb back to health. I truly believed your amnesia had been a blessing. Your insistence on recovering your memories distressed me more than I can say."

She opened her mouth to interrupt again but was stopped by Max's mental tap against her lips. He looped his arm around her shoulders. *He's choking on something. Let him spit it out.*

Leo shifted his briefcase to both arms, holding it across his chest like a shield. "I'm sorry, Delaney. Elizabeth didn't send you the photographs of Stanford; I did."

She stiffened. "You *what*?"

"It was to discourage you from remembering and also to encourage you to initiate the countersuit. I'm sorry," he repeated. "I may have been overzealous in my efforts, and it may seem cruel in retrospect, but I believed it was for your own good."

"For my own good? That's ridiculous. It would have been kinder to simply tell me about Stanford's affairs in the first place."

"Protecting you from his infidelities wasn't the main reason I didn't want you to recover your memories. It was because of Elizabeth's lawsuit."

"I don't understand."

"I was concerned you might remember something about the accident that would make defending you, ah, problematic."

It took her a moment to grasp what he meant. "You thought she was right, didn't you? From the beginning, you believed I *did* cause Stanford's death."

"I suspected there might be something more serious than your marital troubles that had caused your mind to block those memories. I didn't want to know what it was. I didn't want you to know, either, because then you would likely feel obligated to tell the authorities."

She hesitated.

Max gave her another mental tap against her lips. *Don't.*

"And as I've said before," Leo continued, "certain things are best left alone."

"When it comes to my husband's death, I happen to agree with you."

"Thank you, Delaney. I hope that means we can put this unpleasantness behind us."

"Sending those photographs was more than unpleasant, Leo. It was horrible."

"Please. You were willing to forgive your stepdaughter when you thought she might have done it, so I do hope you can find it in your heart to forgive me."

"There's no excuse . . ." She paused when she realized what she was about to say. She'd been willing to excuse everyone else. Leo was a loyal friend. He didn't deserve to be condemned without a chance.

Don't forgive him, Deedee.

He didn't mean any harm, Max, she sent back. *Everyone makes mistakes.*

Come on, let me hit him for you. I hate lawyers.

Don't you dare!

It would help him get rid of his guilt. I'd be doing him a favor. See how miserable he is?

This wasn't funny, yet after everything else that she and Max had gone through, it did seem trivial. "It's Elizabeth you should be apologizing to, Leo. No one deserves to be accused unfairly."

"Yes, of course. I will. Thank you, Delaney. You're an exceptional woman. I—" He stopped and glanced at Max. "Speaking of unfair accusations, I've begun the process of clearing your name, John. It will take time, but we do have the statements from the police who overheard your conversation with Budge. Combined with the other evidence, I believe we have cause for optimism."

MAX WAS QUIET ON THE DRIVE HOME. THE DAMAGE THE police and Virgil had done to the house had been repaired days ago, yet faint traces of turpentine lingered in the air when he unlocked the door. The scent didn't disturb Delaney, because it would always remind her of Max. He dropped his keys in the ceramic dish. That sound reminded her of him, too. In fact, practically everything made her think of him these days. That wasn't surprising, since he had taken up residence in her heart.

Before he could move past the living room, she slid her arms around his waist and leaned back to look up at him. "You're mulling about something. What's going on?"

"Come upstairs, and I'll show you."

"Have you been thinking about what Leo said?"

"You guessed it."

"It's wonderful, isn't it? I'm going to make sure the local newspapers carry the story, even if I need to buy the page space."

"He wouldn't want it made public."

"I meant the review of your conviction, not his confession."

"He didn't confess. He took one look at me, and he chickened out."

"What are you talking about?"

"He's in love with you."

"Leo? No, we're just friends."

"No, take it from me, I know that expression. I feel it on my face whenever I look at you."

She stared at him.

"Why do you seem so surprised? We don't have any secrets. You've felt how I feel. You told me about it before I recognized it."

"You've never said the words."

"Sure. It still scares the shit out of me."

"Why? You must know by now I'd never hurt you."

He dropped his forehead against hers. "It's because I don't want to hurt you, Deedee. I've lived alone for too long. It's taking a while for me to realize this isn't a dream, that I wake up with you in my arms for real. I'm not used to being . . ."

Free? she offered.

"Depends how you define *free*."

"Give it a try. I've got all day. Actually, I've got the rest of my life."

He smiled, swept her into his arms, and headed for the stairs. "I'd rather show you."

She nestled against him, her body softening to welcome his. If he wanted to express himself through sex, she certainly wouldn't object. He was right; she had already sensed what he'd felt.

He didn't carry her into the bedroom. Instead, he went to

his studio and stopped at his easel. "I finished it this morning. What do you think?"

The painting displayed on the easel was the portrait he'd done of her. Her features were the same as before. So were her scars. She was still posed in front of the cloud and the fire, but he'd painted one major addition.

She slid out of his embrace. She barely felt her feet touch the floor as she moved closer. Understanding spread through her even before he began to explain.

"Now, I don't want you to accuse me of getting philosophical or turning all artsy or anything, but I figured something out. That background is split between good and evil like a lot of my stuff is. You're in the middle because you represent the balance."

She held her fingertips over the second figure he'd painted. "And this?"

"That's your shadow."

It wasn't a shadow; it was Max. He placed himself behind her, his arms wrapped around her in an embrace that sheltered yet didn't hide. They weren't leaning on each other. They both stood straight and strong, braced to survive whatever fate might have in store for them. Their appearances were nothing alike. She was fair and he was dark. Her expression was open, his was cautious. She was as solid as sunshine and he swirled with energy like the wind, yet together they were complete.

He was with her. Within her. A part of her forever. It was a depiction of love that no words could equal.

It was the promise their hearts had made the day they had met.

"ELIZABETH?"

She opened her eyes. The world was a blur. Her body was a mass of aches. Pain throbbed through her skull. She wanted nothing more than to go back to sleep.

"Hey." A hand settled on her shoulder. "Are you okay?"

She knew that voice. She squinted until the blur fused into a face. Large nose. Beard stubble on a square jaw. Eyes of amber that reached as deep as his music.

The pain ebbed. "Rick?"

"Yeah." He loomed over her. No, *loom* was the wrong word. He was kneeling at her side, and there was nothing threatening about his size. Even in the dim light, the concern on his face was plain. He touched her temple. "Does your head hurt? You've been drifting in and out."

She blinked a few times, giving herself a chance to take stock. Yes, her head hurt. The agony was there as it always was, but it was retreating to the background. She flexed her limbs carefully. Her joints were stiff, her muscles sore, as if she'd overdone it on the Bowflex and had neglected to cool down.

But those memories were from *before*, when her life was normal. Reality was different now. She knew in her bones that she wasn't yet home. A chill seeped through her back from the floor where she lay. She moved her foot, expecting to feel the slide of stone.

Instead, she felt dirt. Her feet were bare. She looked past Rick. The walls were made of wood. So was the door. A pale strip of light seeped beneath it. The air was muggy rather than damp and it was ripe with the scent of vegetation. Insects whirred. An animal she couldn't identify screeched in the distance.

They weren't in the dungeon anymore. They were in the hut in the jungle.

She attempted to rise when she discovered her wrists were bound together with a plastic bundling tie. Again. Or had they never been in manacles? She groaned.

Rick slid his arm beneath her shoulders and helped her sit up. "Sorry I couldn't get that band off your wrists," he said, as if he guessed what she'd been thinking. "There's no slack in that plastic. It's locked tight."

"Did you see them?"

"Who?"

"The people who brought us here. Who were they? What did they do to us? How did they transport us?"

"I don't know."

"But you were awake. You must have seen something."

"I only woke up once we were here. I heard men outside, talking in Spanish. Couldn't make out much of what they said, but I did pick out your name. They called you Isabella. Is this the place you talked about before? The camp with the rebel soldiers?"

"It must be. The hut's the same."

"Not much to see except dirt and wood, but it seems built as solid as that cell in the castle basement."

"Then you tried to get out?"

He stroked her hair from her cheek. "To tell you the truth, I've been more concerned about you than about where we are. Something strange is going on."

"Something strange? *Strange?* And what would that be? The fact that we seem to have been magically transported from a castle to a jungle camp with no knowledge or memory of what happened?"

"Yeah, that, too, but I was talking about you."

"How so?"

"Your shiner's gone."

"My what?"

"The black eye you got from the rock." He touched the corner of her eye. "The swelling's gone down. There's no bruise."

She explored it herself as much as she was able with her wrists bound. He was right; the eye had healed. She touched her neck. The scratch had healed, too. Again.

"There's nothing left of that stab wound from the sword in your side, either," he said.

"We must have been kept drugged for months."

"By nothing, I mean nothing. Not even a scar."

She lifted her arms and twisted to see her side. She was once more wearing the baggy trousers and linen shirt. Dirt smeared the fabric, but there was no blood. She hooked her little fingers on the hem of the shirt, meaning to pull it up so she could inspect the wound herself, when she registered what he'd said. "How do you know there's no scar?"

"How else? I checked."

She jerked her chin up. Her vision swam at the sudden movement. She inhaled through her teeth. "You examined me while I was unconscious?"

"I was worried. I thought it might have gotten infected or something and that was why you wouldn't wake up. Glad you're okay."

"Thanks."

"Beats me why you are, though. I saw that wound, and it was deep."

She inched sideways until she could turn her back to him. She raised her shirt. Whoever had changed their costumes had been as thorough as the last time. She was once again braless. Which meant other people besides Rick would have seen her bare breasts.

The realization was more than upsetting; it was humiliating. She was no prude, but she decided to whom she showed her body. She would have no control over what was done to her while she was unconscious. People could strip her, examine her as intimately as they wanted, or dress her in whatever they chose and she would have no more say than a rubber doll or a mannequin. They could cart her from place to place like a piece of meat. They could do with her as they pleased and she couldn't stop them. She was completely helpless.

Tears flooded her eyes. Why was this happening to her? What had she done to deserve this? Was Delaney really behind it? Was she retaliating for the lawsuit? Elizabeth still couldn't picture her stepmother organizing anything this vast. No, the only person who might consider going to such lengths to get even was dead.

You defied the king.

She shivered, dismissing the thought before she could follow it. Her father was gone, he had no power over her anymore, and even he wouldn't have stooped to such melodramatic methods. Not for this long. Not without crowing about his cleverness. It had been all about the win with Stanford.

"Elizabeth?"

She blotted her eyes on her sleeve and shoved back the self-pity. She couldn't afford to get emotional. She was awake now and planned to stay that way.

"You're in pain, aren't you?"

"Nothing I can't handle." She focused on her side. The wound appeared to be gone, but the light in the hut was too dim for her to be sure there was no scar.

It didn't make sense. Had they used steroids on her? Was that why she'd healed so quickly? Or had they done plastic surgery to eliminate the evidence so they wouldn't be charged with assault causing bodily harm? Why bother doing either when they planned to execute her?

"For the record, I didn't deliberately peek. But I guess that does as much good as saying I didn't inhale."

"Don't worry about it. Modesty is the least of my concerns." She let her shirt fall back into place. "How long have you been awake?"

"Hard to tell. All I know is it was darker than it is now."

"Then it must be nearing dawn."

"I suppose."

"The other time I was here, they said I would be shot at dawn."

"I won't let that happen."

She blotted her eyes again. She had to stop feeling sorry for herself. She was no longer the only victim of this outrage. "I owe you an apology."

"Why?"

"I involved you in my problems by singling you out at the castle. They imprisoned you with me because I asked you for help."

"Yeah, well, I haven't been much help so far."

"That's not true. Just knowing I'm not alone . . ." Her voice broke. She wasn't sure what she was going to say anyway. Tell him that his presence gave her strength and made her feel alive? Confess her weakness to a man she hardly knew?

They had decided the mental connection they'd experienced initially had been a fluke. There was no hint of it now. She had made assumptions about his character because of his music, but music wouldn't break them out of a locked building. Appealing for help from a minstrel hadn't been logical. It would have been more logical to seek out the help of the castle blacksmith. "How long do you think it is until sunrise?"

"A while. I'm not sure. My sense of time is out of whack."

"Tell me about it. I don't even know what day this is, let alone what month."

"It's December."

"December?" She slid around to face him. "Impossible. That would mean they've kept me for nearly half a year. Someone should have found me by now."

"I'm pretty sure it's December. There were Christmas lights in the bar last time I played there."

"The last thing I remember was being in Willowbank. It was early July."

"Never heard of Willowbank. Where is it?"

"Upstate New York."

"Is that where you're from?"

"Lord, no. I have a condo in Manhattan. Willowbank is the town where my stepmother lives. We had scheduled a meeting."

"In my family, we don't schedule meetings." He shrugged. His shirt stretched tightly across his shoulders. "We sort of show up."

"My stepmother and I had legal matters to discuss." Her attention was caught by what he was wearing. She hadn't taken note of it before, probably because the clothes were so ordinary.

The medieval tunic and leggings costume had been replaced by a plaid shirt and blue jeans. His resemblance to a desperado was stronger than ever: a pair of scuffed cowboy boots covered his feet. "Are those your real clothes?"

He considered her question. "Probably. They feel like it."

"Wouldn't you recognize them?"

"That's something else strange. I never thought much about the Robin Hood outfit while I was wearing it, not until you pointed it out. It seemed right at the time." He pinched a fold of his shirt. "Like Chester."

"Chester?"

"My horse. I didn't think much about that before either, because it seemed right at the time, too, but I don't ride a horse to work. That would be crazy. I drive an F-150. When it works, anyway. She's getting temperamental in her old age."

She regarded him blankly.

"The F-150. It's a Ford pickup."

"But you said . . ." She pressed the heels of her hands to her forehead. "Do you actually own a horse?"

"Uh-huh, and his name actually is Chester, but I keep him at my parents' farm."

"Then why was he at the castle?"

"Whoever snatched me must have taken him, too, but that seems even harder to believe than the rest of this."

"We must have been given hallucinogens."

"Seems like it." He tugged her hands away from her face. "Whatever drugs they used are seriously messing with our minds. Things that shouldn't make sense do make sense, the same way they do in dreams."

"You think any of this makes *sense*?"

"Maybe not the whole picture, but the details do."

"I can't believe anyone is mad enough to assume they'll get away with this."

"They're doing a good job of it so far." He turned her hands to one side and then the other while he scrutinized the strip of plastic around her wrists. "Elizabeth, why would anyone want to lock you up?"

"I wish I knew."

"You've been mixed up in this longer than I have, and you're the only one they've bothered to bind. Both times. You must be at the center of the trouble."

"Don't you think if I knew I'd tell you? Do you think I volunteered to be treated like this? In the real world, I have respect. I have power. I have manicures and wear pearls and heels and *underwear*. Nobody pushes me around. If they try, they find out fast that I push back."

"I'll bet."

"And as soon as we get out of here, I won't rest until every single person who had any role in this kidnapping is caught and convicted and has to serve the maximum sentence allowed by law, even if it means I have to build the damn jail myself."

He rubbed his thumbs over the plastic tie. "What do you do, back in the real world?"

"I run Grayecorp. It's a property development company."

"In Manhattan?"

"That's where we're based, but we have interests all over the continent."

"Sounds like you're a regular Donald Trump."

"I'm not in his league. Not yet, that is."

"But you're rich, right?"

Not a fraction as wealthy as she would have been if her father had lived long enough to follow through on his promise. Instead, Delaney had inherited the fortune she'd had no right to claim. But thinking of the events surrounding Stanford's accident was enough to bring back the headache. Elizabeth sucked air through her teeth again. "The definition of rich is relative."

"Only rich people would say that. If you're poor, it's as plain as the holes in your pockets. So you're loaded, aren't you?"

"I have money, yes. Enough to pay a substantial ransom, but no one appears willing to negotiate. Whoever's doing this to us doesn't seem to be motivated by profit."

"Well, if it's a ransom they're after, I can't help you there. I pick up extra cash in the summer working construction, but those jobs are pretty scarce at this time of year. By the time I split what I take in from my bar gigs with the guys who play backup for me, I don't clear much more than my rent money. Maybe I should ride Chester to work after all. He'd probably be more reliable than the truck, and hay would be cheaper than gas. I could strap my gear to the saddle and—" He broke off suddenly. "Hell, I should have thought of it before."

"What?"

"My gear." He released her hands and twisted to reach for something in the shadows at the base of the wall. When he straightened to face her once more, he was holding a guitar.

She started. "Where did that come from?"

"It was here when I woke up." He shifted to sit cross-legged and laid the instrument flat across his lap. He ran his thumb lightly over the strings.

"Is it yours?"

He tapped the body. "Absolutely. See those scratches?"

Four short parallel lines dulled the gleam of the varnish. "Vaguely."

"That's where Daisy landed on it back when she was a puppy. She was chasing a cricket."

"You have a dog as well as a horse?"

"Yep. A dog, a horse, and a truck. I'm livin' every American boy's dream."

"Is she with your parents, too?"

"No, I don't take her out there much. She's scared of the barn cats." He turned one of the tuning pegs. "Most days she hangs out with my landlady almost as much as she hangs with me. Probably lying on the couch eating bonbons by now. You like dogs?"

"As I've had no experience with them, I neither like nor dislike them."

"You never wanted one? Not even when you were a kid?"

"There were many things I wanted as a child, but I grew out of them," she said. Or, to be more accurate, she grew out of the desire to ask for them. She frowned as he continued to fiddle with his guitar. "Since they brought your instrument with you, then they really did plan for you to play the part of a minstrel. Or, in our current circumstances, a musician."

"I suppose so."

"You had a different instrument in the castle. Wasn't that one a lute?"

"That wasn't a lute; it was a balalaika."

"Was that yours as well?"

"Uh-huh. It belonged to a friend of mine I used to jam with.

He was Russian, but he was into country. It's got an interesting sound, like a mandolin, only richer. I don't use it as often as the guitar."

"As much as I enjoyed your music, we should be concentrating on planning our escape. We don't know how long we'll have before dawn—" She stopped when he chuckled. "This isn't funny, Rick."

"Sure, it is. You assumed I was fixed on serenading you instead of helping you."

"I wouldn't have put it like that."

"And you're figuring a guitar won't do us much good." He gave the tuning peg another twist. "Whoever left it here must have figured the same thing."

She realized he wasn't tightening the string; he was loosening it. As soon there was enough slack to unhook it, he pulled it free, set the guitar aside, and yanked off his boots. When he pulled off his socks, her curiosity peaked. "What on earth are you doing?"

"The socks are for padding." He wrapped one sock over his knuckles and coiled one end of the guitar string around it. He repeated the procedure with his other hand, then shifted closer. "Hold out your arms."

"What? Why?"

"I'm going to saw off that plastic tie."

Realization dawned. The guitar string he had removed was one of the lower ones and was, in fact, a metal wire that had been wound with more metal. The tight ridges from the winding weren't sharp, but they would be much harder than plastic. She extended her arms immediately. "I'm sorry, Rick. I, uh, didn't know what to think."

"Uh-huh, you thought I was an idiot."

"Of course not. Quite the opposite. This is brilliant."

"Let's see if it works first. It may take a while." He angled one elbow between her arms, fitted the wire against the plastic, and drew it across. His arm bumped into her shoulder. "Could you turn sideways? I'll get better leverage."

She rotated so that her legs were perpendicular to his. After a few more bumps, she swung her legs across his thighs so that she could hold her wrists directly over his lap. "How's that?"

He uncoiled the wire from his right hand temporarily so

that he could slip his arm beneath hers and bring it up between them. He did a few experimental strokes across the plastic, then settled into a firm, back-and-forth rhythm. As he'd warned, it did take a while—the ridged wire wore the plastic away rather than cut it—but eventually a groove did begin to form. "Okay," he said. "Looks like we're in business."

The progress was slow but steady. Elizabeth told herself to ignore the proximity of their bodies. It wasn't easy because he was a large man. He smelled surprisingly good for someone who had been around a horse and had been tossed in a dungeon and a dirt-floored hut. As a matter of fact, he smelled as if they were in bed. She caught a whiff of cotton that reminded her of crisp, freshly laundered sheets. And his skin exuded a mellow, early-morning scent, reminiscent of a man still warm and relaxed from a night's sleep.

But the way he smelled was no more relevant than the way the muscles in his thighs flexed beneath hers, or the way his forearm came so close to her breasts on each down stroke that she could feel his body heat. Breasts that he'd seen naked. She glanced at his bent head. The hair at his nape had a slight curl to it and was long enough to fall partly over his collar. She didn't normally care for the look of long hair on a man, yet on Rick it seemed perfect. She could all too easily imagine how the curls would wrap around her fingertips . . .

"Does that hurt?"

"No. Why?"

"You moaned."

"Headache." She focused on the wire. It had begun to squeak as it moved across the plastic. The groove was deepening more quickly as it heated from the friction. The undersides of her thighs were heating, too, from the contact with his legs. "This was creative thinking. I'm glad now that you're a Luddite."

"To be honest, I don't think all technology is evil. I've got nothing against power tools, only cell phones."

"And computers."

"Yeah, but I do love my TV remote."

"Apart from news broadcasts, I don't watch television."

"Say it ain't so. You don't watch TV? No Jerry Springer? No Monday Night Football?"

"I don't have time."

"Too busy talking on your BlackBerry with the rest of the Borg Collective?" His elbow rubbed along the upper crease of her thigh. "Oops. Sorry."

"I usually don't leave the office until after ten."

"Huh. Lots of nights that's when I start working."

"With your songwriting talent, I'm surprised you have to play in bars to make a living."

"Thanks, but my songs aren't exactly popular. Seems audiences like them better the drunker they get. A lot of the time I do covers of old standards so I don't get pelted with peanuts."

"Nonsense. Your songs are powerfully moving. Your melodies are haunting. You're also a very skillful musician. You should have an exceptional career."

He paused. "You know about music?"

"I studied piano in my youth." How simple a statement that was. It didn't begin to describe the long hours of daily practice or the years of devotion. Or how precious that dream had once been. Another example of a desire she grew out of.

"I always wished I could play the piano when I was a kid, but this old guitar was all my folks could afford." He resumed sawing. "Just as well, because I wouldn't be able to take a piano with me when I went to gigs, 'specially if I start going green and use Chester instead of the truck. What kind of music did you play? Ten to one it was the stuffy stuff."

"I wouldn't put it like that. Many of the men we consider classic composers were the rock stars of their day, quite scandalous and cutting-edge. Don't you like classical music?"

"Can't say as I never listened to it much."

"Don't let the packaging drive you off. The passion comes through, whatever format is being used. Good music is universal. It has the ability to take you out of yourself."

"Take you out of yourself," he repeated. "That's a good way to put it. That's pretty well what mine does for me."

"I believe music does even more than that. It's a kind of sharing that crosses all boundaries, whether they're time or place or genre. I learned to play the classics, so that's what moves me the most easily. Any emotion you can name has been expressed by the masters, and they do it on a level beyond words. When it's right, it can slip straight past your conscious thoughts and . . ." She trailed off when she realized he had stopped sawing again. "What?"

"It's good to hear you talk about emotions. Most of the time you seem to avoid them."

"They have their place."

"Uh-huh?"

"They're an integral part of the best music. However, they're counterproductive in crisis situations."

"You ever get a melody in your head that you can't get out? Like, if you hear a song first thing in the morning, you're stuck with it for the rest of the day?"

"From time to time. Why?"

"It's as useless to ignore what you're feeling. Seems to me you might as well give in and hum along." He dropped the guitar string, fitted a hand around each of her wrists, and gave them a sharp tug.

The plastic bundling tie snapped and fell off.

Her hands were free.

Finally. Yes. Yes. *Yes!*

The relief that crashed through her was out of all proportion to the situation. Regaining the use of her hands wouldn't matter if she and Rick couldn't find a way out of their prison. They weren't yet out of danger. This wasn't over.

But he'd given her hope. That was more than she'd had an hour ago. From what she understood, it was more than she'd had in five months. She wiggled her fingers, delighting in the simple ability to move as she wanted. She was no longer completely helpless. "Thank you, Rick."

He smiled. It was a full-face smile, not a one-sided quirk of his lips. The corners of his eyes crinkled. His cheeks lifted. And to the left of his mouth, a dimple appeared. "You're welcome, Lady Elspeth Isabella Elizabeth."

She flexed her fingers again, then touched his dimple. His beard stubble was softer than she would have expected. It rasped gently against her skin. She wondered what it would feel like against her lips.

Which was an incredibly inappropriate thought. As she'd told him, she shouldn't allow herself to get emotional. They were in a life-and-death situation, and even if they weren't, she certainly shouldn't consider kissing him, no matter how enjoyable it would be to, well, hum along, as he put it. The more time they spent together, the more obvious it was that they had nothing whatsoever in common. In the real world, they probably would have never met.

His smile faded. "Do you hear that?"

All she could hear was her heartbeat. She dropped her hand. He couldn't have heard her thoughts, could he? "What?"

He tilted his head. "It sounds like a helicopter."

She held her breath so that she could listen. There was a distant throb. It was unmistakably mechanical, and it was growing louder fast. It wasn't long before the ground beneath her vibrated in time with the engine.

They weren't the only ones who had noticed the noise. Men's voices came from outside. Footsteps pounded past the hut. Someone shouted orders in Spanish. Within seconds, the entire camp was abuzz with activity.

Rick yanked on his socks and boots.

"What's going on?" she asked.

"From what I can make out of what they're saying, they think it's a raid."

"A raid? As in police?"

"Or the army." The noise of the helicopter increased rapidly. It seemed to be coming from directly above the camp. Rick raised his voice. "Either one's good news for us as long as we don't get caught in a—"

His words were drowned out by a rapid burst of gunfire from overhead.

"Cross fire!" he yelled. "Get down!"

Elizabeth didn't have the chance to absorb what he said before his body slammed into hers, knocking her on her back.

Bullets tore through the roof. Splinters flew from the walls. Rick dragged himself on top of her as dust and wood chips rained down on them.

Answering gunfire erupted from everywhere as the guerrillas or drug smugglers or whatever they were fought back. There was a high-pitched whistle that ended in an explosion. The ground shook. Men screamed. More explosions followed as rapidly as the gunfire. Soon a new noise joined the din: the whooshing crackle of flames. Black smoke wafted into the hut through the bullet holes.

Elizabeth struggled for air. Her vision dimmed. Frantic to stay conscious, she pushed at Rick's shoulders. "Let me up!"

"It's not safe." He cupped his hand protectively over the top of her head. "We need to stay put until the firing stops."

"No! The smoke! I can't breathe!"

He couldn't have heard her. The battle that raged around them was too loud.

She fisted her hand to pound his back, but didn't have the strength to lift her arm. The energy she'd awakened with had dwindled. It wasn't the smoke that was sapping her strength. The darkness that spread over her was coming from within.

It was happening again. She was slipping away. She splayed her fingers, trying to stay with him. "Rick, please, don't let me go to sleep! I have to stay awake!"

Her plea went unanswered. He couldn't hear her. She couldn't even hear herself over the earsplitting noise. Another explosion shook the ground. The wall beside them burst inward. The bullet-riddled roof collapsed, burying them under a pile of burning debris.

Rick! Get up!

He didn't move. A roof beam lay across his shoulders. His body was a deadweight on hers.

The void opened. Elizabeth screamed her resistance. No! She couldn't give up now. Rescue was within reach. She knew it. She felt it. All she had to do was stay alive. Someone was bound to find them.

ALAN CHECKED HIS WATCH, THEN AIMED THE REMOTE AT the TV on the wall to switch off the news and pushed himself out of the chair. He needed to get moving if he was going to make the game. The Rangers were playing the Bruins tonight and Grayecorp had season tickets on the blue line. He wasn't much of a hockey fan himself, but Sherri Silver was Canadian so what else could he expect? She also happened to be the only daughter of a man who owned a very lucrative gold mine.

Alan considered himself quite accomplished in the art of seducing poor little rich girls, but being shackled to Elizabeth cramped his style. If he'd been free to pursue Sherri openly, he would have had her in his bed months ago, but playing the sympathy card was slow work. The main reason he'd managed to get as far with her as he had was because she was impressed by his devotion to his fiancée. She was also impressed by his choice of fiancée. Sherri's father had begun as a common prospector, wandering around the wilds of Northern Quebec, before he'd struck it rich. Her family had wealth, but no roots or pedigree like Elizabeth's. Sherri was intelligent enough, but she had no competitive streak; she was more like a guppy than a shark. He suspected she felt flattered by his attention, since any comparison between the two women wouldn't favor Sherri. She couldn't open the doors Elizabeth could, or provide access to the kind of power that controlling Grayecorp would give him.

But Alan was at the point where he couldn't afford the luxury of being choosy. His expenses were mounting. So were the demands from his creditors. The project he'd initiated on the expectation of Elizabeth's financial backing was in danger of falling through unless he found alternate financing. He needed to hedge his bets. Unlike the turnip he was still engaged to, Sherri was fully capable of signing a check.

"Damn you, Elizabeth," he muttered, pulling on his coat. "I've given you more time than you deserve. You've got no right to do this to me."

He eyed the equipment that kept her alive. The hums and beeps were getting on his nerves. They were as relentless as she used to be. Too bad Lidstone got scared off by Delaney—pulling the plugs would have been the perfect solution, particularly if someone else had done it. Even the fraction of Elizabeth's estate Alan would get through a palimony suit would have been better than nothing. He shifted his gaze to the bed. "Why can't you just die?"

She moved her hand.

Alan froze. He couldn't have seen what he'd thought he had. It must have been an optical illusion, or maybe a reflection of his own hand in the metal bed rail. He rubbed his face and looked again.

There was no mistake. Elizabeth was holding her right hand an inch above the mattress.

Alan glanced behind him to make sure the door of her room was shut, then stepped closer to the bed. He kept his arms at his sides. "Elizabeth?"

Her breathing became ragged. Her body stiffened with her efforts to keep her hand in the air.

The occasional twitches he'd witnessed during his previous visits were nothing compared to what he was seeing now. She had never moved her hand before. This didn't appear to be the result of an involuntary reflex. The gesture seemed deliberate. It was more life than she'd displayed in five months.

Could Delaney be right? Was it possible for Elizabeth to wake up? Hell, if she did, there was little chance of Sherri taking out her checkbook. He'd assured her that his fiancée's death was imminent.

He needed time to consider a fallback position. He also had better watch what he said around Elizabeth. "Can you hear me, darling?"

She spread her fingers, as if she were grasping for something. An alarm dinged from the direction of the monitors.

Alan glanced over his shoulder again, then grabbed her hand and pushed it back to the bed.

She put up no resistance. Whatever strength she'd managed to dredge up appeared to desert her. Her hand went limp. Her body relaxed.

So did his. By the time the door swung open behind him, the sounds from the monitors had reverted to their typical monotonous pattern. "Mr. Rashotte! What's going on?"

Alan blanked his expression before he looked at the nurse. It was Beryl tonight, one of the older ones. He didn't like her. She was too rigid. She reminded him of a traffic cop. "Hello, Beryl. I didn't see you when I came in. Is something wrong?"

"There was a sudden increase in Miss Graye's heart rate." She went to the other side of the bed to take Elizabeth's pulse. "Didn't you hear the alarm?"

"An alarm? No, I don't think so. What's wrong with her heart?"

Beryl didn't reply immediately. She frowned at the monitors. "Nothing, now. Her pulse rate appears to be back to normal."

"That's odd."

"Yes, it is. Didn't you notice anything unusual a few minutes ago?"

He shook his head. "I'm afraid I didn't."

"Any agitation? Any movement?"

"She was the same as always. Could those machines be malfunctioning?"

Her frown deepened. "I'll make a note to have the technician check the equipment in the morning."

"That's reassuring. Elizabeth's so dependent on them, I'd hate to think what could happen if they broke down."

"Are you certain you didn't see any change in her?"

"Sorry, no. Not a thing."